POKÉMON ADVENTURES:
DIAMOND AND PEARL/
PLATINUM
Volume 5
Perfect Square Edition

Story by **HIDENORI KUSAKA**
Art by **SATOSHI YAMAMOTO**

© 2012 Pokémon.
© 1995-2012 Nintendo/Creatures Inc./GAME FREAK inc.
TM, ®, and character names are trademarks of Nintendo.
POCKET MONSTERS SPECIAL Vol. 5 (34)
by Hidenori KUSAKA, Satoshi YAMAMOTO
All rights reserved.
Original Japanese edition published by SHOGAKUKAN.
English translation rights in the United States of America, Canada, United Kingdom,
Ireland, Australia and New Zealand arranged with SHOGAKUKAN.

Translation/Katherine Schilling
Touch-up & Lettering/Annaliese Christman
Design/Yukiko Whitley
Editor/Annette Roman

The stories, characters and incidents mentioned
in this publication are entirely fictional.

Printed in the U.S.A.

Published by VIZ Media, LLC
P.O. Box 77010
San Francisco, CA 94107

10 9 8 7 6 5 4 3 2
First printing, June 2012
Second printing, June 2014

www.perfectsquare.com   www.viz.com

Art

Satoshi Yamamoto

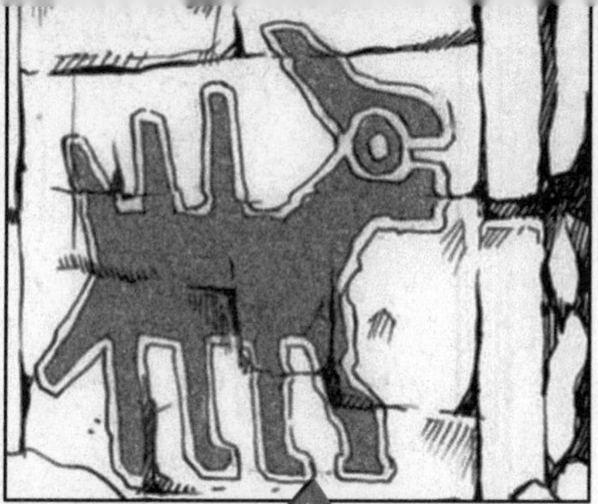

Pokémon™ Adventures Diamond and Pearl Platinum

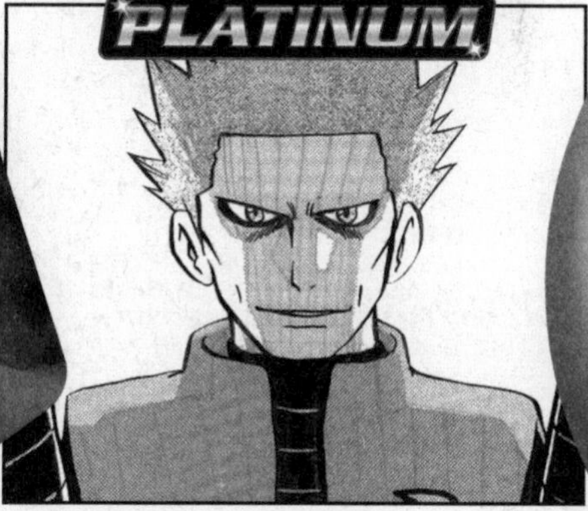

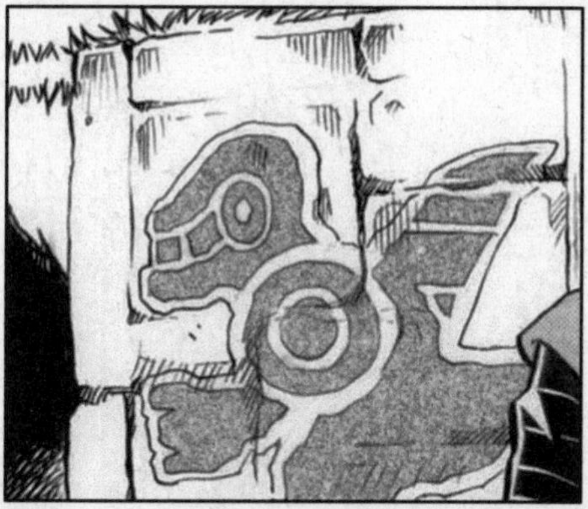

Story

Hidenori Kusaka

Our Story So Far...

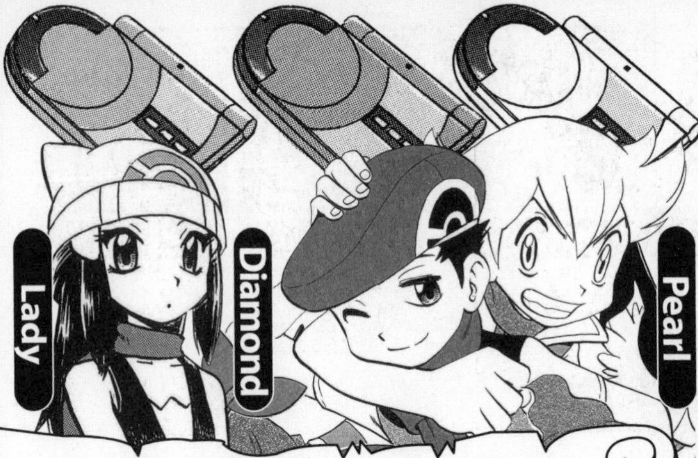
Lady
Diamond
Pearl

A STORY ABOUT YOUNG PEOPLE EN-TRUSTED WITH POKÉ-DEXES BY THE WORLD'S LEADING POKÉMON RE-SEARCH-ERS. TOGETHER WITH THEIR POKÉMON, THEY TRAVEL, DO BATTLE, AND EVOLVE!

SOME PLACE IN SOME TIME... THE DAY HAS COME FOR A YOUNG LADY, THE ONLY DAUGHTER OF THE BERLITZ FAMILY, THE WEALTHIEST IN THE SINNOH REGION, TO EMBARK ON A JOURNEY. IN ORDER TO MAKE A SPECIAL EMBLEM BEARING HER FAMILY CREST, SHE MUST PERSONALLY FIND AND GATHER THE MATERIALS AT THE PEAK OF MT. CORONET. SHE SETS OUT ON HER JOURNEY WITH THE INTENTION OF MEETING UP WITH TWO BODYGUARDS ASSIGNED TO ESCORT HER.

MEANWHILE, POKÉMON TRAINERS PEARL AND DIAMOND, WHO DREAM OF BECOMING STAND-UP COMEDIANS, ENTER A COMEDY CONTEST IN JUBILIFE AND WIN THE SPECIAL MERIT AWARD. BUT THEIR PRIZE OF AN ALL-EXPENSES PAID TRIP GETS SWITCHED WITH THE CONTRACT FOR LADY'S BODYGUARDS!

THUS PEARL AND DIAMOND THINK LADY IS THEIR TOUR GUIDE, AND LADY THINKS THEY ARE HER BODY-GUARDS! DESPITE THE CASES OF MISTAKEN IDENTITY, THE TRIO TRAVEL TOGETHER QUITE HAPPILY THROUGH THE VAST COUNTRYSIDE.

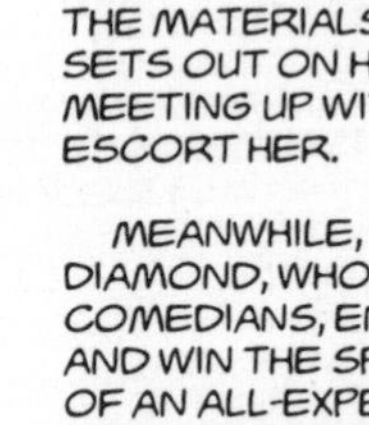

Paka & Uji

THE REAL BODYGUARDS HIRED TO ESCORT LADY.

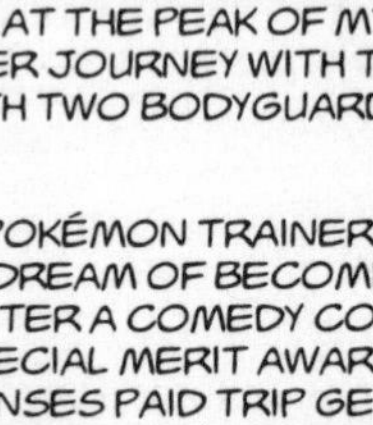

Sebastian

THE BERLITZ FAMILY BUTLER, WHO IS ALWAYS WORRYING ABOUT LADY.

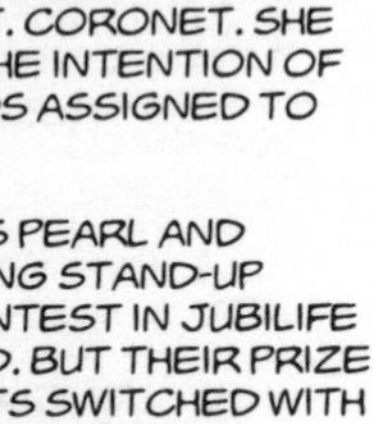

Mr. Berlitz

LADY'S FATHER, WHO ASSISTS PROFESSOR ROWAN.

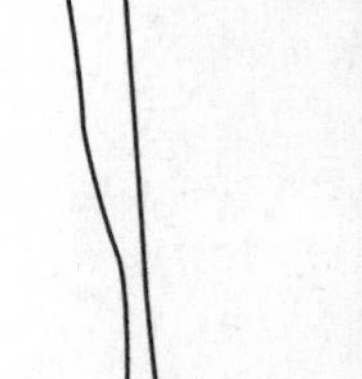

Professor Rowan

A LEADING RESEARCHER OF POKÉMON EVOLUTION. HE CAN BE QUITE INTIMIDATING!

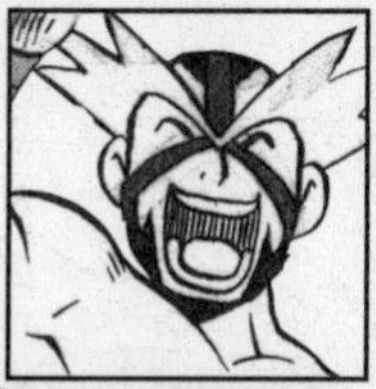

Wake

PASTORIA CITY'S GYM LEADER, KNOWN AS THE TORRENTIAL MASKED MASTER.

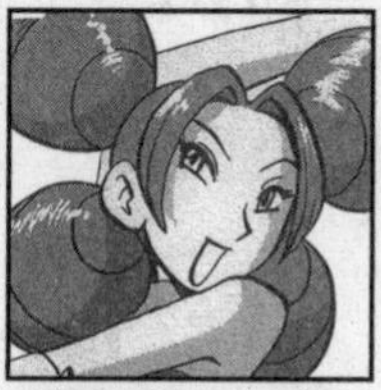

Fantina

THE ALLURING SOULFUL DANCER OF HEARTHOME.

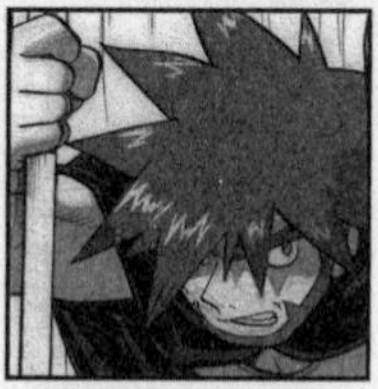

Byron

CANALAVE CITY'S GYM LEADER AND FATHER OF OREBURGH CITY'S GYM LEADER, ROARK.

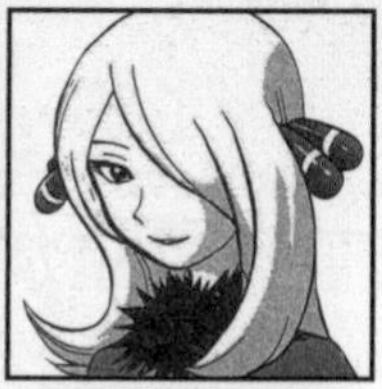

Cynthia

A MYSTERIOUS WOMAN WHO SEEMS TO BE INVESTIGATING A MYSTERY.

MEANWHILE, THE TWO BODYGUARDS SENT TO ESCORT LADY THINK SHE HAS BEEN KIDNAPPED BY DIAMOND AND PEARL AND ARE HOT ON THEIR HEELS. TO TOP IT ALL OFF, MYSTERIOUS TEAM GALACTIC IS BUSY CREATING TROUBLE IN THE SINNOH REGION BY CONSTRUCTING A GALACTIC BOMB! THEY PLAN TO EXTORT THE MONEY FOR THEIR NEFARIOUS PROJECT FROM THE WEALTHY BERLITZ FAMILY!

WHEN TEAM GALACTIC FAILS TO KIDNAP LADY, THEY GO AFTER HER FATHER, SIR BERLITZ, AND PROFESSOR ROWAN! THEN, WHEN LADY LEARNS HER FATHER HAS GONE MISSING WHILE ATTENDING A POKÉMON CONFERENCE IN CANALAVE CITY, SHE RACES THERE WITH DIAMOND AND PEARL, BURSTS INTO A POKÉMON GYM, AND BEGINS TO BATTLE...!

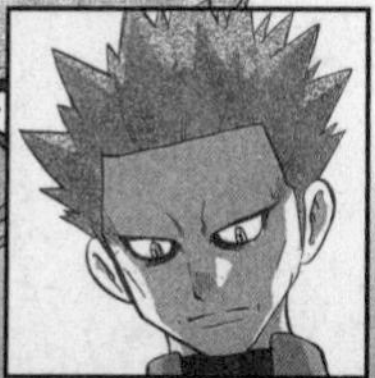

Cyrus

TEAM GALACTIC'S BOSS. AN OVERBEARING, INTENSE MAN.

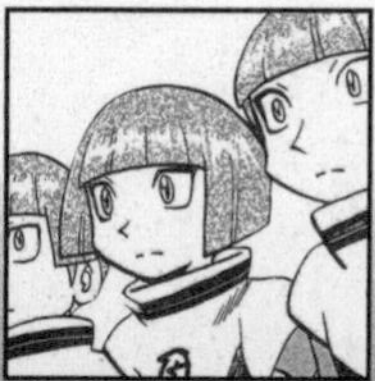

Galactic Grunts

THE TEAM GALACTIC TROOPS, WHO CARRY OUT THEIR LEADER'S BIDDING WITHOUT QUESTION. CREEPY!

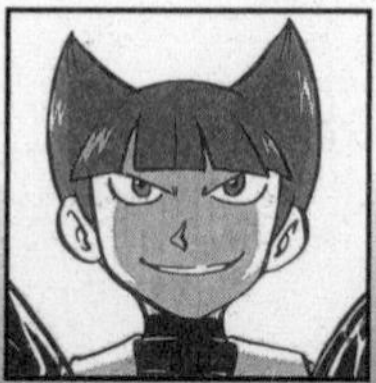

Saturn

HE IS IN CHARGE OF THE BOMB AND RARELY STEPS ONTO THE BATTLEFIELD HIMSELF.

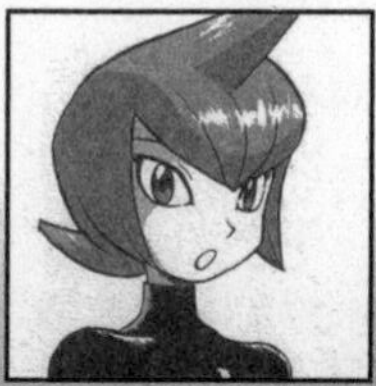

Mars

A TEAM GALACTIC LEADER. HER PERSONALITY IS HARD TO PIN DOWN.

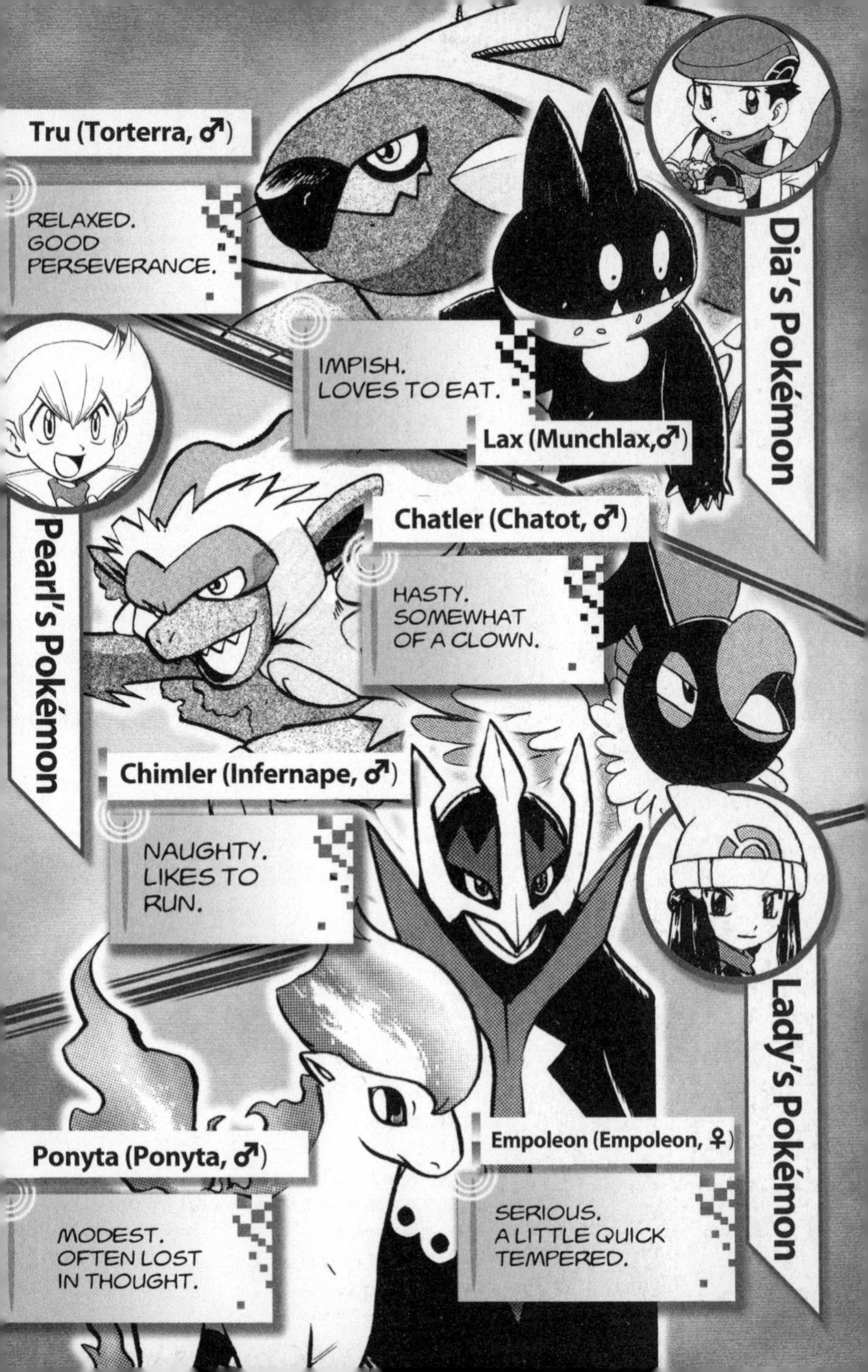

Dia's Pokémon
Tru (Torterra, ♂)
RELAXED. GOOD PERSEVERANCE.
Lax (Munchlax,♂)
IMPISH. LOVES TO EAT.
Pearl's Pokémon
Chatler (Chatot, ♂)
HASTY. SOMEWHAT OF A CLOWN.
Chimler (Infernape, ♂)
NAUGHTY. LIKES TO RUN.
Lady's Pokémon
Empoleon (Empoleon, ♀)
SERIOUS. A LITTLE QUICK TEMPERED.
Ponyta (Ponyta, ♂)
MODEST. OFTEN LOST IN THOUGHT.

Pokémon Adventures Diamond and Pearl Platinum 5

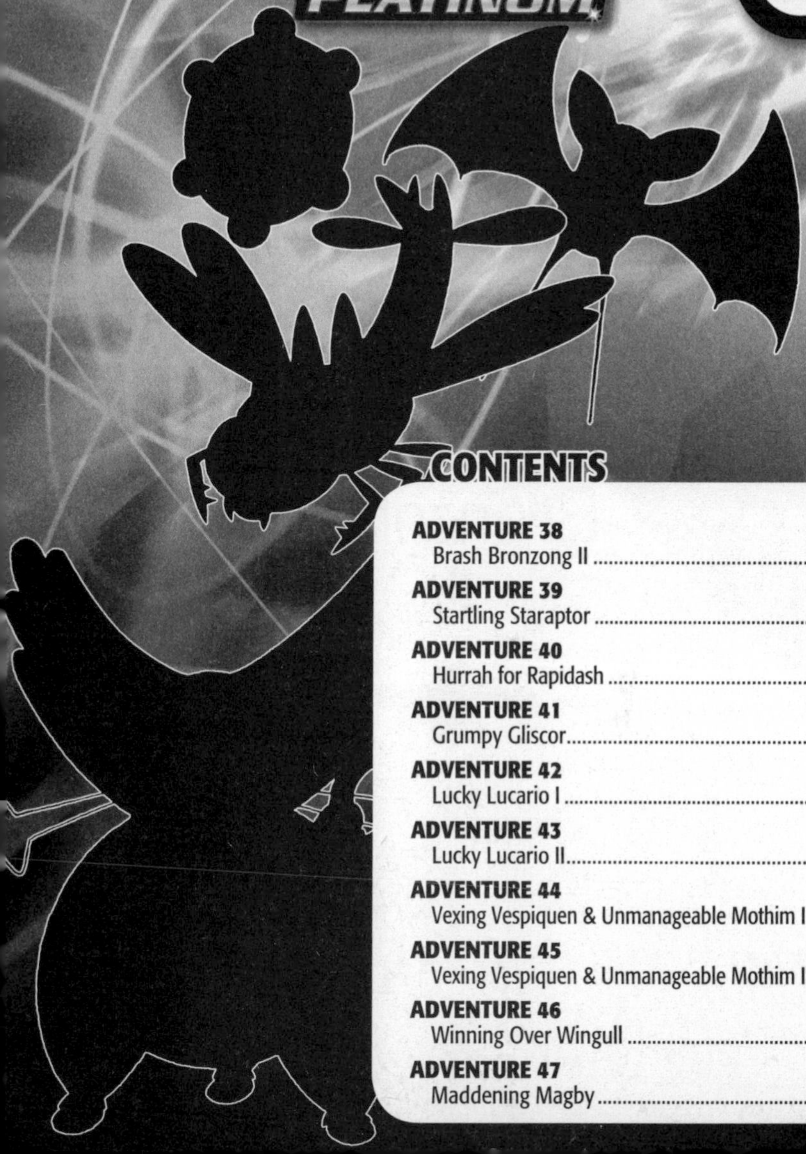

CONTENTS

38

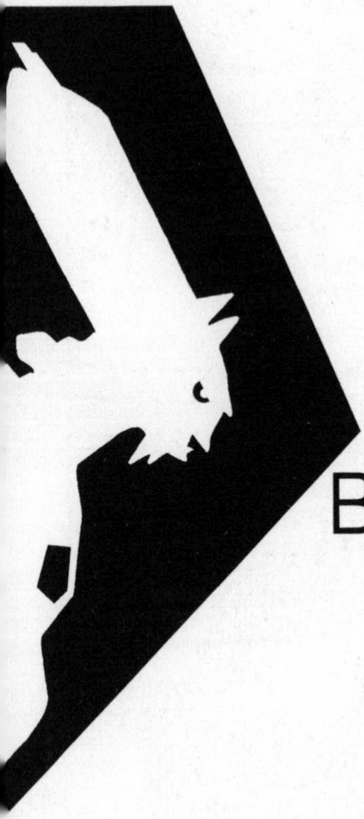

Brash Bronzong II

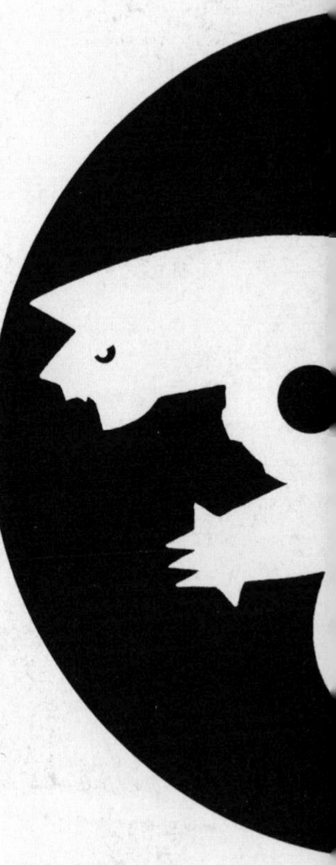

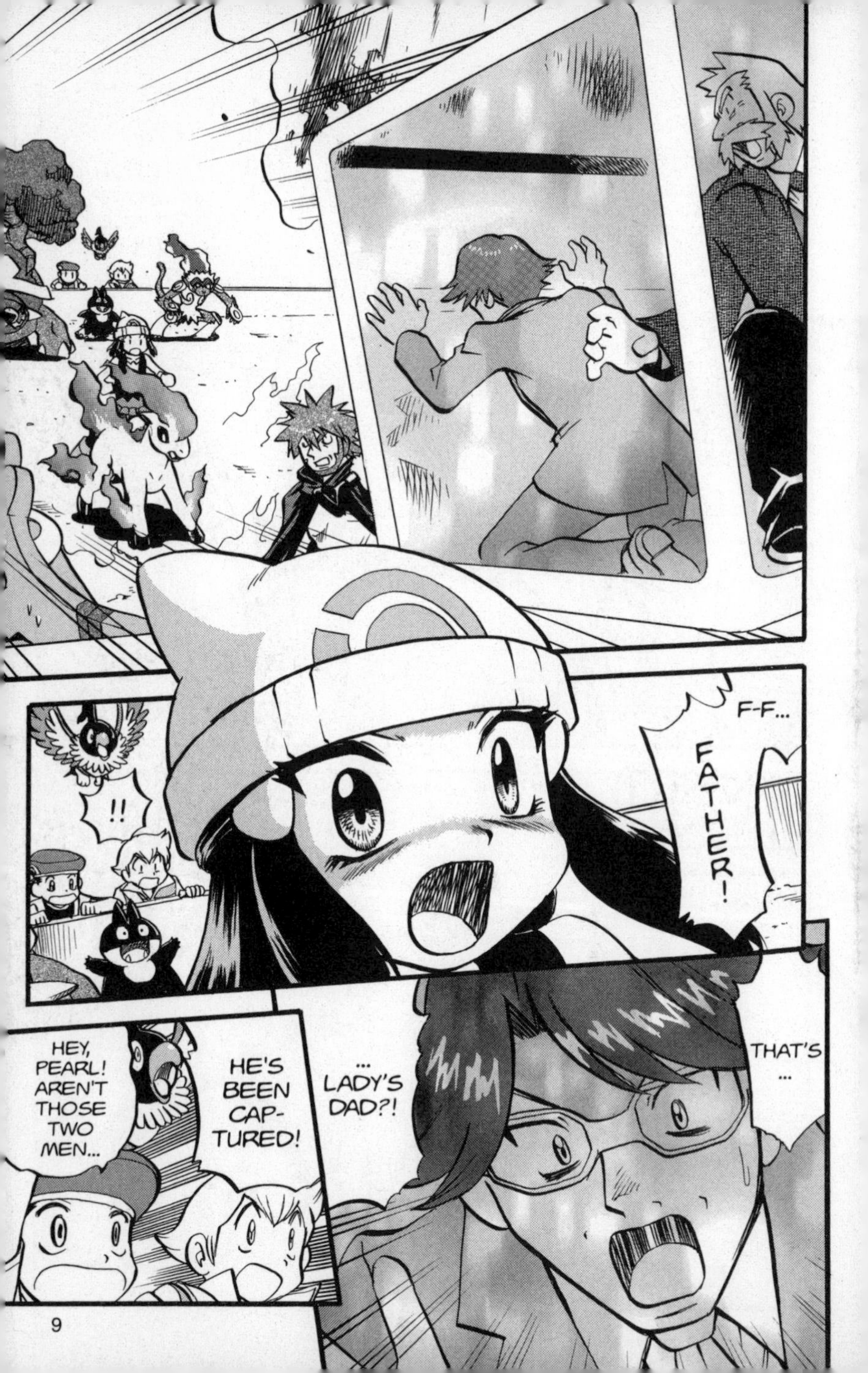

F-F...
FATHER!
!!
THAT'S ...
... LADY'S DAD?!
HE'S BEEN CAP-TURED!
HEY, PEARL! AREN'T THOSE TWO MEN...

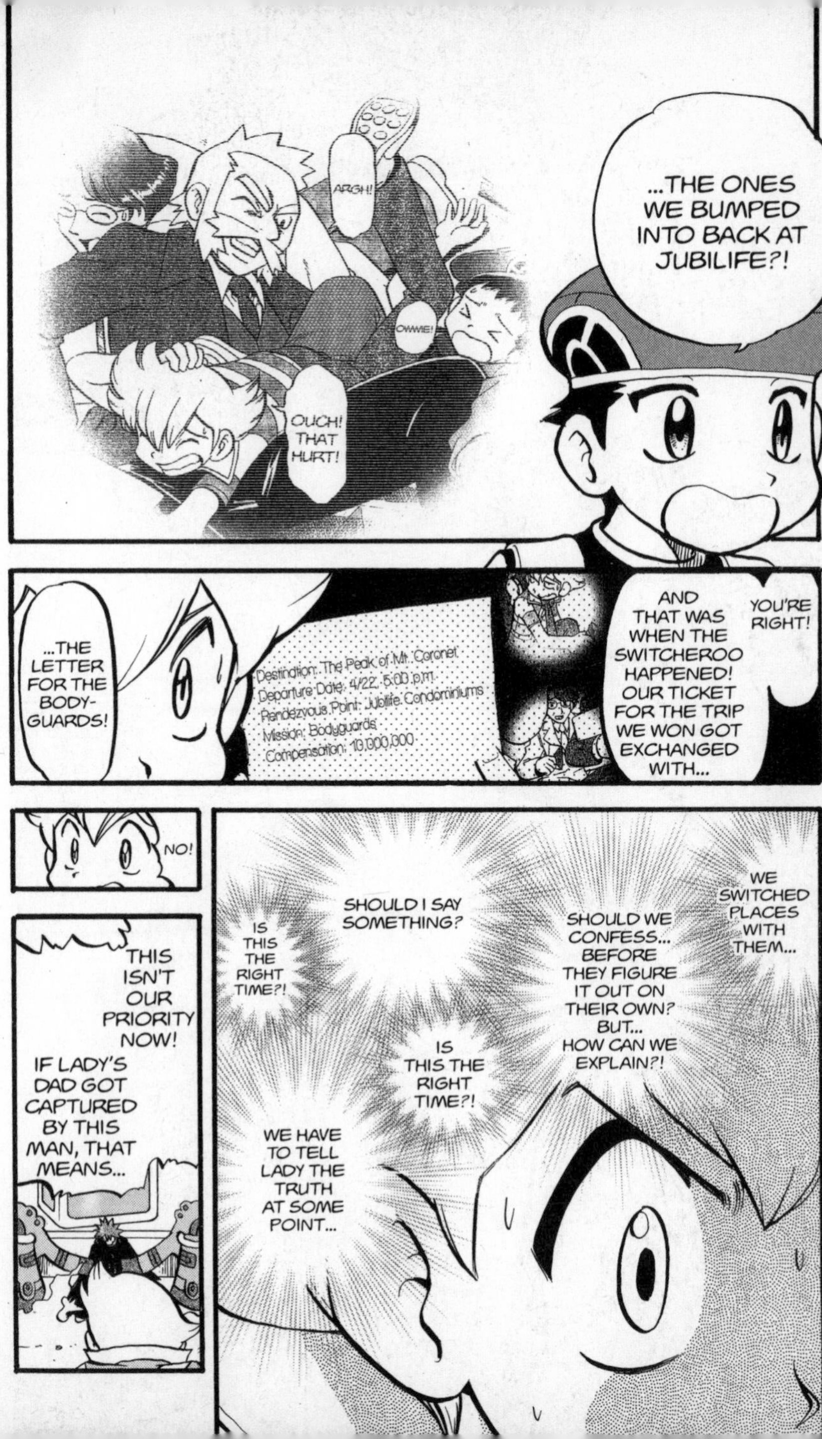
...THE ONES WE BUMPED INTO BACK AT JUBILIFE?!
ARGH!
OWWIE!
OUCH! THAT HURT!
YOU'RE RIGHT!
AND THAT WAS WHEN THE SWITCHEROO HAPPENED! OUR TICKET FOR THE TRIP WE WON GOT EXCHANGED WITH...
Destination: The Peak of Mt. Coronet
Departure Date: 4/22, 5:00 p.m.
Rendezvous Point: Jubilife Condominiums
Mission: Bodyguards
Compensation: 10,000,000
...THE LETTER FOR THE BODY-GUARDS!
WE SWITCHED PLACES WITH THEM...
SHOULD WE CONFESS... BEFORE THEY FIGURE IT OUT ON THEIR OWN? BUT... HOW CAN WE EXPLAIN?!
SHOULD I SAY SOMETHING?
IS THIS THE RIGHT TIME?!
IS THIS THE RIGHT TIME?!
WE HAVE TO TELL LADY THE TRUTH AT SOME POINT...
NO!
THIS ISN'T OUR PRIORITY NOW!
IF LADY'S DAD GOT CAPTURED BY THIS MAN, THAT MEANS...

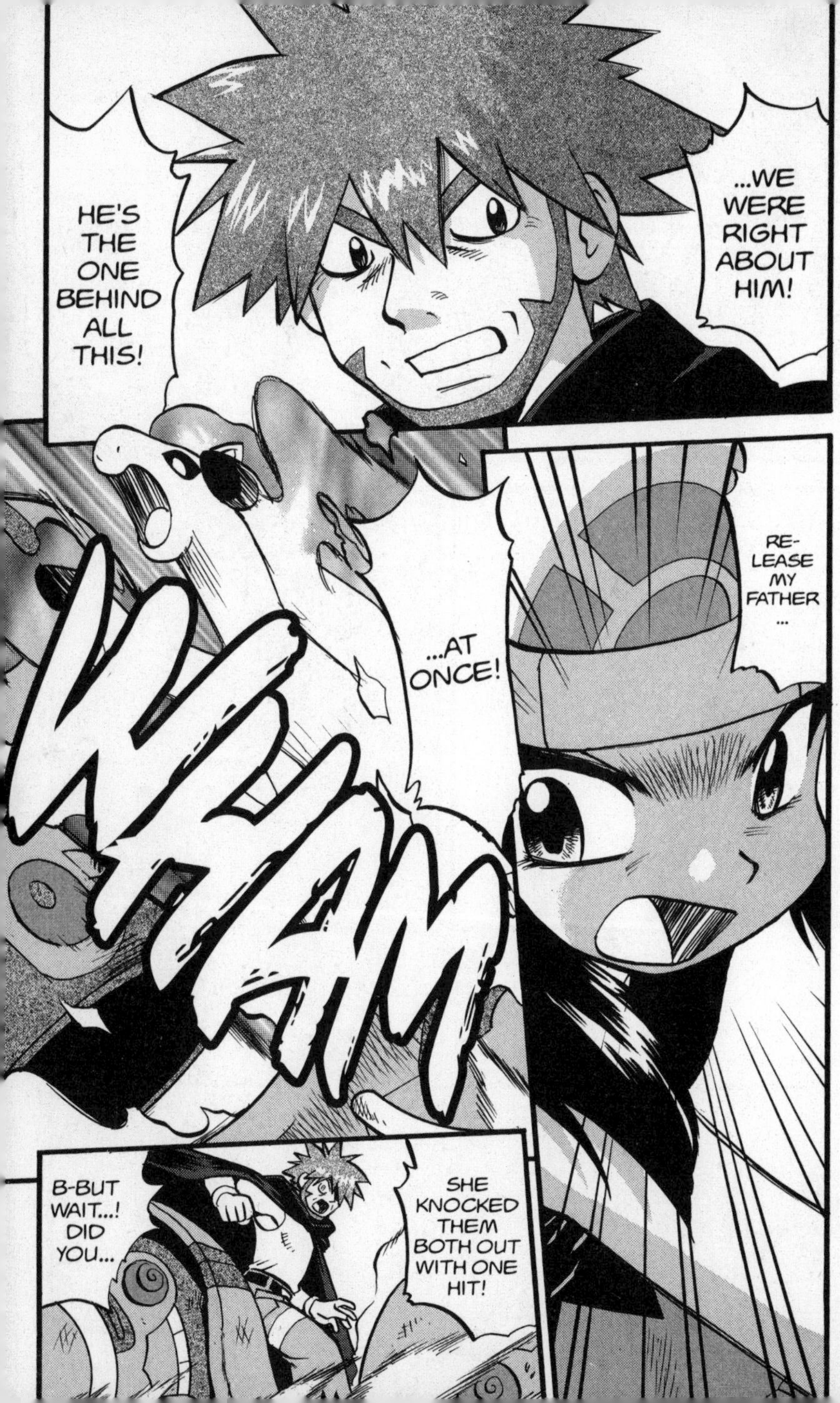
...WE WERE RIGHT ABOUT HIM!
HE'S THE ONE BEHIND ALL THIS!
RE-LEASE MY FATHER...
...AT ONCE!
WHAM
SHE KNOCKED THEM BOTH OUT WITH ONE HIT!
B-BUT WAIT...! DID YOU...

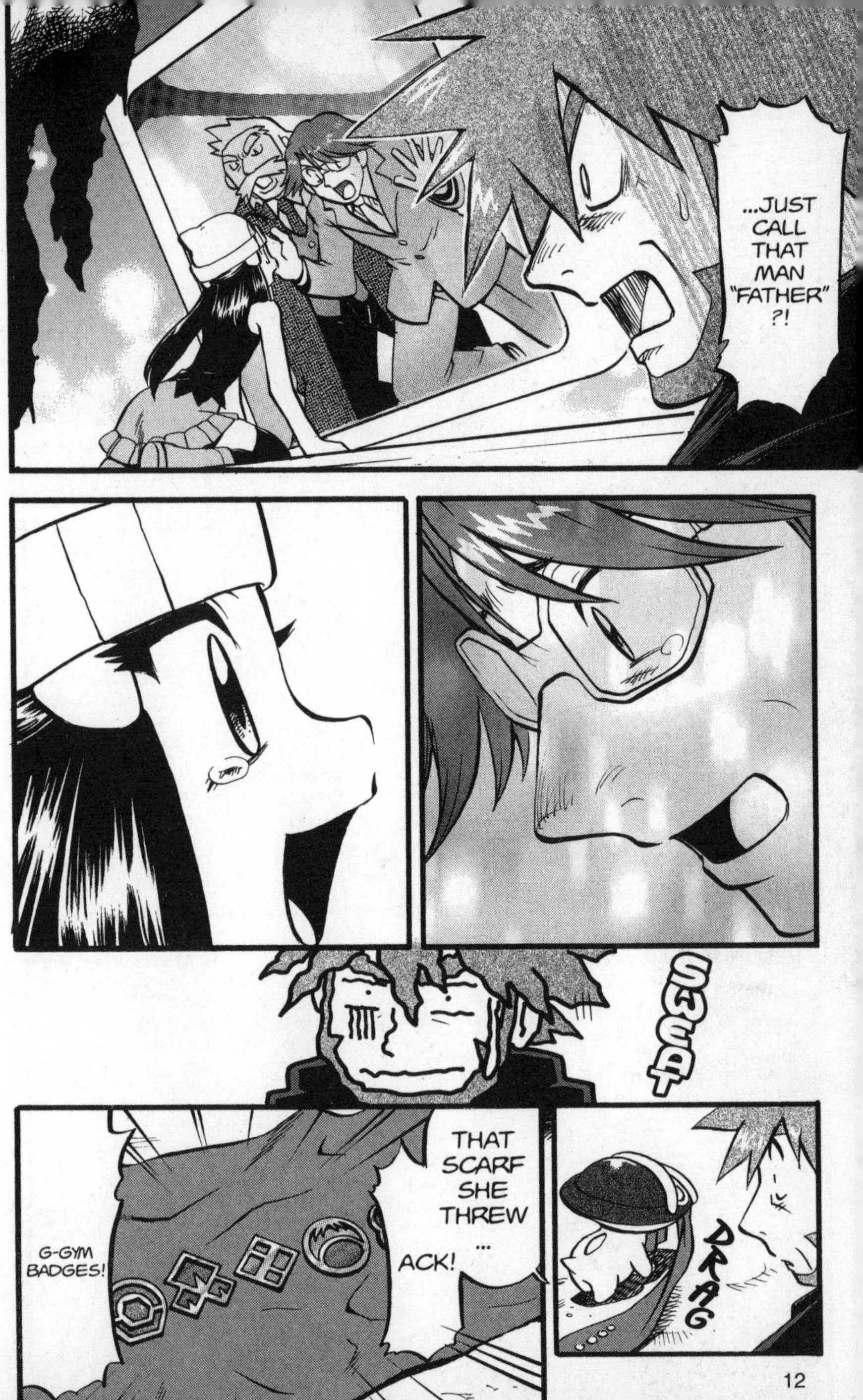

...JUST CALL THAT MAN "FATHER" ?!
SWEAT
DRAG
THAT SCARF SHE THREW ...
ACK!
G-GYM BADGES!

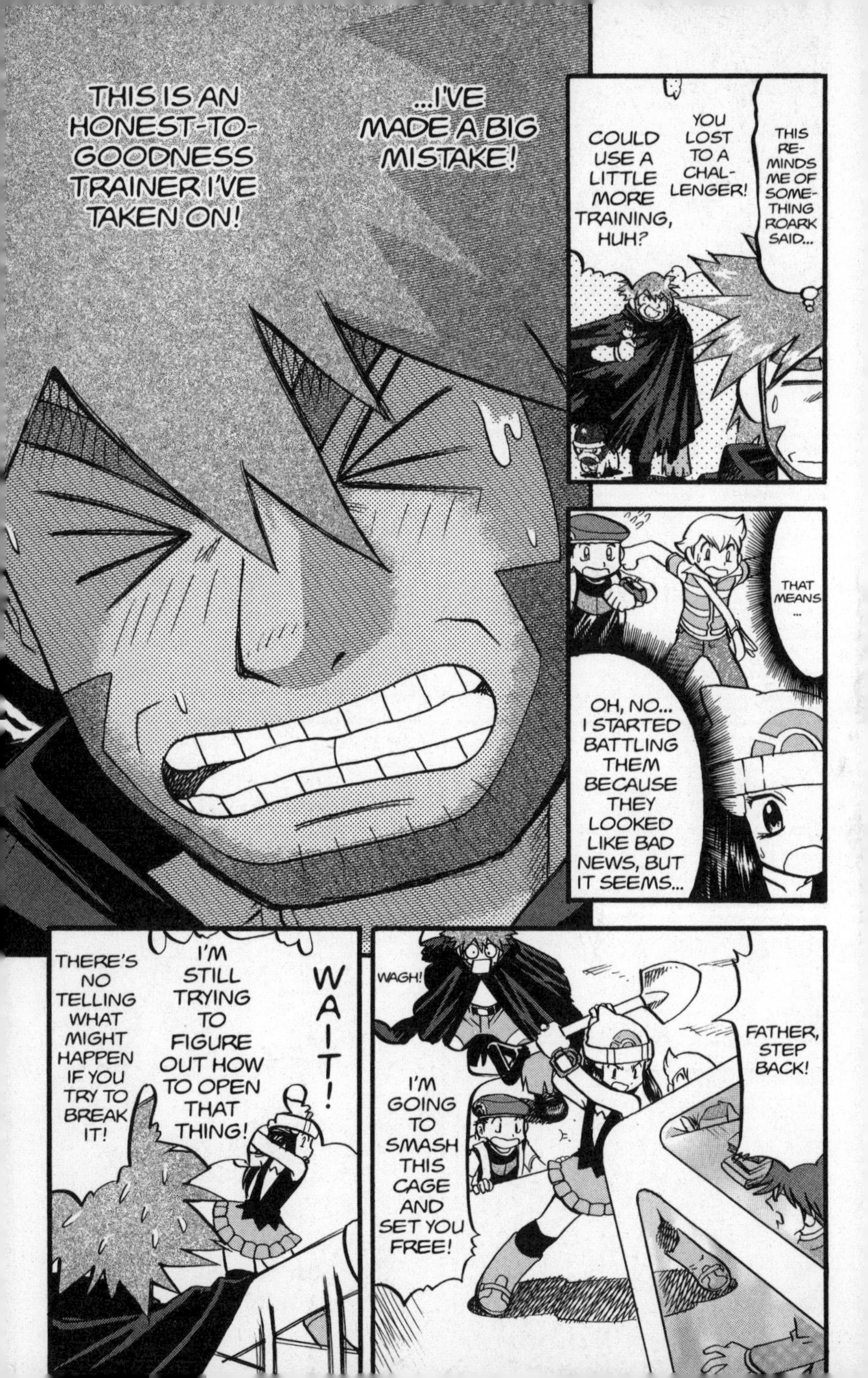
THIS REMINDS ME OF SOMETHING ROARK SAID...
YOU LOST TO A CHALLENGER!
COULD USE A LITTLE MORE TRAINING, HUH?
THAT MEANS...
OH, NO... I STARTED BATTLING THEM BECAUSE THEY LOOKED LIKE BAD NEWS, BUT IT SEEMS...
...I'VE MADE A BIG MISTAKE!
THIS IS AN HONEST-TO-GOODNESS TRAINER I'VE TAKEN ON!
FATHER, STEP BACK!
WAGH!
I'M GOING TO SMASH THIS CAGE AND SET YOU FREE!
WAIT!
I'M STILL TRYING TO FIGURE OUT HOW TO OPEN THAT THING!
THERE'S NO TELLING WHAT MIGHT HAPPEN IF YOU TRY TO BREAK IT!

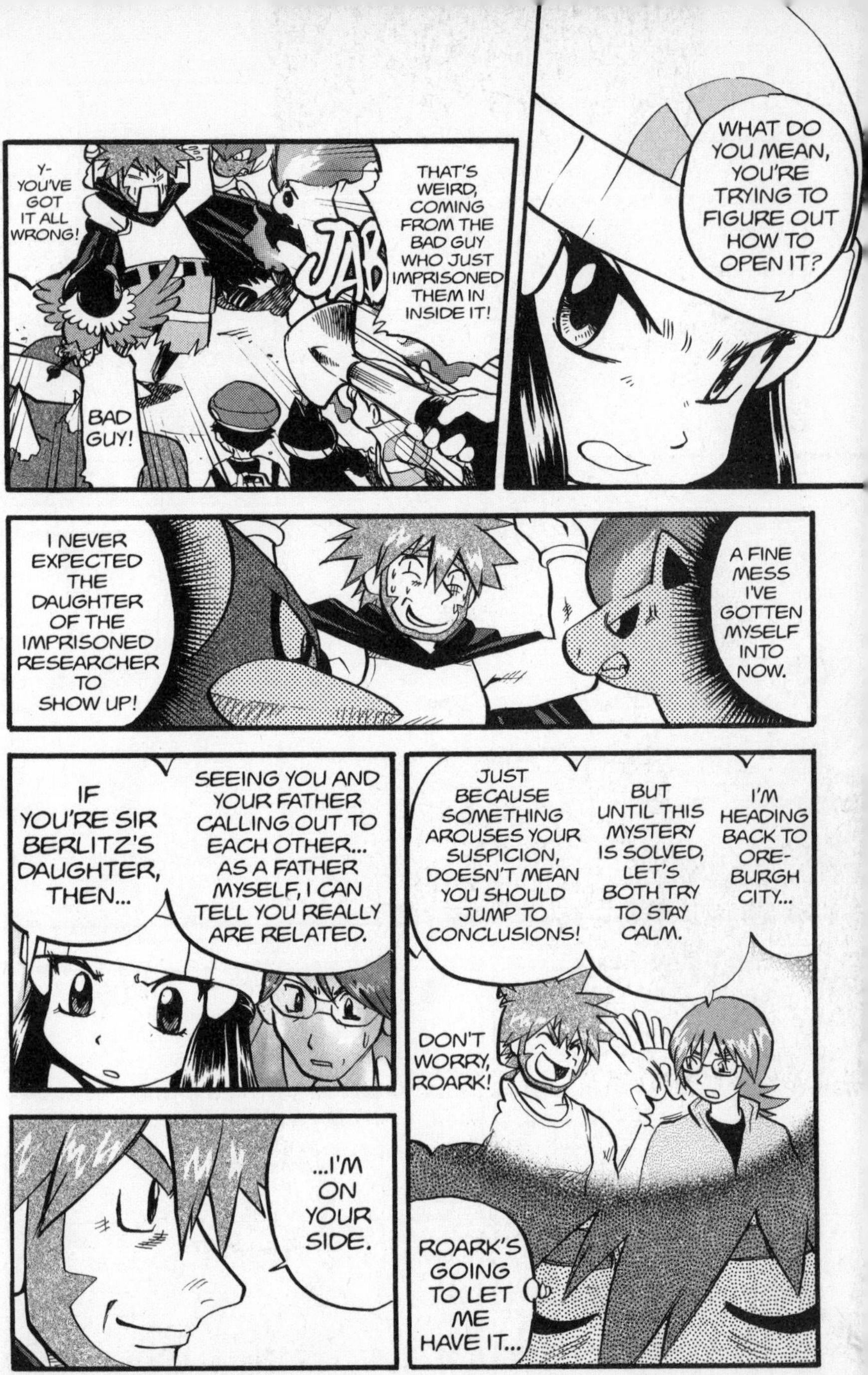
WHAT DO YOU MEAN, YOU'RE TRYING TO FIGURE OUT HOW TO OPEN IT?
THAT'S WEIRD, COMING FROM THE BAD GUY WHO JUST IMPRISONED THEM IN INSIDE IT!
JAB
Y-YOU'VE GOT IT ALL WRONG!
BAD GUY!
A FINE MESS I'VE GOTTEN MYSELF INTO NOW.
I NEVER EXPECTED THE DAUGHTER OF THE IMPRISONED RESEARCHER TO SHOW UP!
I'M HEADING BACK TO ORE-BURGH CITY...
BUT UNTIL THIS MYSTERY IS SOLVED, LET'S BOTH TRY TO STAY CALM.
JUST BECAUSE SOMETHING AROUSES YOUR SUSPICION, DOESN'T MEAN YOU SHOULD JUMP TO CONCLUSIONS!
DON'T WORRY, ROARK!
ROARK'S GOING TO LET ME HAVE IT...
SEEING YOU AND YOUR FATHER CALLING OUT TO EACH OTHER... AS A FATHER MYSELF, I CAN TELL YOU REALLY ARE RELATED.
IF YOU'RE SIR BERLITZ'S DAUGHTER, THEN...
...I'M ON YOUR SIDE.

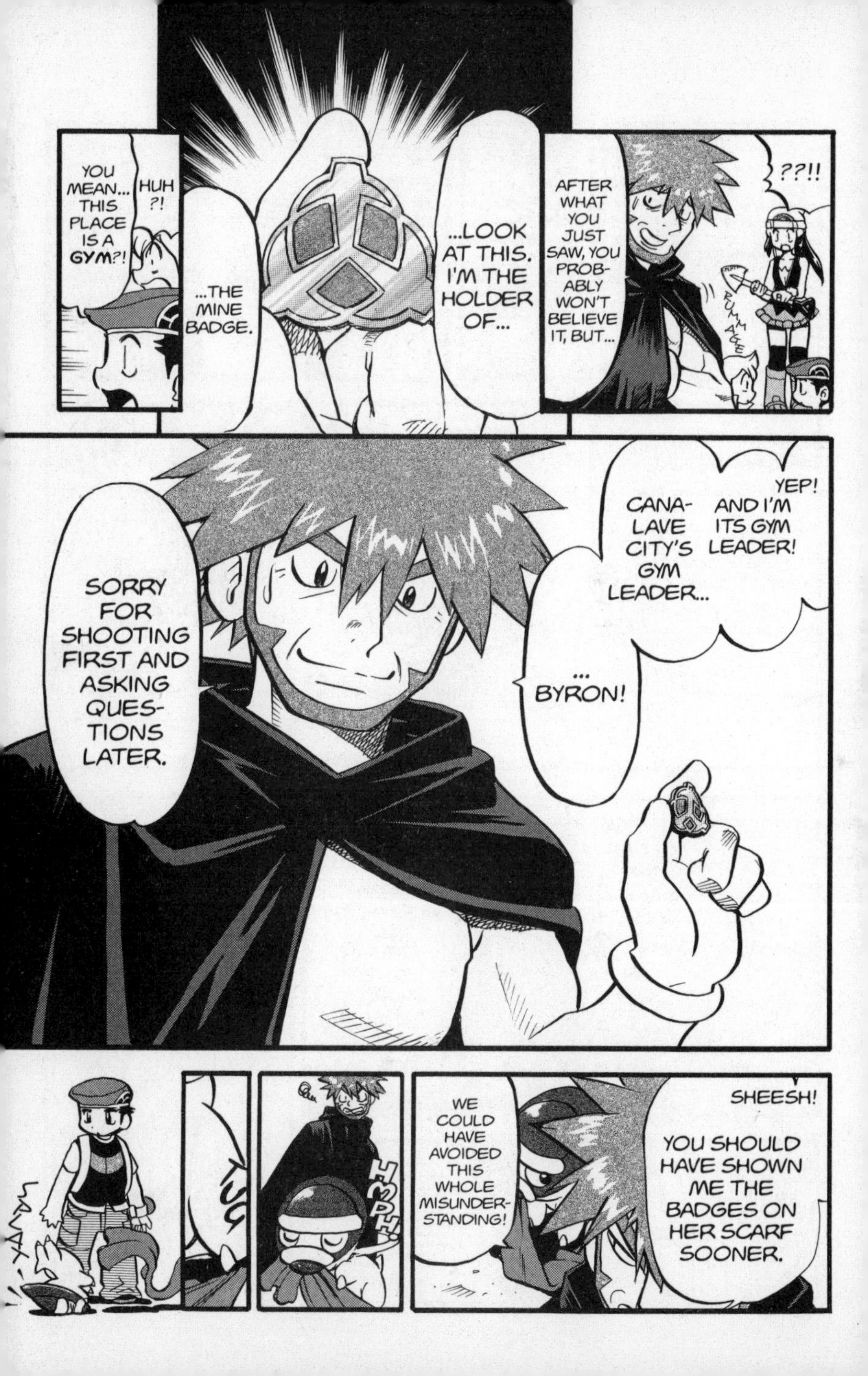
??!!
AFTER WHAT YOU JUST SAW, YOU PROBABLY WON'T BELIEVE IT, BUT...
RUMMAGE
...LOOK AT THIS. I'M THE HOLDER OF...
...THE MINE BADGE.
HUH?!
YOU MEAN... THIS PLACE IS A GYM?!
YEP! AND I'M ITS GYM LEADER!
CANALAVE CITY'S GYM LEADER...
...BYRON!
SORRY FOR SHOOTING FIRST AND ASKING QUESTIONS LATER.
SHEESH!
YOU SHOULD HAVE SHOWN ME THE BADGES ON HER SCARF SOONER.
WE COULD HAVE AVOIDED THIS WHOLE MISUNDERSTANDING!
HMPH!
TUG

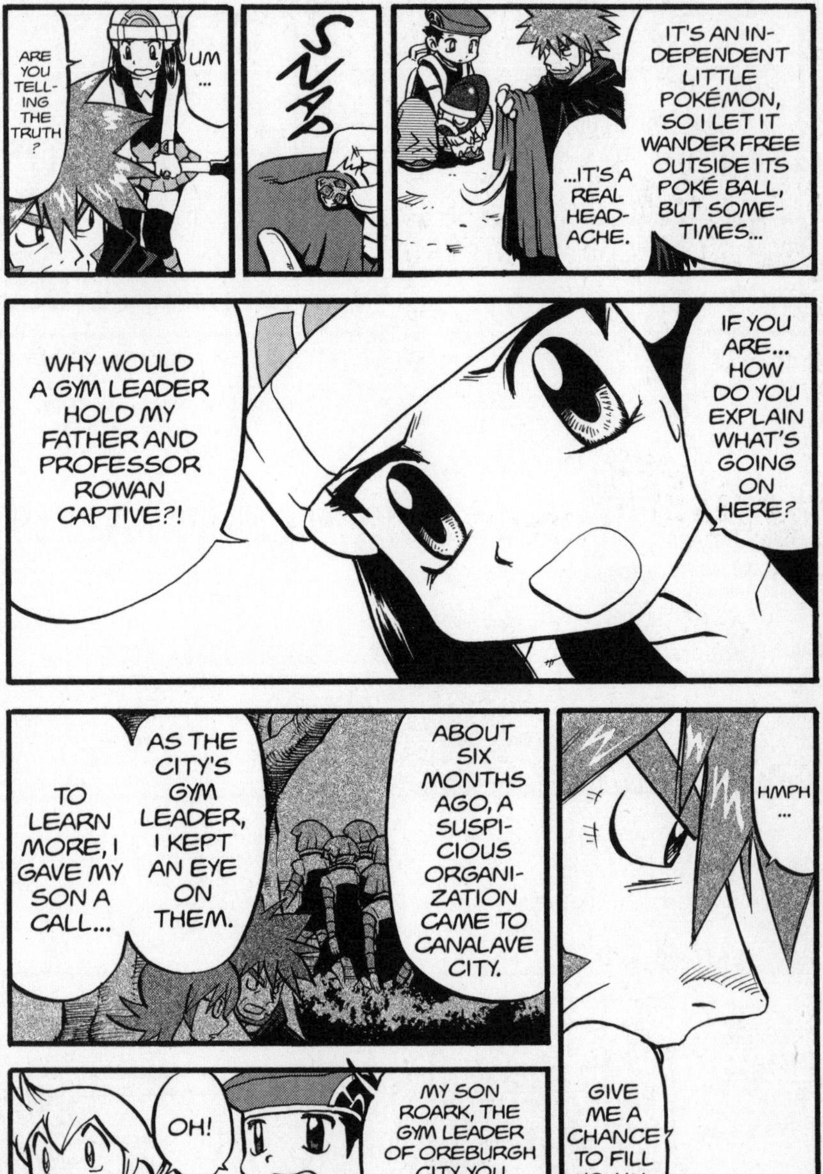
IT'S AN INDEPENDENT LITTLE POKÉMON, SO I LET IT WANDER FREE OUTSIDE ITS POKÉ BALL, BUT SOMETIMES...
...IT'S A REAL HEADACHE.
SNAP
UM ...
ARE YOU TELLING THE TRUTH?
IF YOU ARE... HOW DO YOU EXPLAIN WHAT'S GOING ON HERE?
WHY WOULD A GYM LEADER HOLD MY FATHER AND PROFESSOR ROWAN CAPTIVE?!
HMPH ...
GIVE ME A CHANCE TO FILL YOU IN.
ABOUT SIX MONTHS AGO, A SUSPICIOUS ORGANIZATION CAME TO CANALAVE CITY.
AS THE CITY'S GYM LEADER, I KEPT AN EYE ON THEM.
TO LEARN MORE, I GAVE MY SON A CALL...
MY SON ROARK, THE GYM LEADER OF OREBURGH CITY. YOU BATTLED HIM.
OH!

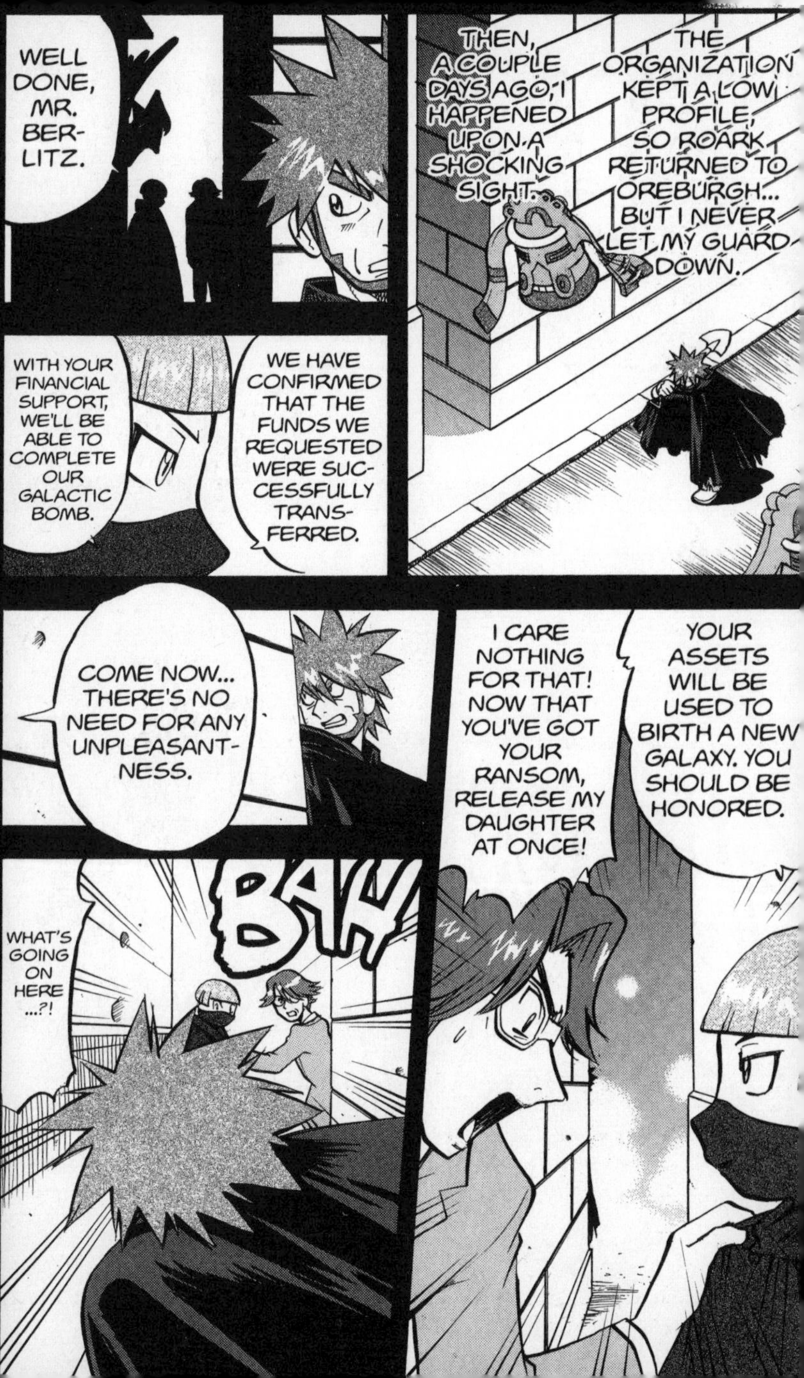
THE ORGANIZATION KEPT A LOW PROFILE, SO ROARK RETURNED TO OREBURGH... BUT I NEVER LET MY GUARD DOWN.
THEN, A COUPLE DAYS AGO, I HAPPENED UPON A SHOCKING SIGHT.
WELL DONE, MR. BER-LITZ.
WE HAVE CONFIRMED THAT THE FUNDS WE REQUESTED WERE SUC-CESSFULLY TRANS-FERRED.
WITH YOUR FINANCIAL SUPPORT, WE'LL BE ABLE TO COMPLETE OUR GALACTIC BOMB.
YOUR ASSETS WILL BE USED TO BIRTH A NEW GALAXY. YOU SHOULD BE HONORED.
I CARE NOTHING FOR THAT! NOW THAT YOU'VE GOT YOUR RANSOM, RELEASE MY DAUGHTER AT ONCE!
COME NOW... THERE'S NO NEED FOR ANY UNPLEASANT-NESS.
BAH
WHAT'S GOING ON HERE ...?!

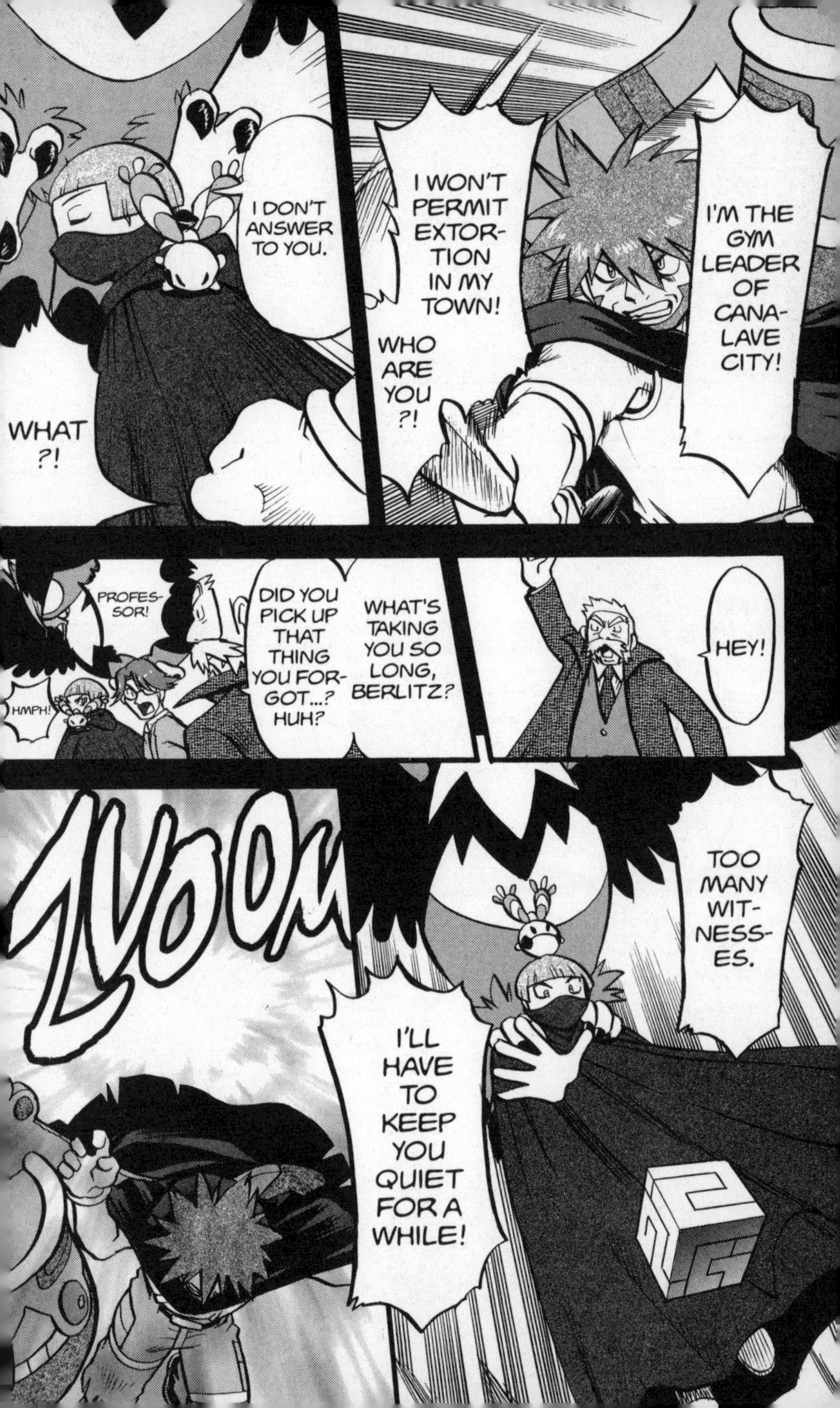
I'M THE GYM LEADER OF CANALAVE CITY!
I WON'T PERMIT EXTORTION IN MY TOWN!
WHO ARE YOU?!
I DON'T ANSWER TO YOU.
WHAT?!
HEY!
WHAT'S TAKING YOU SO LONG, BERLITZ?
DID YOU PICK UP THAT THING YOU FORGOT...? HUH?
PROFESSOR!
HMPH!
TOO MANY WITNESSES.
I'LL HAVE TO KEEP YOU QUIET FOR A WHILE!

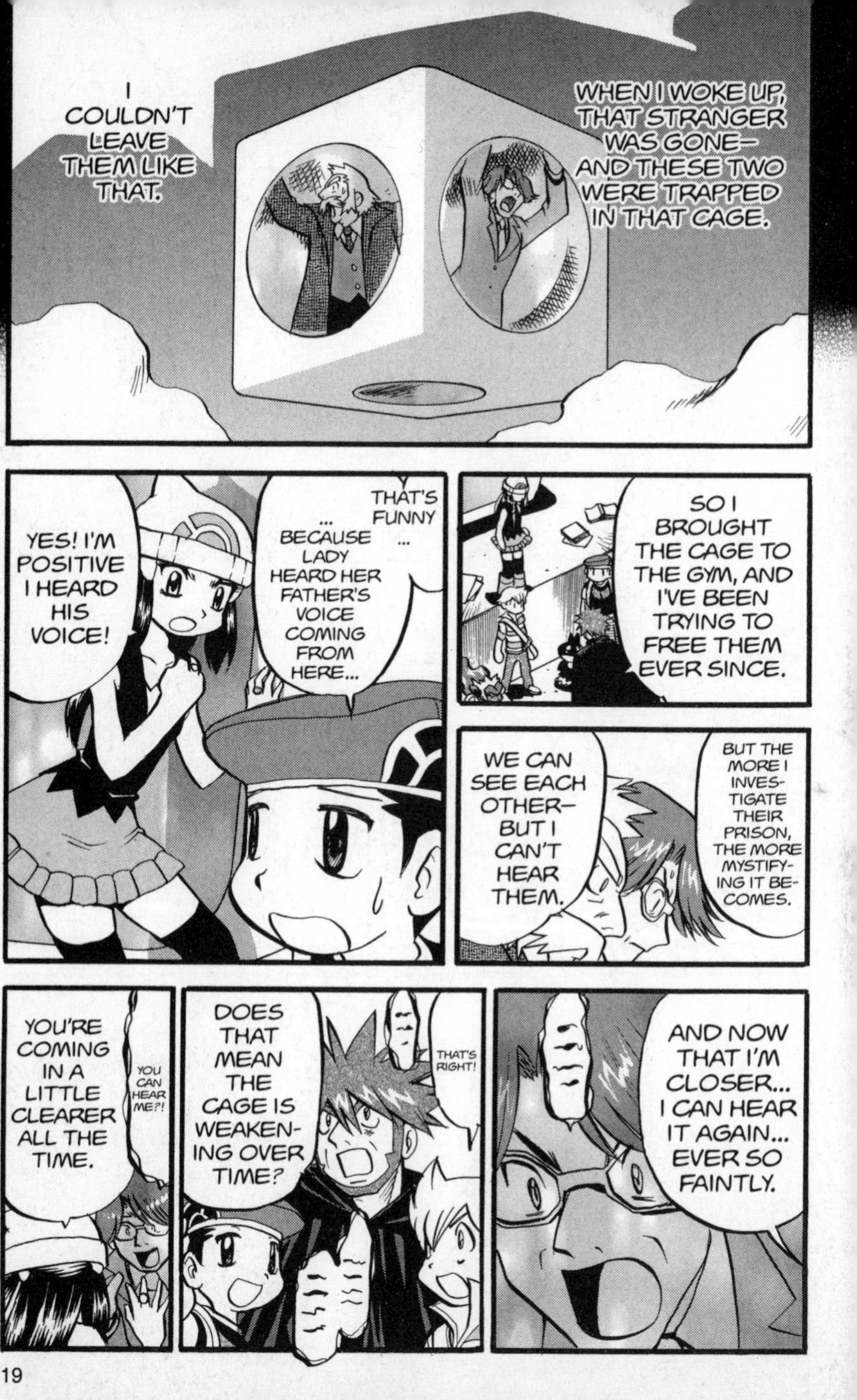
WHEN I WOKE UP, THAT STRANGER WAS GONE— AND THESE TWO WERE TRAPPED IN THAT CAGE.
I COULDN'T LEAVE THEM LIKE THAT.
SO I BROUGHT THE CAGE TO THE GYM, AND I'VE BEEN TRYING TO FREE THEM EVER SINCE.
BUT THE MORE I INVESTIGATE THEIR PRISON, THE MORE MYSTIFYING IT BECOMES.
WE CAN SEE EACH OTHER— BUT I CAN'T HEAR THEM.
THAT'S FUNNY ... ... BECAUSE LADY HEARD HER FATHER'S VOICE COMING FROM HERE...
YES! I'M POSITIVE I HEARD HIS VOICE!
AND NOW THAT I'M CLOSER... I CAN HEAR IT AGAIN... EVER SO FAINTLY.
THAT'S RIGHT!
DOES THAT MEAN THE CAGE IS WEAKENING OVER TIME?
YOU CAN HEAR ME?!
YOU'RE COMING IN A LITTLE CLEARER ALL THE TIME.

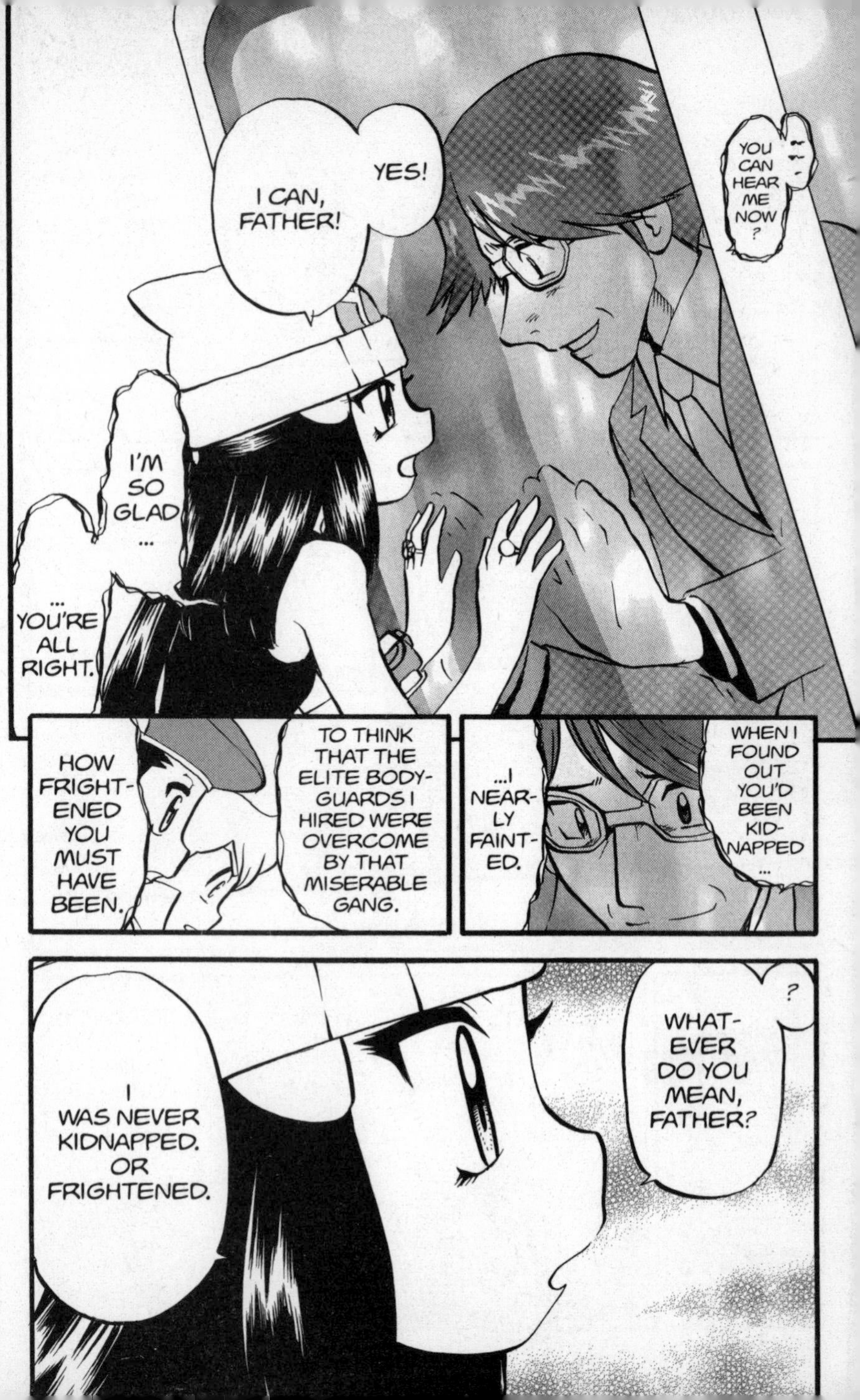
YOU CAN HEAR ME NOW?
YES!
I CAN, FATHER!
I'M SO GLAD...
...YOU'RE ALL RIGHT.
WHEN I FOUND OUT YOU'D BEEN KIDNAPPED...
...I NEARLY FAINTED.
TO THINK THAT THE ELITE BODYGUARDS I HIRED WERE OVERCOME BY THAT MISERABLE GANG.
HOW FRIGHTENED YOU MUST HAVE BEEN.
?
WHATEVER DO YOU MEAN, FATHER?
I WAS NEVER KIDNAPPED. OR FRIGHTENED.

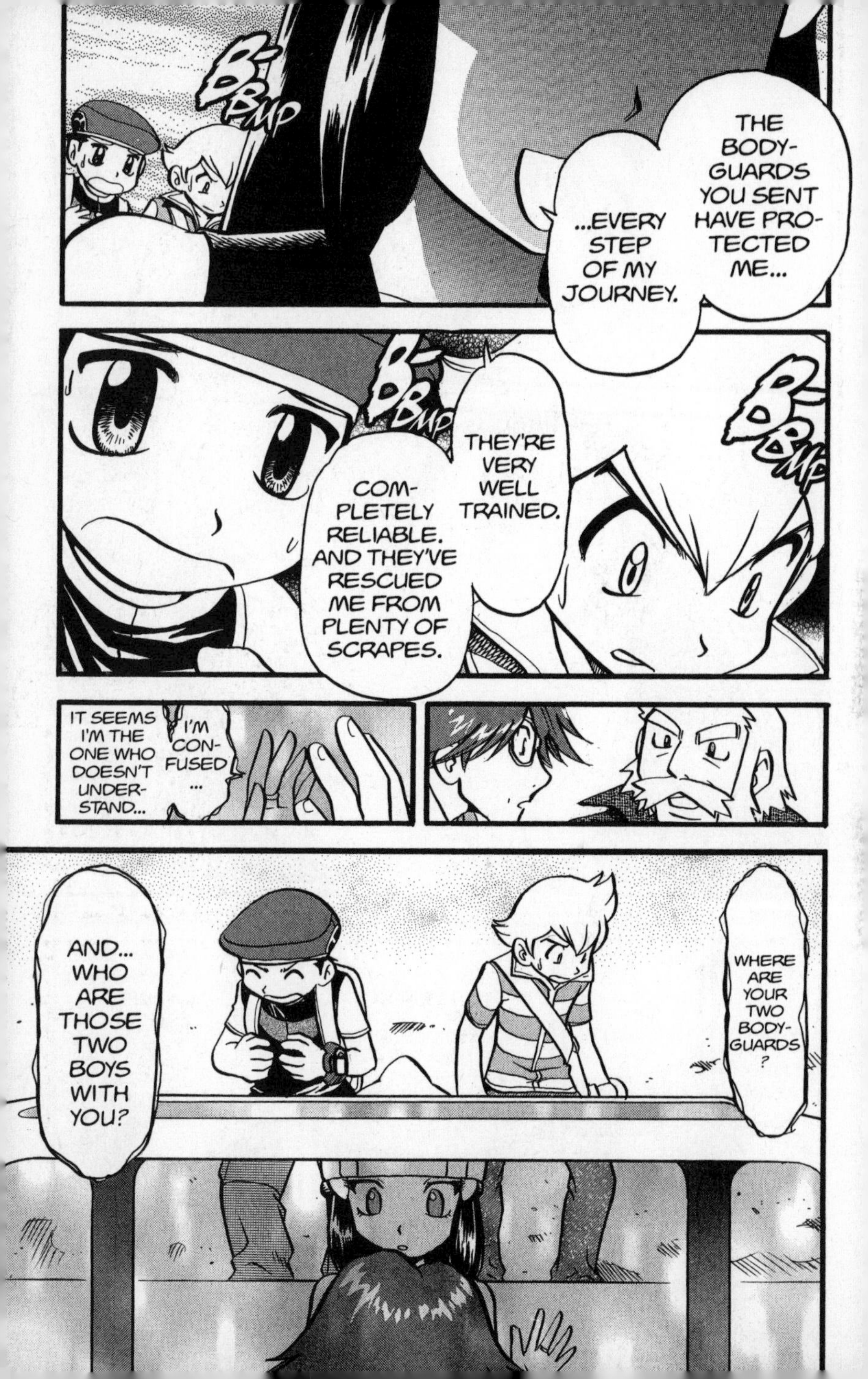
THE BODYGUARDS YOU SENT HAVE PROTECTED ME...
...EVERY STEP OF MY JOURNEY.
B-BMP
B-BMP
THEY'RE VERY WELL TRAINED.
COMPLETELY RELIABLE. AND THEY'VE RESCUED ME FROM PLENTY OF SCRAPES.
B-BMP
I'M CONFUSED...
IT SEEMS I'M THE ONE WHO DOESN'T UNDERSTAND...
WHERE ARE YOUR TWO BODYGUARDS?
AND... WHO ARE THOSE TWO BOYS WITH YOU?

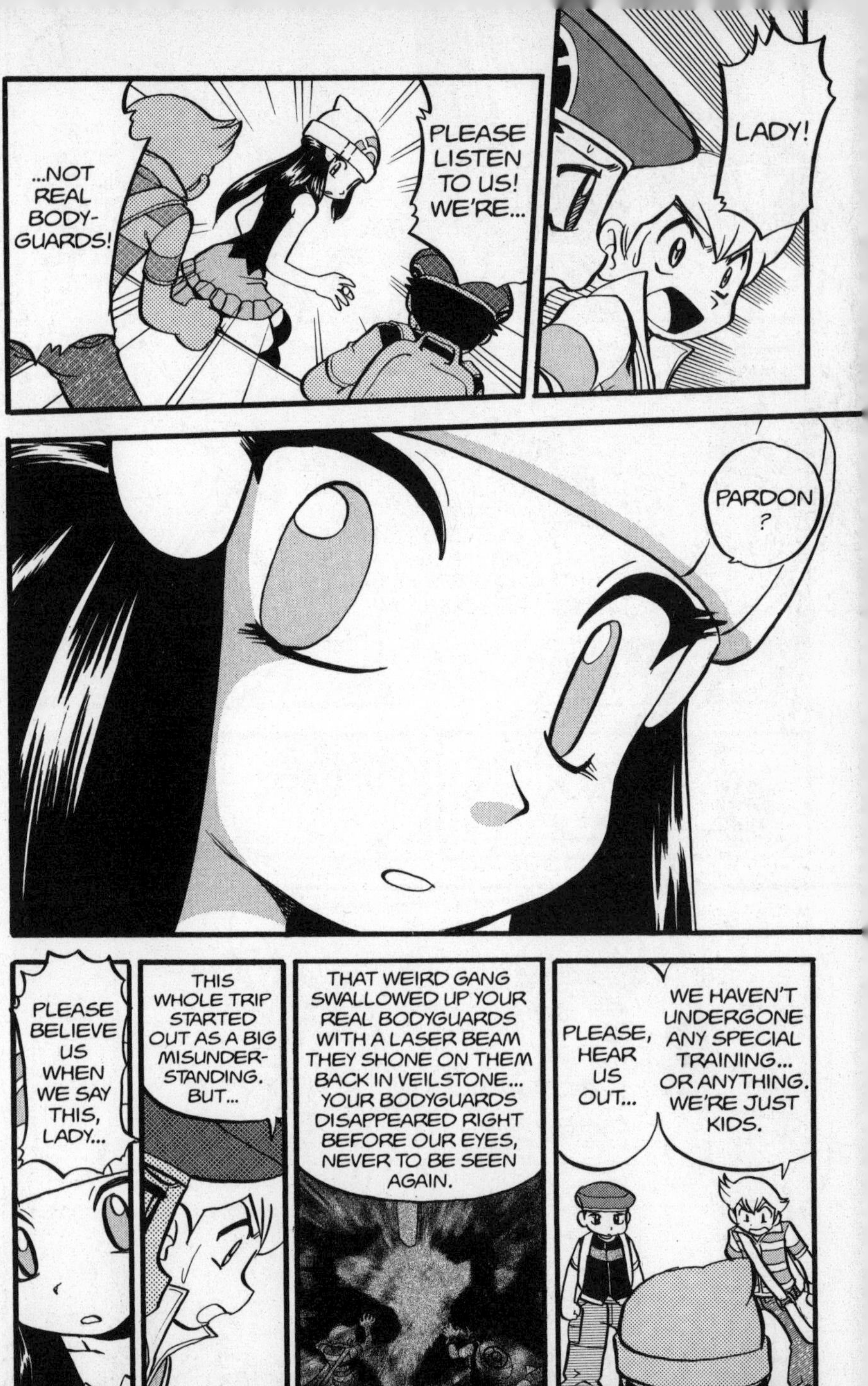
LADY!
PLEASE LISTEN TO US! WE'RE...
...NOT REAL BODY-GUARDS!
PARDON?
WE HAVEN'T UNDERGONE ANY SPECIAL TRAINING... OR ANYTHING. WE'RE JUST KIDS.
PLEASE, HEAR US OUT...
THAT WEIRD GANG SWALLOWED UP YOUR REAL BODYGUARDS WITH A LASER BEAM THEY SHONE ON THEM BACK IN VEILSTONE... YOUR BODYGUARDS DISAPPEARED RIGHT BEFORE OUR EYES, NEVER TO BE SEEN AGAIN.
THIS WHOLE TRIP STARTED OUT AS A BIG MISUNDER-STANDING. BUT...
PLEASE BELIEVE US WHEN WE SAY THIS, LADY...

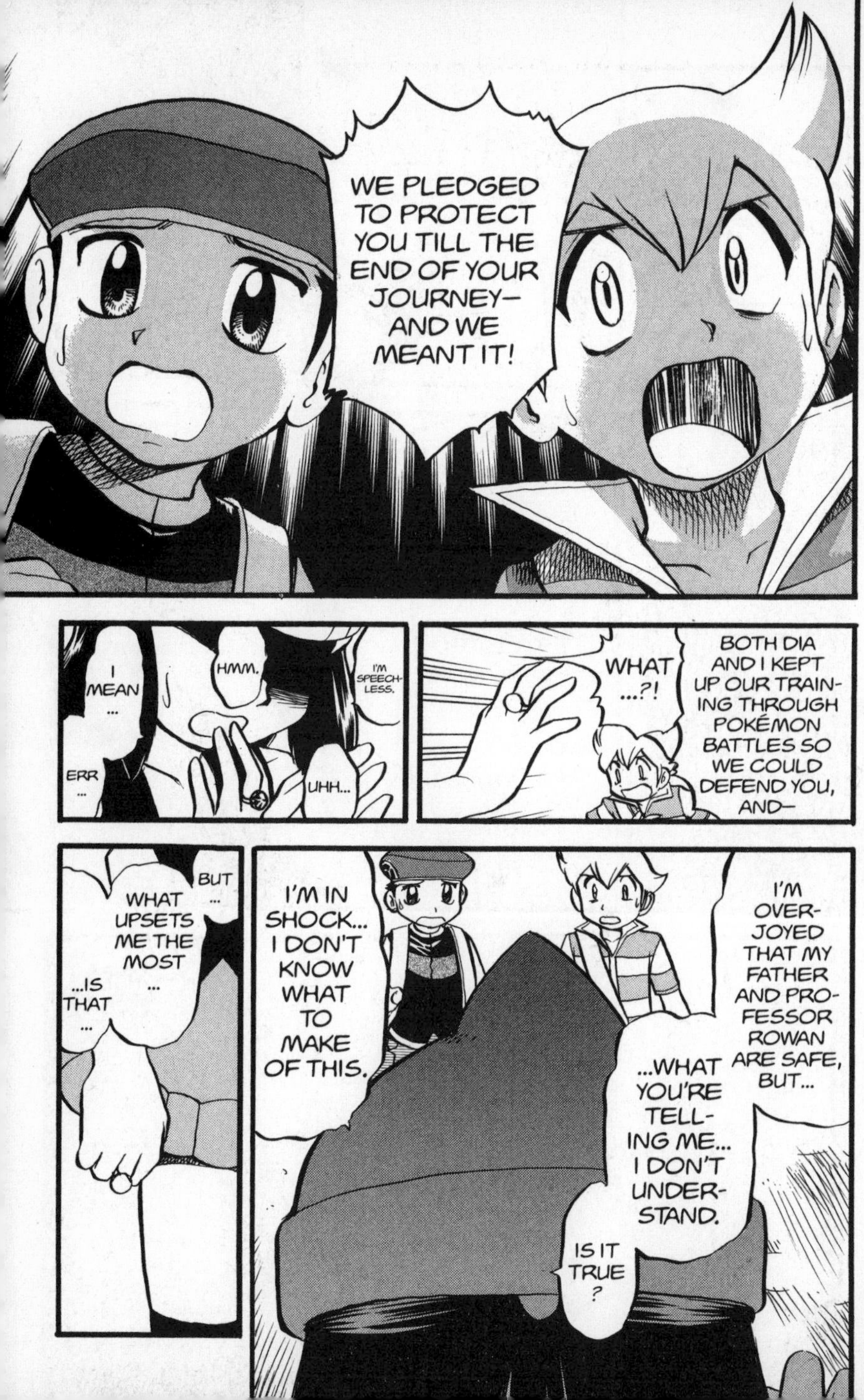
WE PLEDGED TO PROTECT YOU TILL THE END OF YOUR JOURNEY—AND WE MEANT IT!
BOTH DIA AND I KEPT UP OUR TRAIN-ING THROUGH POKÉMON BATTLES SO WE COULD DEFEND YOU, AND—
WHAT ...?!
I'M SPEECH-LESS.
HMM.
I MEAN ...
UHH...
ERR ...
I'M OVER-JOYED THAT MY FATHER AND PRO-FESSOR ROWAN ARE SAFE, BUT...
I'M IN SHOCK... I DON'T KNOW WHAT TO MAKE OF THIS.
...WHAT YOU'RE TELL-ING ME... I DON'T UNDER-STAND.
IS IT TRUE?
BUT ...
WHAT UPSETS ME THE MOST ...
...IS THAT ...

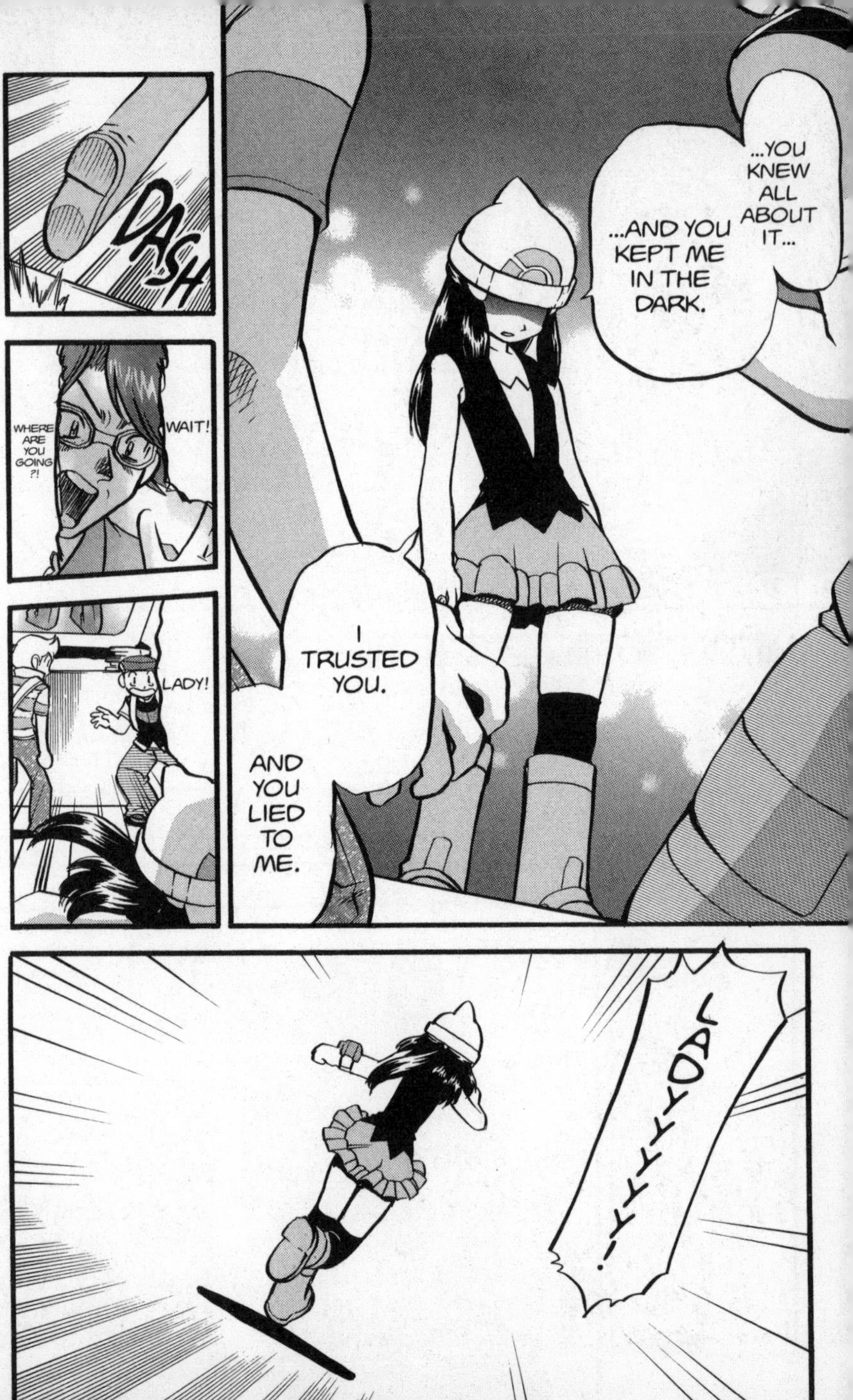
...YOU KNEW ALL ABOUT IT...
...AND YOU KEPT ME IN THE DARK.
I TRUSTED YOU.
AND YOU LIED TO ME.
DASH
WAIT!
WHERE ARE YOU GOING?!
LADY!
LADYYYYYY—!

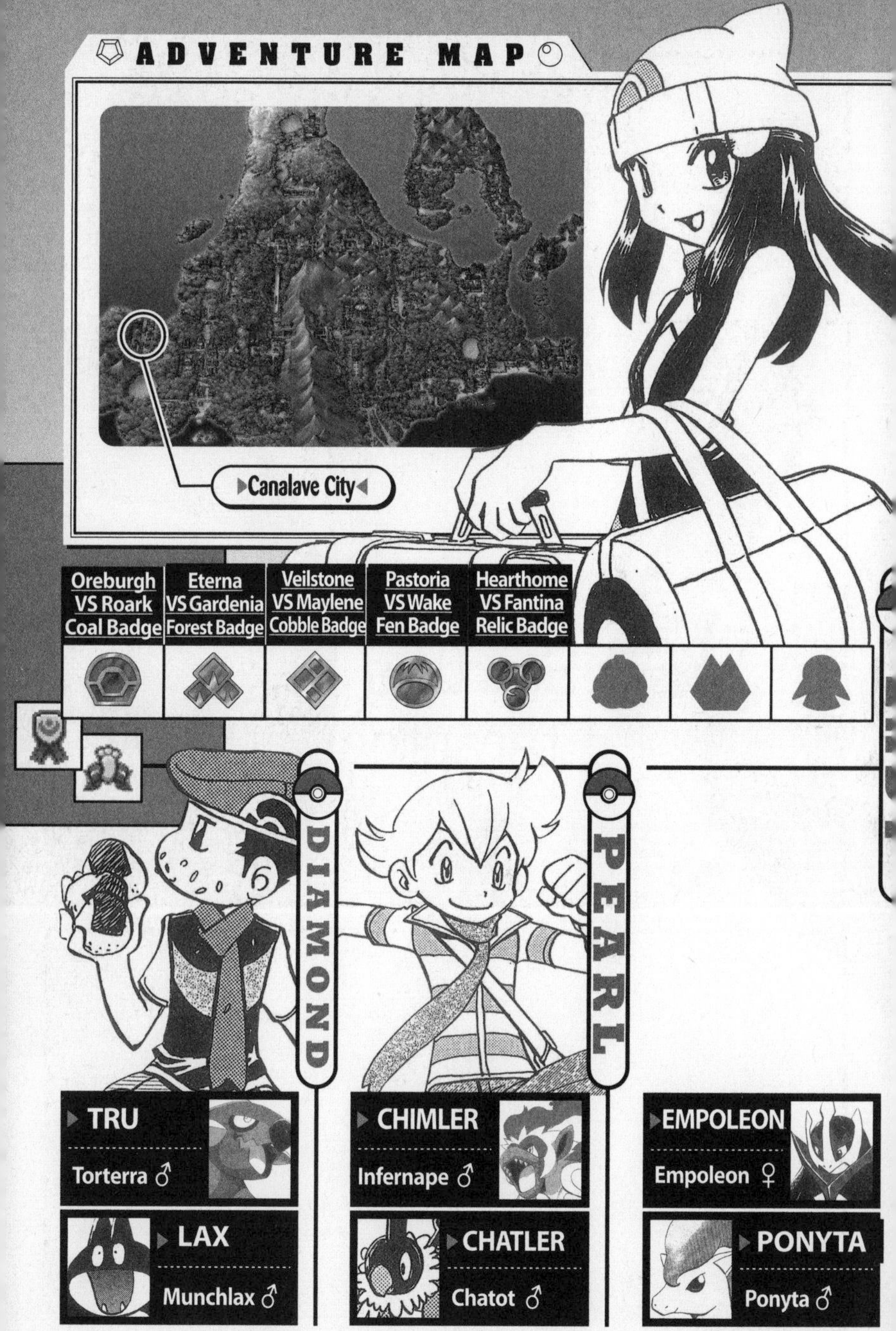
ADVENTURE MAP
Canalave City
Oreburgh
VS Roark
Coal Badge
Eterna
VS Gardenia
Forest Badge
Veilstone
VS Maylene
Cobble Badge
Pastoria
VS Wake
Fen Badge
Hearthome
VS Fantina
Relic Badge
DIAMOND
PEARL
TRU
Torterra ♂
LAX
Munchlax ♂
CHIMLER
Infernape ♂
CHATLER
Chatot ♂
EMPOLEON
Empoleon ♀
PONYTA
Ponyta ♂

39

Startling
Staraptor

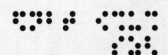

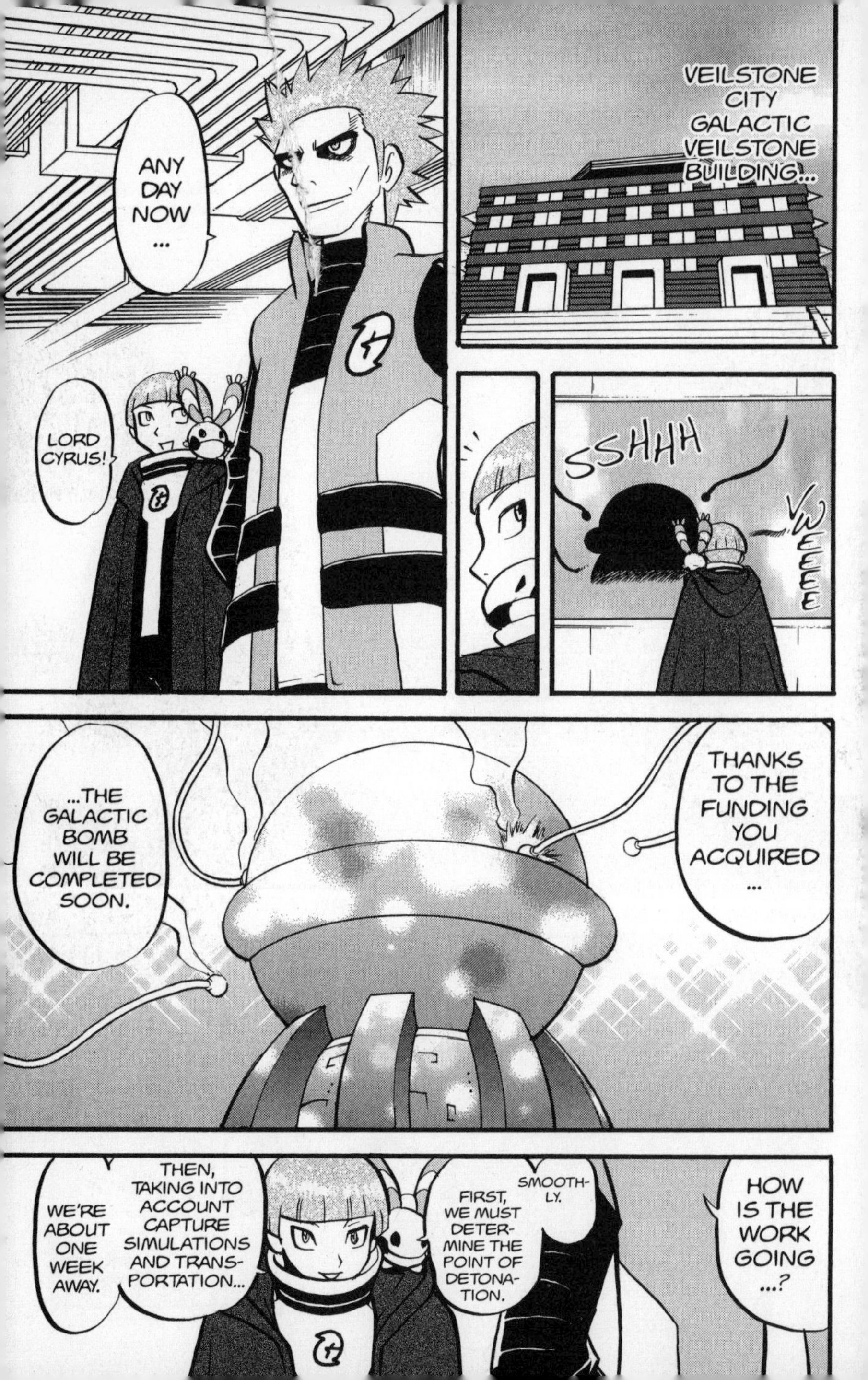
VEILSTONE CITY GALACTIC VEILSTONE BUILDING...
SSHHH
VWEEEE
ANY DAY NOW...
LORD CYRUS!
THANKS TO THE FUNDING YOU ACQUIRED...
...THE GALACTIC BOMB WILL BE COMPLETED SOON.
HOW IS THE WORK GOING...?
SMOOTH-LY.
FIRST, WE MUST DETER-MINE THE POINT OF DETONA-TION.
THEN, TAKING INTO ACCOUNT CAPTURE SIMULATIONS AND TRANS-PORTATION...
WE'RE ABOUT ONE WEEK AWAY.

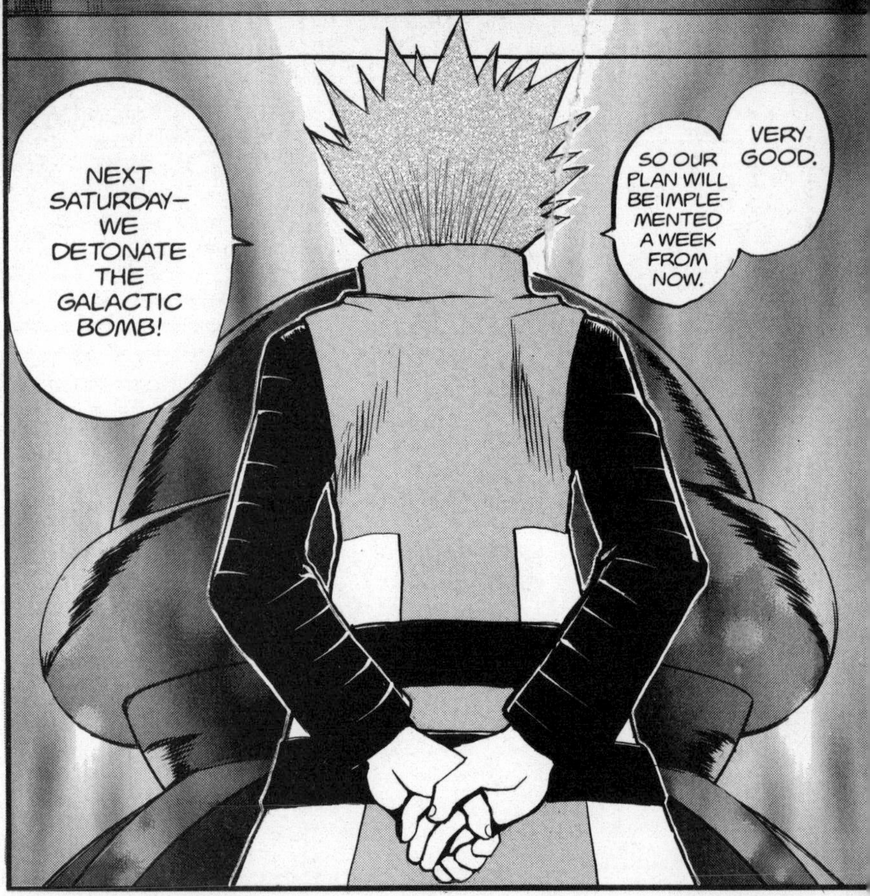
VERY GOOD.
SO OUR PLAN WILL BE IMPLE-MENTED A WEEK FROM NOW.
NEXT SATURDAY—WE DETONATE THE GALACTIC BOMB!

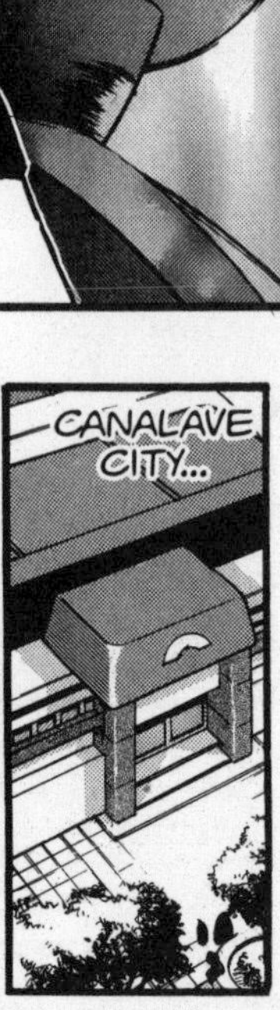
CANALAVE CITY...

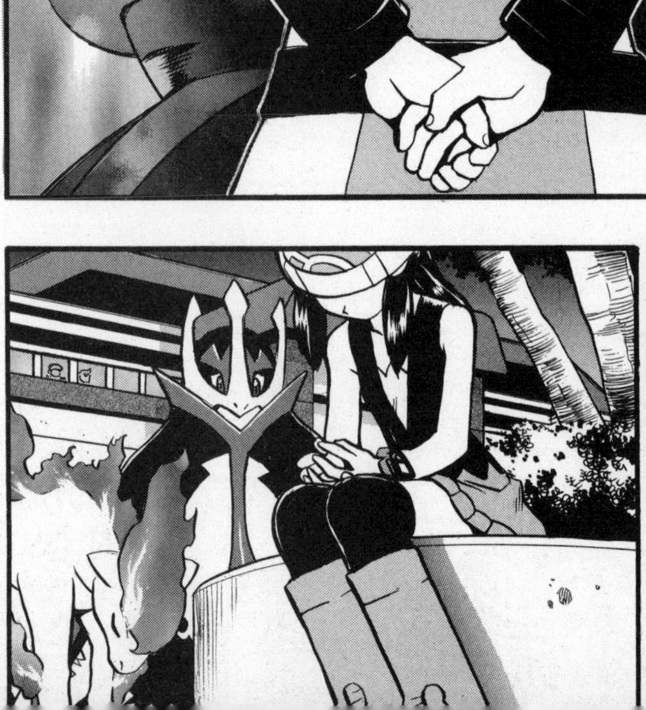

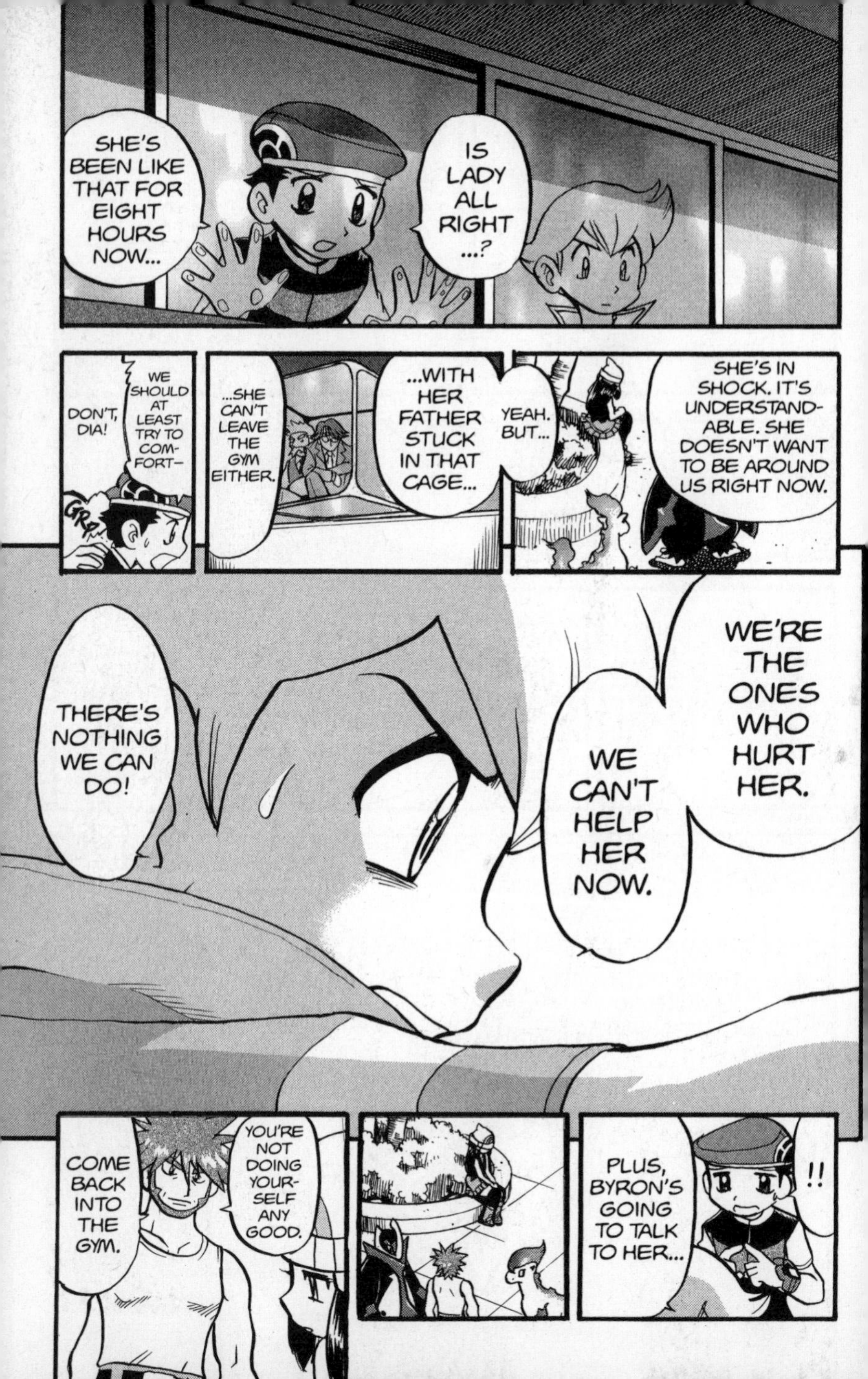
IS LADY ALL RIGHT ...?
SHE'S BEEN LIKE THAT FOR EIGHT HOURS NOW...
SHE'S IN SHOCK. IT'S UNDERSTANDABLE. SHE DOESN'T WANT TO BE AROUND US RIGHT NOW.
YEAH. BUT...
...WITH HER FATHER STUCK IN THAT CAGE...
...SHE CAN'T LEAVE THE GYM EITHER.
WE SHOULD AT LEAST TRY TO COMFORT–
DON'T, DIA!
GRP
WE'RE THE ONES WHO HURT HER.
WE CAN'T HELP HER NOW.
THERE'S NOTHING WE CAN DO!
!!
PLUS, BYRON'S GOING TO TALK TO HER...
YOU'RE NOT DOING YOURSELF ANY GOOD.
COME BACK INTO THE GYM.

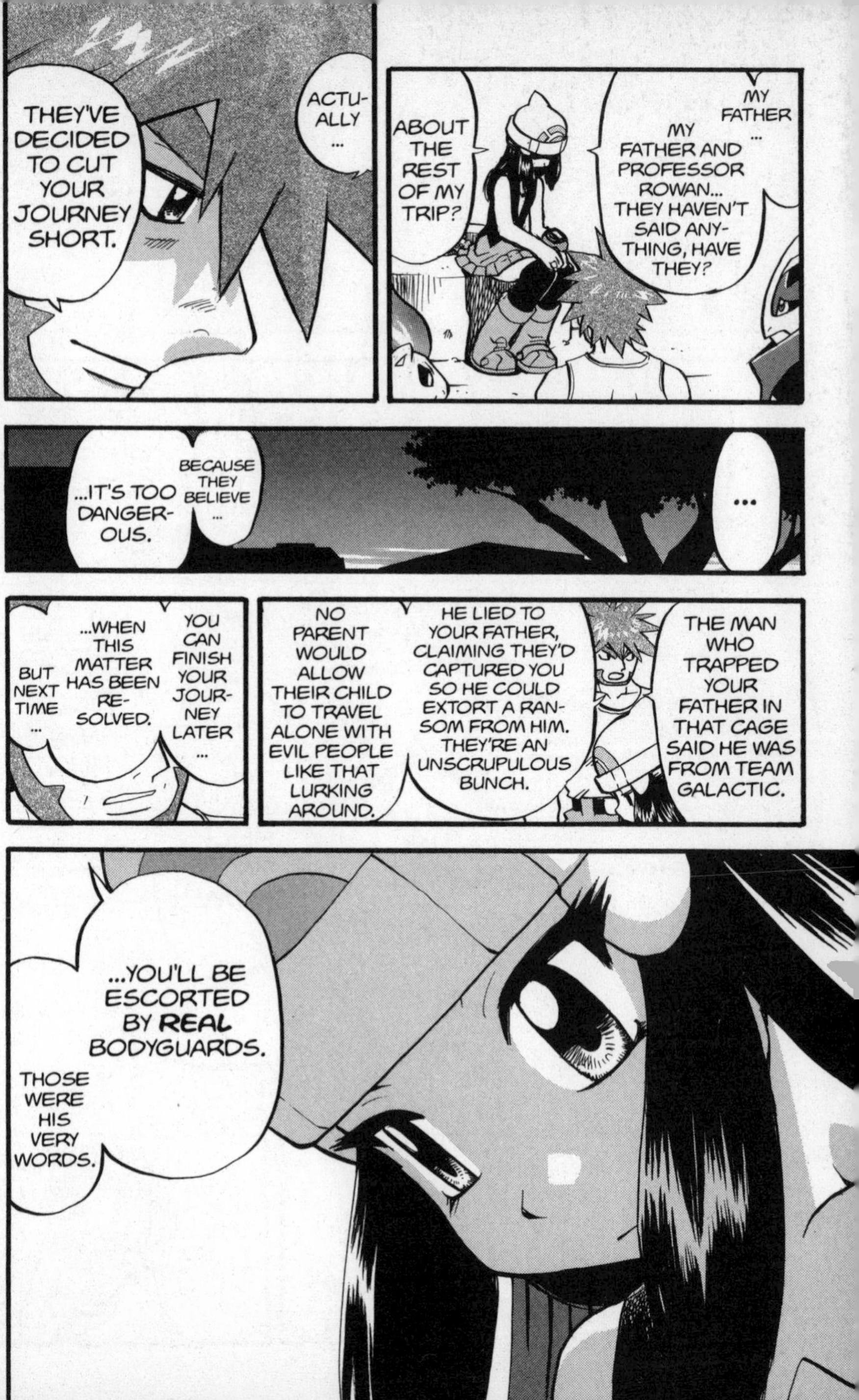
MY FATHER ...
MY FATHER AND PROFESSOR ROWAN... THEY HAVEN'T SAID ANYTHING, HAVE THEY?
ABOUT THE REST OF MY TRIP?
ACTUALLY ...
THEY'VE DECIDED TO CUT YOUR JOURNEY SHORT.
...
BECAUSE THEY BELIEVE ...
...IT'S TOO DANGEROUS.
THE MAN WHO TRAPPED YOUR FATHER IN THAT CAGE SAID HE WAS FROM TEAM GALACTIC.
HE LIED TO YOUR FATHER, CLAIMING THEY'D CAPTURED YOU SO HE COULD EXTORT A RANSOM FROM HIM. THEY'RE AN UNSCRUPULOUS BUNCH.
NO PARENT WOULD ALLOW THEIR CHILD TO TRAVEL ALONE WITH EVIL PEOPLE LIKE THAT LURKING AROUND.
YOU CAN FINISH YOUR JOURNEY LATER ...
...WHEN THIS MATTER HAS BEEN RESOLVED.
BUT NEXT TIME ...
...YOU'LL BE ESCORTED BY **REAL** BODYGUARDS.
THOSE WERE HIS VERY WORDS.

UNFOR-TUNATELY, THIS IS WHERE YOU THREE PART WAYS.
THEY'LL BE GOING BACK TO THEIR OWN HOMES.
ALONG WITH... PEARL AND DIAMOND?
NO.
AS SOON AS YOUR FATHER AND PRO-FESSOR ROWAN GET OUT OF THAT CAGE...
...YOU'LL BE RE-TURNING TO SAND-GEM TOWN.
BUT IT'S LATE NOW...
IF YOU DON'T WANT TO RETURN TO THE GYM...
...WE HAVE ACCOM-MODATIONS WHERE YOU CAN SPEND THE NIGHT.
PONYTA ...
EMPO-LEON ...
WHAT SHOULD I DO?
MY HEART IS SO HEAVY... AND I'M SO TIRED...
I CAN'T STAND TO... THINK ABOUT IT...ANY-MORE...
FWOMP

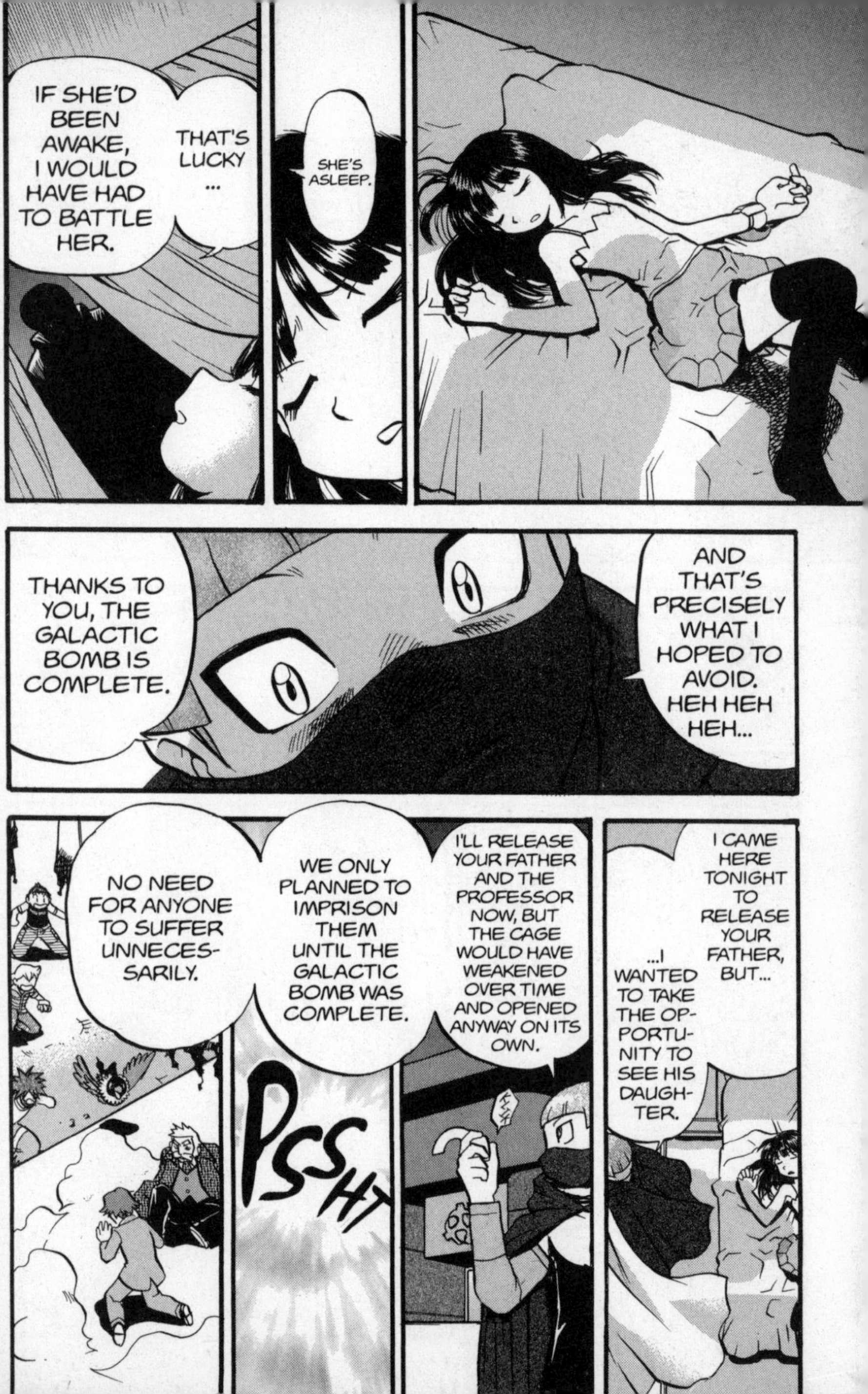
SHE'S ASLEEP.
THAT'S LUCKY ...
IF SHE'D BEEN AWAKE, I WOULD HAVE HAD TO BATTLE HER.
AND THAT'S PRECISELY WHAT I HOPED TO AVOID. HEH HEH HEH...
THANKS TO YOU, THE GALACTIC BOMB IS COMPLETE.
I CAME HERE TONIGHT TO RELEASE YOUR FATHER, BUT...
...I WANTED TO TAKE THE OPPORTUNITY TO SEE HIS DAUGHTER.
I'LL RELEASE YOUR FATHER AND THE PROFESSOR NOW, BUT THE CAGE WOULD HAVE WEAKENED OVER TIME AND OPENED ANYWAY ON ITS OWN.
WE ONLY PLANNED TO IMPRISON THEM UNTIL THE GALACTIC BOMB WAS COMPLETE.
NO NEED FOR ANYONE TO SUFFER UNNECESSARILY.
PSSHT

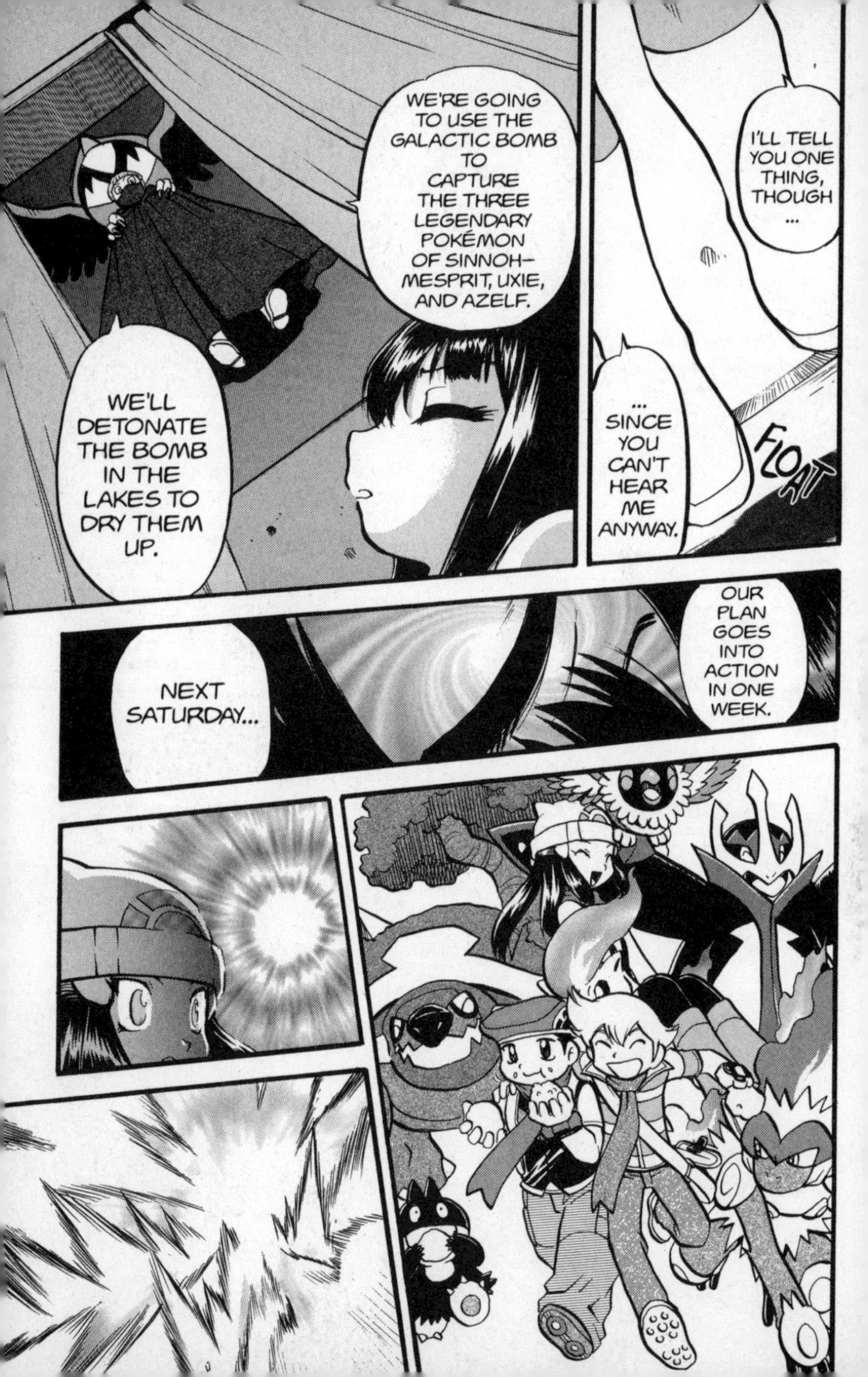
I'LL TELL YOU ONE THING, THOUGH ...
... SINCE YOU CAN'T HEAR ME ANYWAY.
FLOAT
WE'RE GOING TO USE THE GALACTIC BOMB TO CAPTURE THE THREE LEGENDARY POKÉMON OF SINNOH—MESPRIT, UXIE, AND AZELF.
WE'LL DETONATE THE BOMB IN THE LAKES TO DRY THEM UP.
OUR PLAN GOES INTO ACTION IN ONE WEEK.
NEXT SATURDAY...

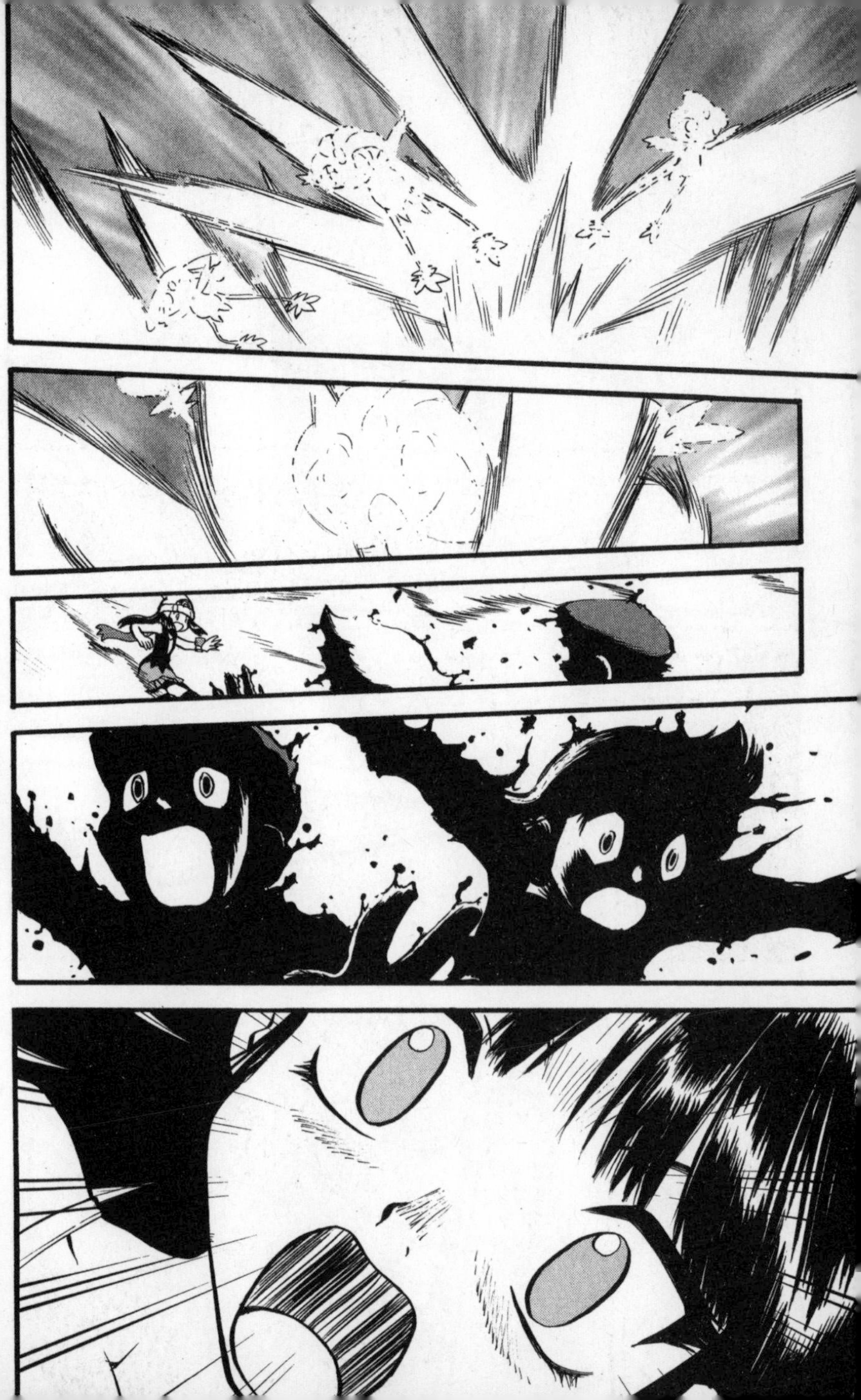

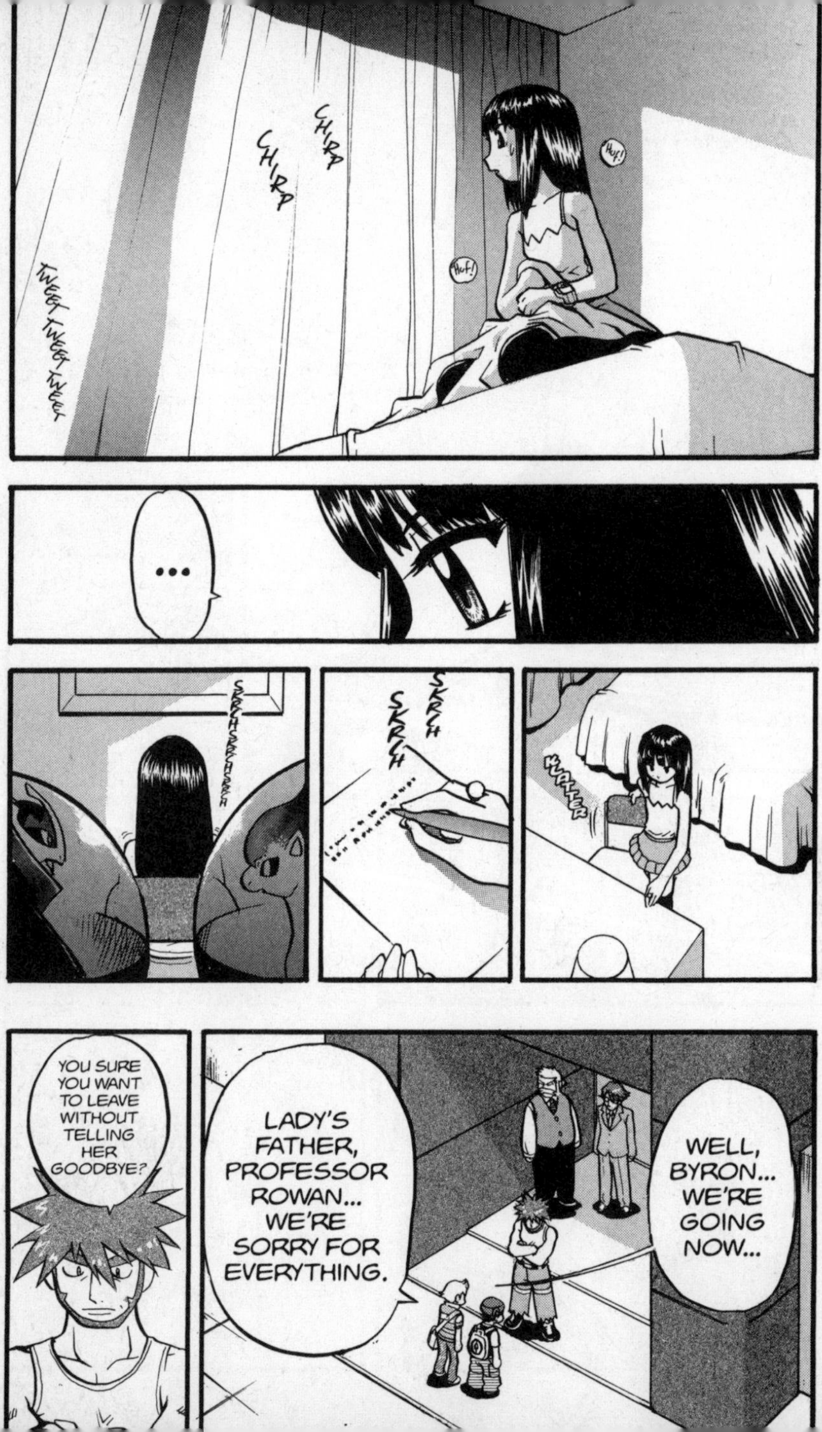
CHIRP
CHIRP
Huf!
Huf!
TWEET TWEET TWEET TWEET
...
KLATTER
SKRCH
SKRCH
SKRCHSKRCHSKRCH
WELL, BYRON... WE'RE GOING NOW...
LADY'S FATHER, PROFESSOR ROWAN... WE'RE SORRY FOR EVERYTHING.
YOU SURE YOU WANT TO LEAVE WITHOUT TELLING HER GOODBYE?

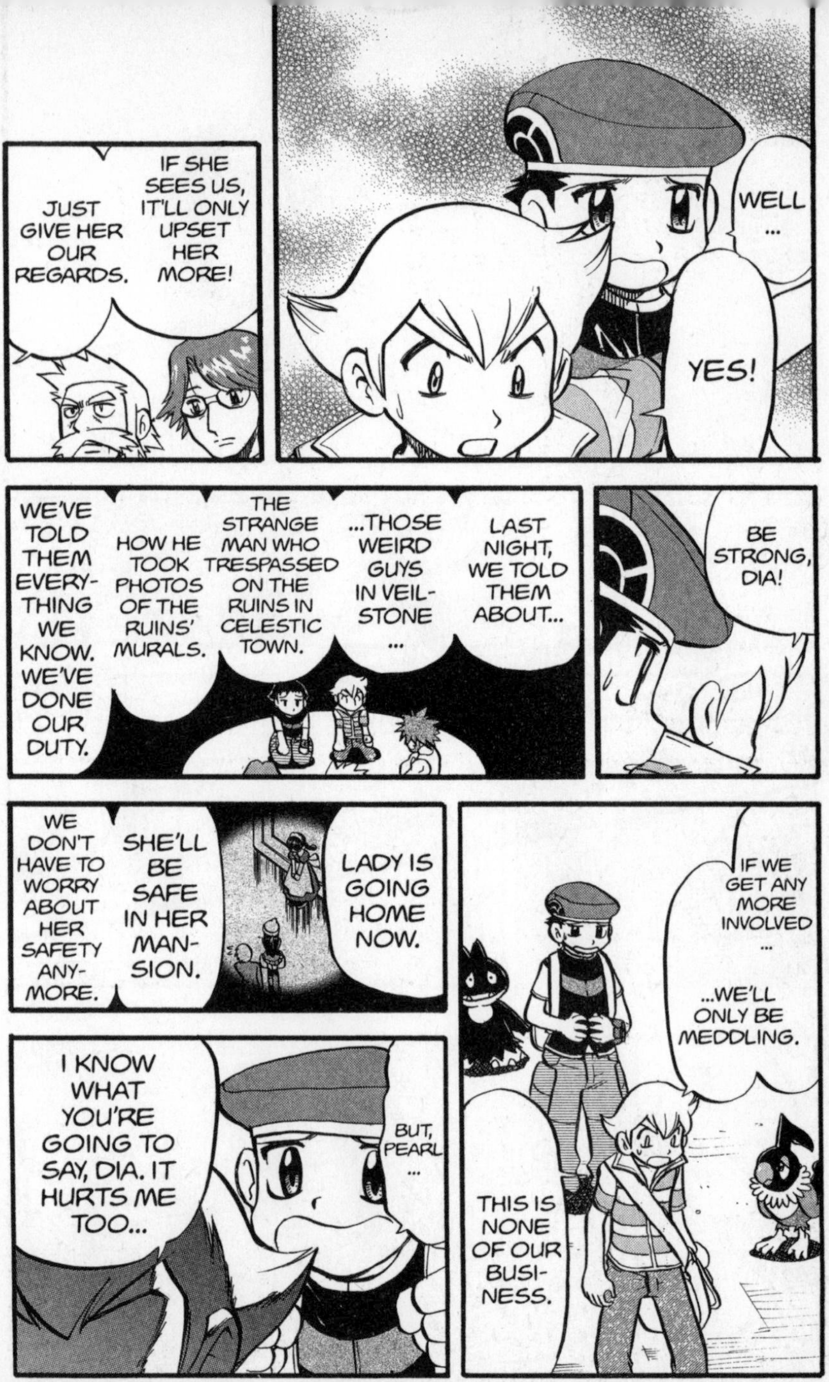
WELL ...
YES!
IF SHE SEES US, IT'LL ONLY UPSET HER MORE!
JUST GIVE HER OUR REGARDS.
BE STRONG, DIA!
LAST NIGHT, WE TOLD THEM ABOUT...
...THOSE WEIRD GUYS IN VEIL-STONE ...
THE STRANGE MAN WHO TRESPASSED ON THE RUINS IN CELESTIC TOWN.
HOW HE TOOK PHOTOS OF THE RUINS' MURALS.
WE'VE TOLD THEM EVERY-THING WE KNOW. WE'VE DONE OUR DUTY.
IF WE GET ANY MORE INVOLVED ...
...WE'LL ONLY BE MEDDLING.
THIS IS NONE OF OUR BUSI-NESS.
LADY IS GOING HOME NOW.
SHE'LL BE SAFE IN HER MAN-SION.
WE DON'T HAVE TO WORRY ABOUT HER SAFETY ANY-MORE.
BUT, PEARL ...
I KNOW WHAT YOU'RE GOING TO SAY, DIA. IT HURTS ME TOO...

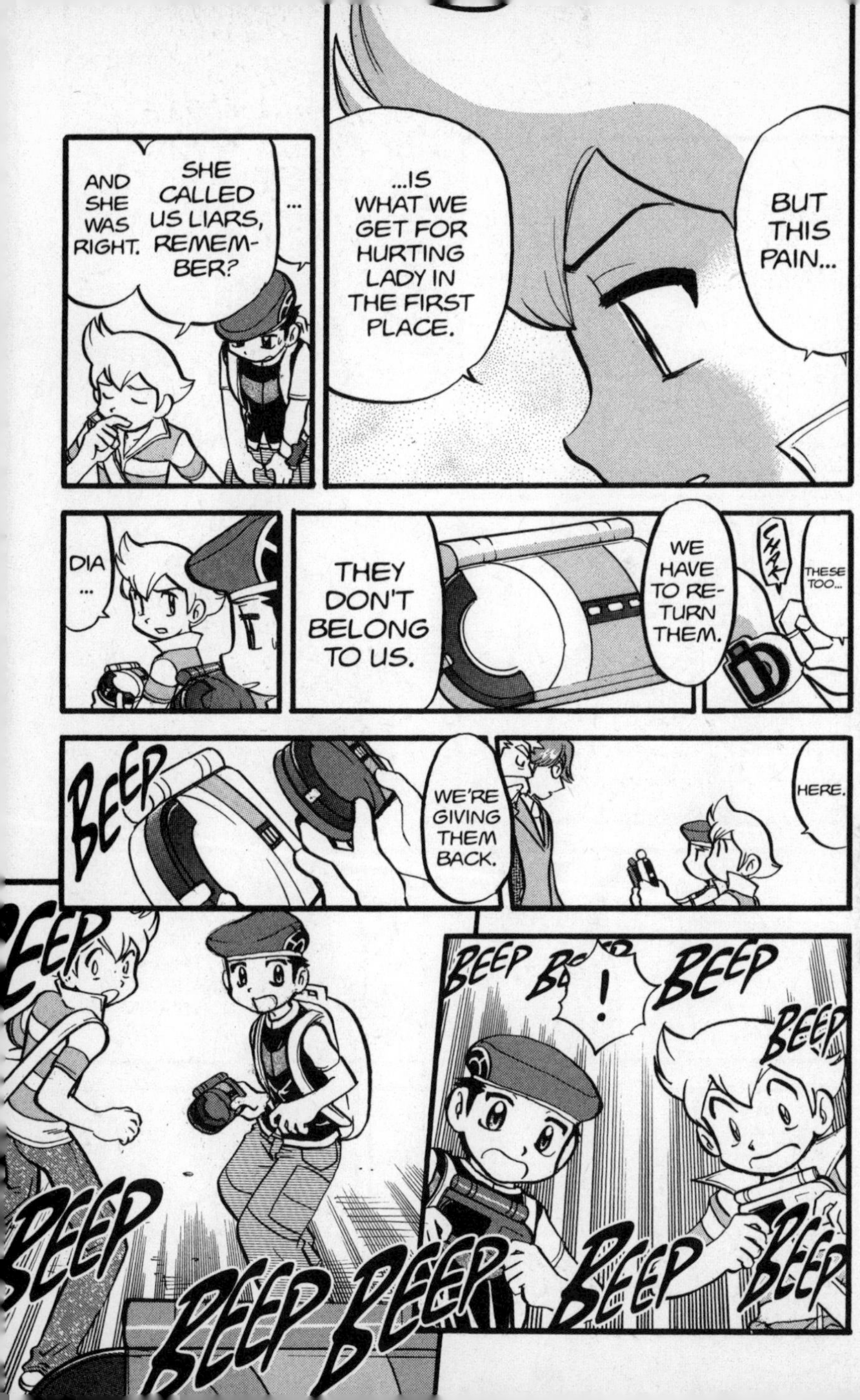
BUT THIS PAIN...
...IS WHAT WE GET FOR HURTING LADY IN THE FIRST PLACE.
SHE CALLED US LIARS, REMEMBER?
...
AND SHE WAS RIGHT.
THESE TOO...
CHAK
WE HAVE TO RETURN THEM.
THEY DON'T BELONG TO US.
DIA...
HERE.
WE'RE GIVING THEM BACK.
BEEP
BEEP
BEEP
!
BEEP
BEEP
BEEP
BEEP
BEEP
BEEP
BEEP
BEEP

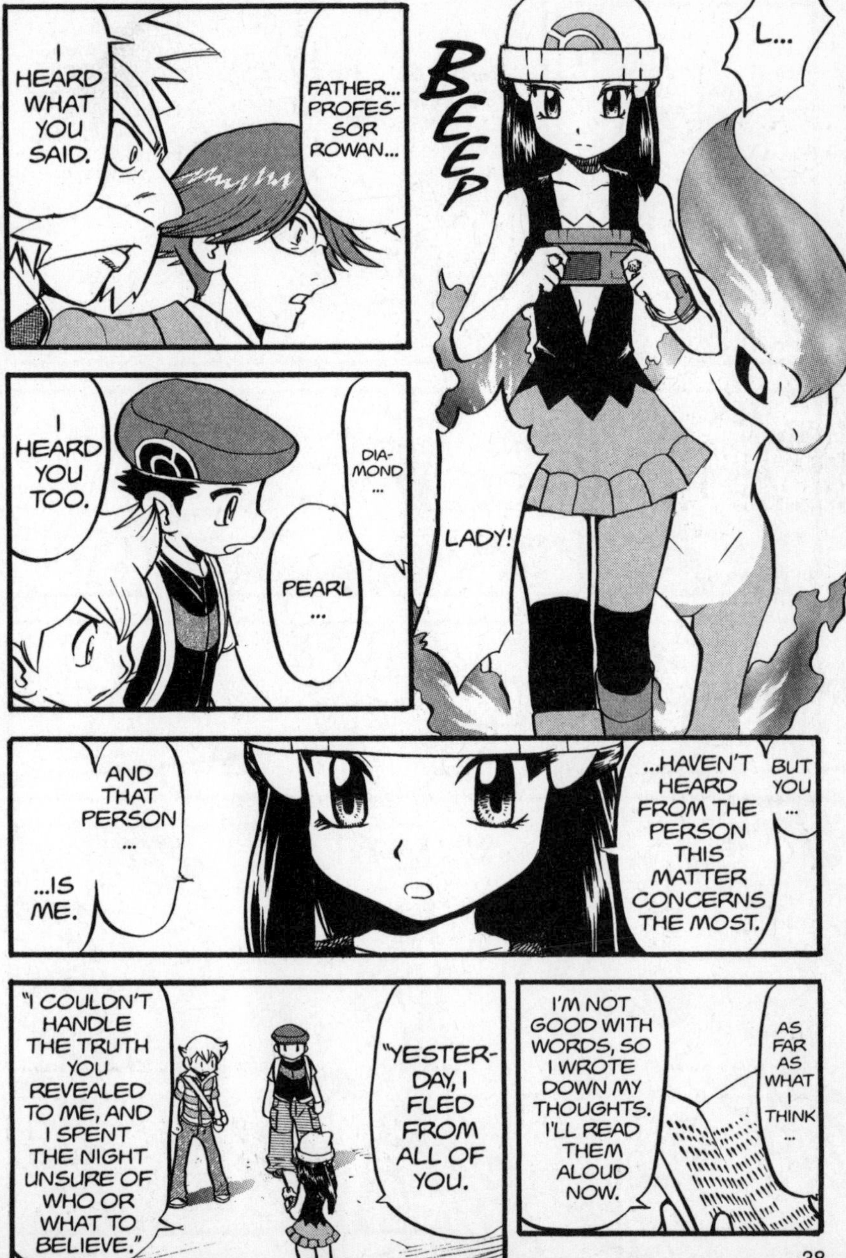
L...
BEEP
LADY!
FATHER... PROFESSOR ROWAN...
I HEARD WHAT YOU SAID.
DIAMOND...
PEARL...
I HEARD YOU TOO.
BUT YOU...
...HAVEN'T HEARD FROM THE PERSON THIS MATTER CONCERNS THE MOST.
AND THAT PERSON...
...IS ME.
AS FAR AS WHAT I THINK...
I'M NOT GOOD WITH WORDS, SO I WROTE DOWN MY THOUGHTS. I'LL READ THEM ALOUD NOW.
"YESTERDAY, I FLED FROM ALL OF YOU.
"I COULDN'T HANDLE THE TRUTH YOU REVEALED TO ME, AND I SPENT THE NIGHT UNSURE OF WHO OR WHAT TO BELIEVE."

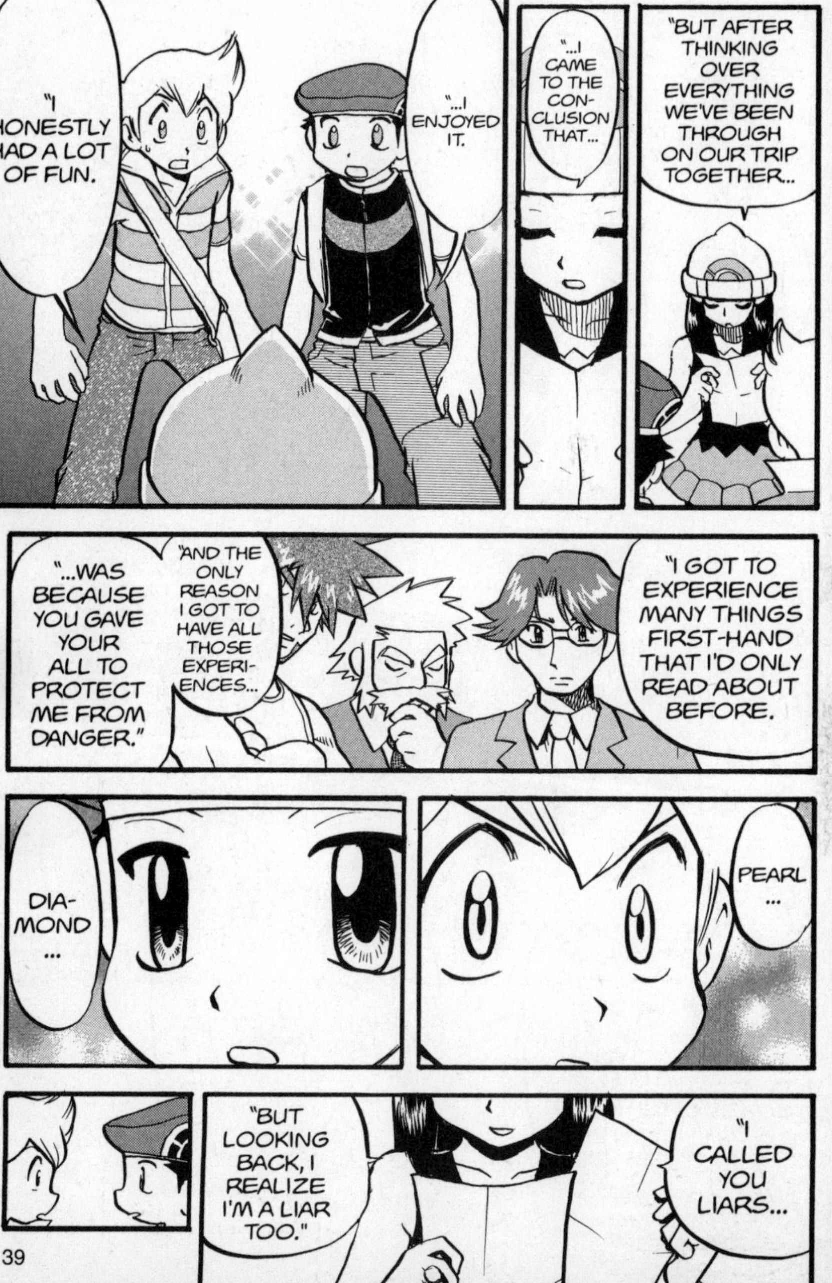
"BUT AFTER THINKING OVER EVERYTHING WE'VE BEEN THROUGH ON OUR TRIP TOGETHER...
"...I CAME TO THE CON-CLUSION THAT...
"...I ENJOYED IT.
"I HONESTLY HAD A LOT OF FUN.
"I GOT TO EXPERIENCE MANY THINGS FIRST-HAND THAT I'D ONLY READ ABOUT BEFORE.
"AND THE ONLY REASON I GOT TO HAVE ALL THOSE EXPERI-ENCES...
"...WAS BECAUSE YOU GAVE YOUR ALL TO PROTECT ME FROM DANGER."
PEARL ...
DIA-MOND ...
"I CALLED YOU LIARS...
"BUT LOOKING BACK, I REALIZE I'M A LIAR TOO."

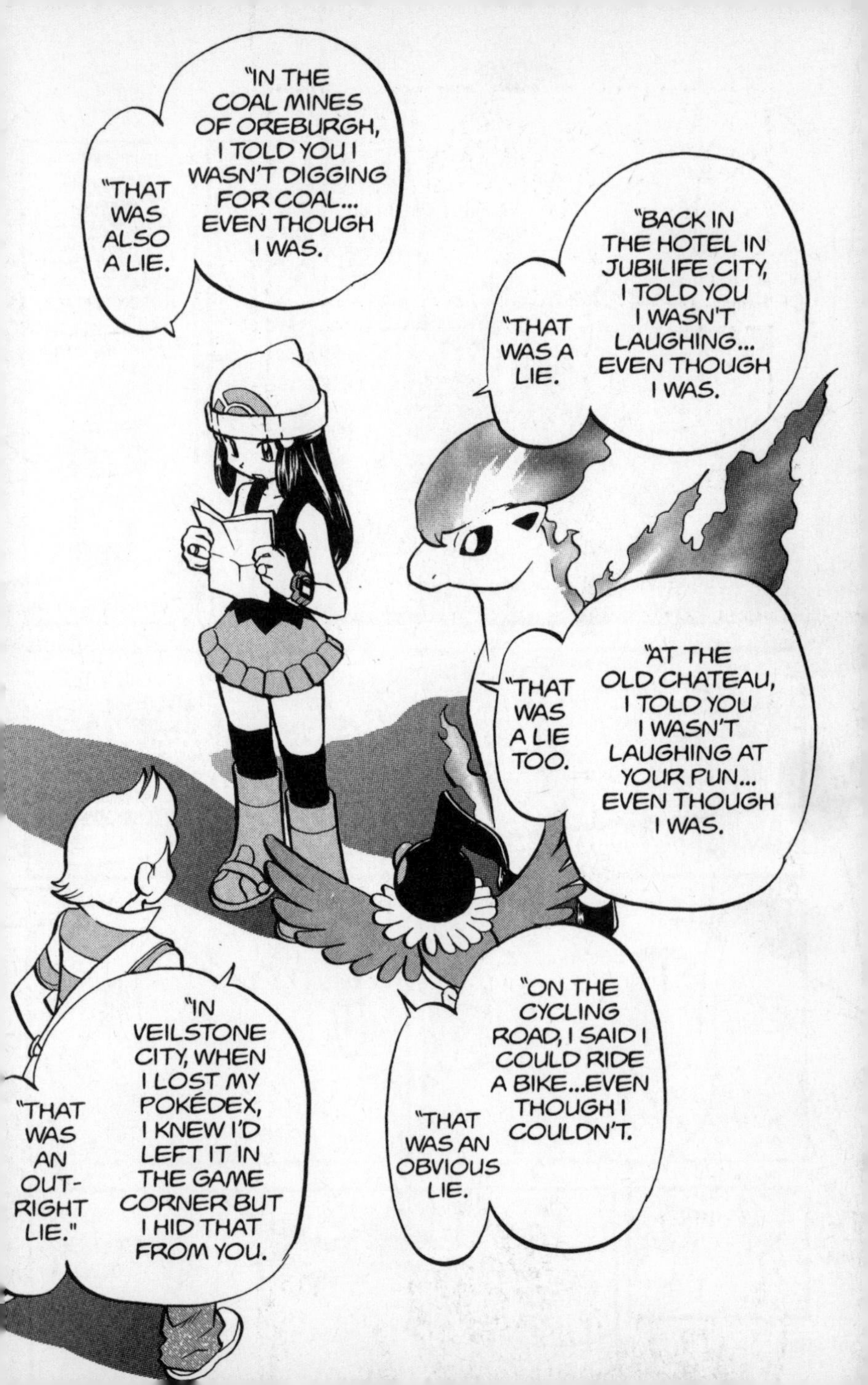
"BACK IN THE HOTEL IN JUBILIFE CITY, I TOLD YOU I WASN'T LAUGHING... EVEN THOUGH I WAS.
"THAT WAS A LIE.
"IN THE COAL MINES OF OREBURGH, I TOLD YOU I WASN'T DIGGING FOR COAL... EVEN THOUGH I WAS.
"THAT WAS ALSO A LIE.
"AT THE OLD CHATEAU, I TOLD YOU I WASN'T LAUGHING AT YOUR PUN... EVEN THOUGH I WAS.
"THAT WAS A LIE TOO.
"ON THE CYCLING ROAD, I SAID I COULD RIDE A BIKE...EVEN THOUGH I COULDN'T.
"THAT WAS AN OBVIOUS LIE.
"IN VEILSTONE CITY, WHEN I LOST MY POKÉDEX, I KNEW I'D LEFT IT IN THE GAME CORNER BUT I HID THAT FROM YOU.
"THAT WAS AN OUT-RIGHT LIE."

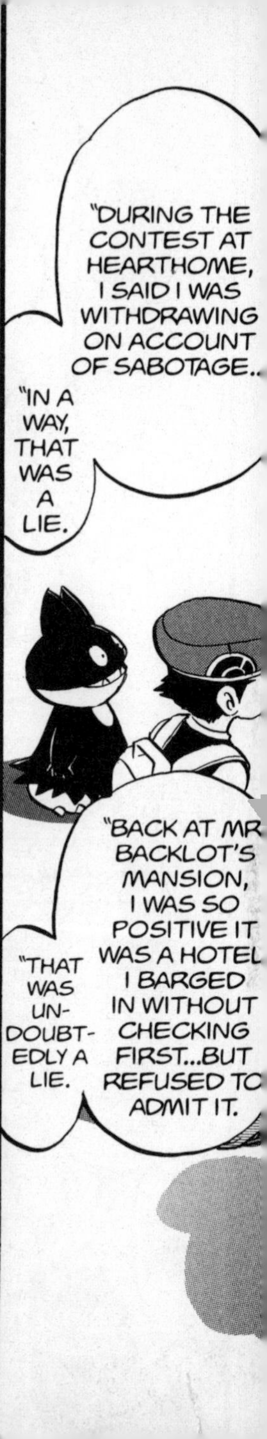
"DURING THE CONTEST AT HEARTHOME, I SAID I WAS WITHDRAWING ON ACCOUNT OF SABOTAGE..
"IN A WAY, THAT WAS A LIE.
"BACK AT MR BACKLOT'S MANSION, I WAS SO POSITIVE IT WAS A HOTEL I BARGED IN WITHOUT CHECKING FIRST...BUT REFUSED TO ADMIT IT.
"THAT WAS UNDOUBTEDLY A LIE.

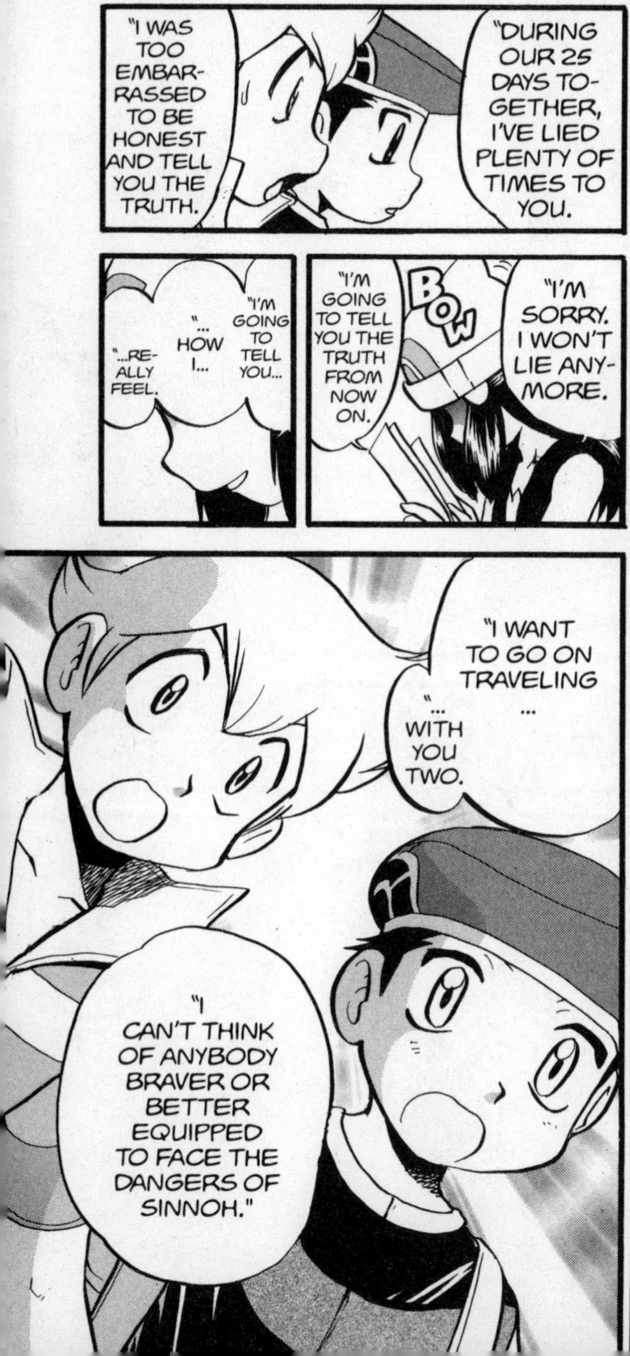
"DURING OUR 25 DAYS TOGETHER, I'VE LIED PLENTY OF TIMES TO YOU.
"I WAS TOO EMBARRASSED TO BE HONEST AND TELL YOU THE TRUTH.
"I'M SORRY. I WON'T LIE ANYMORE.
BOW
"I'M GOING TO TELL YOU THE TRUTH FROM NOW ON.
"I'M GOING TO TELL YOU...
"...HOW I...
"...REALLY FEEL.
"I WANT TO GO ON TRAVELING...
"...WITH YOU TWO.
"I CAN'T THINK OF ANYBODY BRAVER OR BETTER EQUIPPED TO FACE THE DANGERS OF SINNOH."

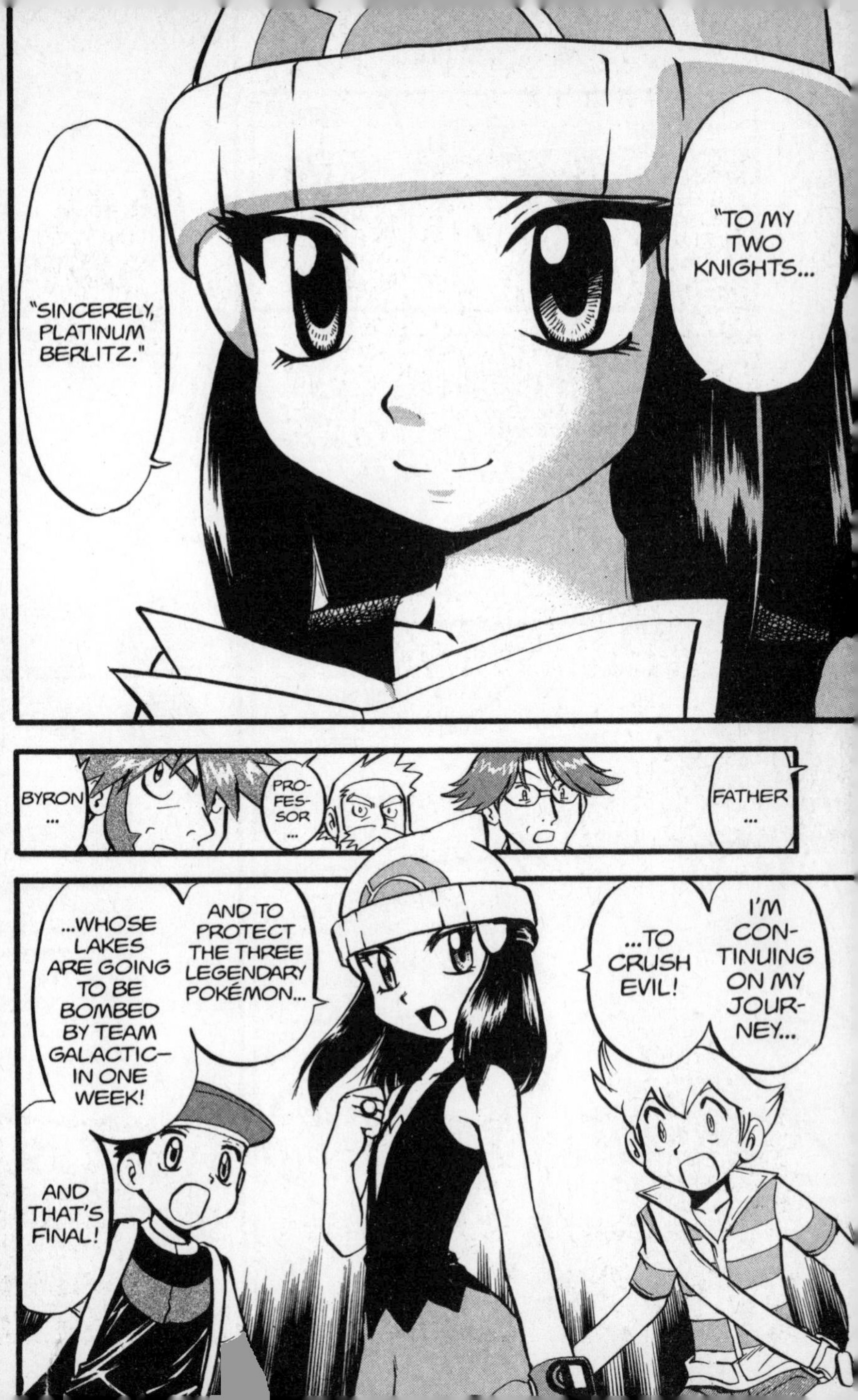
"TO MY TWO KNIGHTS...
"SINCERELY, PLATINUM BERLITZ."
FATHER ...
PRO-FES-SOR ...
BYRON ...
I'M CON-TINUING ON MY JOUR-NEY...
...TO CRUSH EVIL!
AND TO PROTECT THE THREE LEGENDARY POKÉMON...
...WHOSE LAKES ARE GOING TO BE BOMBED BY TEAM GALACTIC— IN ONE WEEK!
AND THAT'S FINAL!

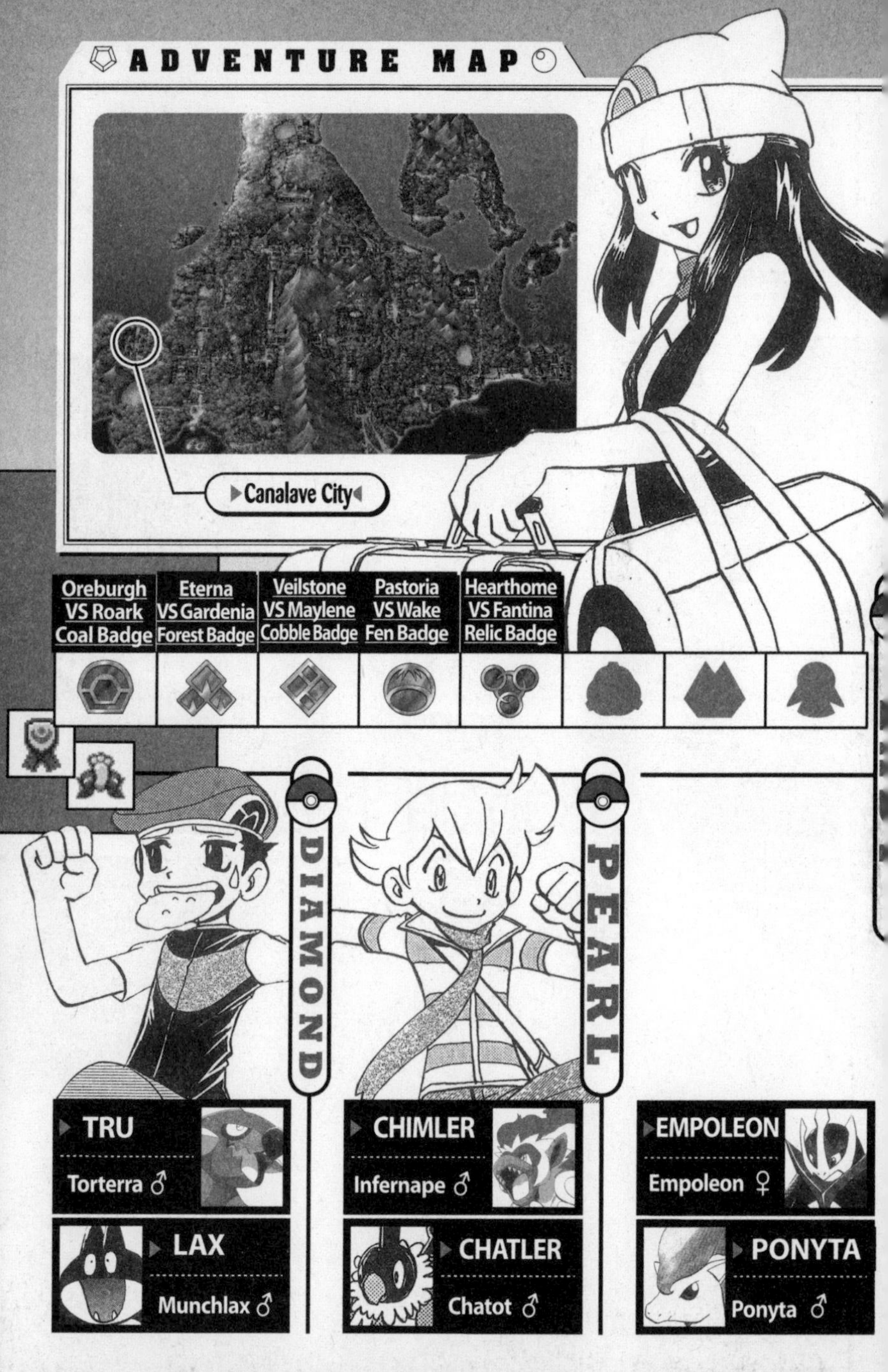

ADVENTURE MAP
Canalave City
Oreburgh
VS Roark
Coal Badge
Eterna
VS Gardenia
Forest Badge
Veilstone
VS Maylene
Cobble Badge
Pastoria
VS Wake
Fen Badge
Hearthome
VS Fantina
Relic Badge
DIAMOND
PEARL
TRU
Torterra ♂
LAX
Munchlax ♂
CHIMLER
Infernape ♂
CHATLER
Chatot ♂
EMPOLEON
Empoleon ♀
PONYTA
Ponyta ♂

40

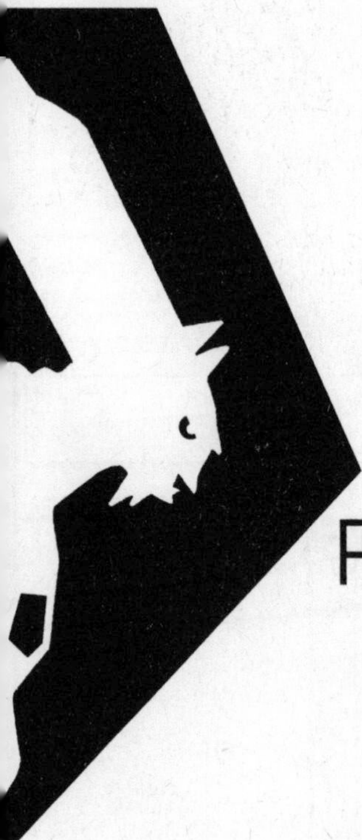

Hurrah for Rapidash

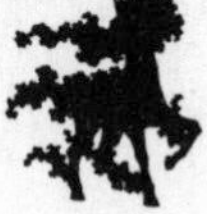

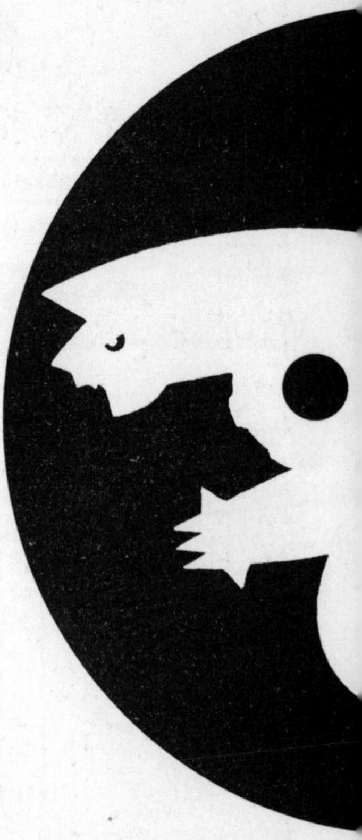

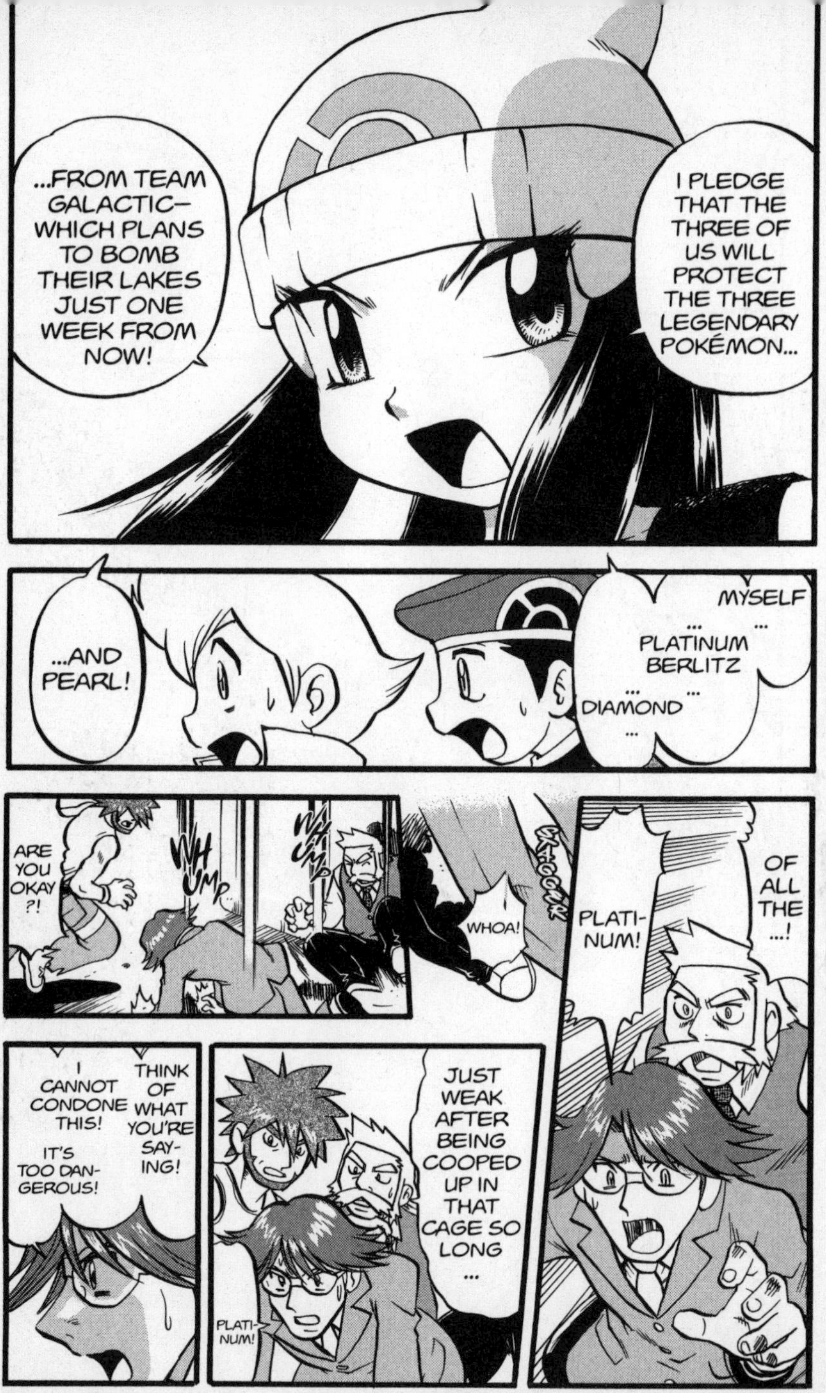
I PLEDGE THAT THE THREE OF US WILL PROTECT THE THREE LEGENDARY POKÉMON...
...FROM TEAM GALACTIC—WHICH PLANS TO BOMB THEIR LAKES JUST ONE WEEK FROM NOW!
MYSELF ... PLATINUM BERLITZ ... DIAMOND ...
...AND PEARL!
OF ALL THE ...!
PLATI-NUM!
STAGGER
WHOA!
WHUMP
WHUMP
ARE YOU OKAY ?!
JUST WEAK AFTER BEING COOPED UP IN THAT CAGE SO LONG ...
PLATI-NUM!
THINK OF WHAT YOU'RE SAY-ING!
I CANNOT CONDONE THIS!
IT'S TOO DAN-GEROUS!

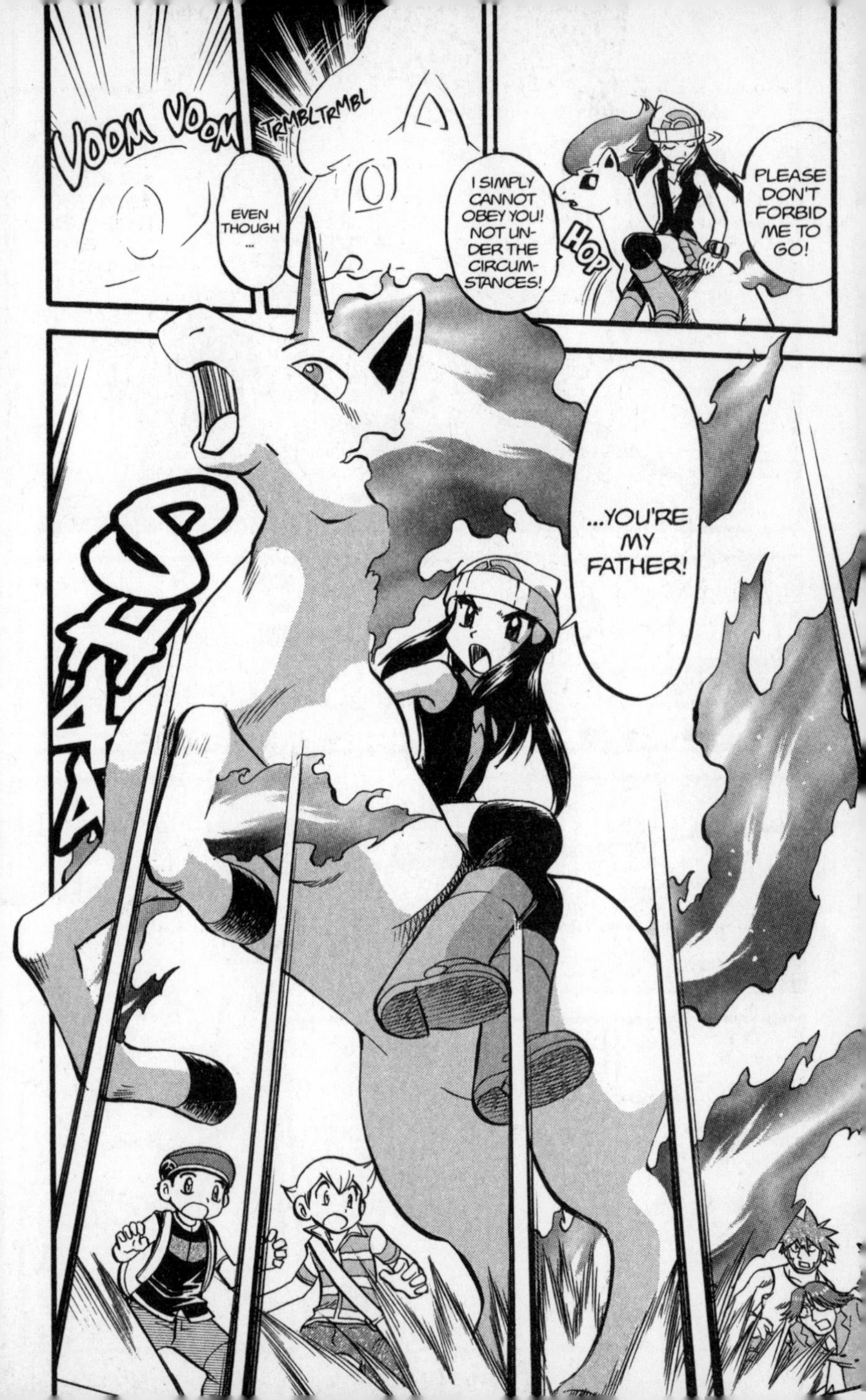
PLEASE DON'T FORBID ME TO GO!
I SIMPLY CANNOT OBEY YOU! NOT UNDER THE CIRCUMSTANCES!
HOP
TRMBLTRMBL
EVEN THOUGH ...
VOOM VOOM
...YOU'RE MY FATHER!

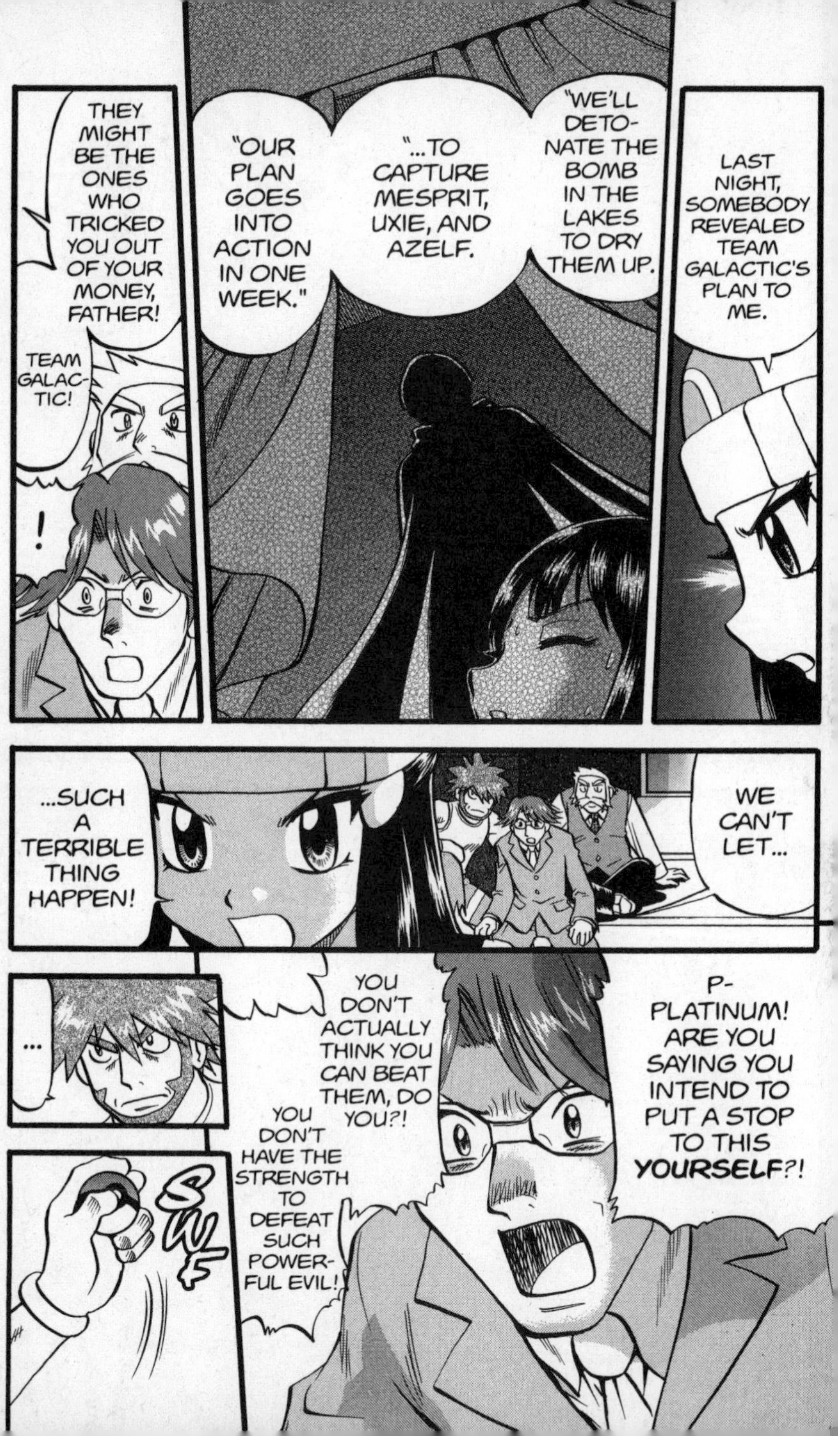
LAST NIGHT, SOMEBODY REVEALED TEAM GALACTIC'S PLAN TO ME.
"WE'LL DETONATE THE BOMB IN THE LAKES TO DRY THEM UP.
"...TO CAPTURE MESPRIT, UXIE, AND AZELF.
"OUR PLAN GOES INTO ACTION IN ONE WEEK."
THEY MIGHT BE THE ONES WHO TRICKED YOU OUT OF YOUR MONEY, FATHER!
TEAM GALACTIC!
!
WE CAN'T LET...
...SUCH A TERRIBLE THING HAPPEN!
P-PLATINUM! ARE YOU SAYING YOU INTEND TO PUT A STOP TO THIS **YOURSELF**?!
YOU DON'T ACTUALLY THINK YOU CAN BEAT THEM, DO YOU?!
YOU DON'T HAVE THE STRENGTH TO DEFEAT SUCH POWERFUL EVIL!
...
SWF

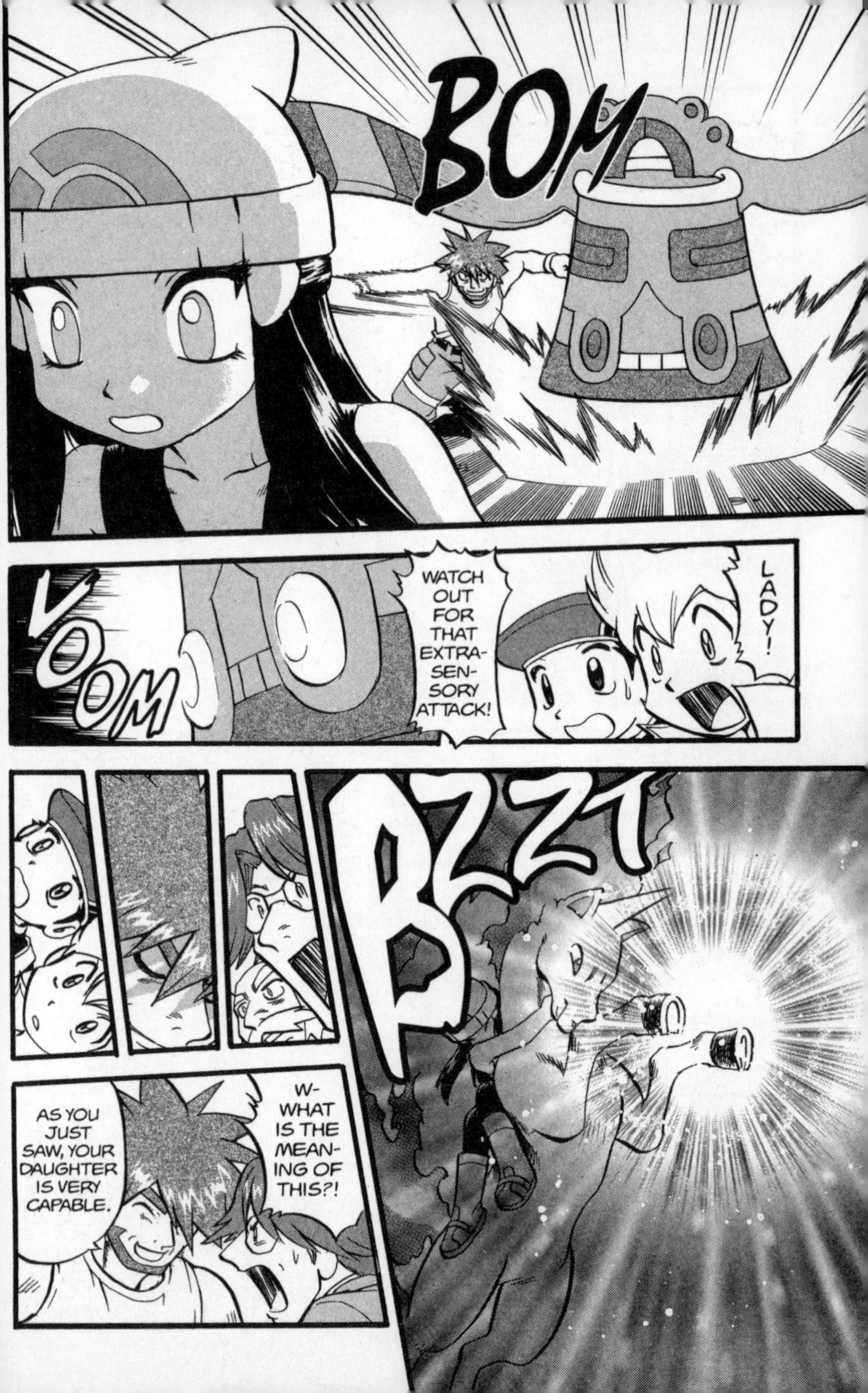
BOM
LADY!
WATCH OUT FOR THAT EXTRA-SENSORY ATTACK!
VOOM
BZZT
W-WHAT IS THE MEANING OF THIS?!
AS YOU JUST SAW, YOUR DAUGHTER IS VERY CAPABLE.

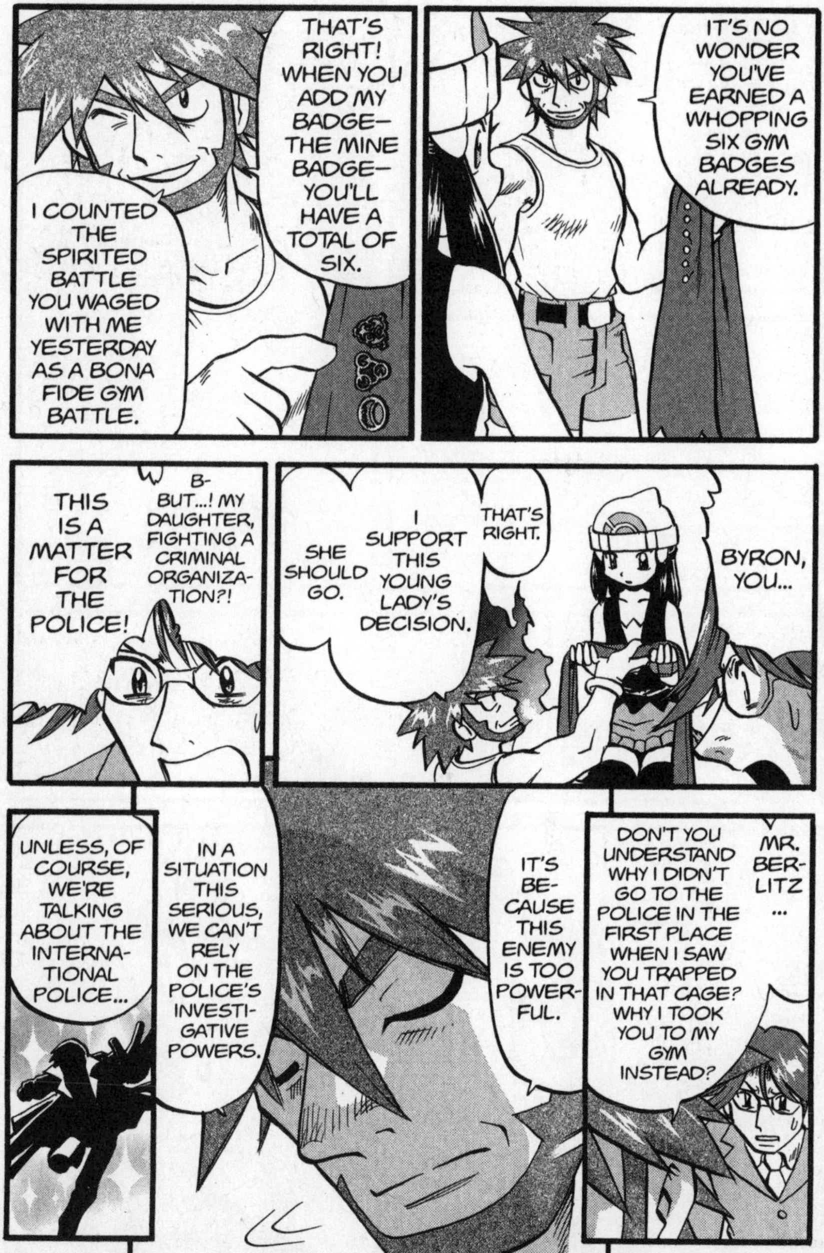
IT'S NO WONDER YOU'VE EARNED A WHOPPING SIX GYM BADGES ALREADY.
THAT'S RIGHT! WHEN YOU ADD MY BADGE— THE MINE BADGE— YOU'LL HAVE A TOTAL OF SIX.
I COUNTED THE SPIRITED BATTLE YOU WAGED WITH ME YESTERDAY AS A BONA FIDE GYM BATTLE.
BYRON, YOU...
THAT'S RIGHT.
I SUPPORT THIS YOUNG LADY'S DECISION.
SHE SHOULD GO.
B- BUT...! MY DAUGHTER, FIGHTING A CRIMINAL ORGANIZA- TION?!
THIS IS A MATTER FOR THE POLICE!
MR. BER- LITZ ...
DON'T YOU UNDERSTAND WHY I DIDN'T GO TO THE POLICE IN THE FIRST PLACE WHEN I SAW YOU TRAPPED IN THAT CAGE? WHY I TOOK YOU TO MY GYM INSTEAD?
IT'S BE- CAUSE THIS ENEMY IS TOO POWER- FUL.
IN A SITUATION THIS SERIOUS, WE CAN'T RELY ON THE POLICE'S INVESTI- GATIVE POWERS.
UNLESS, OF COURSE, WE'RE TALKING ABOUT THE INTERNA- TIONAL POLICE...

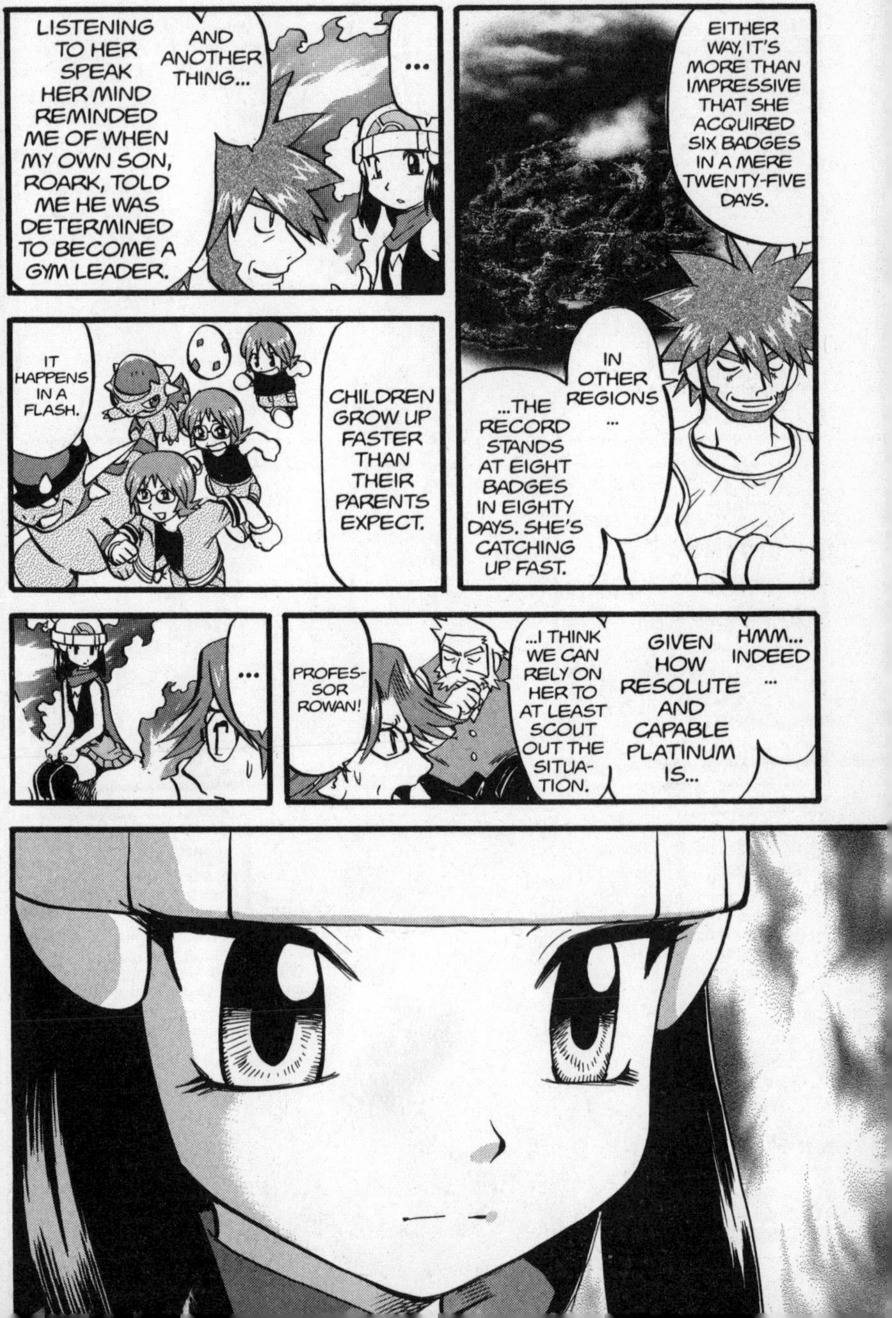
EITHER WAY, IT'S MORE THAN IMPRESSIVE THAT SHE ACQUIRED SIX BADGES IN A MERE TWENTY-FIVE DAYS.
IN OTHER REGIONS...
...THE RECORD STANDS AT EIGHT BADGES IN EIGHTY DAYS. SHE'S CATCHING UP FAST.
...
AND ANOTHER THING...
LISTENING TO HER SPEAK HER MIND REMINDED ME OF WHEN MY OWN SON, ROARK, TOLD ME HE WAS DETERMINED TO BECOME A GYM LEADER.
CHILDREN GROW UP FASTER THAN THEIR PARENTS EXPECT.
IT HAPPENS IN A FLASH.
HMM... INDEED...
GIVEN HOW RESOLUTE AND CAPABLE PLATINUM IS...
...I THINK WE CAN RELY ON HER TO AT LEAST SCOUT OUT THE SITUATION.
PROFESSOR ROWAN!
...

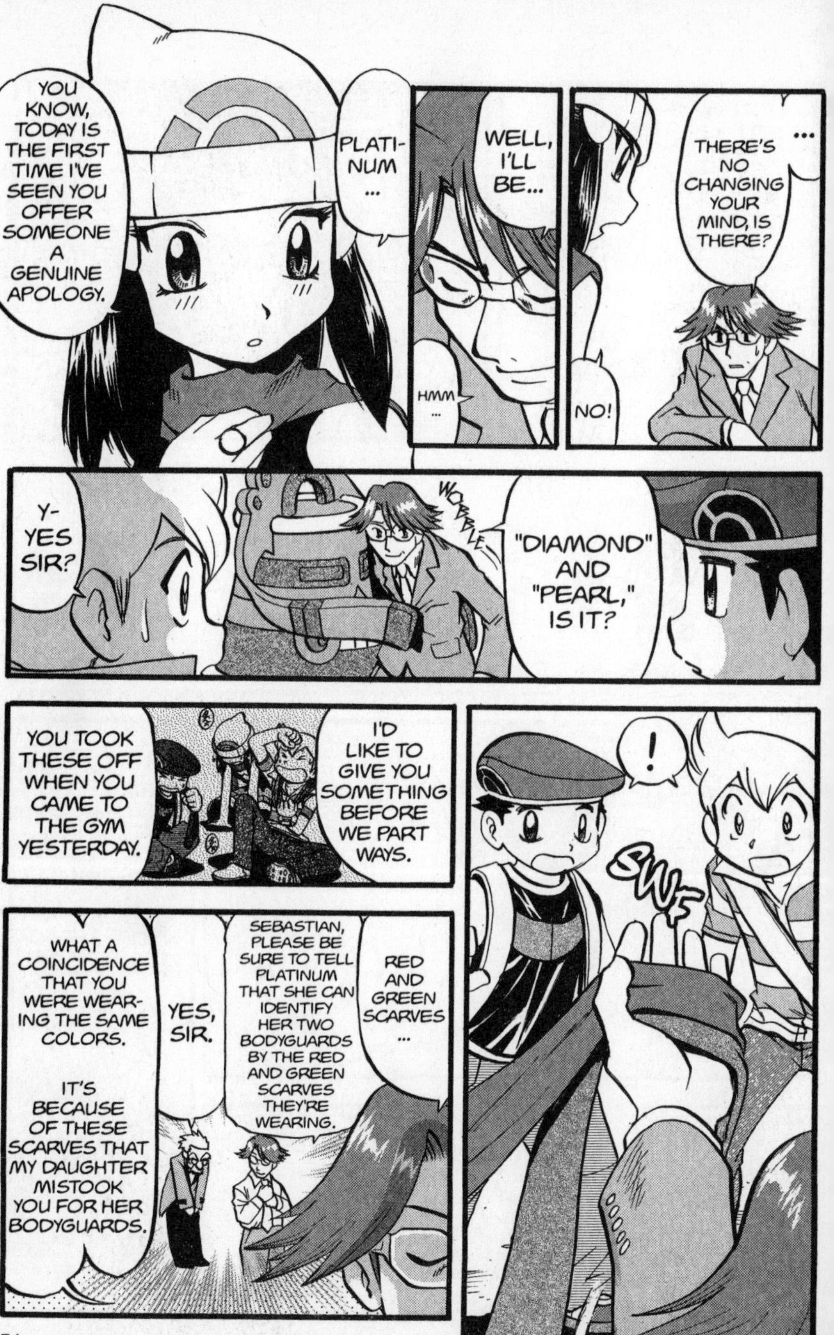
...
THERE'S NO CHANGING YOUR MIND, IS THERE?
NO!
WELL, I'LL BE...
HMM...
PLATI-NUM ...
YOU KNOW, TODAY IS THE FIRST TIME I'VE SEEN YOU OFFER SOMEONE A GENUINE APOLOGY.
"DIAMOND" AND "PEARL," IS IT?
WOBBLE
Y-YES SIR?
!
SWF
I'D LIKE TO GIVE YOU SOMETHING BEFORE WE PART WAYS.
YOU TOOK THESE OFF WHEN YOU CAME TO THE GYM YESTERDAY.
RED AND GREEN SCARVES ...
SEBASTIAN, PLEASE BE SURE TO TELL PLATINUM THAT SHE CAN IDENTIFY HER TWO BODYGUARDS BY THE RED AND GREEN SCARVES THEY'RE WEARING.
YES, SIR.
WHAT A COINCIDENCE THAT YOU WERE WEAR-ING THE SAME COLORS.
IT'S BECAUSE OF THESE SCARVES THAT MY DAUGHTER MISTOOK YOU FOR HER BODYGUARDS.

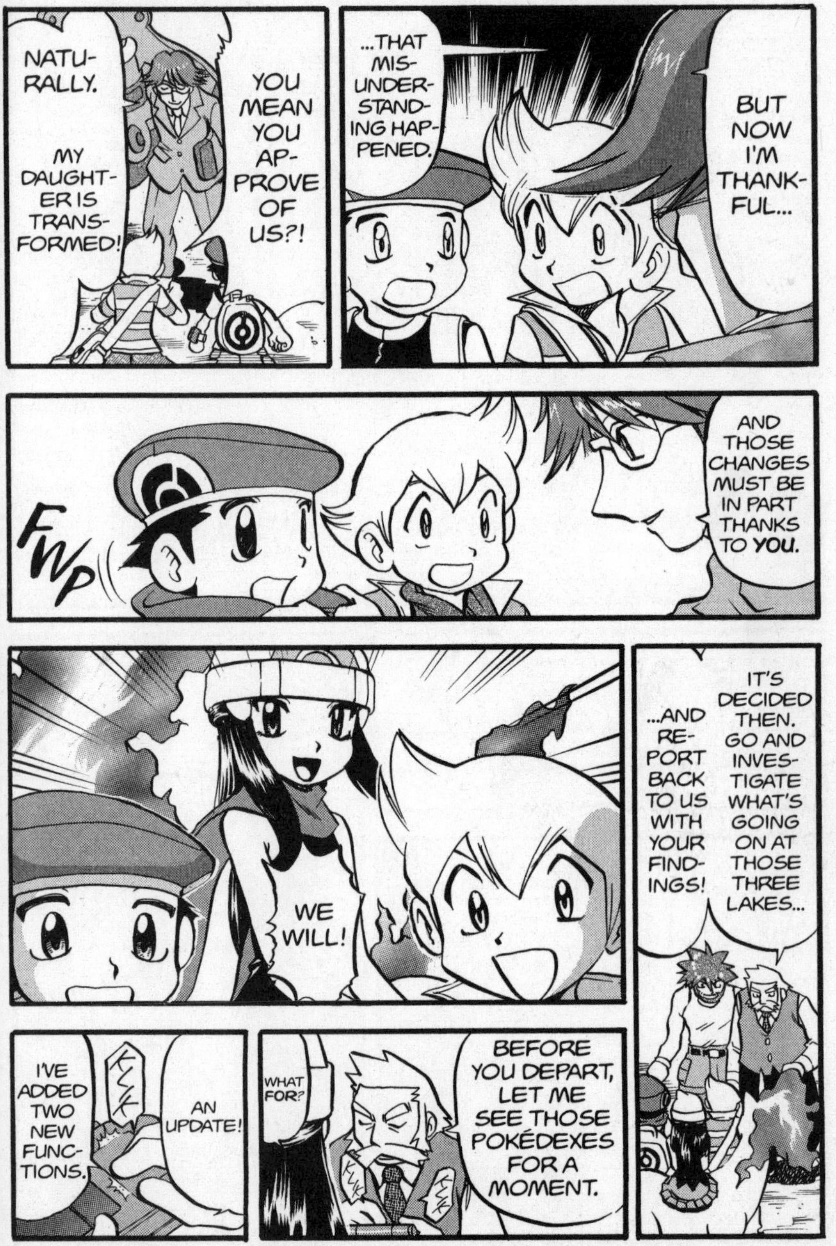
BUT NOW I'M THANKFUL...
...THAT MISUNDERSTANDING HAPPENED.
YOU MEAN YOU APPROVE OF US?!
NATURALLY.
MY DAUGHTER IS TRANSFORMED!
AND THOSE CHANGES MUST BE IN PART THANKS TO **YOU**.
FWP
IT'S DECIDED THEN. GO AND INVESTIGATE WHAT'S GOING ON AT THOSE THREE LAKES...
...AND REPORT BACK TO US WITH YOUR FINDINGS!
WE WILL!
BEFORE YOU DEPART, LET ME SEE THOSE POKÉDEXES FOR A MOMENT.
WHAT FOR?
KLIK
KLIK
AN UPDATE!
KLIK
I'VE ADDED TWO NEW FUNCTIONS.

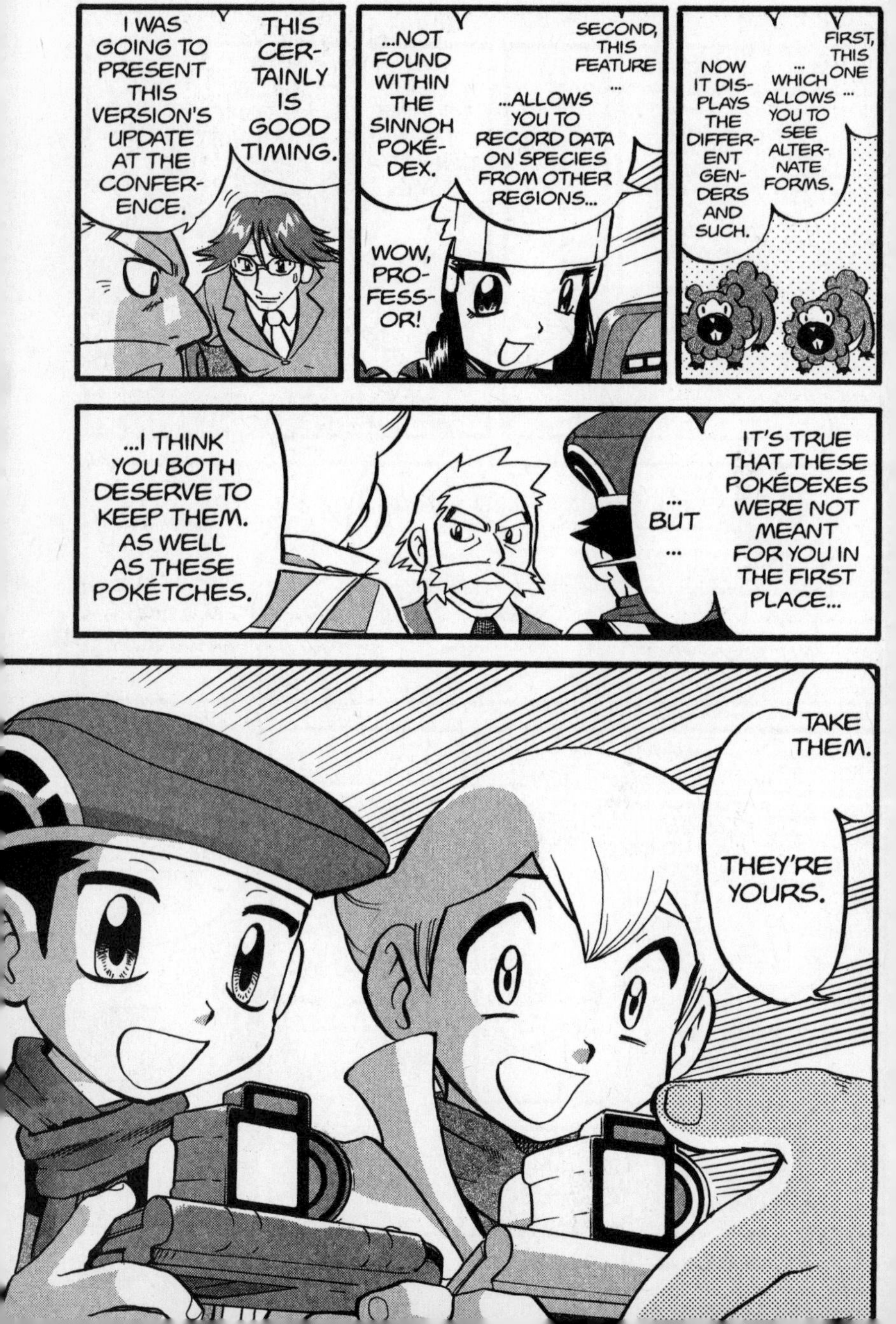
FIRST, THIS ONE ...
...WHICH ALLOWS YOU TO SEE ALTERNATE FORMS.
NOW IT DISPLAYS THE DIFFERENT GENDERS AND SUCH.
SECOND, THIS FEATURE ...
...ALLOWS YOU TO RECORD DATA ON SPECIES FROM OTHER REGIONS...
...NOT FOUND WITHIN THE SINNOH POKÉDEX.
WOW, PROFESSOR!
THIS CERTAINLY IS GOOD TIMING.
I WAS GOING TO PRESENT THIS VERSION'S UPDATE AT THE CONFERENCE.
IT'S TRUE THAT THESE POKÉDEXES WERE NOT MEANT FOR YOU IN THE FIRST PLACE...
...BUT...
...I THINK YOU BOTH DESERVE TO KEEP THEM. AS WELL AS THESE POKÉTCHES.
TAKE THEM.
THEY'RE YOURS.

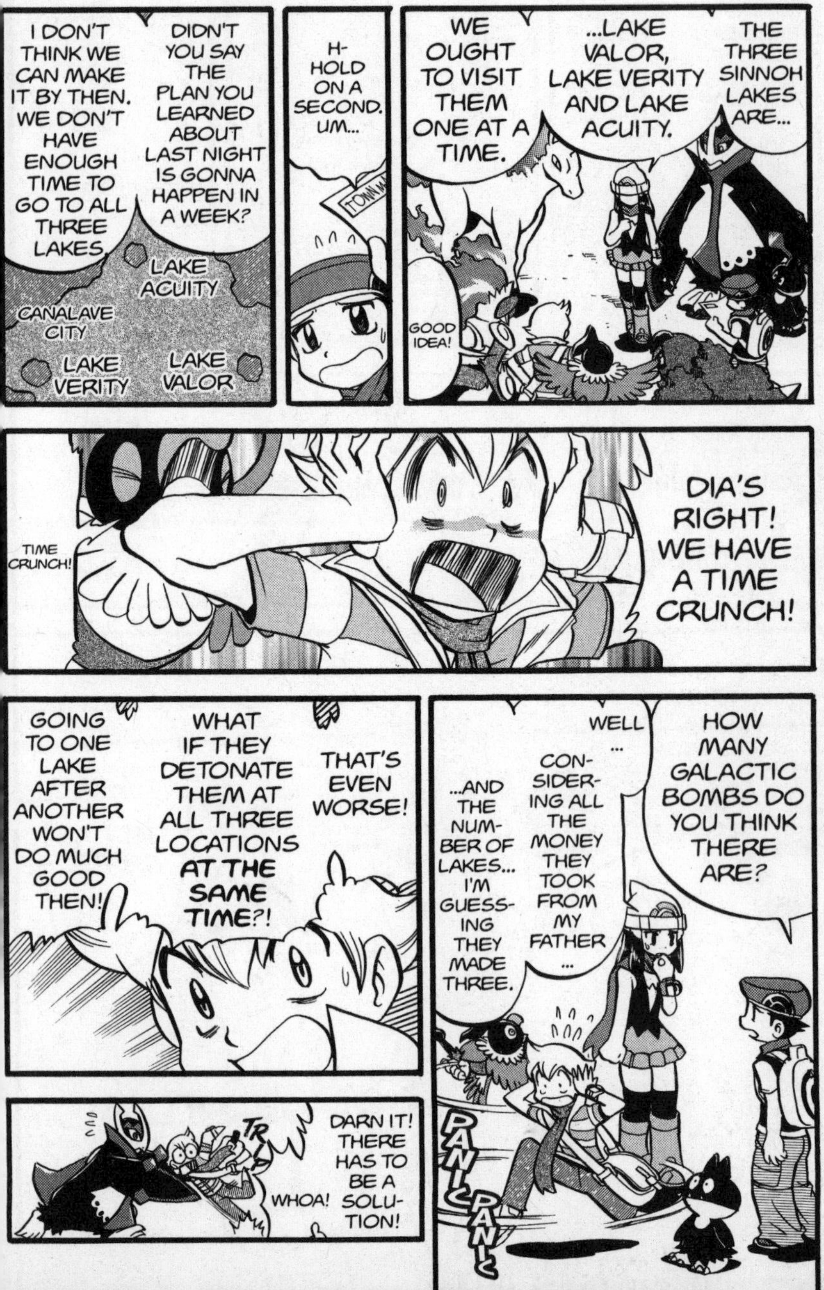
THE THREE SINNOH LAKES ARE...
...LAKE VALOR, LAKE VERITY AND LAKE ACUITY.
WE OUGHT TO VISIT THEM ONE AT A TIME.
GOOD IDEA!
H-HOLD ON A SECOND. UM...
DIDN'T YOU SAY THE PLAN YOU LEARNED ABOUT LAST NIGHT IS GONNA HAPPEN IN A WEEK?
I DON'T THINK WE CAN MAKE IT BY THEN. WE DON'T HAVE ENOUGH TIME TO GO TO ALL THREE LAKES.
LAKE ACUITY
CANALAVE CITY
LAKE VERITY
LAKE VALOR
DIA'S RIGHT! WE HAVE A TIME CRUNCH!
TIME CRUNCH!
HOW MANY GALACTIC BOMBS DO YOU THINK THERE ARE?
WELL...
CONSIDERING ALL THE MONEY THEY TOOK FROM MY FATHER...
...AND THE NUMBER OF LAKES... I'M GUESSING THEY MADE THREE.
PANIC
PANIC
PANIC
THAT'S EVEN WORSE!
WHAT IF THEY DETONATE THEM AT ALL THREE LOCATIONS AT THE SAME TIME?!
GOING TO ONE LAKE AFTER ANOTHER WON'T DO MUCH GOOD THEN!
DARN IT! THERE HAS TO BE A SOLUTION!
WHOA!

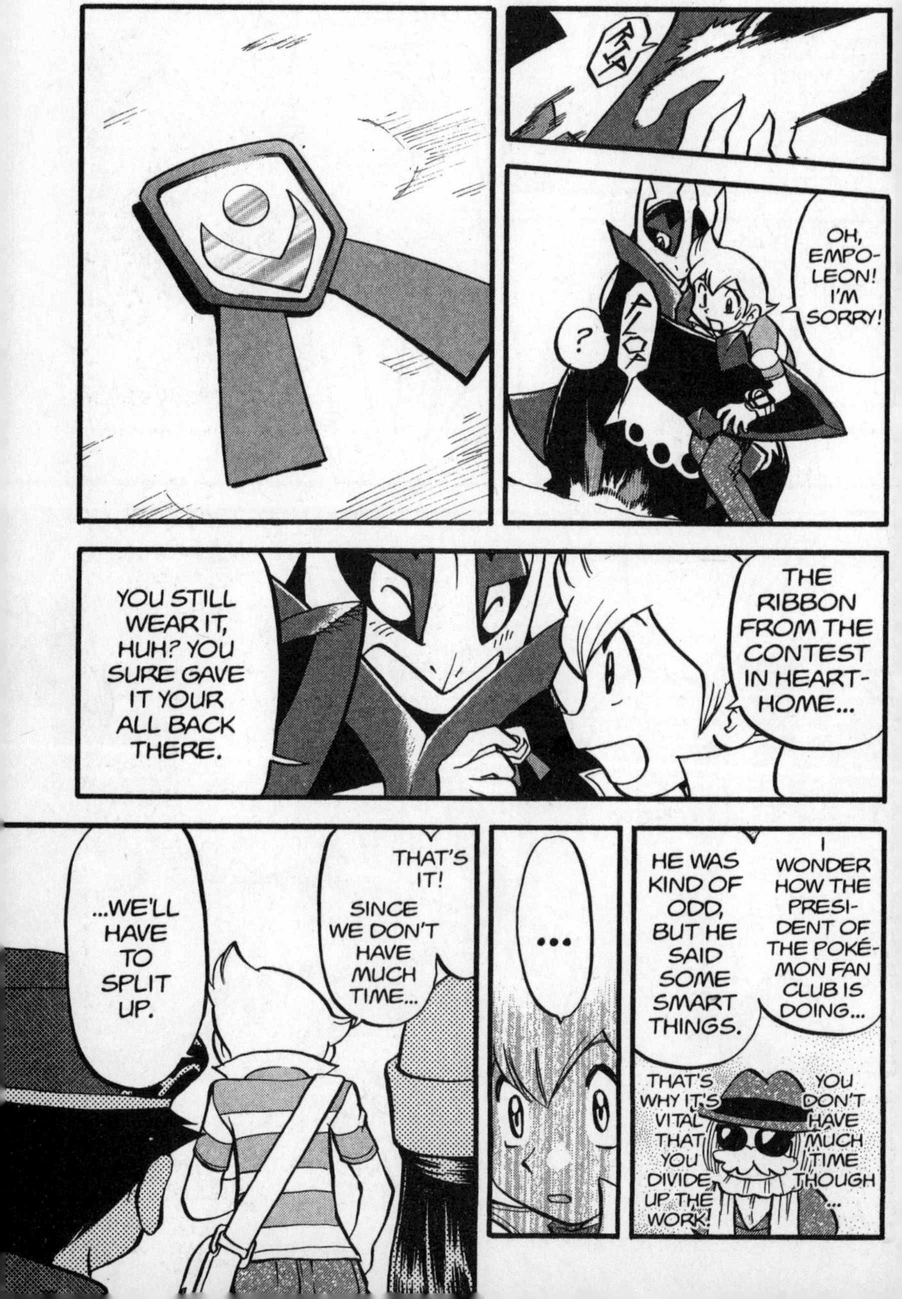
RIP
PLOP
?
OH, EMPO-LEON! I'M SORRY!
THE RIBBON FROM THE CONTEST IN HEART-HOME...
YOU STILL WEAR IT, HUH? YOU SURE GAVE IT YOUR ALL BACK THERE.
I WONDER HOW THE PRESI-DENT OF THE POKÉ-MON FAN CLUB IS DOING...
HE WAS KIND OF ODD, BUT HE SAID SOME SMART THINGS.
YOU DON'T HAVE MUCH TIME THOUGH...
THAT'S WHY IT'S VITAL THAT YOU DIVIDE UP THE WORK!
...
THAT'S IT!
SINCE WE DON'T HAVE MUCH TIME...
...WE'LL HAVE TO SPLIT UP.

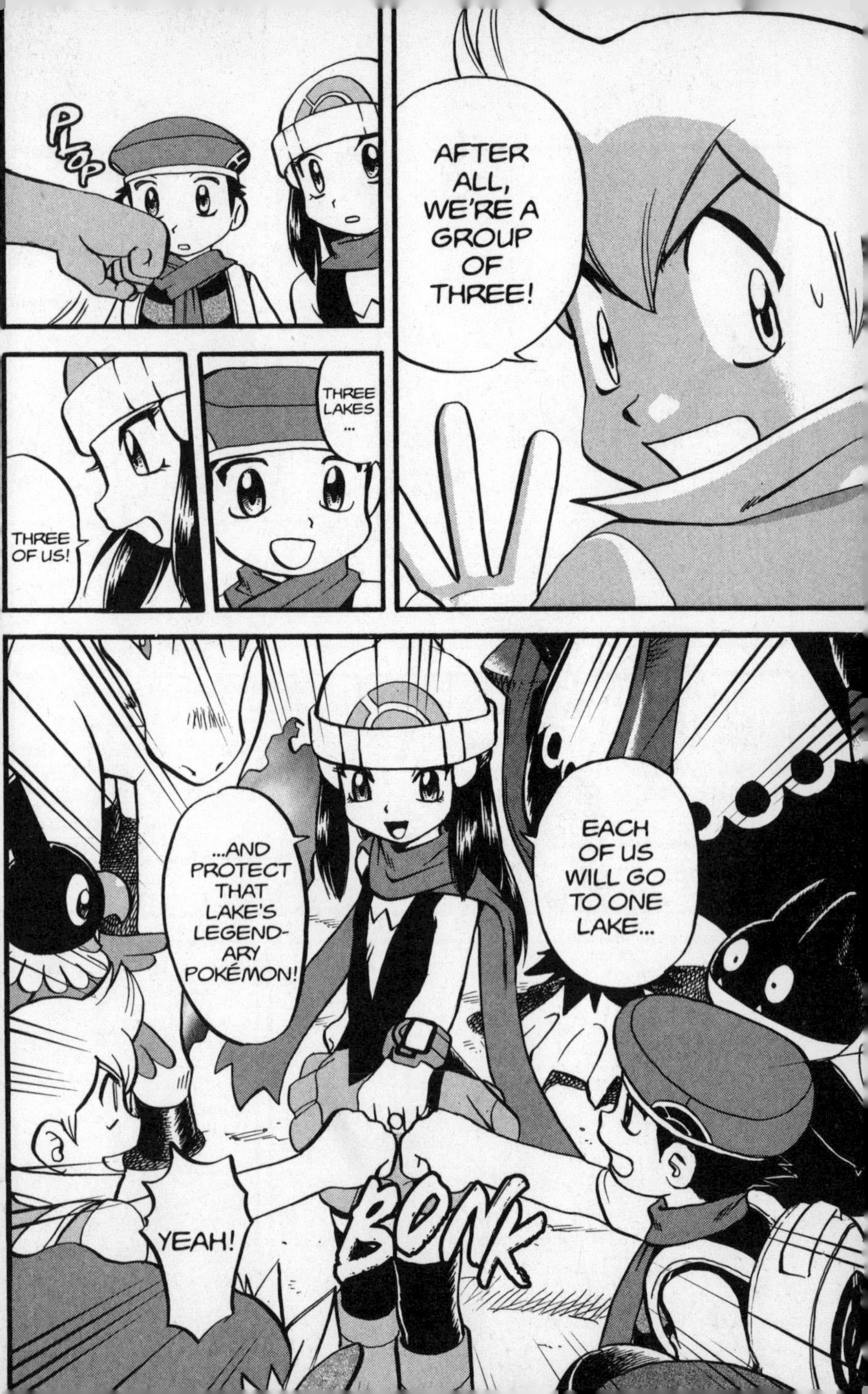
AFTER ALL, WE'RE A GROUP OF THREE!
PLOP
THREE LAKES...
THREE OF US!
EACH OF US WILL GO TO ONE LAKE...
...AND PROTECT THAT LAKE'S LEGENDARY POKÉMON!
BONK
YEAH!

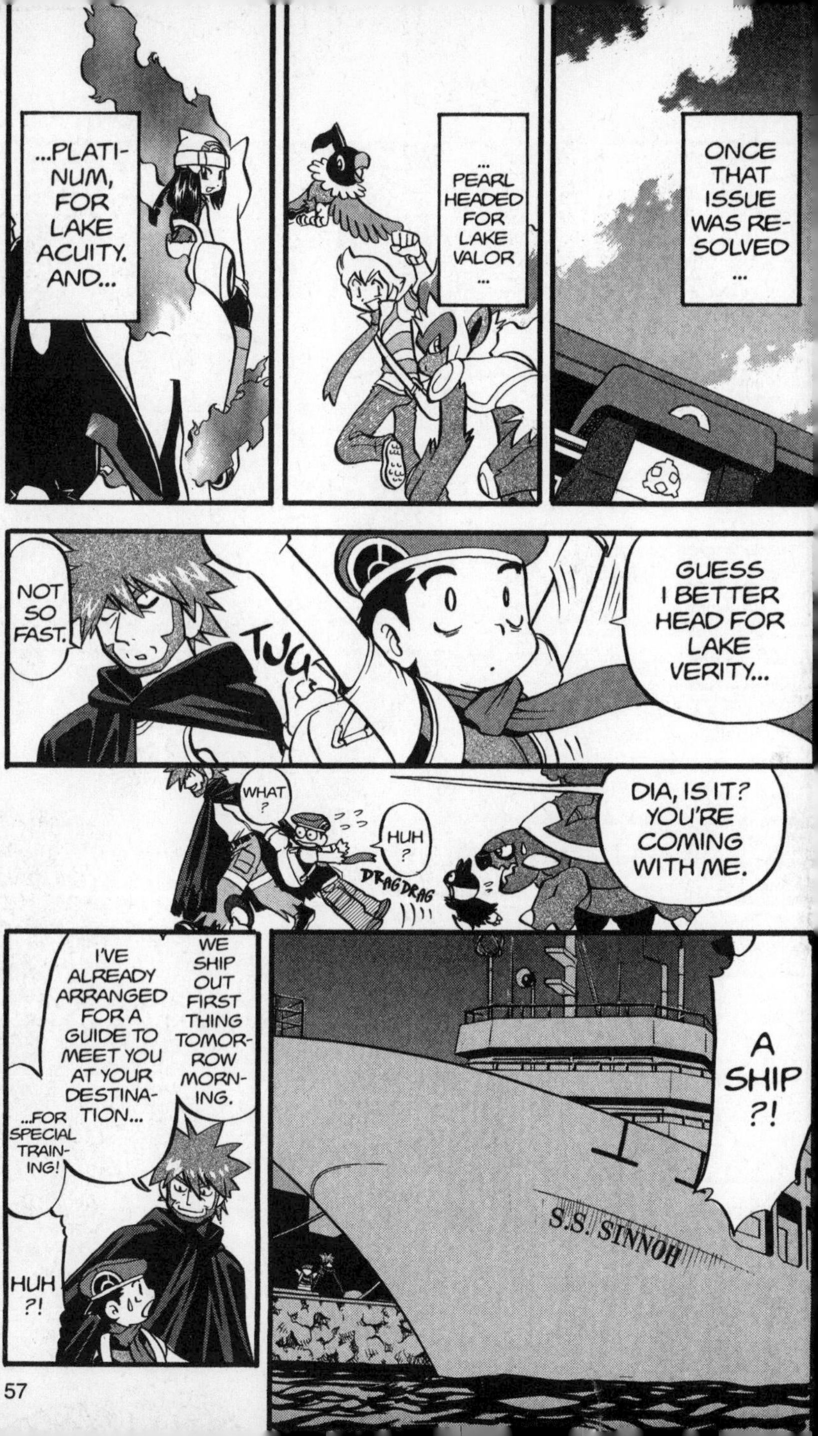
ONCE THAT ISSUE WAS RESOLVED ...
... PEARL HEADED FOR LAKE VALOR ...
...PLATINUM, FOR LAKE ACUITY. AND...
GUESS I BETTER HEAD FOR LAKE VERITY...
NOT SO FAST.
DIA, IS IT? YOU'RE COMING WITH ME.
DRAG DRAG
HUH?
WHAT?
A SHIP ?!
S.S. SINNOH
WE SHIP OUT FIRST THING TOMORROW MORNING.
I'VE ALREADY ARRANGED FOR A GUIDE TO MEET YOU AT YOUR DESTINATION...
...FOR SPECIAL TRAINING!
HUH ?!

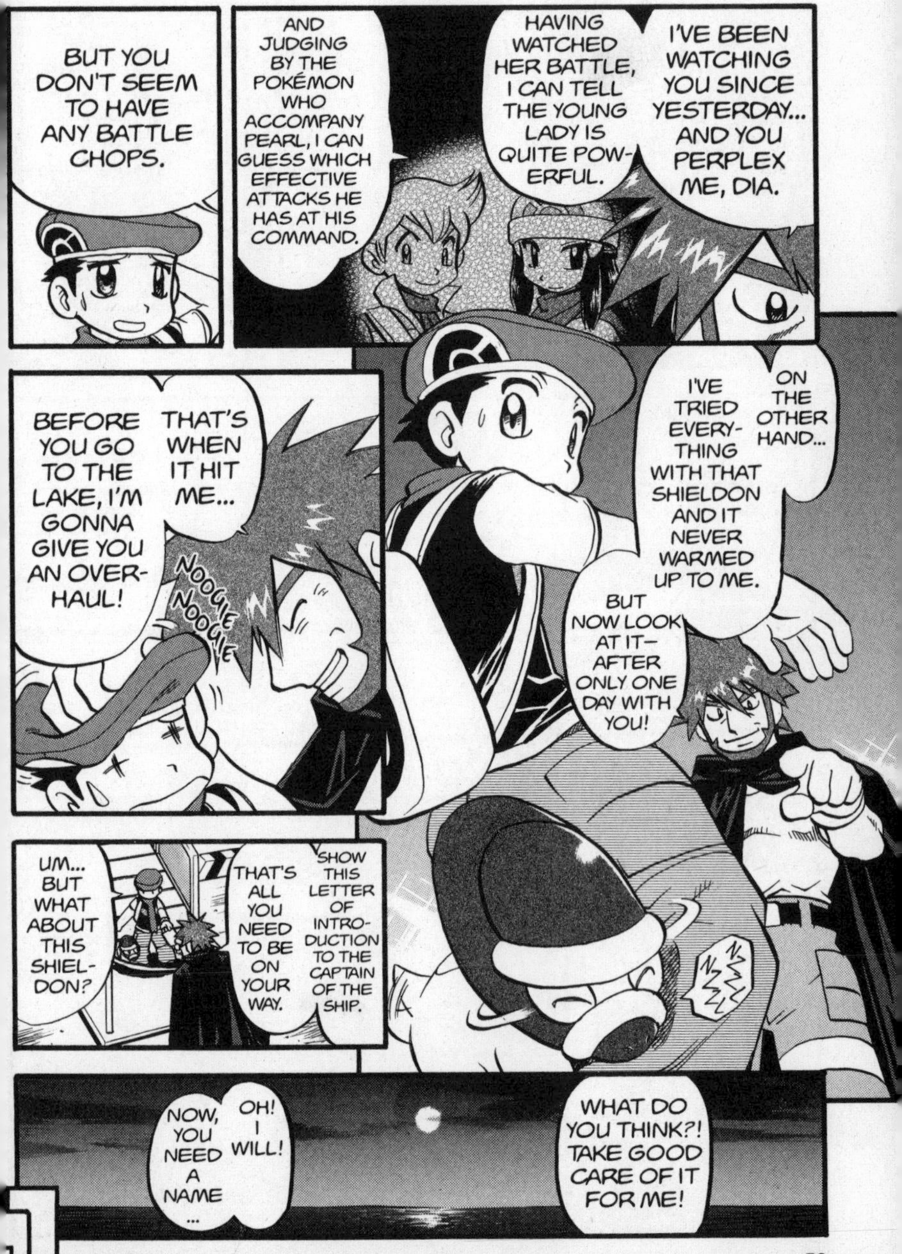
I'VE BEEN WATCHING YOU SINCE YESTERDAY... AND YOU PERPLEX ME, DIA.
HAVING WATCHED HER BATTLE, I CAN TELL THE YOUNG LADY IS QUITE POW-ERFUL.
AND JUDGING BY THE POKÉMON WHO ACCOMPANY PEARL, I CAN GUESS WHICH EFFECTIVE ATTACKS HE HAS AT HIS COMMAND.
BUT YOU DON'T SEEM TO HAVE ANY BATTLE CHOPS.
ON THE OTHER HAND...
I'VE TRIED EVERY-THING WITH THAT SHIELDON AND IT NEVER WARMED UP TO ME.
BUT NOW LOOK AT IT— AFTER ONLY ONE DAY WITH YOU!
NZZZ NZZZ
THAT'S WHEN IT HIT ME...
BEFORE YOU GO TO THE LAKE, I'M GONNA GIVE YOU AN OVER-HAUL!
NOOGIE NOOGIE
SHOW THIS LETTER OF INTRO-DUCTION TO THE CAPTAIN OF THE SHIP.
THAT'S ALL YOU NEED TO BE ON YOUR WAY.
UM... BUT WHAT ABOUT THIS SHIEL-DON?
WHAT DO YOU THINK?! TAKE GOOD CARE OF IT FOR ME!
OH! I WILL!
NOW, YOU NEED A NAME ...

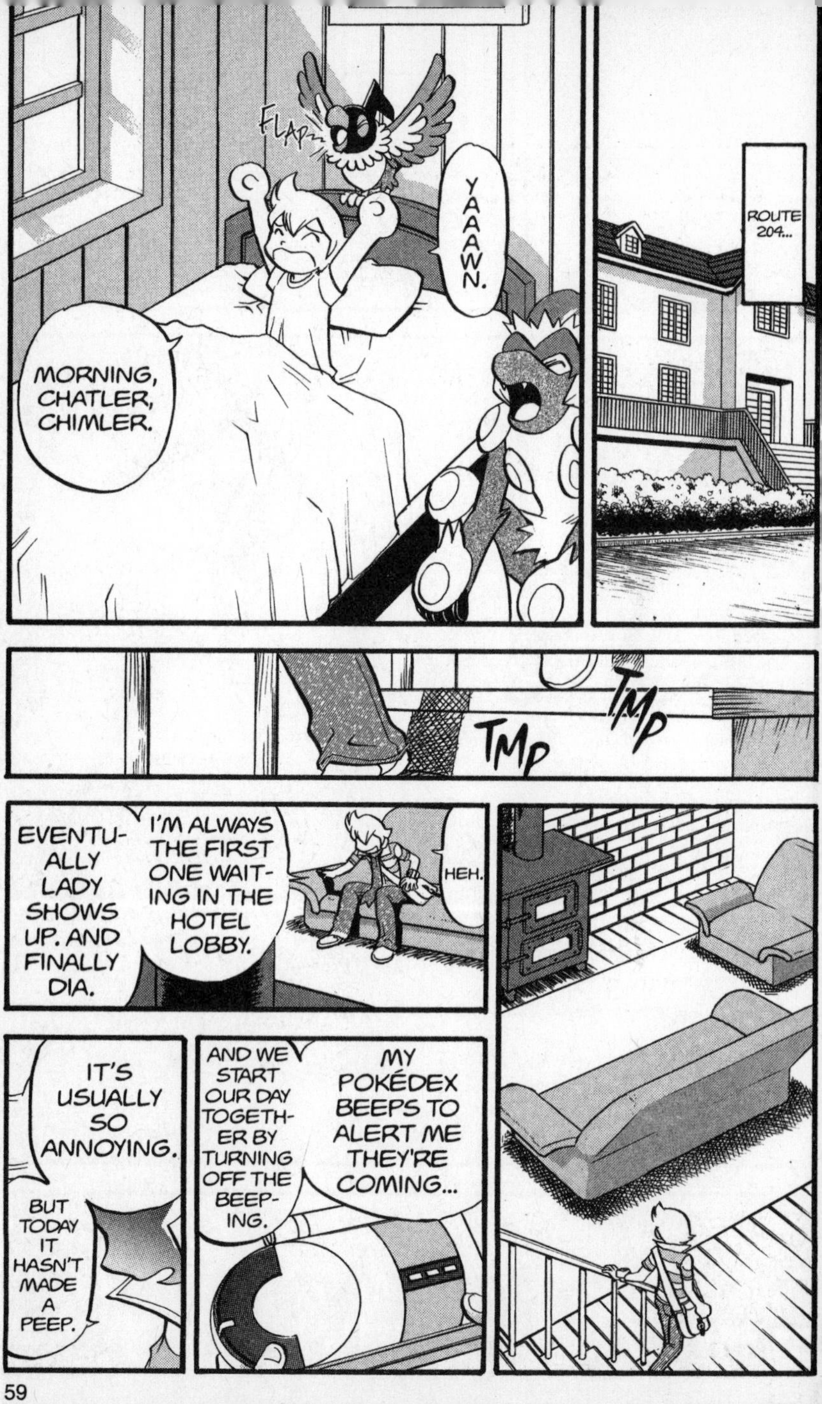
ROUTE 204...
YAAAAWN.
FLAP
MORNING, CHATLER, CHIMLER.
TMP
TMP
HEH.
I'M ALWAYS THE FIRST ONE WAITING IN THE HOTEL LOBBY.
EVENTUALLY LADY SHOWS UP. AND FINALLY DIA.
MY POKÉDEX BEEPS TO ALERT ME THEY'RE COMING...
AND WE START OUR DAY TOGETHER BY TURNING OFF THE BEEPING.
IT'S USUALLY SO ANNOYING.
BUT TODAY IT HASN'T MADE A PEEP.

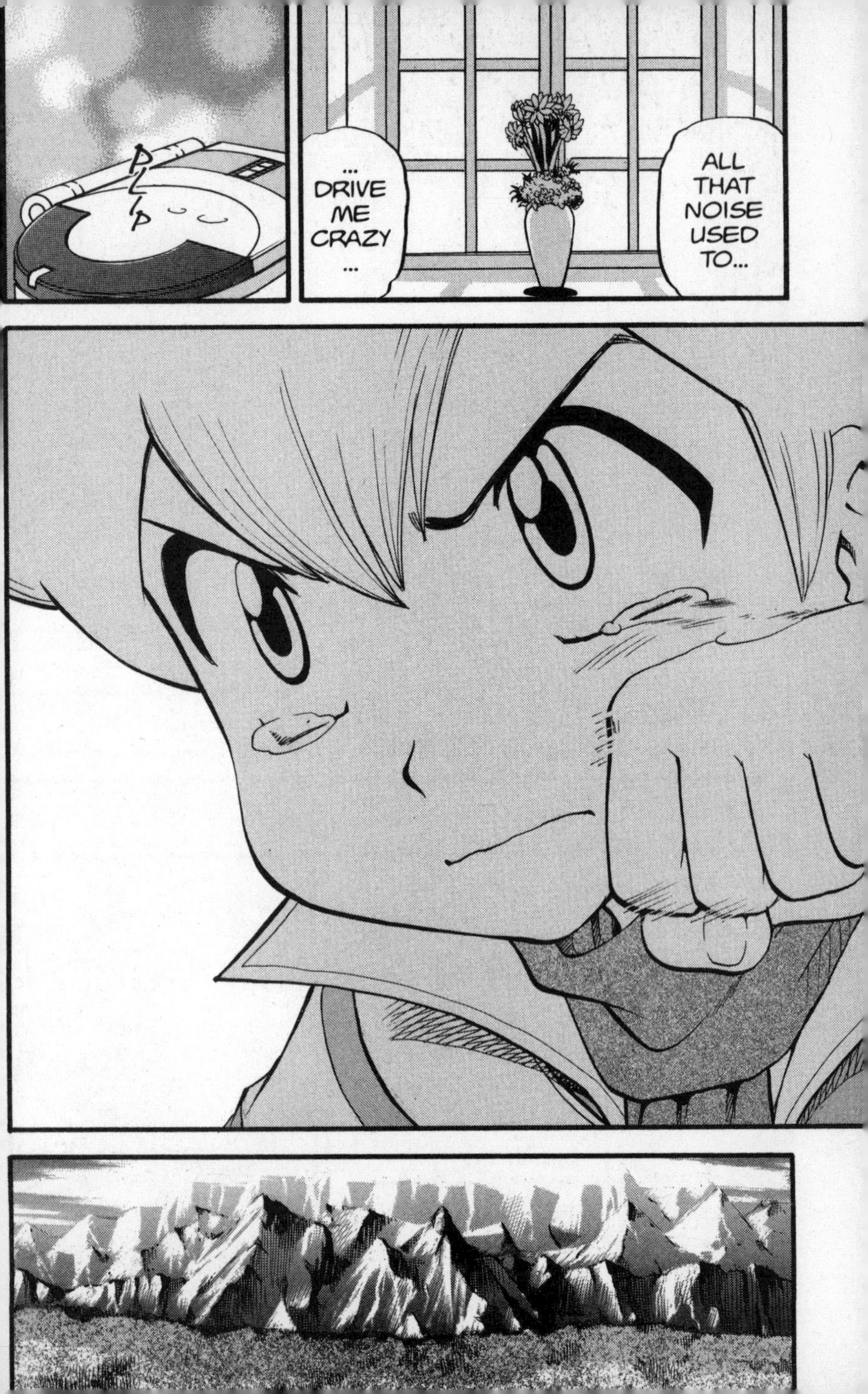
ALL THAT NOISE USED TO...
... DRIVE ME CRAZY ...
PLIP

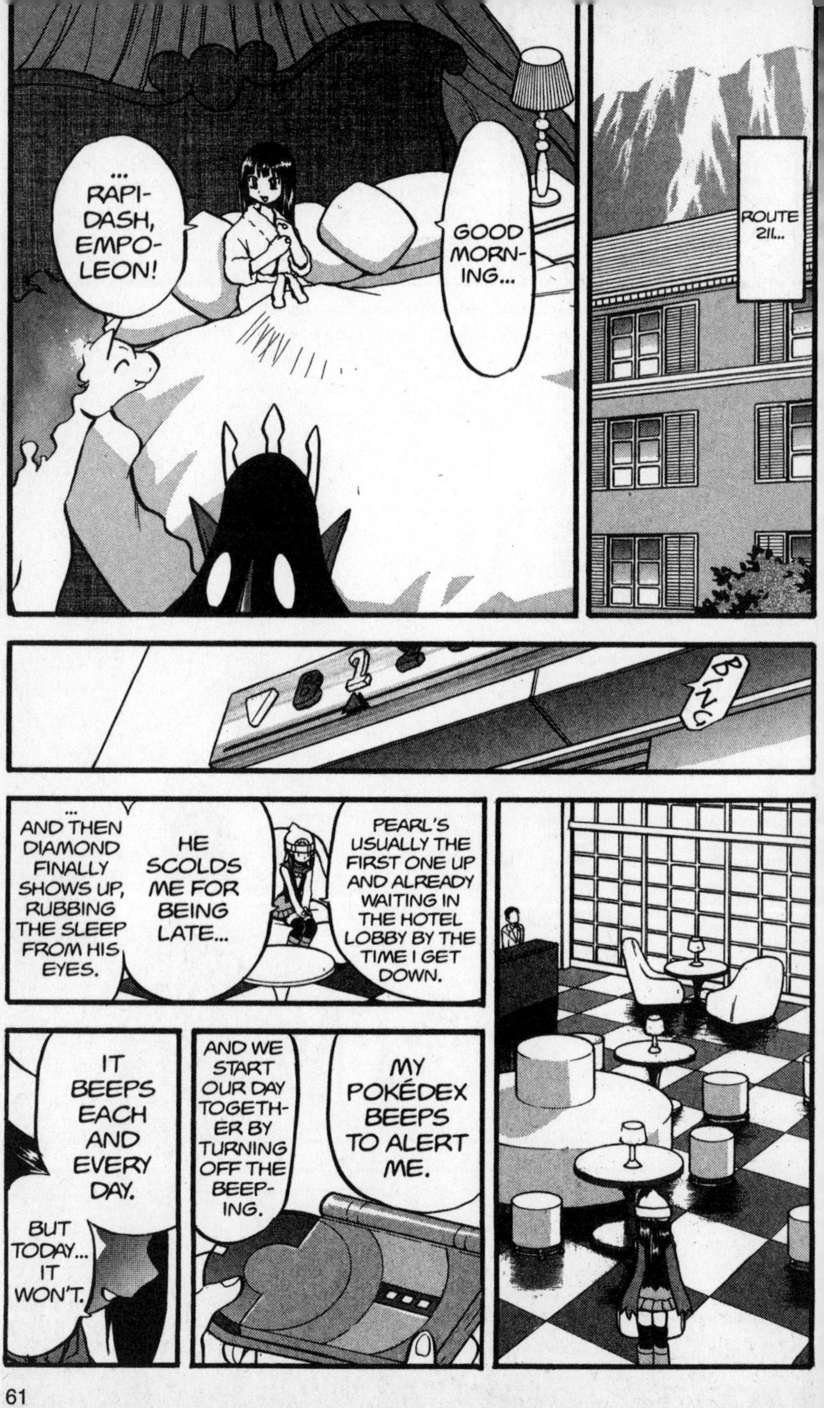
ROUTE 211...
GOOD MORNING...
... RAPIDASH, EMPOLEON!
BING
PEARL'S USUALLY THE FIRST ONE UP AND ALREADY WAITING IN THE HOTEL LOBBY BY THE TIME I GET DOWN.
HE SCOLDS ME FOR BEING LATE...
... AND THEN DIAMOND FINALLY SHOWS UP, RUBBING THE SLEEP FROM HIS EYES.
MY POKÉDEX BEEPS TO ALERT ME.
AND WE START OUR DAY TOGETHER BY TURNING OFF THE BEEPING.
IT BEEPS EACH AND EVERY DAY.
BUT TODAY... IT WON'T.

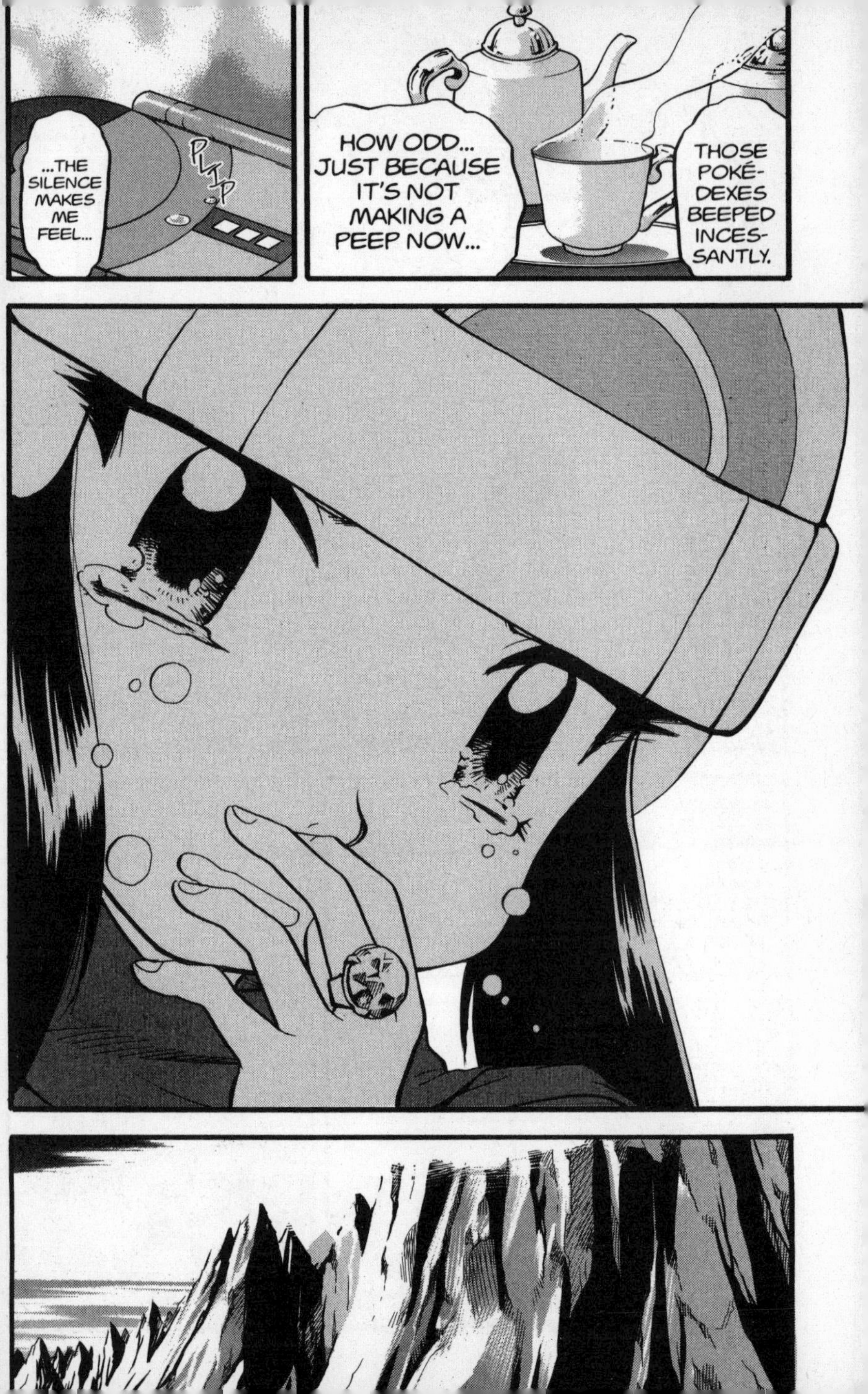
THOSE POKÉDEXES BEEPED INCESSANTLY.
HOW ODD... JUST BECAUSE IT'S NOT MAKING A PEEP NOW...
PLIP
...THE SILENCE MAKES ME FEEL...

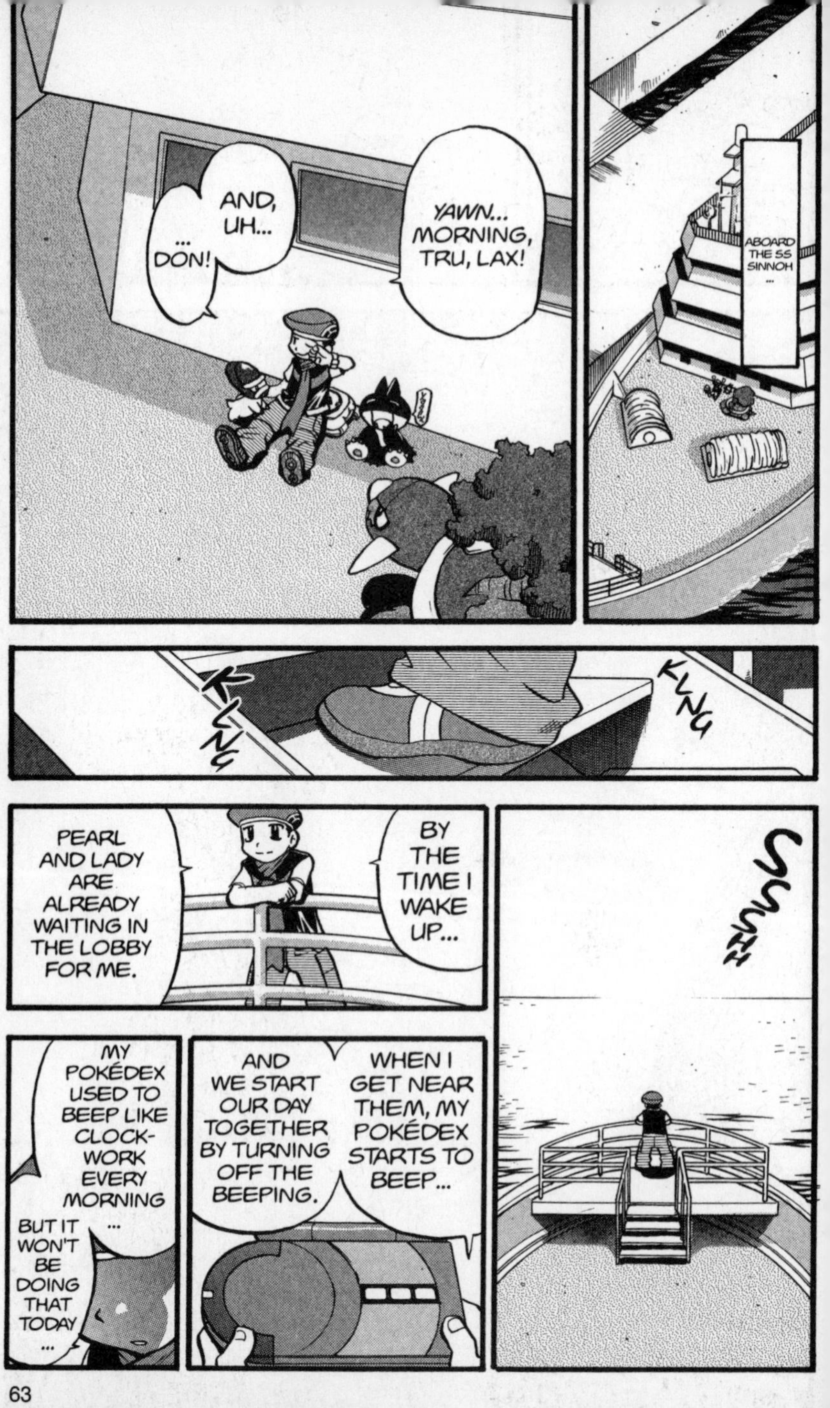
ABOARD THE SS SINNOH ...
YAWN... MORNING, TRU, LAX!
AND, UH... ... DON!
KLNG
KLNG
SSSHHH
BY THE TIME I WAKE UP...
PEARL AND LADY ARE ALREADY WAITING IN THE LOBBY FOR ME.
WHEN I GET NEAR THEM, MY POKÉDEX STARTS TO BEEP...
AND WE START OUR DAY TOGETHER BY TURNING OFF THE BEEPING.
MY POKÉDEX USED TO BEEP LIKE CLOCK-WORK EVERY MORNING ...
BUT IT WON'T BE DOING THAT TODAY ...

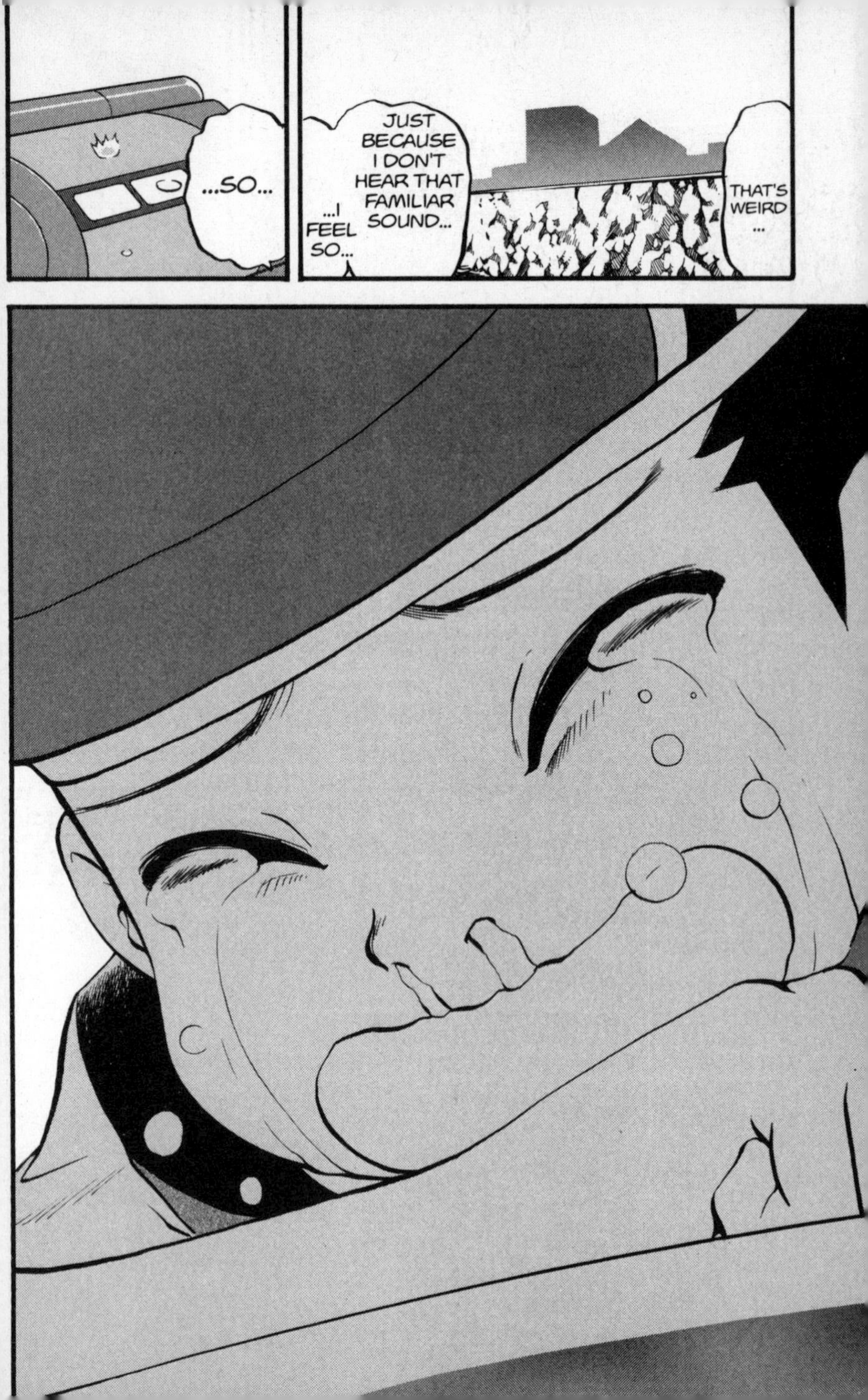
THAT'S WEIRD...
JUST BECAUSE I DON'T HEAR THAT FAMILIAR SOUND...
...I FEEL SO...
...SO...

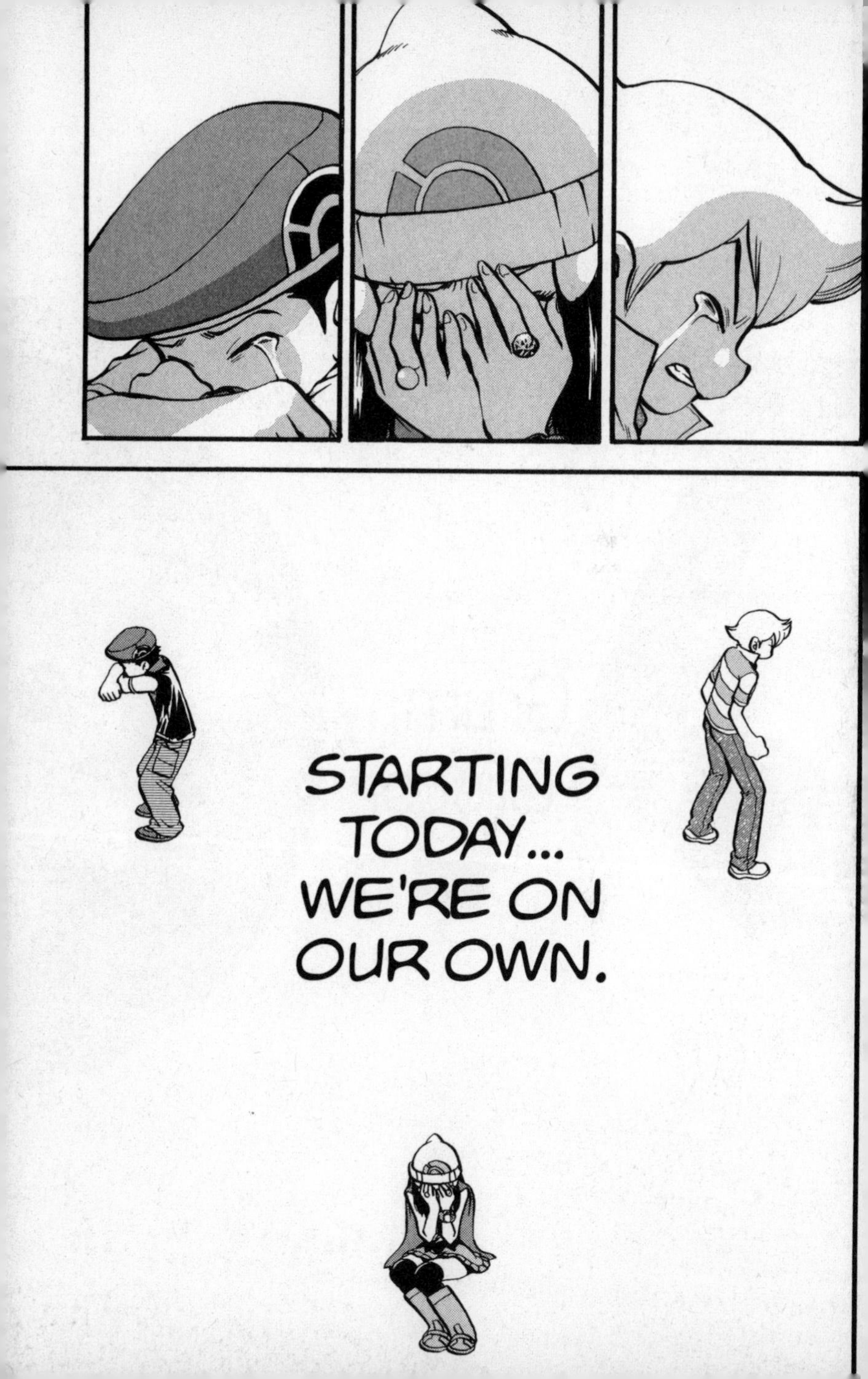
STARTING TODAY... WE'RE ON OUR OWN.

41

Grumpy
Gliscor

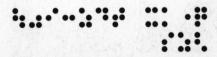

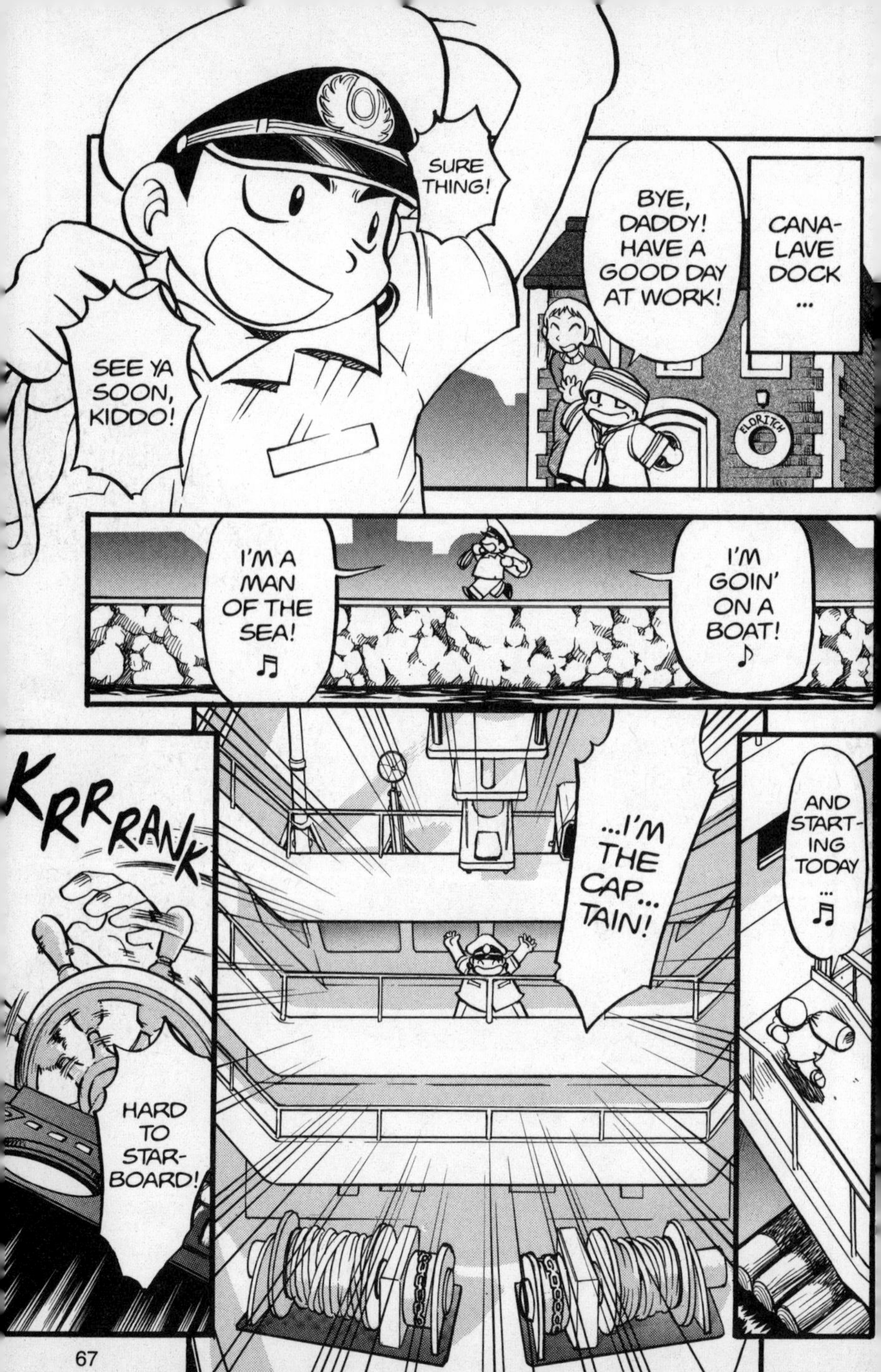
CANA-
LAVE
DOCK
...
BYE, DADDY! HAVE A GOOD DAY AT WORK!
ELDRITCH
SURE THING!
SEE YA SOON, KIDDO!
I'M GOIN' ON A BOAT! ♪
I'M A MAN OF THE SEA! ♬
AND START-ING TODAY ... ♬
...I'M THE CAP... TAIN!
KRRRANK
HARD TO STAR-BOARD!

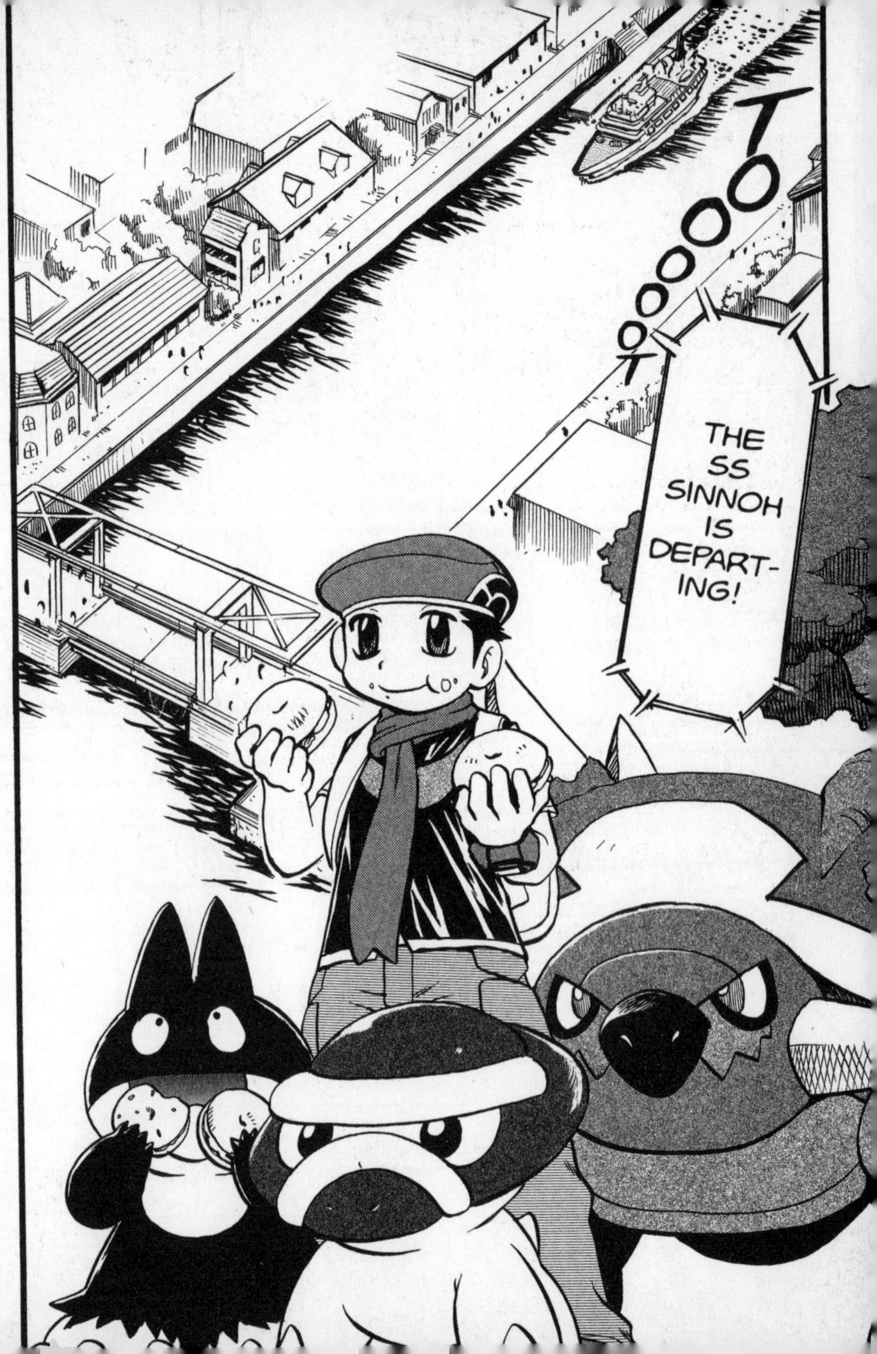
TOOOOOOT
THE SS SINNOH IS DEPART-ING!

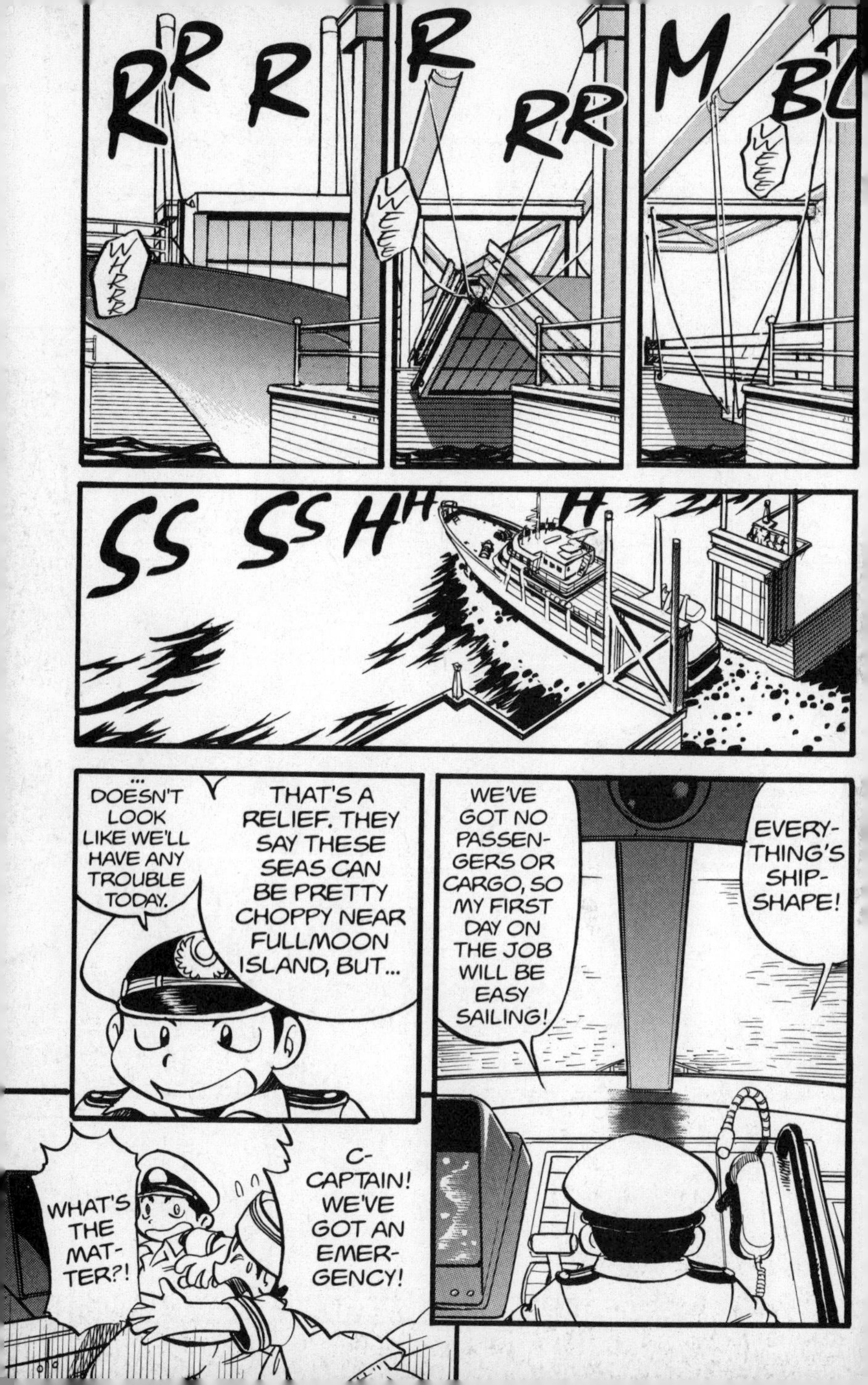
RRR R R RR M BO
WEEE
WEEE
WHRRR
SS SSHHH
EVERY-THING'S SHIP-SHAPE!
WE'VE GOT NO PASSEN-GERS OR CARGO, SO MY FIRST DAY ON THE JOB WILL BE EASY SAILING!
THAT'S A RELIEF. THEY SAY THESE SEAS CAN BE PRETTY CHOPPY NEAR FULLMOON ISLAND, BUT...
... DOESN'T LOOK LIKE WE'LL HAVE ANY TROUBLE TODAY.
C-CAPTAIN! WE'VE GOT AN EMER-GENCY!
WHAT'S THE MAT-TER?!

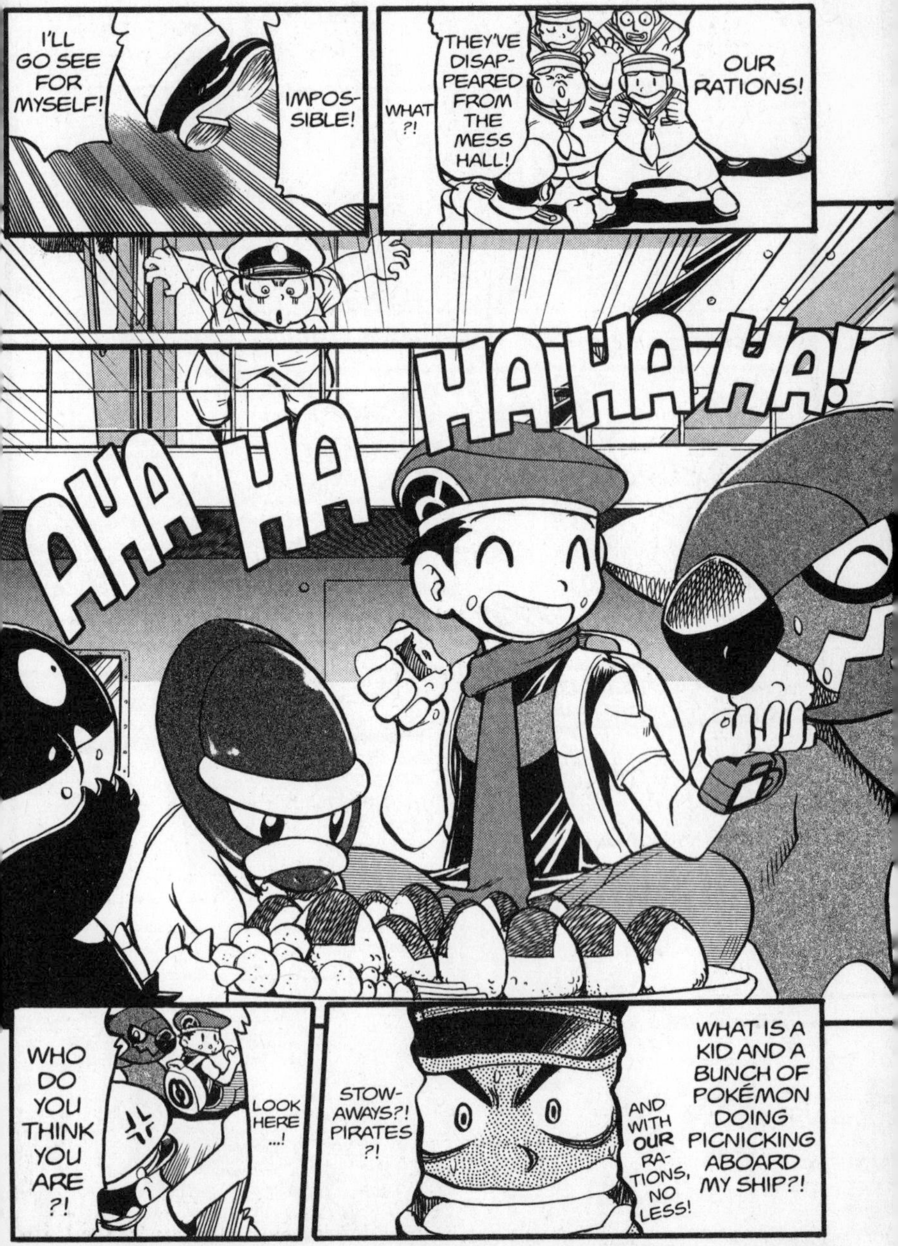
OUR RATIONS!
THEY'VE DISAPPEARED FROM THE MESS HALL!
WHAT?!
IMPOSSIBLE!
I'LL GO SEE FOR MYSELF!
AHA HA HA HA HA HA!
WHAT IS A KID AND A BUNCH OF POKÉMON DOING PICNICKING ABOARD MY SHIP?!
AND WITH **OUR** RATIONS, NO LESS!
STOWAWAYS?! PIRATES?!
LOOK HERE...!
WHO DO YOU THINK YOU ARE?!

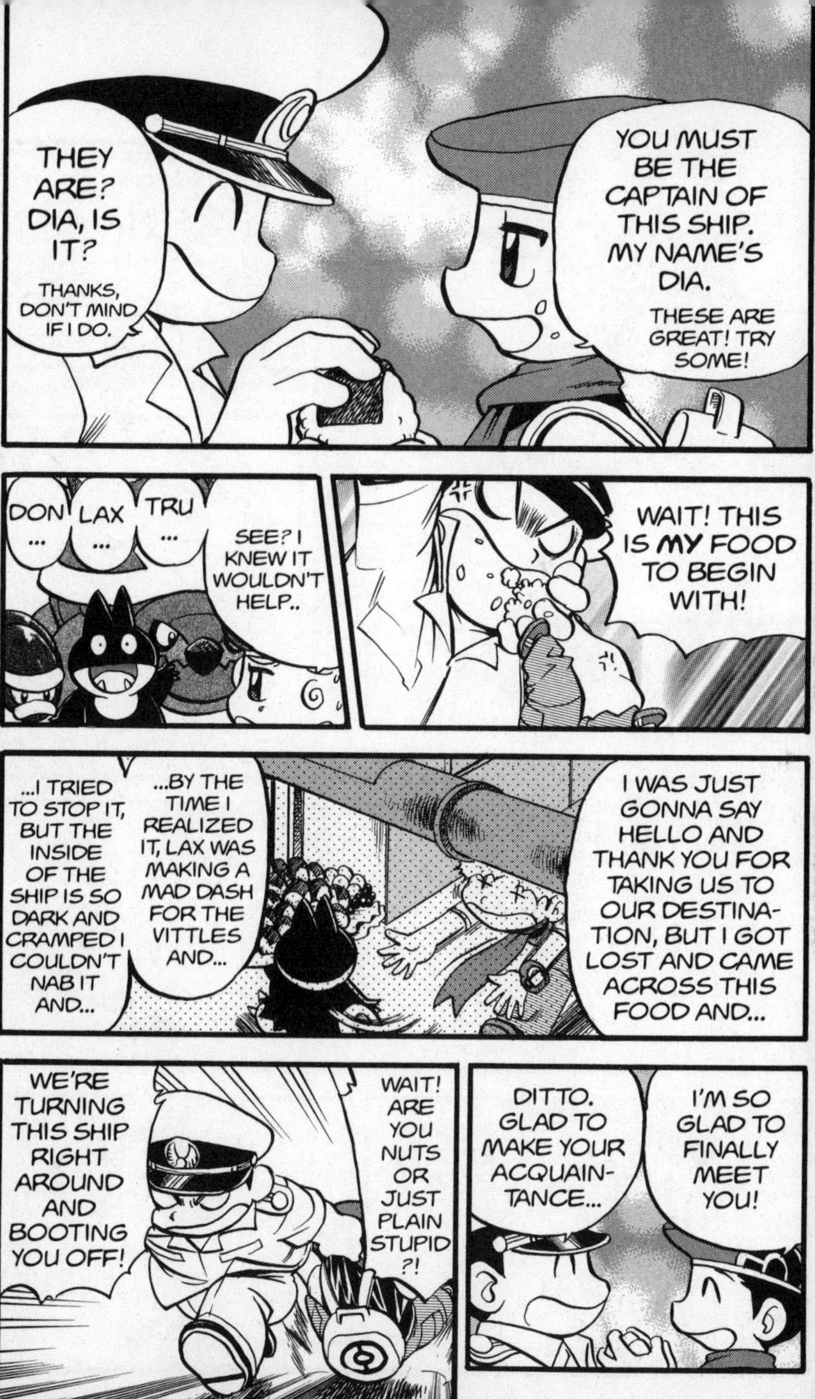
YOU MUST BE THE CAPTAIN OF THIS SHIP. MY NAME'S DIA.
THESE ARE GREAT! TRY SOME!
THEY ARE? DIA, IS IT?
THANKS, DON'T MIND IF I DO.
WAIT! THIS IS **MY** FOOD TO BEGIN WITH!
SEE? I KNEW IT WOULDN'T HELP..
TRU ...
LAX ...
DON ...
I WAS JUST GONNA SAY HELLO AND THANK YOU FOR TAKING US TO OUR DESTINA-TION, BUT I GOT LOST AND CAME ACROSS THIS FOOD AND...
...BY THE TIME I REALIZED IT, LAX WAS MAKING A MAD DASH FOR THE VITTLES AND...
...I TRIED TO STOP IT, BUT THE INSIDE OF THE SHIP IS SO DARK AND CRAMPED I COULDN'T NAB IT AND...
I'M SO GLAD TO FINALLY MEET YOU!
DITTO. GLAD TO MAKE YOUR ACQUAIN-TANCE...
WAIT! ARE YOU NUTS OR JUST PLAIN STUPID?!
WE'RE TURNING THIS SHIP RIGHT AROUND AND BOOTING YOU OFF!

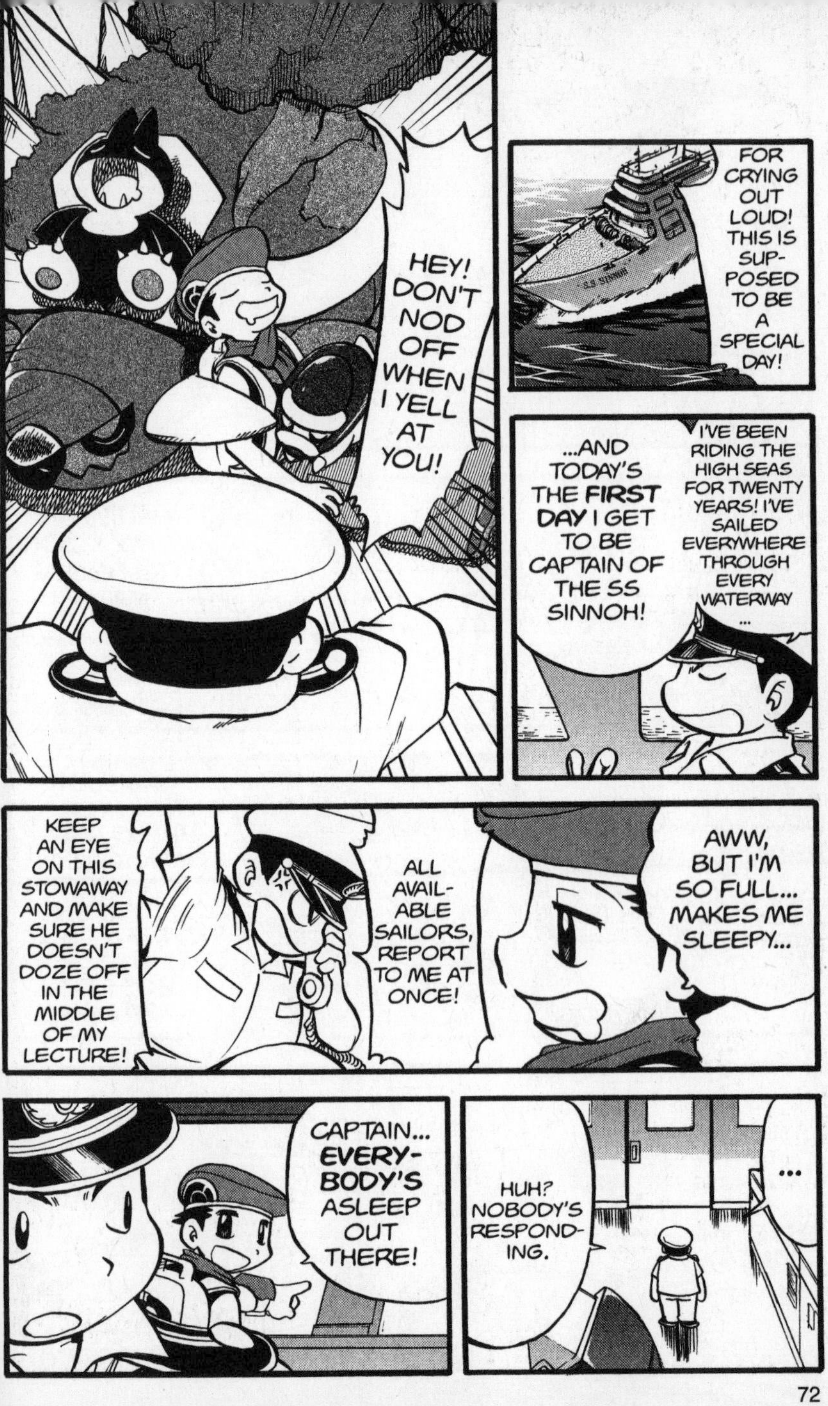
FOR CRYING OUT LOUD! THIS IS SUP-POSED TO BE A SPECIAL DAY!
I'VE BEEN RIDING THE HIGH SEAS FOR TWENTY YEARS! I'VE SAILED EVERYWHERE THROUGH EVERY WATERWAY ...
...AND TODAY'S THE **FIRST DAY** I GET TO BE CAPTAIN OF THE SS SINNOH!
HEY! DON'T NOD OFF WHEN I YELL AT YOU!
AWW, BUT I'M SO FULL... MAKES ME SLEEPY...
ALL AVAIL-ABLE SAILORS, REPORT TO ME AT ONCE!
KEEP AN EYE ON THIS STOWAWAY AND MAKE SURE HE DOESN'T DOZE OFF IN THE MIDDLE OF MY LECTURE!
...
HUH? NOBODY'S RESPOND-ING.
CAPTAIN... **EVERY-BODY'S** ASLEEP OUT THERE!

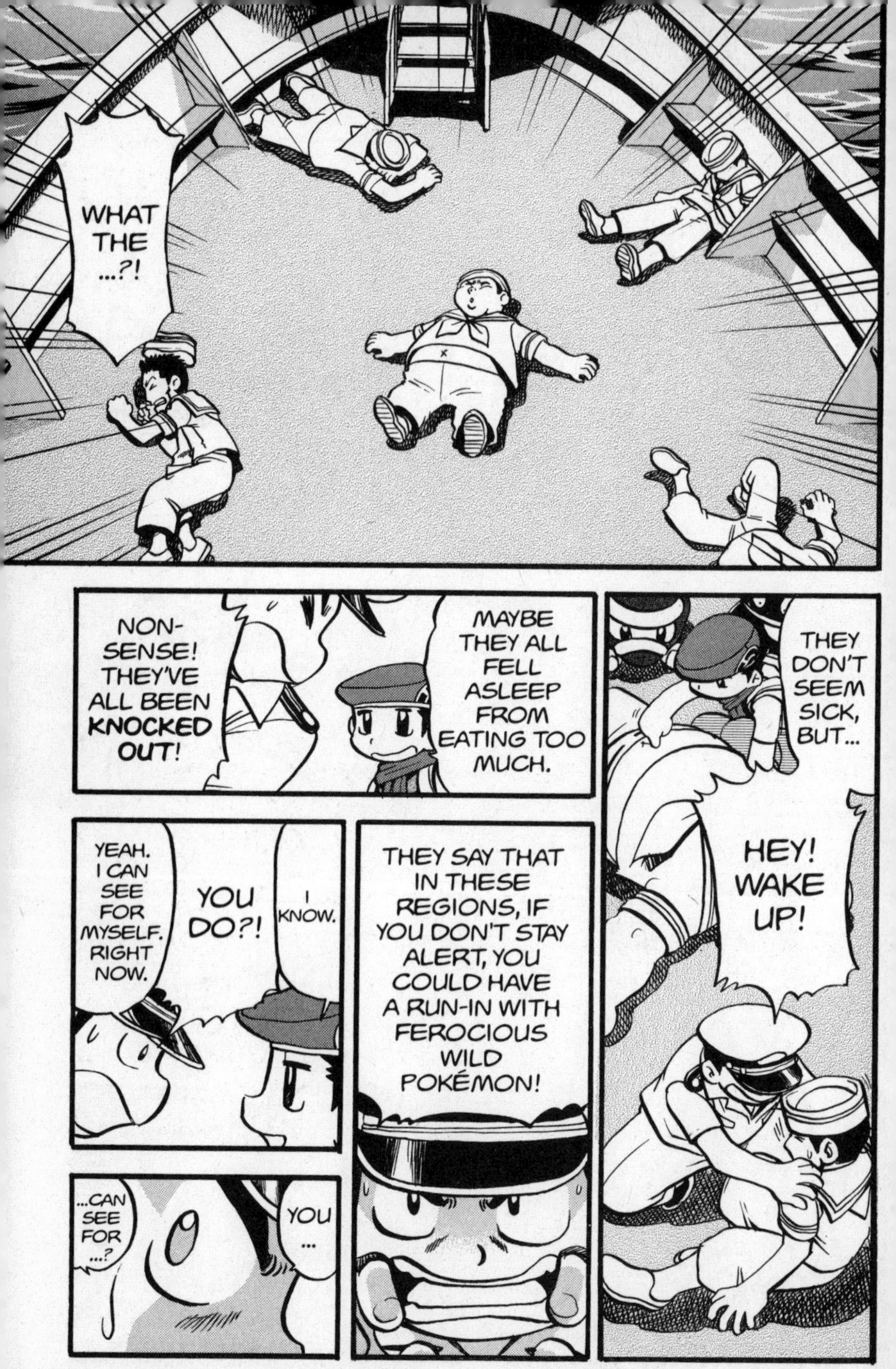
WHAT THE ...?!
THEY DON'T SEEM SICK, BUT...
HEY! WAKE UP!
MAYBE THEY ALL FELL ASLEEP FROM EATING TOO MUCH.
NON-SENSE! THEY'VE ALL BEEN KNOCKED OUT!
THEY SAY THAT IN THESE REGIONS, IF YOU DON'T STAY ALERT, YOU COULD HAVE A RUN-IN WITH FEROCIOUS WILD POKÉMON!
I KNOW.
YOU DO?!
YEAH. I CAN SEE FOR MYSELF. RIGHT NOW.
YOU ...
...CAN SEE FOR ...?

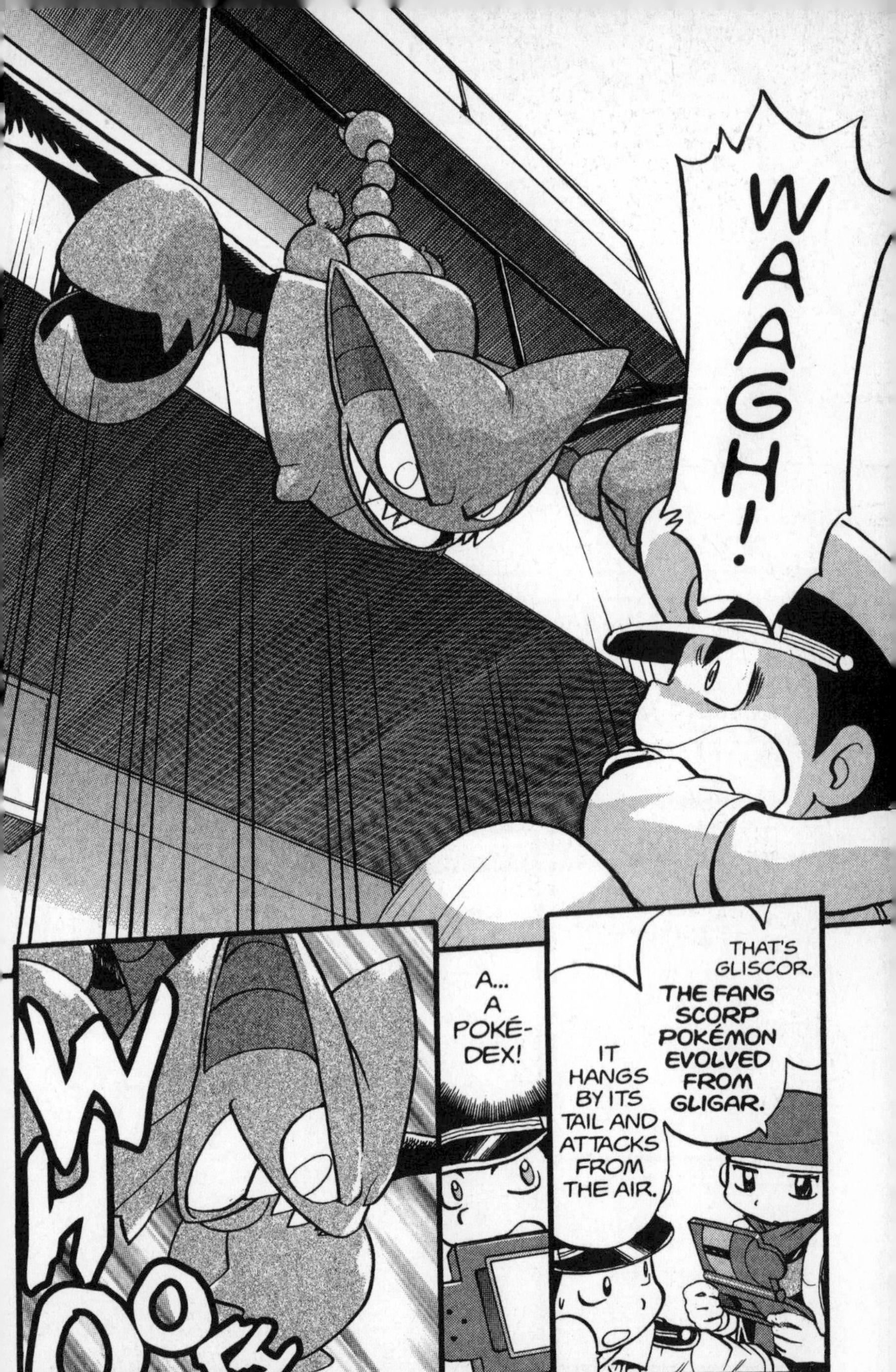
WAAGH!
THAT'S GLISCOR. THE FANG SCORP POKÉMON EVOLVED FROM GLIGAR.
A... A POKÉ-DEX!
IT HANGS BY ITS TAIL AND ATTACKS FROM THE AIR.
WHOOSH

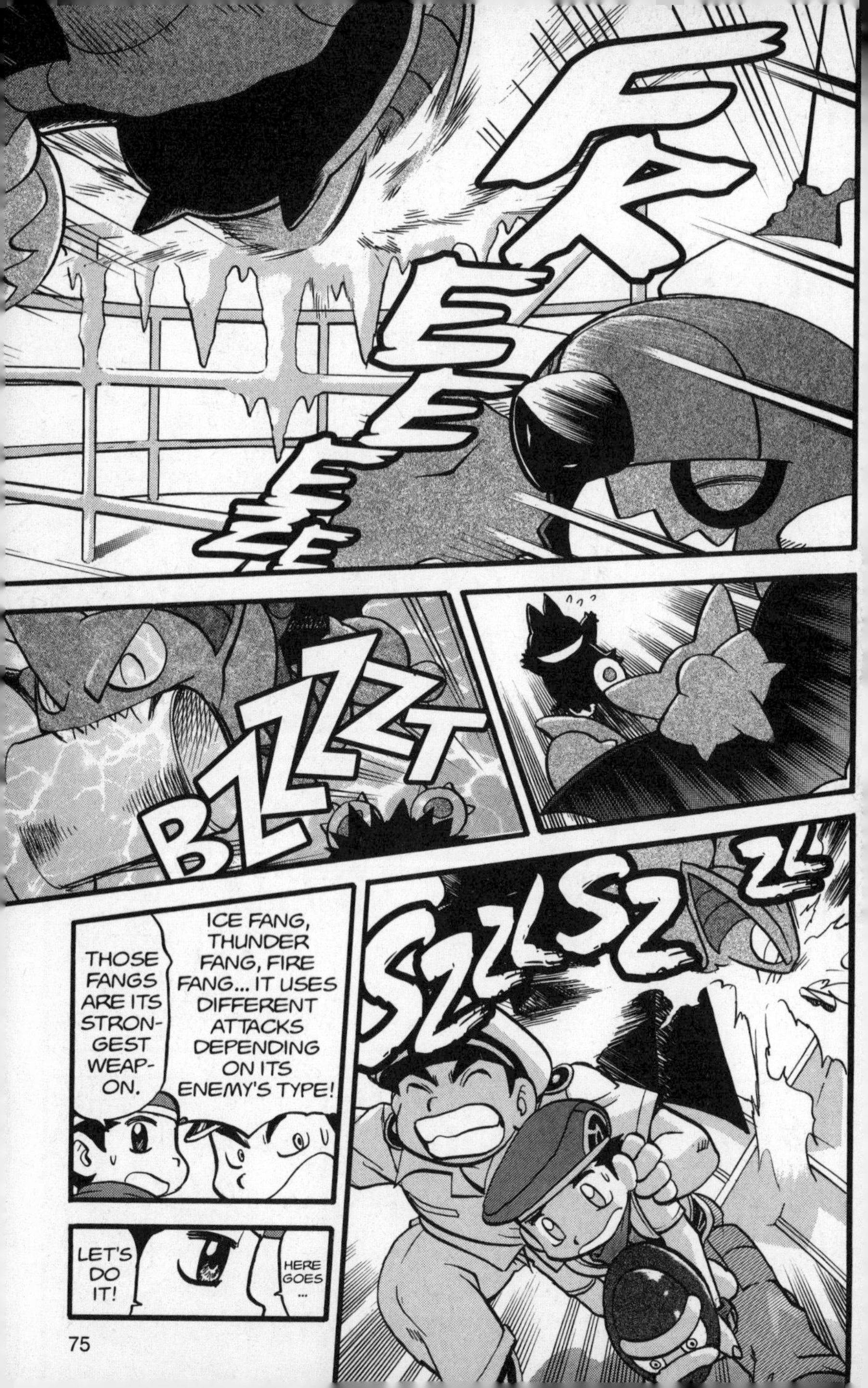
FREEEZE
BZZZZT
SZZSZZ
ICE FANG, THUNDER FANG, FIRE FANG... IT USES DIFFERENT ATTACKS DEPENDING ON ITS ENEMY'S TYPE!
THOSE FANGS ARE ITS STRON-GEST WEAP-ON.
HERE GOES...
LET'S DO IT!

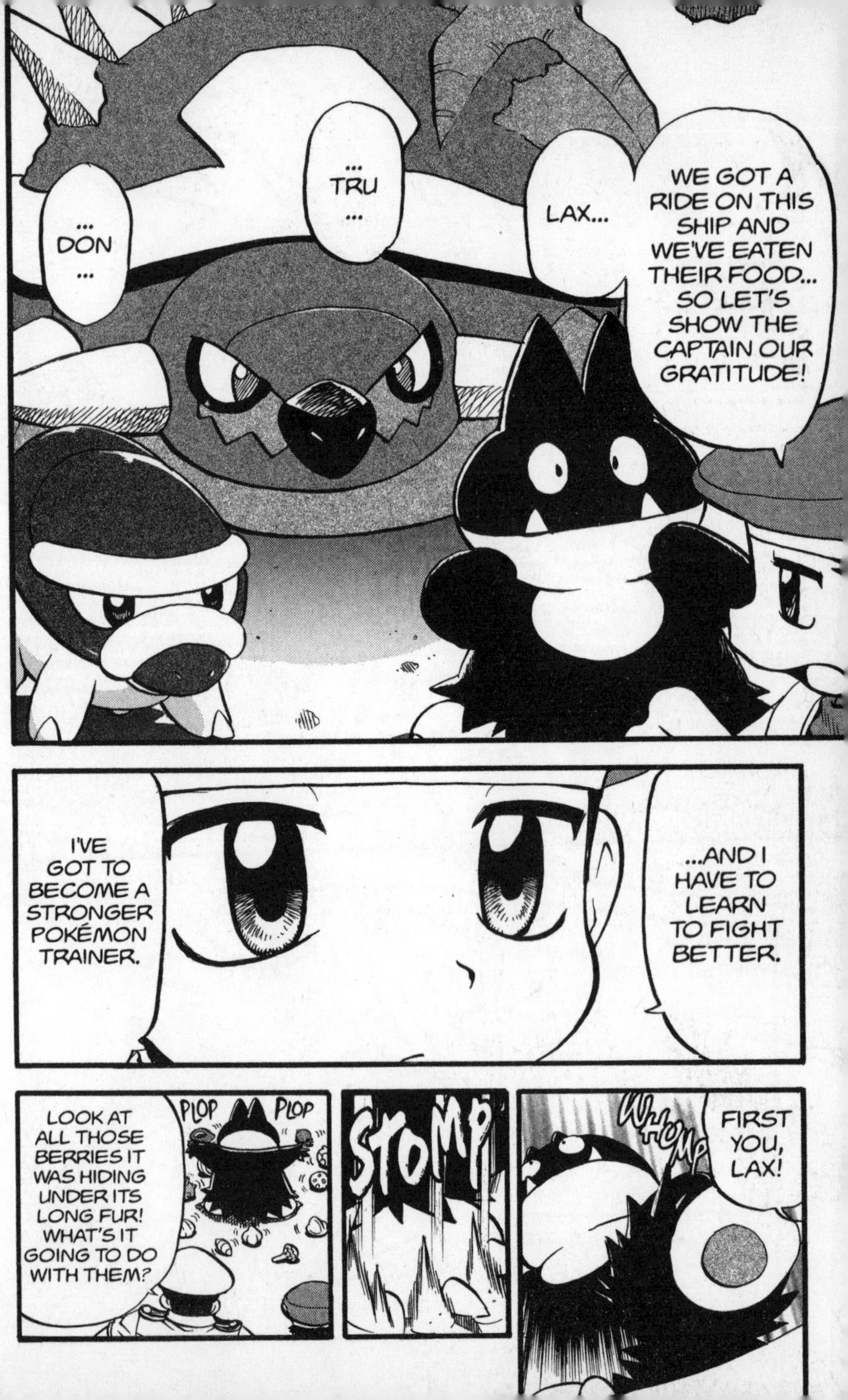
WE GOT A RIDE ON THIS SHIP AND WE'VE EATEN THEIR FOOD... SO LET'S SHOW THE CAPTAIN OUR GRATITUDE!
LAX...
... TRU ...
... DON ...
I'VE GOT TO BECOME A STRONGER POKÉMON TRAINER.
...AND I HAVE TO LEARN TO FIGHT BETTER.
WHOMP
FIRST YOU, LAX!
STOMP
PLOP PLOP
LOOK AT ALL THOSE BERRIES IT WAS HIDING UNDER ITS LONG FUR! WHAT'S IT GOING TO DO WITH THEM?

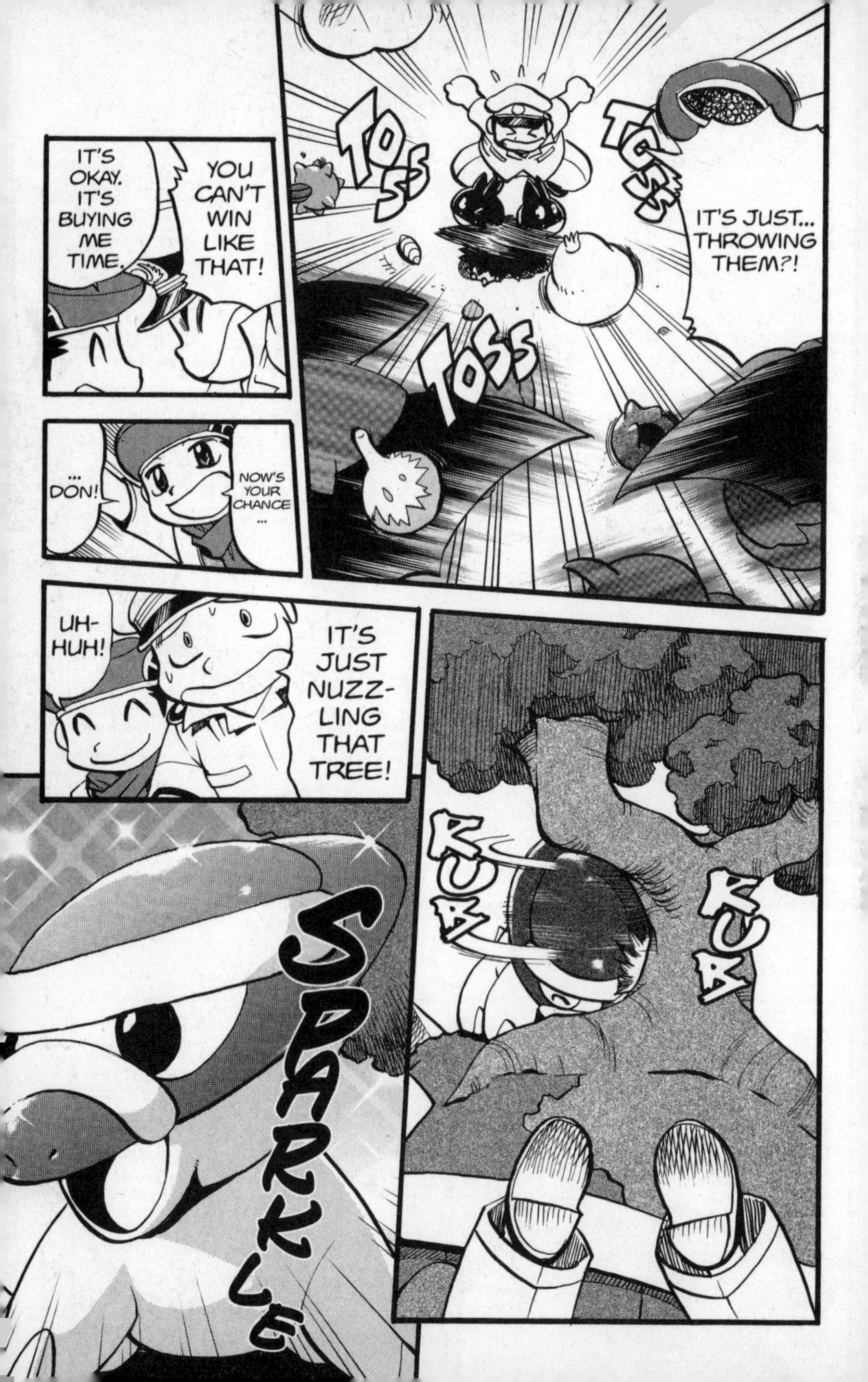
TOSS
TOSS
IT'S JUST... THROWING THEM?!
TOSS
YOU CAN'T WIN LIKE THAT!
IT'S OKAY. IT'S BUYING ME TIME.
NOW'S YOUR CHANCE...
...DON!
RUB
RUB
IT'S JUST NUZZ-LING THAT TREE!
UH-HUH!
SPARKLE

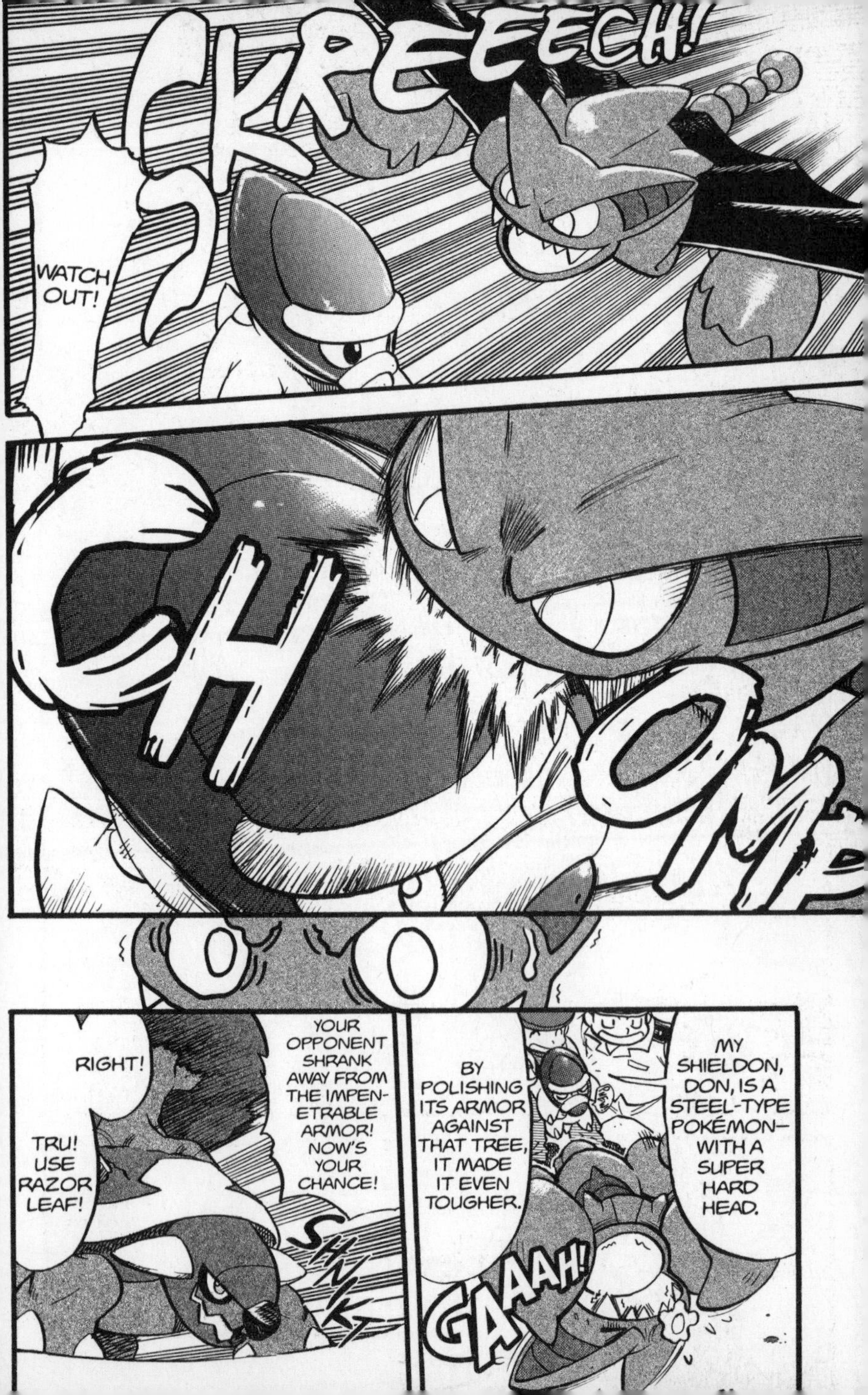
SKREEECH!
WATCH OUT!
CHOMP
MY SHIELDON, DON, IS A STEEL-TYPE POKÉMON—WITH A SUPER HARD HEAD.
BY POLISHING ITS ARMOR AGAINST THAT TREE, IT MADE IT EVEN TOUGHER.
GAAAH!
YOUR OPPONENT SHRANK AWAY FROM THE IMPEN-ETRABLE ARMOR! NOW'S YOUR CHANCE!
RIGHT!
TRU! USE RAZOR LEAF!
SHNIKT

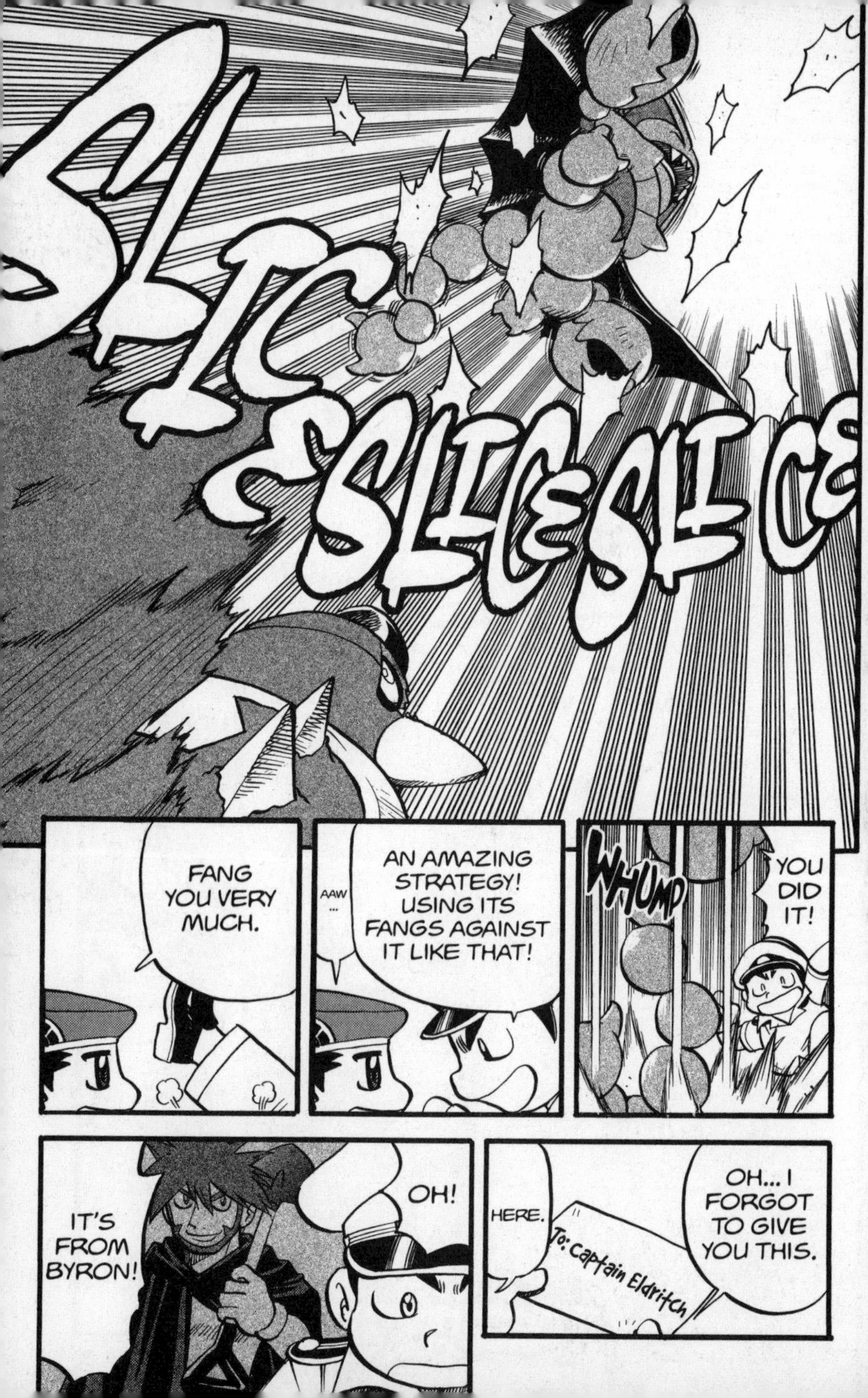
SLICE SLICE SLICE
YOU DID IT!
WHUMP
AN AMAZING STRATEGY! USING ITS FANGS AGAINST IT LIKE THAT!
AAW...
FANG YOU VERY MUCH.
OH... I FORGOT TO GIVE YOU THIS.
HERE.
To: Captain Eldritch
OH!
IT'S FROM BYRON!

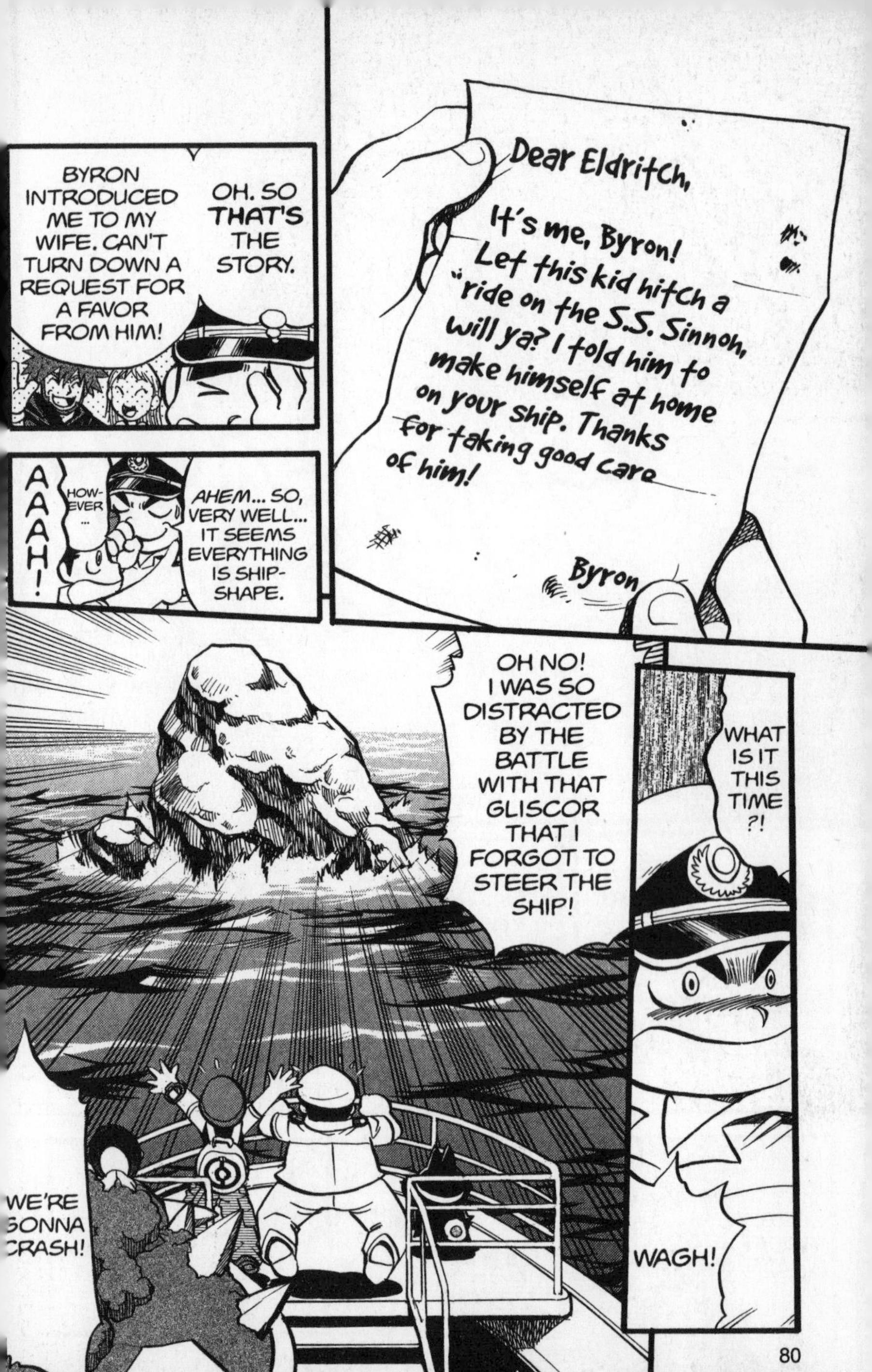
Dear Eldritch,
It's me, Byron! Let this kid hitch a ride on the S.S. Sinnoh, will ya? I told him to make himself at home on your ship. Thanks for taking good care of him!
Byron
OH. SO THAT'S THE STORY.
BYRON INTRODUCED ME TO MY WIFE. CAN'T TURN DOWN A REQUEST FOR A FAVOR FROM HIM!
AHEM... SO, VERY WELL... IT SEEMS EVERYTHING IS SHIP-SHAPE.
HOW-EVER ...
AAAAH!
WHAT IS IT THIS TIME ?!
WAGH!
OH NO! I WAS SO DISTRACTED BY THE BATTLE WITH THAT GLISCOR THAT I FORGOT TO STEER THE SHIP!
WE'RE GONNA CRASH!

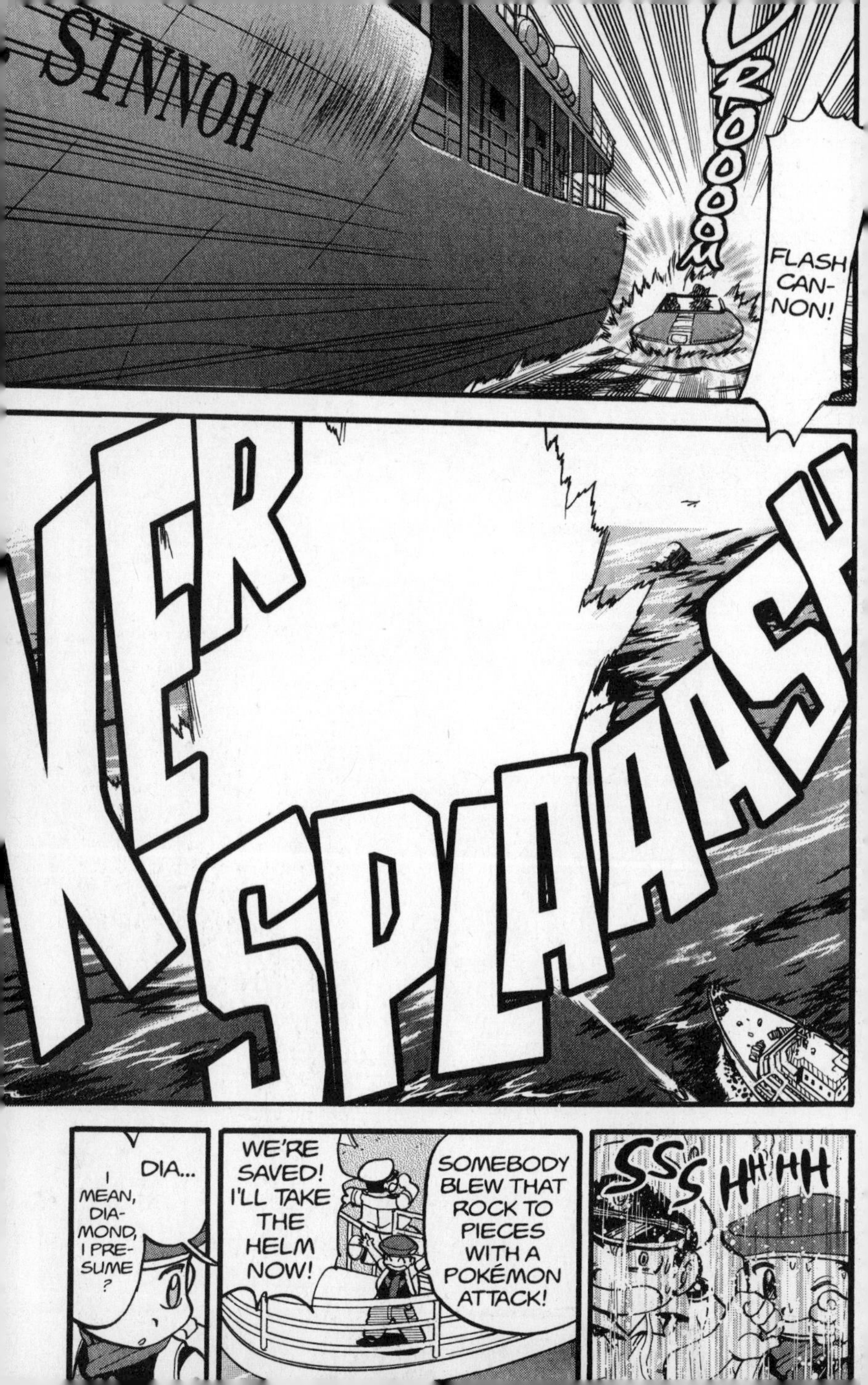
SINNOH
FLASH CANNON!
VROOOOOM
KER SPLAASH
SSSHHHHH
SOMEBODY BLEW THAT ROCK TO PIECES WITH A POKÉMON ATTACK!
WE'RE SAVED! I'LL TAKE THE HELM NOW!
DIA...
I MEAN, DIAMOND, I PRESUME?

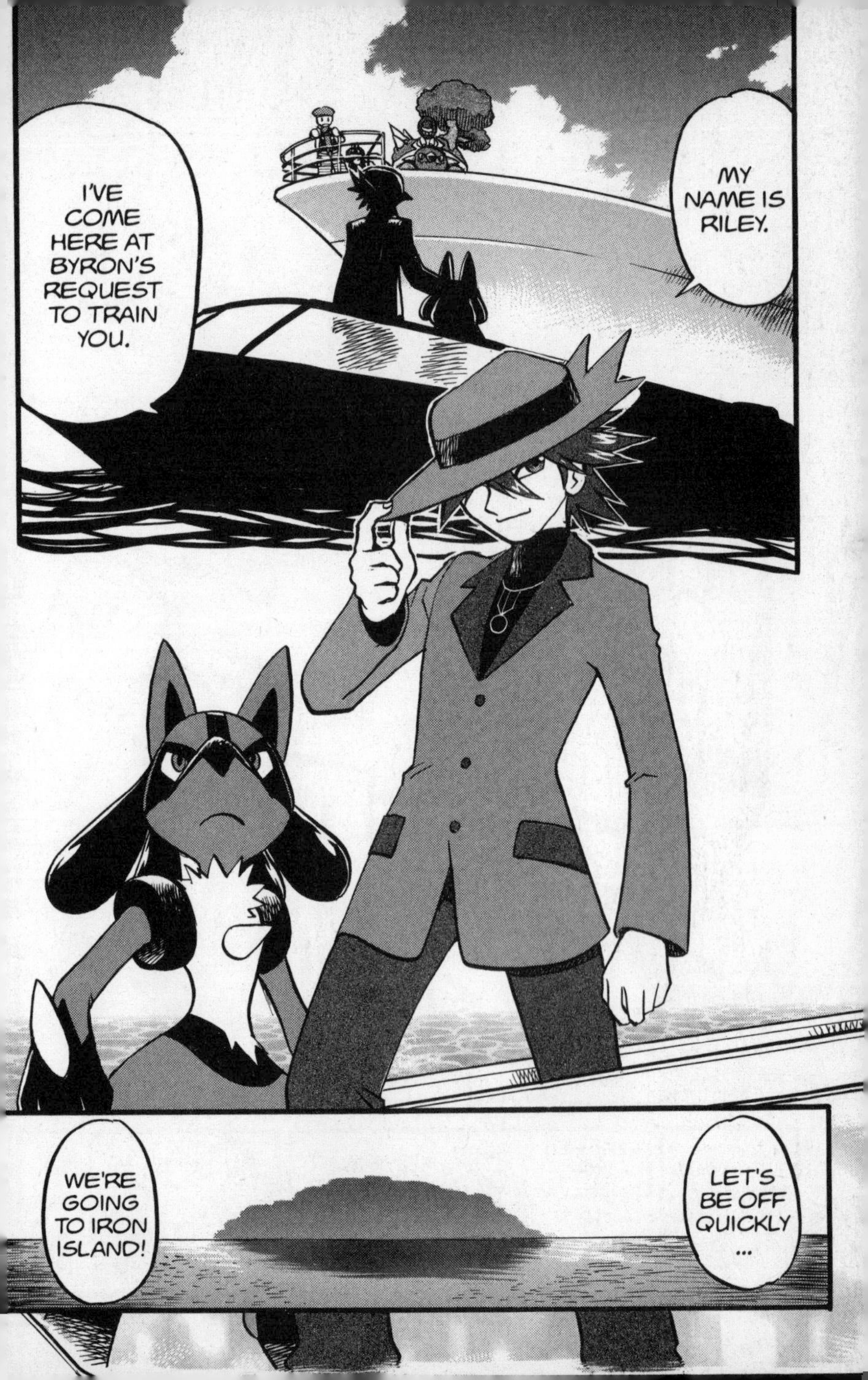
MY NAME IS RILEY.
I'VE COME HERE AT BYRON'S REQUEST TO TRAIN YOU.
LET'S BE OFF QUICKLY ...
WE'RE GOING TO IRON ISLAND!

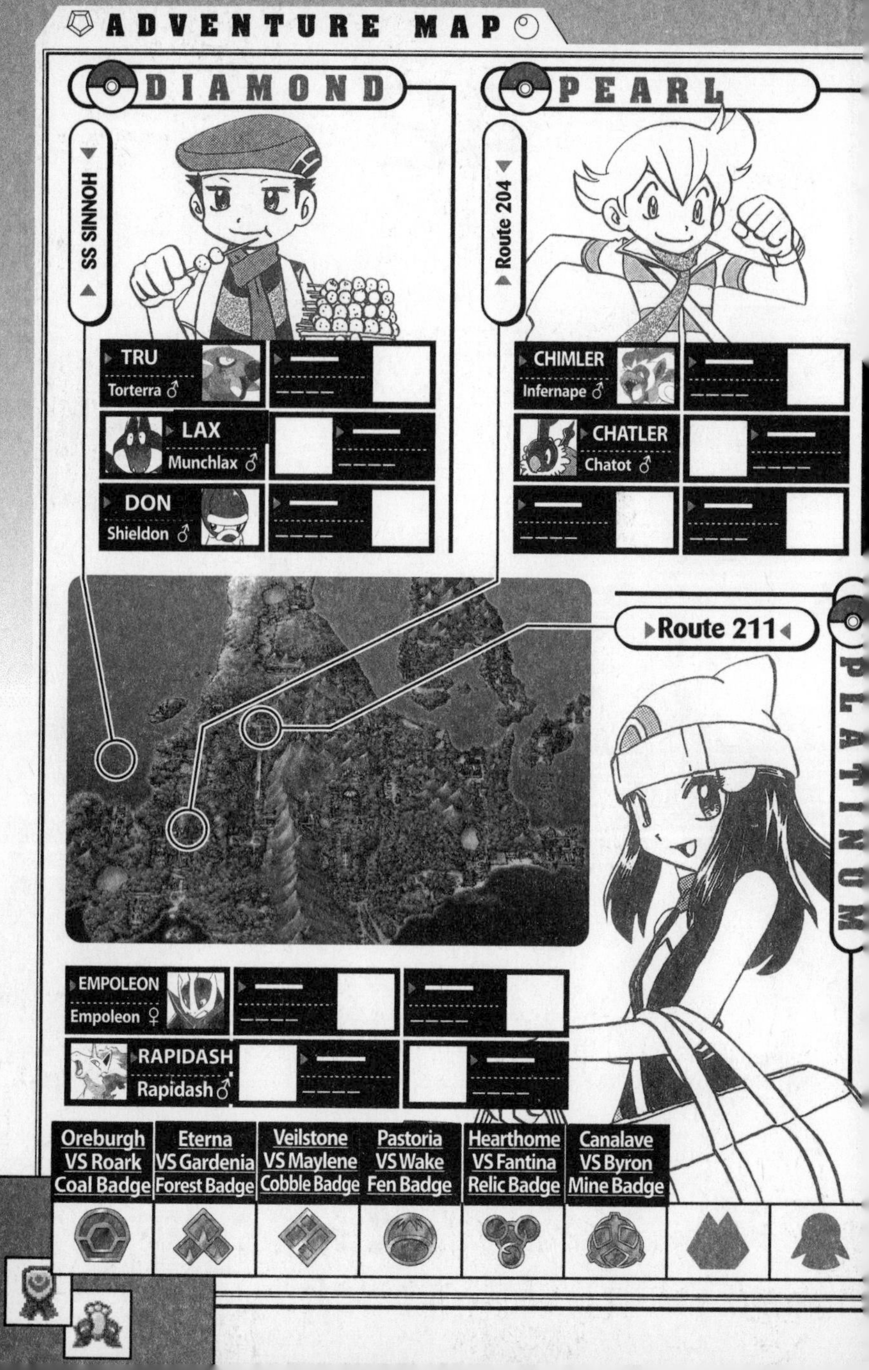
ADVENTURE MAP
DIAMOND
SS SINNOH
TRU
Torterra ♂
LAX
Munchlax ♂
DON
Shieldon ♂
PEARL
Route 204
CHIMLER
Infernape ♂
CHATLER
Chatot ♂
Route 211
PLATINUM
EMPOLEON
Empoleon ♀
RAPIDASH
Rapidash ♂
Oreburgh
VS Roark
Coal Badge
Eterna
VS Gardenia
Forest Badge
Veilstone
VS Maylene
Cobble Badge
Pastoria
VS Wake
Fen Badge
Hearthome
VS Fantina
Relic Badge
Canalave
VS Byron
Mine Badge

42

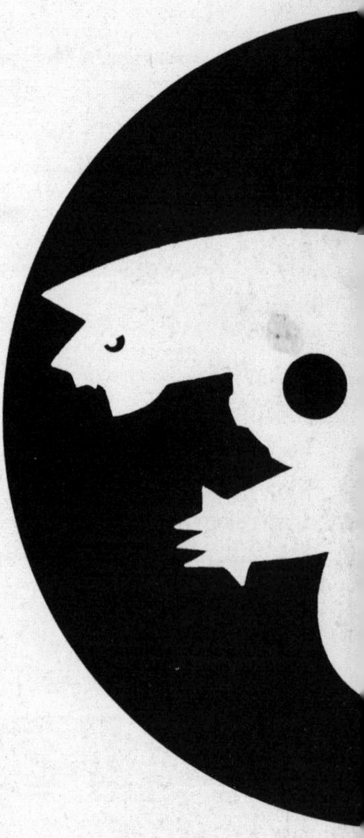

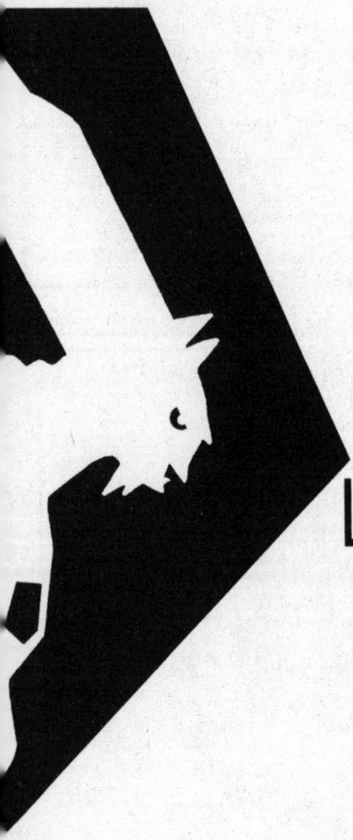

Lucky Lucario I

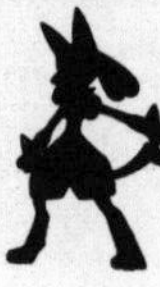

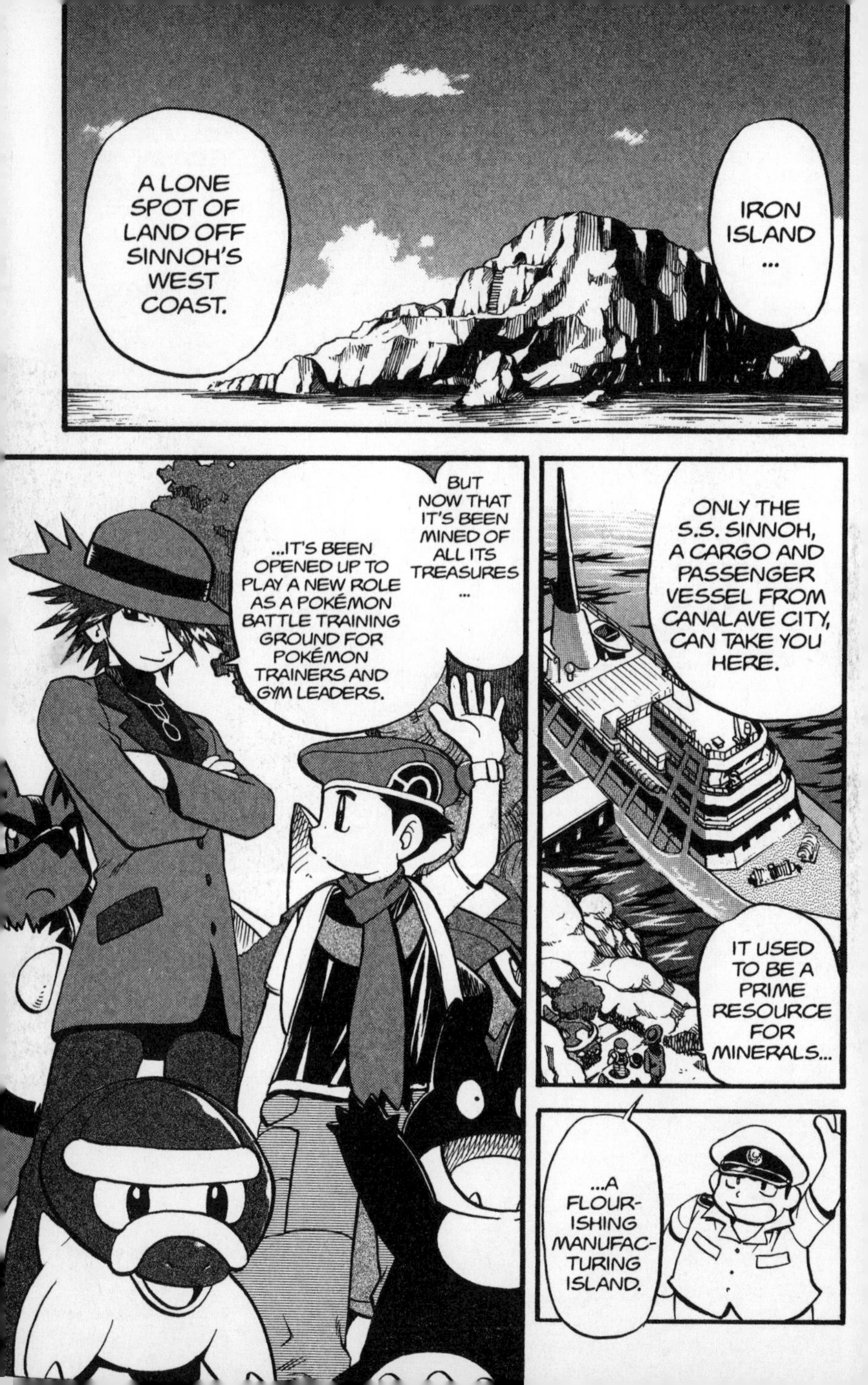
IRON ISLAND ...
A LONE SPOT OF LAND OFF SINNOH'S WEST COAST.
ONLY THE S.S. SINNOH, A CARGO AND PASSENGER VESSEL FROM CANALAVE CITY, CAN TAKE YOU HERE.
IT USED TO BE A PRIME RESOURCE FOR MINERALS...
...A FLOUR-ISHING MANUFAC-TURING ISLAND.
BUT NOW THAT IT'S BEEN MINED OF ALL ITS TREASURES ...
...IT'S BEEN OPENED UP TO PLAY A NEW ROLE AS A POKÉMON BATTLE TRAINING GROUND FOR POKÉMON TRAINERS AND GYM LEADERS.

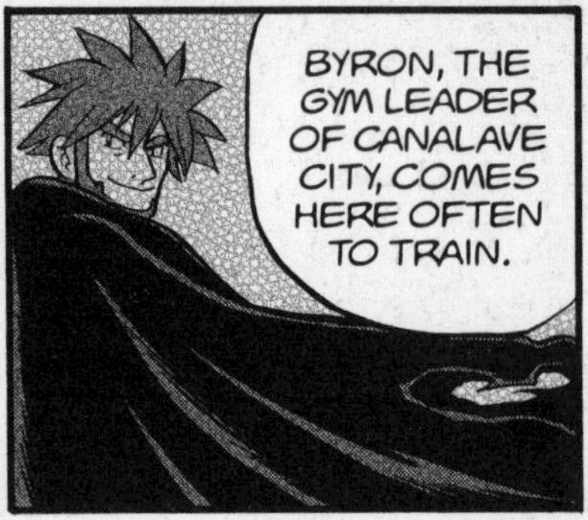
BYRON, THE GYM LEADER OF CANALAVE CITY, COMES HERE OFTEN TO TRAIN.
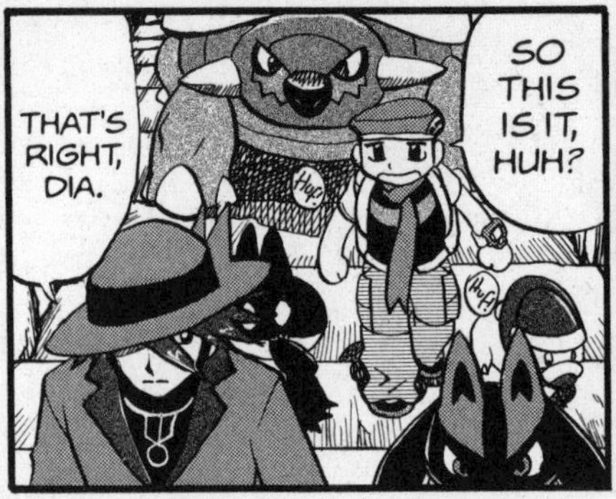
SO THIS IS IT, HUH?
THAT'S RIGHT, DIA.
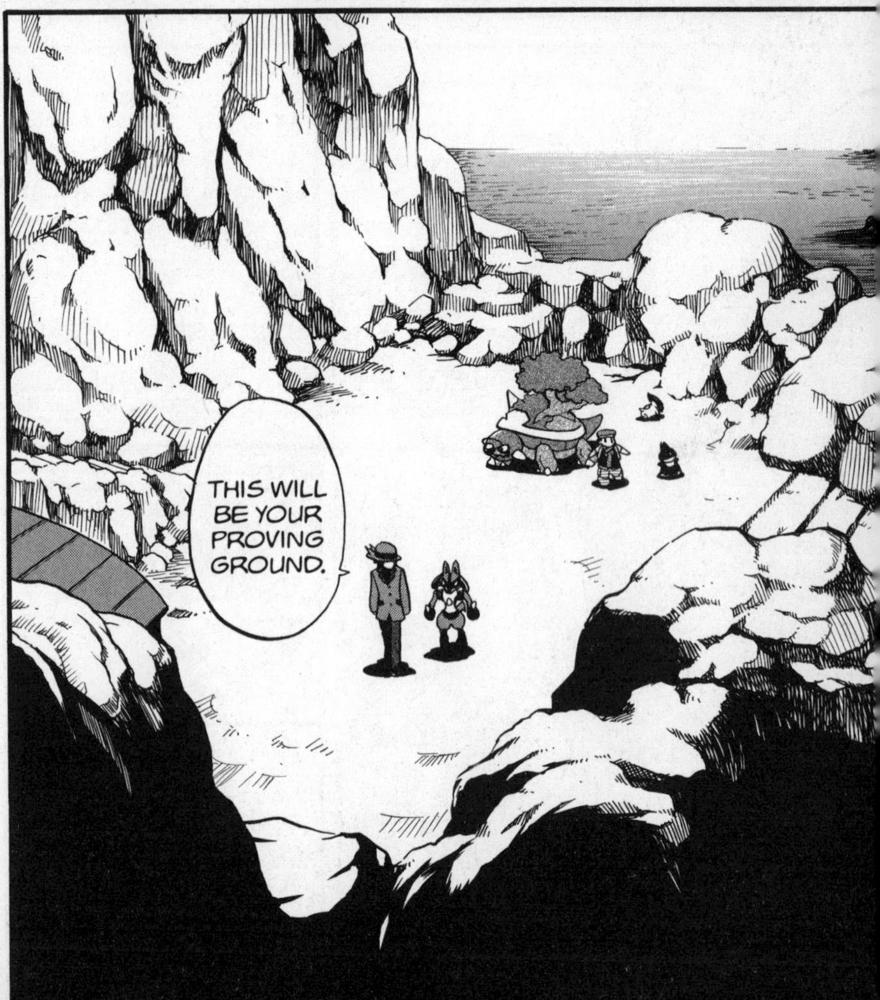
THIS WILL BE YOUR PROVING GROUND.

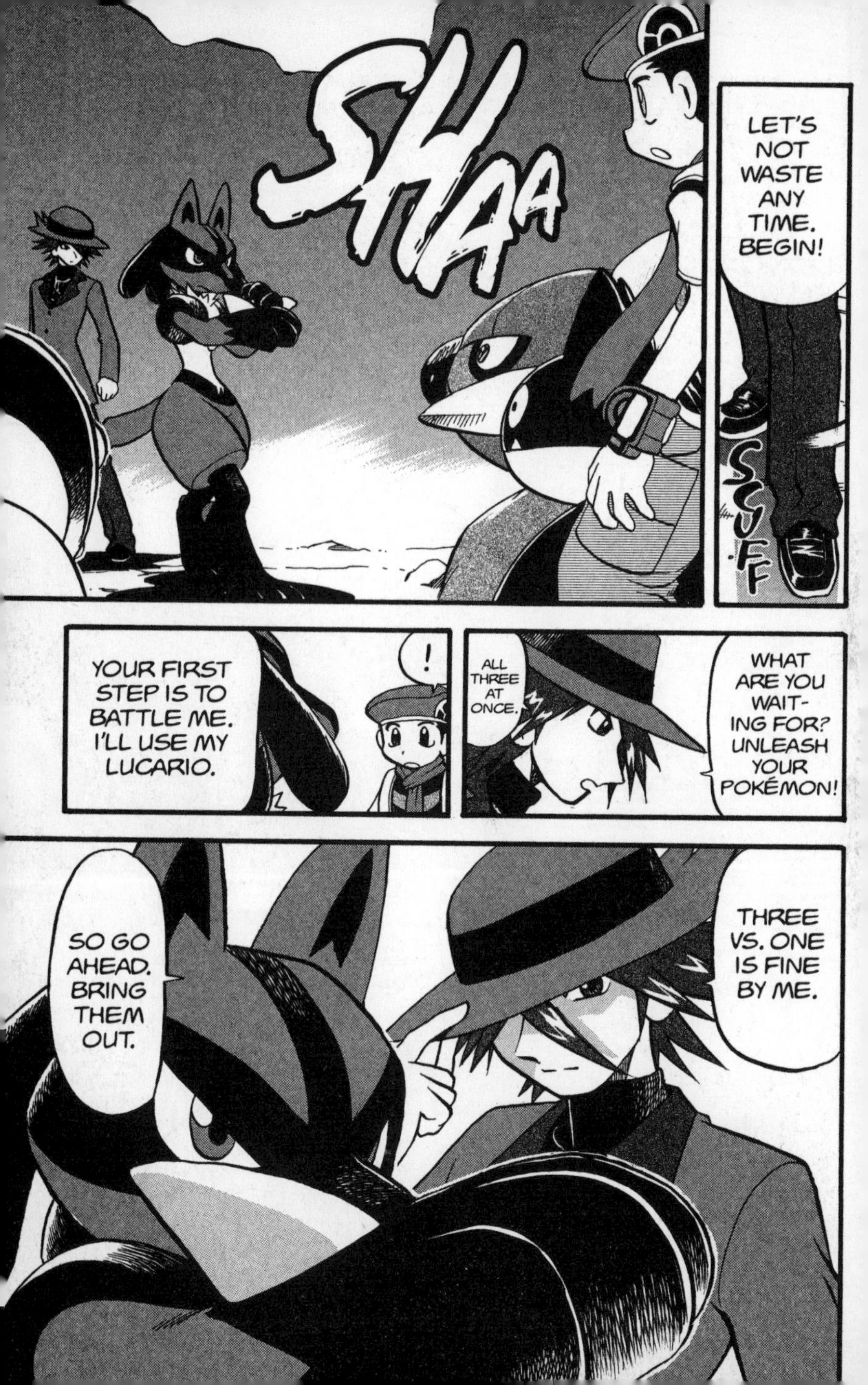
LET'S NOT WASTE ANY TIME. BEGIN!
SCUFF
SHAA
WHAT ARE YOU WAITING FOR? UNLEASH YOUR POKÉMON!
ALL THREE AT ONCE.
!
YOUR FIRST STEP IS TO BATTLE ME. I'LL USE MY LUCARIO.
THREE VS. ONE IS FINE BY ME.
SO GO AHEAD. BRING THEM OUT.

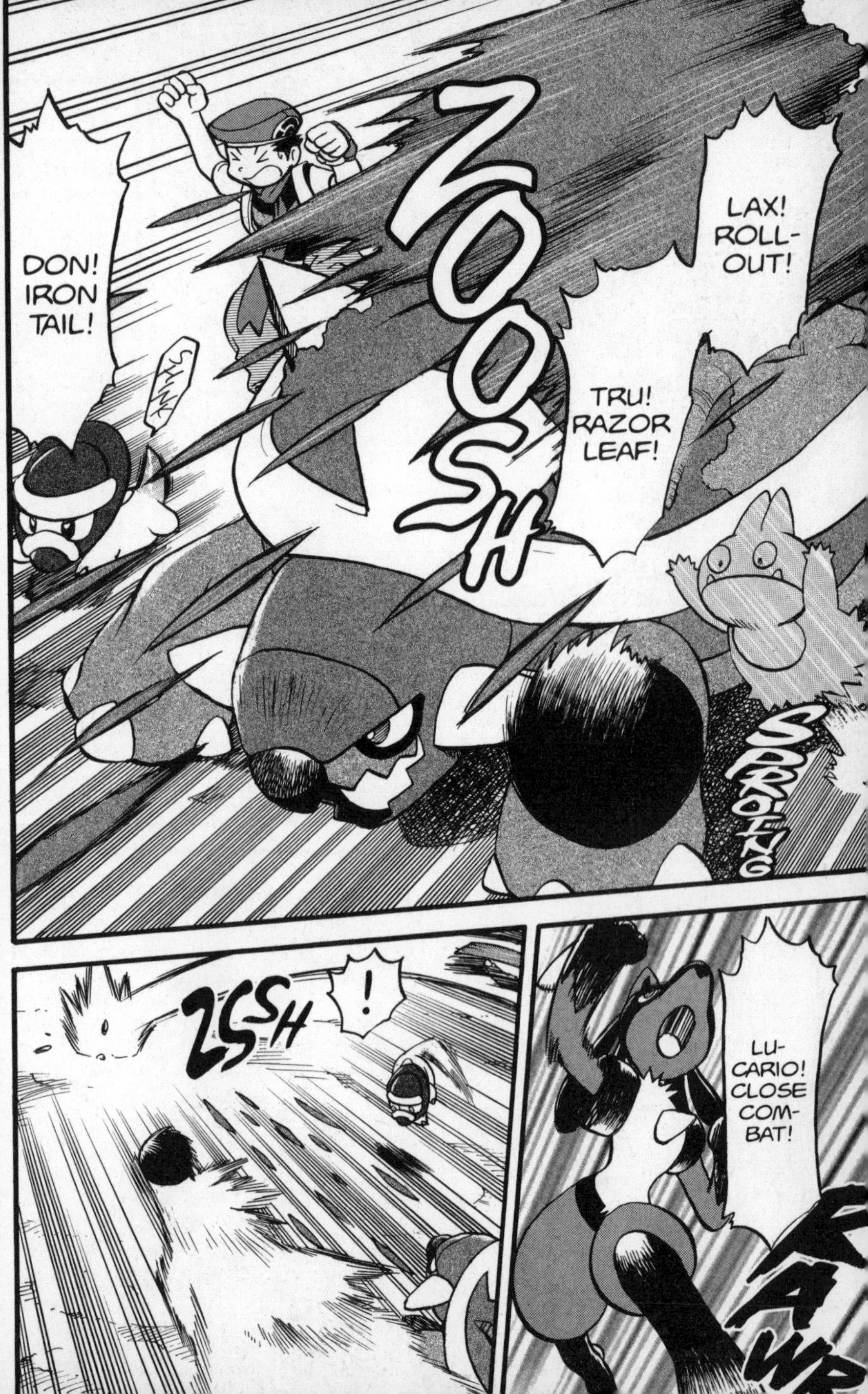
LAX! ROLL-OUT!
TRU! RAZOR LEAF!
WOOOSH
DON! IRON TAIL!
SHINK
SPROING
LU-CARIO! CLOSE COM-BAT!
KAWR
!
ZSSH

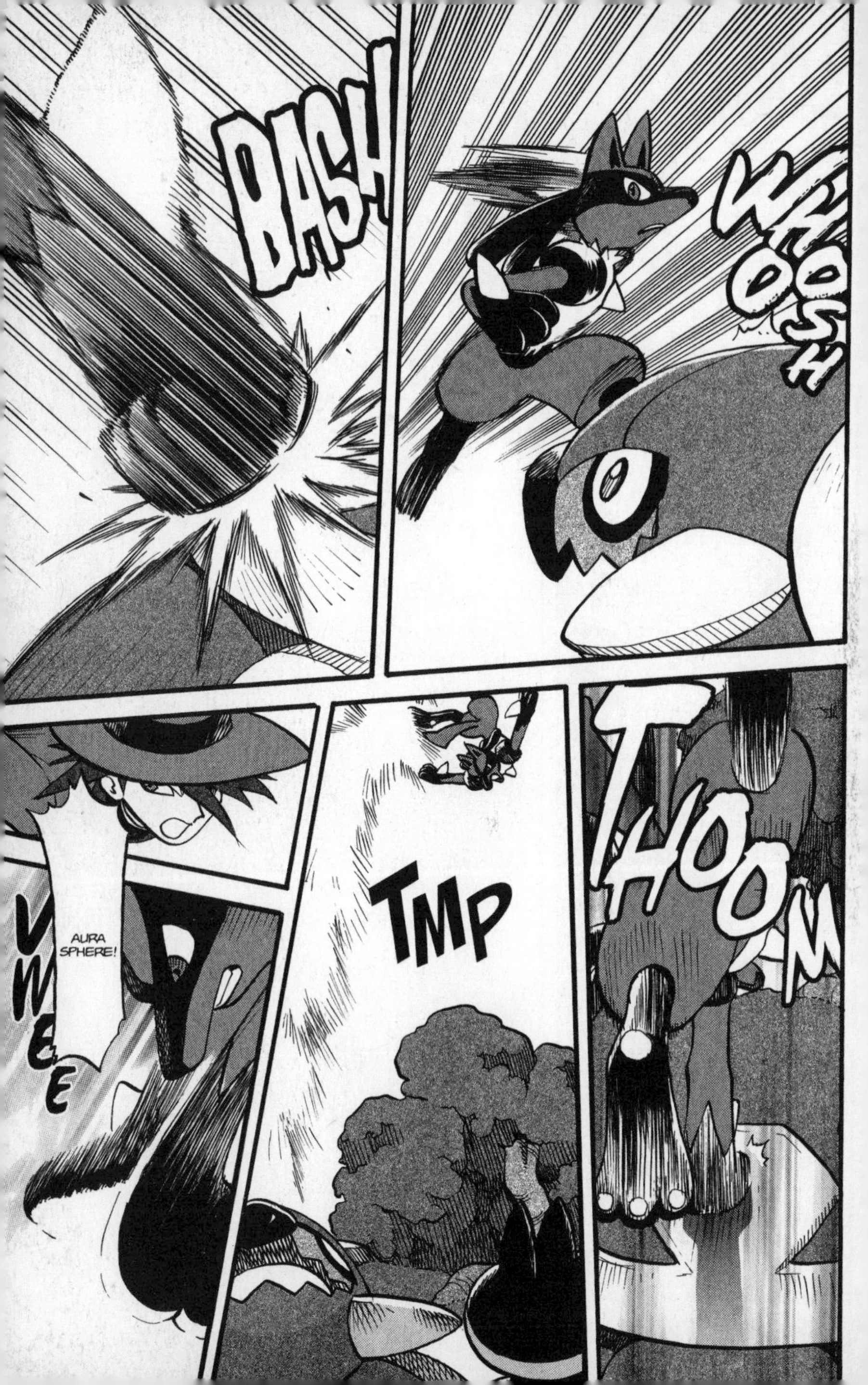
WHOOSH
BASH!
THOOM
TMP
AURA SPHERE!
VWEEE

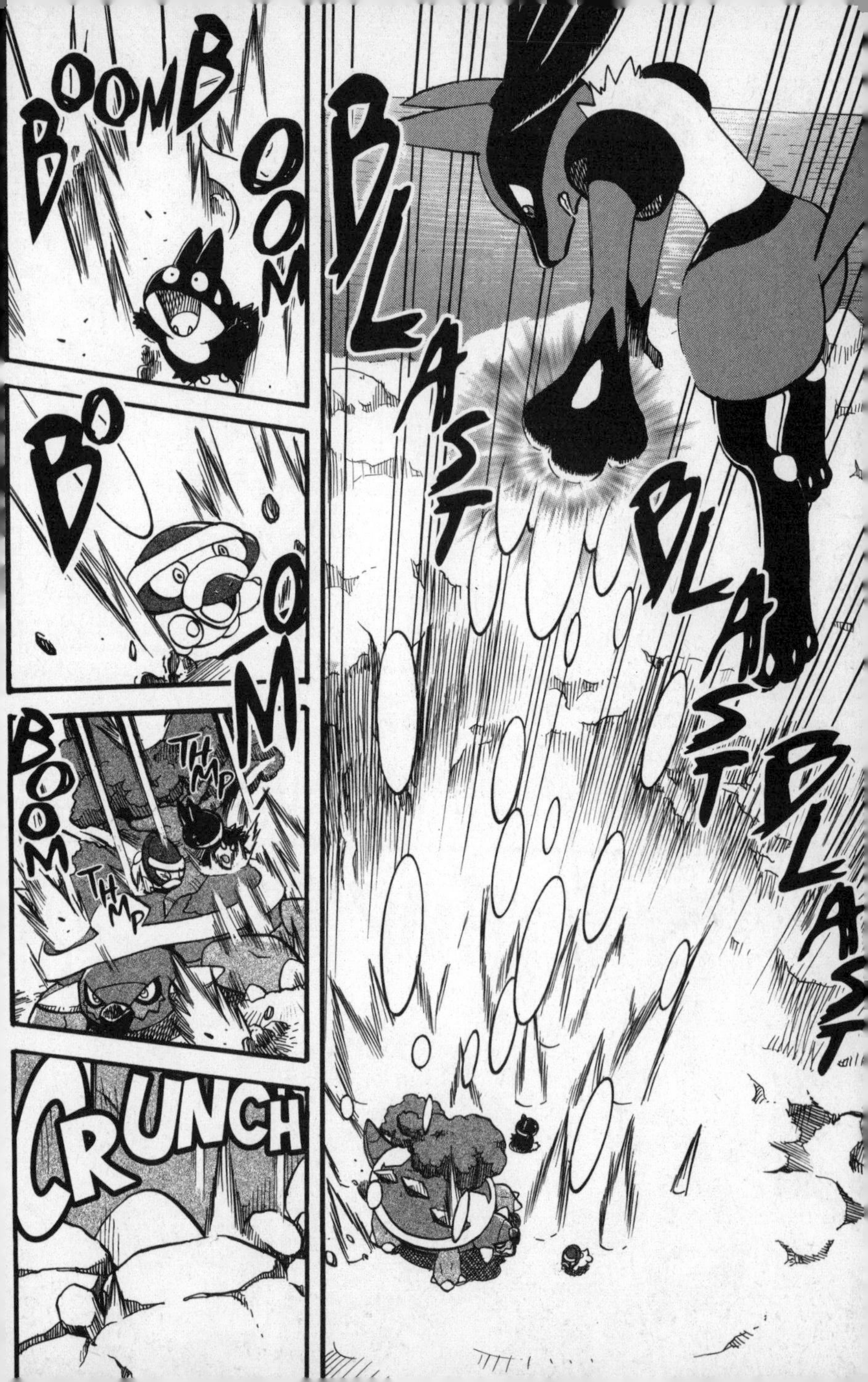
BLAST
BLAST
BLAST
BOOM
BOOM
BOOM
BOOM
THMP
THMP
CRUNCH

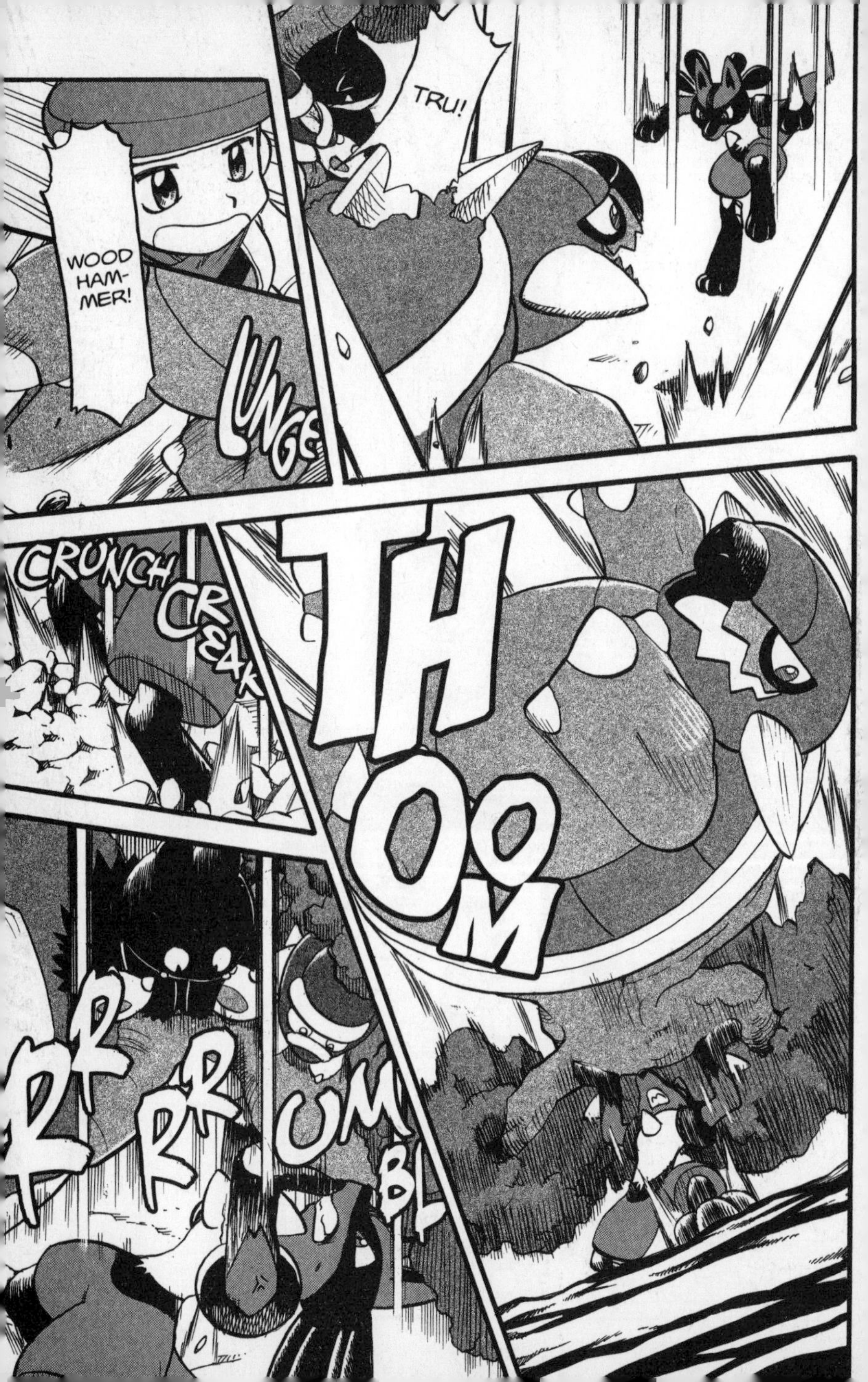
TRU!
WOOD HAMMER!
LUNGE
THOOOM
CRUNCH
CREAK
RR RR RUMBL

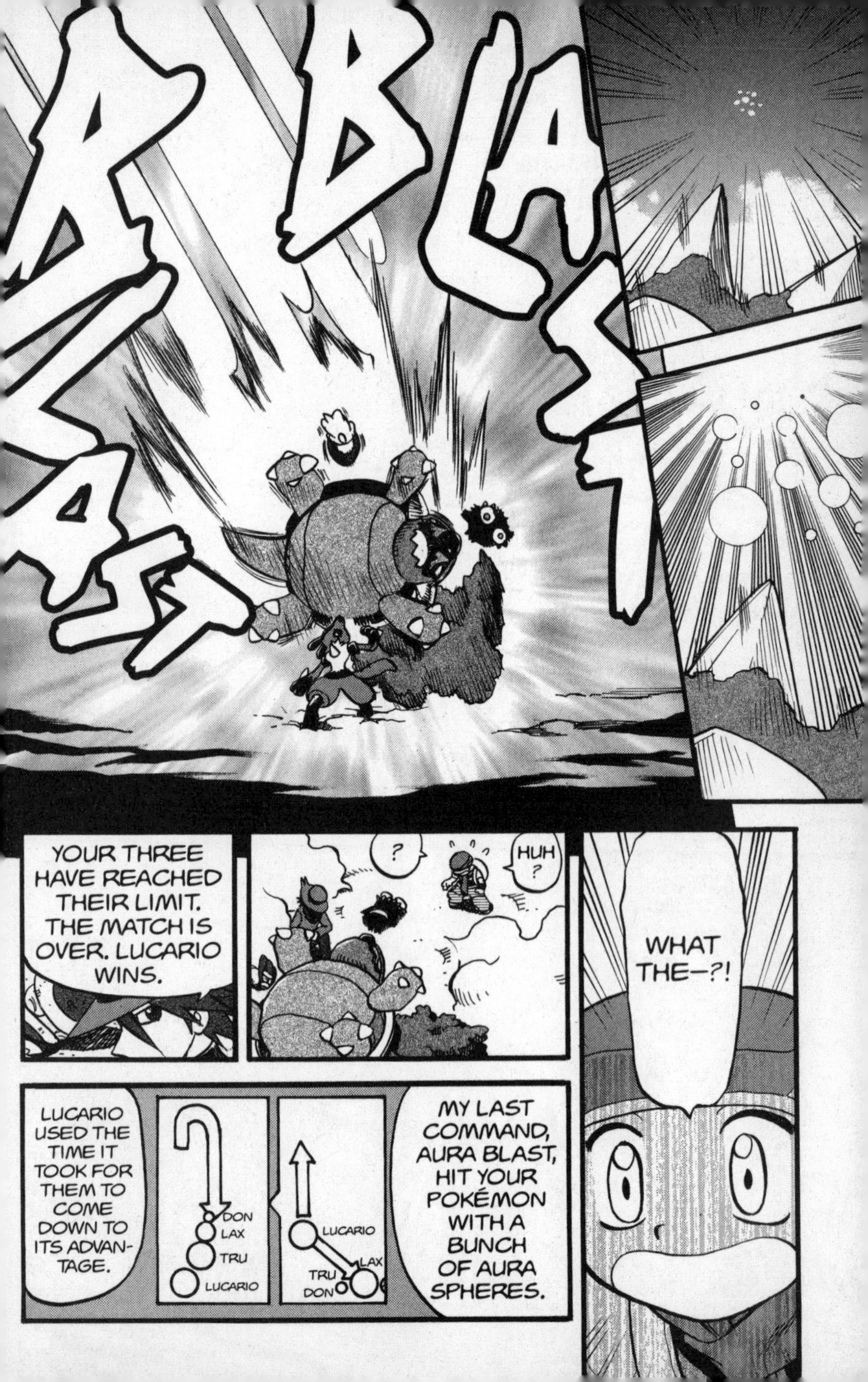
BLAST
WHAT THE–?!
HUH ?
?
YOUR THREE HAVE REACHED THEIR LIMIT. THE MATCH IS OVER. LUCARIO WINS.
MY LAST COMMAND, AURA BLAST, HIT YOUR POKÉMON WITH A BUNCH OF AURA SPHERES.
LUCARIO
LAX
TRU
DON
DON
LAX
TRU
LUCARIO
LUCARIO USED THE TIME IT TOOK FOR THEM TO COME DOWN TO ITS ADVANTAGE.

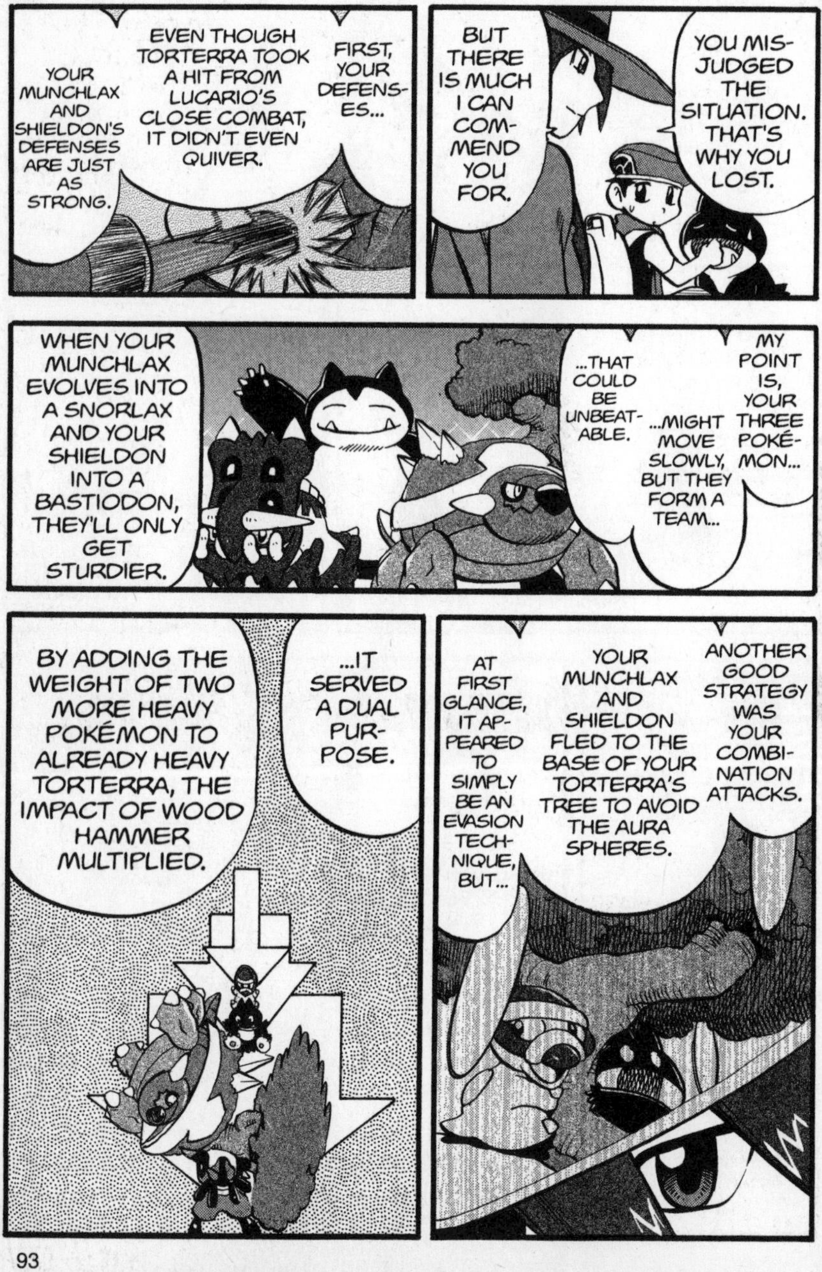
YOU MISJUDGED THE SITUATION. THAT'S WHY YOU LOST.
BUT THERE IS MUCH I CAN COMMEND YOU FOR.
FIRST, YOUR DEFENSES...
EVEN THOUGH TORTERRA TOOK A HIT FROM LUCARIO'S CLOSE COMBAT, IT DIDN'T EVEN QUIVER.
YOUR MUNCHLAX AND SHIELDON'S DEFENSES ARE JUST AS STRONG.
MY POINT IS, YOUR THREE POKÉMON...
...MIGHT MOVE SLOWLY, BUT THEY FORM A TEAM...
...THAT COULD BE UNBEATABLE.
WHEN YOUR MUNCHLAX EVOLVES INTO A SNORLAX AND YOUR SHIELDON INTO A BASTIODON, THEY'LL ONLY GET STURDIER.
ANOTHER GOOD STRATEGY WAS YOUR COMBINATION ATTACKS.
YOUR MUNCHLAX AND SHIELDON FLED TO THE BASE OF YOUR TORTERRA'S TREE TO AVOID THE AURA SPHERES.
AT FIRST GLANCE, IT APPEARED TO SIMPLY BE AN EVASION TECHNIQUE, BUT...
...IT SERVED A DUAL PURPOSE.
BY ADDING THE WEIGHT OF TWO MORE HEAVY POKÉMON TO ALREADY HEAVY TORTERRA, THE IMPACT OF WOOD HAMMER MULTIPLIED.

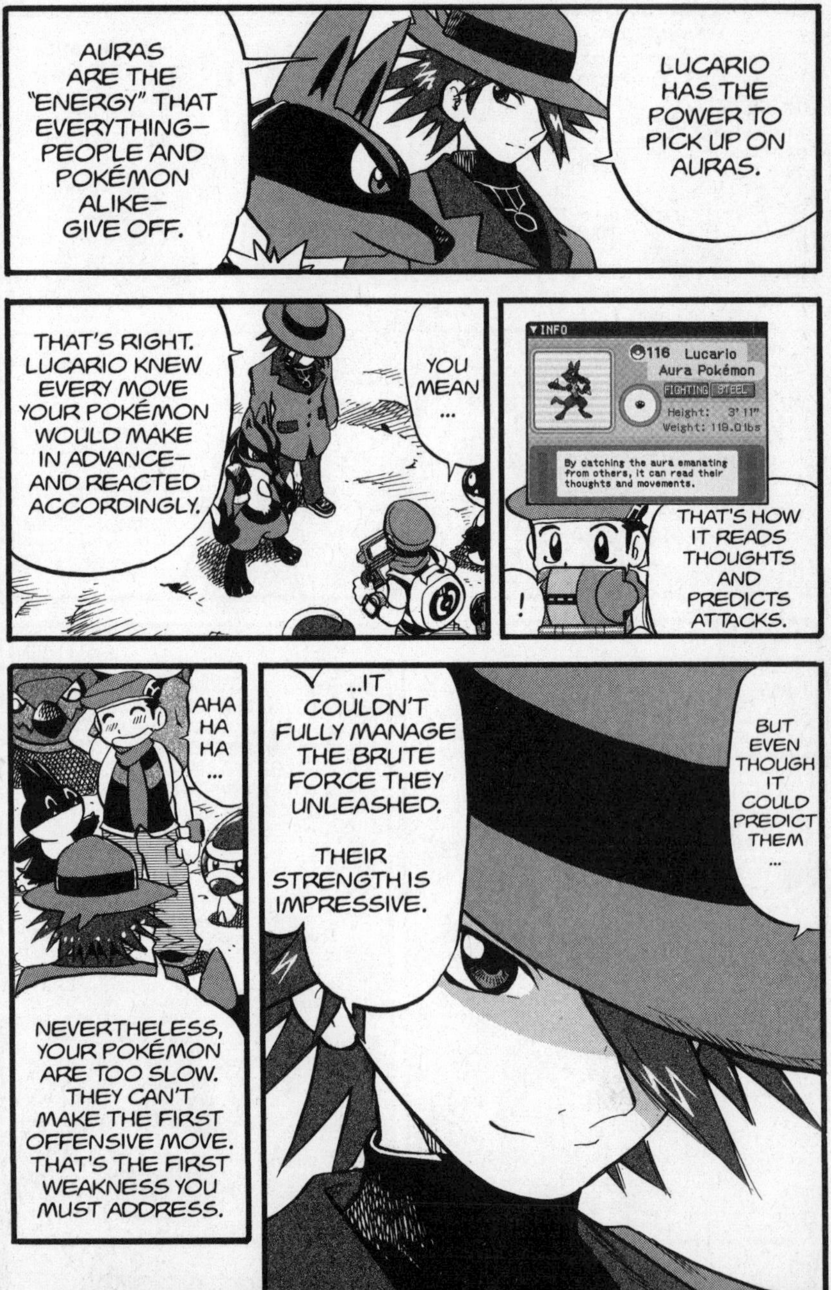
LUCARIO HAS THE POWER TO PICK UP ON AURAS.
AURAS ARE THE "ENERGY" THAT EVERYTHING—PEOPLE AND POKÉMON ALIKE—GIVE OFF.
INFO
116 Lucario
Aura Pokémon
FIGHTING STEEL
Height: 3' 11"
Weight: 119.0 lbs
By catching the aura emanating from others, it can read their thoughts and movements.
!
THAT'S HOW IT READS THOUGHTS AND PREDICTS ATTACKS.
YOU MEAN ...
THAT'S RIGHT. LUCARIO KNEW EVERY MOVE YOUR POKÉMON WOULD MAKE IN ADVANCE—AND REACTED ACCORDINGLY.
BUT EVEN THOUGH IT COULD PREDICT THEM ...
...IT COULDN'T FULLY MANAGE THE BRUTE FORCE THEY UNLEASHED.
THEIR STRENGTH IS IMPRESSIVE.
AHA HA HA ...
NEVERTHELESS, YOUR POKÉMON ARE TOO SLOW. THEY CAN'T MAKE THE FIRST OFFENSIVE MOVE. THAT'S THE FIRST WEAKNESS YOU MUST ADDRESS.

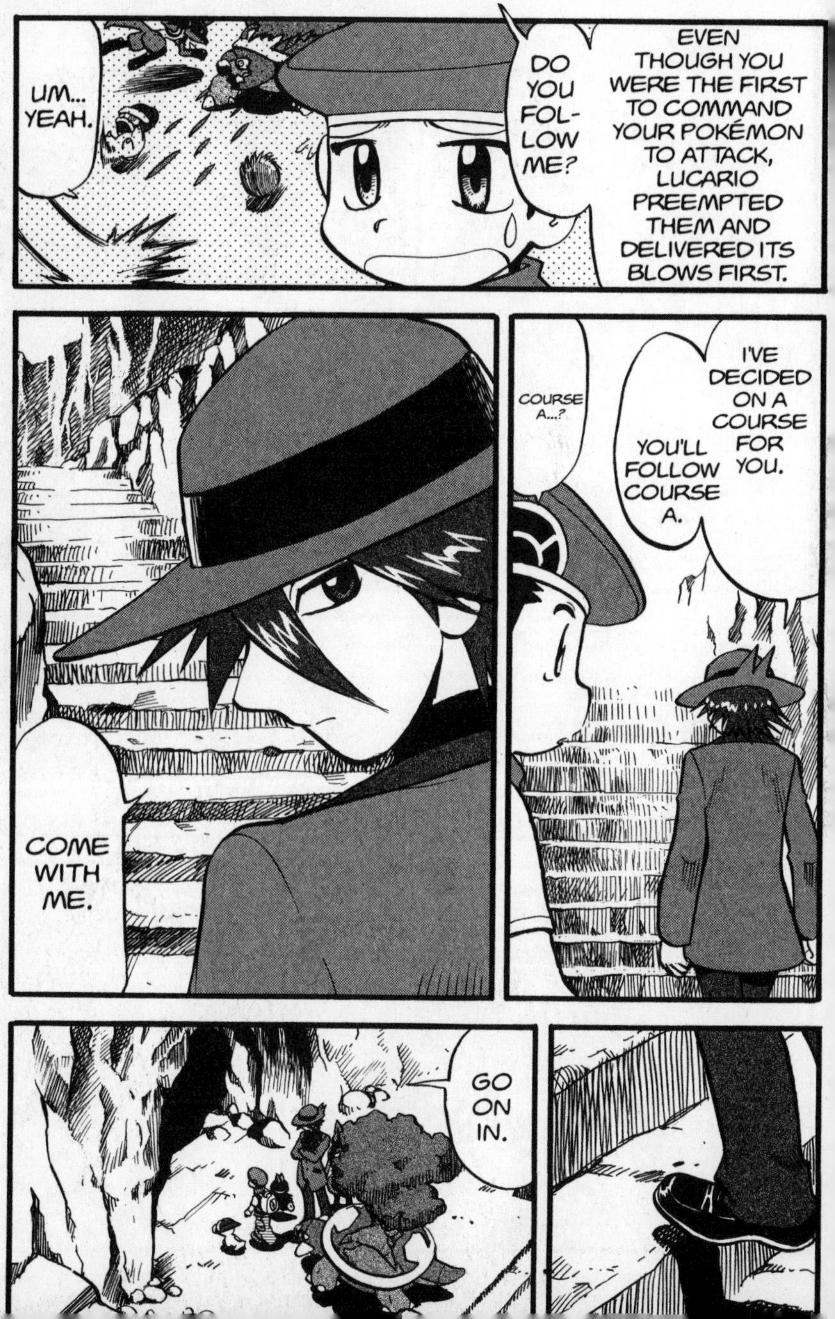
EVEN THOUGH YOU WERE THE FIRST TO COMMAND YOUR POKÉMON TO ATTACK, LUCARIO PREEMPTED THEM AND DELIVERED ITS BLOWS FIRST.
DO YOU FOL-LOW ME?
UM... YEAH.
I'VE DECIDED ON A COURSE FOR YOU.
YOU'LL FOLLOW COURSE A.
COURSE A...?
COME WITH ME.
GO ON IN.

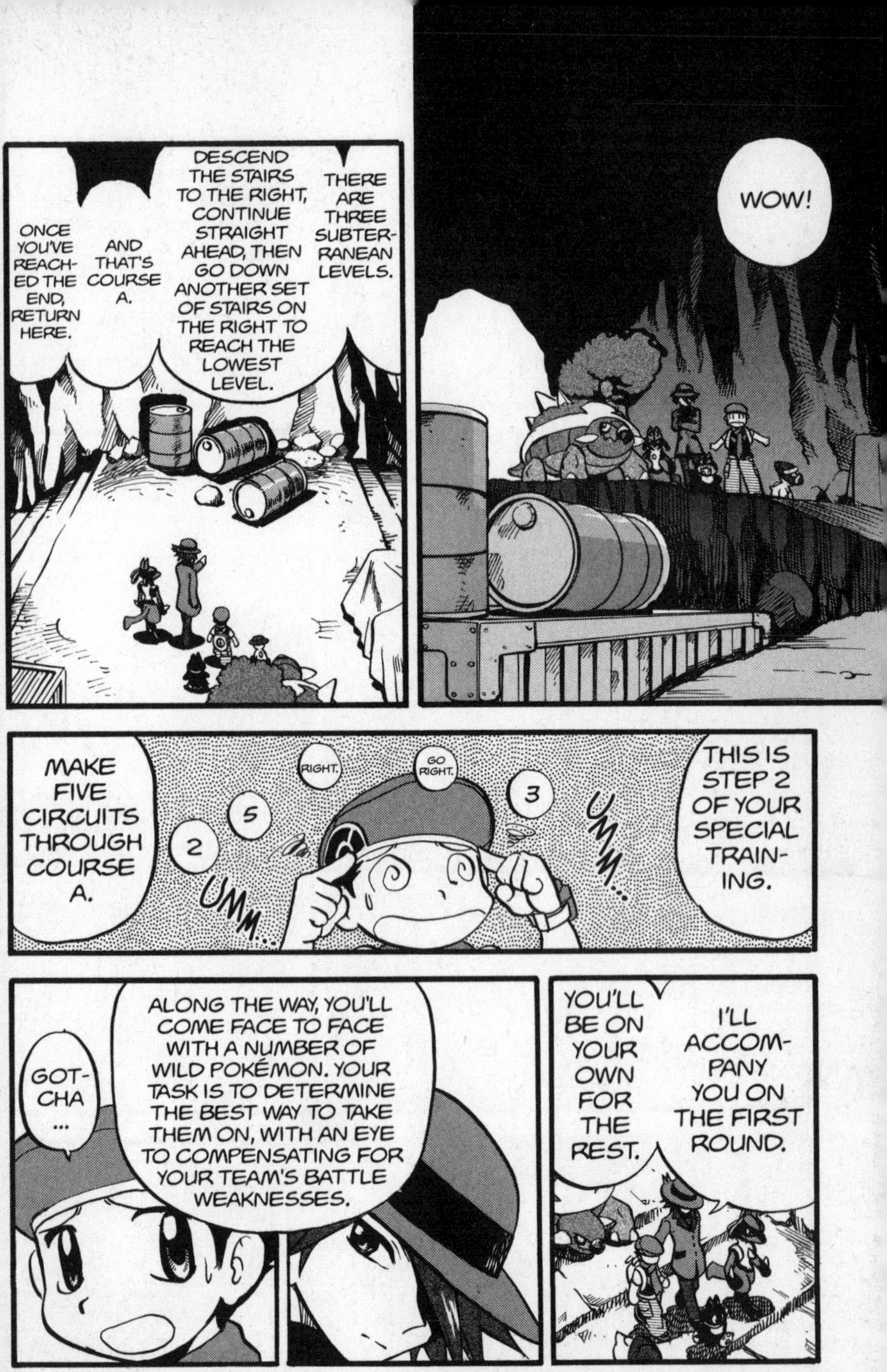
WOW!
THERE ARE THREE SUBTERRANEAN LEVELS.
DESCEND THE STAIRS TO THE RIGHT, CONTINUE STRAIGHT AHEAD, THEN GO DOWN ANOTHER SET OF STAIRS ON THE RIGHT TO REACH THE LOWEST LEVEL.
AND THAT'S COURSE A.
ONCE YOU'VE REACHED THE END, RETURN HERE.
THIS IS STEP 2 OF YOUR SPECIAL TRAINING.
UMM...
GO RIGHT.
3
RIGHT.
5
2
UMM...
MAKE FIVE CIRCUITS THROUGH COURSE A.
I'LL ACCOMPANY YOU ON THE FIRST ROUND.
YOU'LL BE ON YOUR OWN FOR THE REST.
ALONG THE WAY, YOU'LL COME FACE TO FACE WITH A NUMBER OF WILD POKÉMON. YOUR TASK IS TO DETERMINE THE BEST WAY TO TAKE THEM ON, WITH AN EYE TO COMPENSATING FOR YOUR TEAM'S BATTLE WEAKNESSES.
GOTCHA...

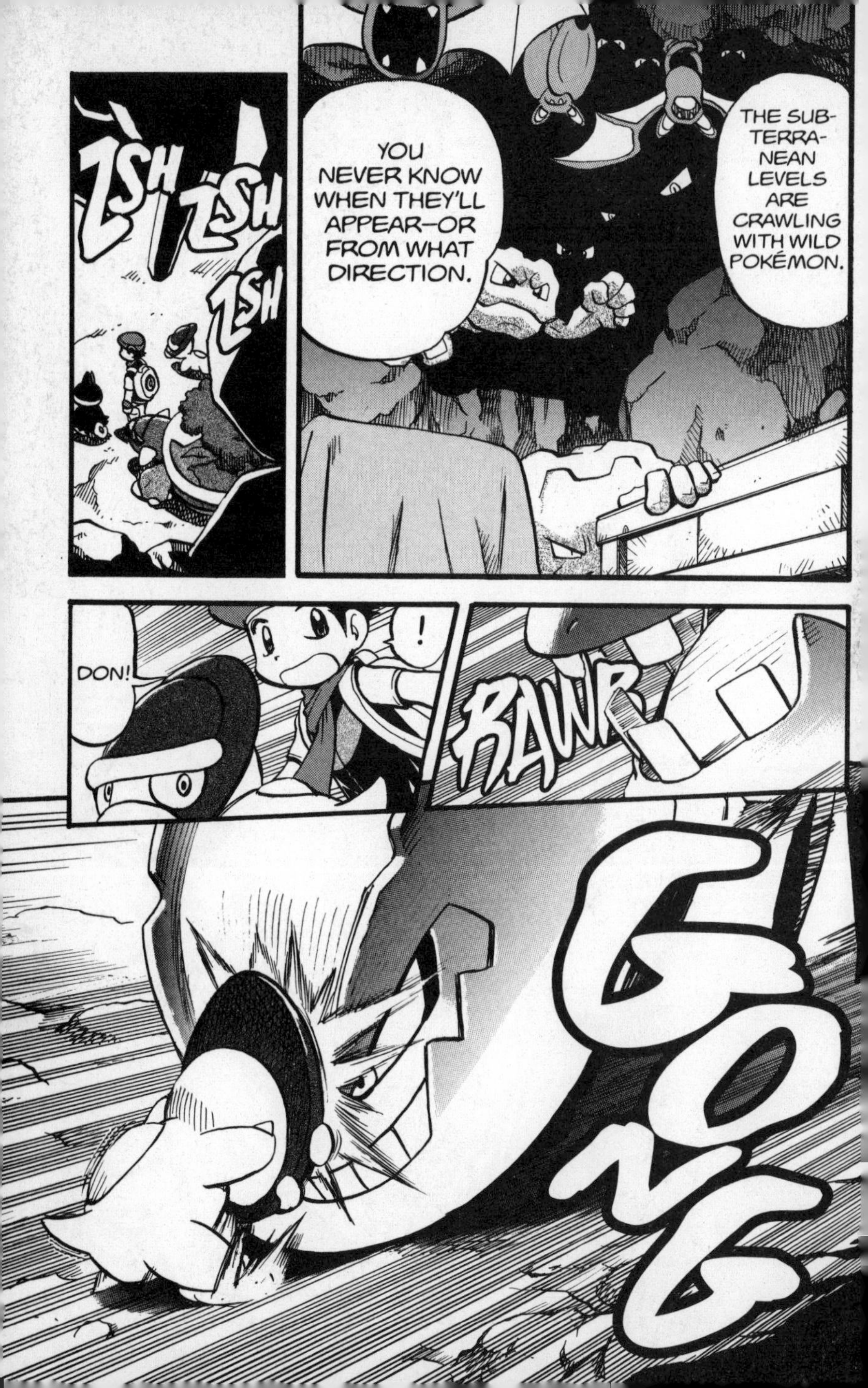
THE SUB-TERRA-NEAN LEVELS ARE CRAWLING WITH WILD POKÉMON.
YOU NEVER KNOW WHEN THEY'LL APPEAR—OR FROM WHAT DIRECTION.
ZSH
ZSH
ZSH
RAWR
!
DON!
GONG

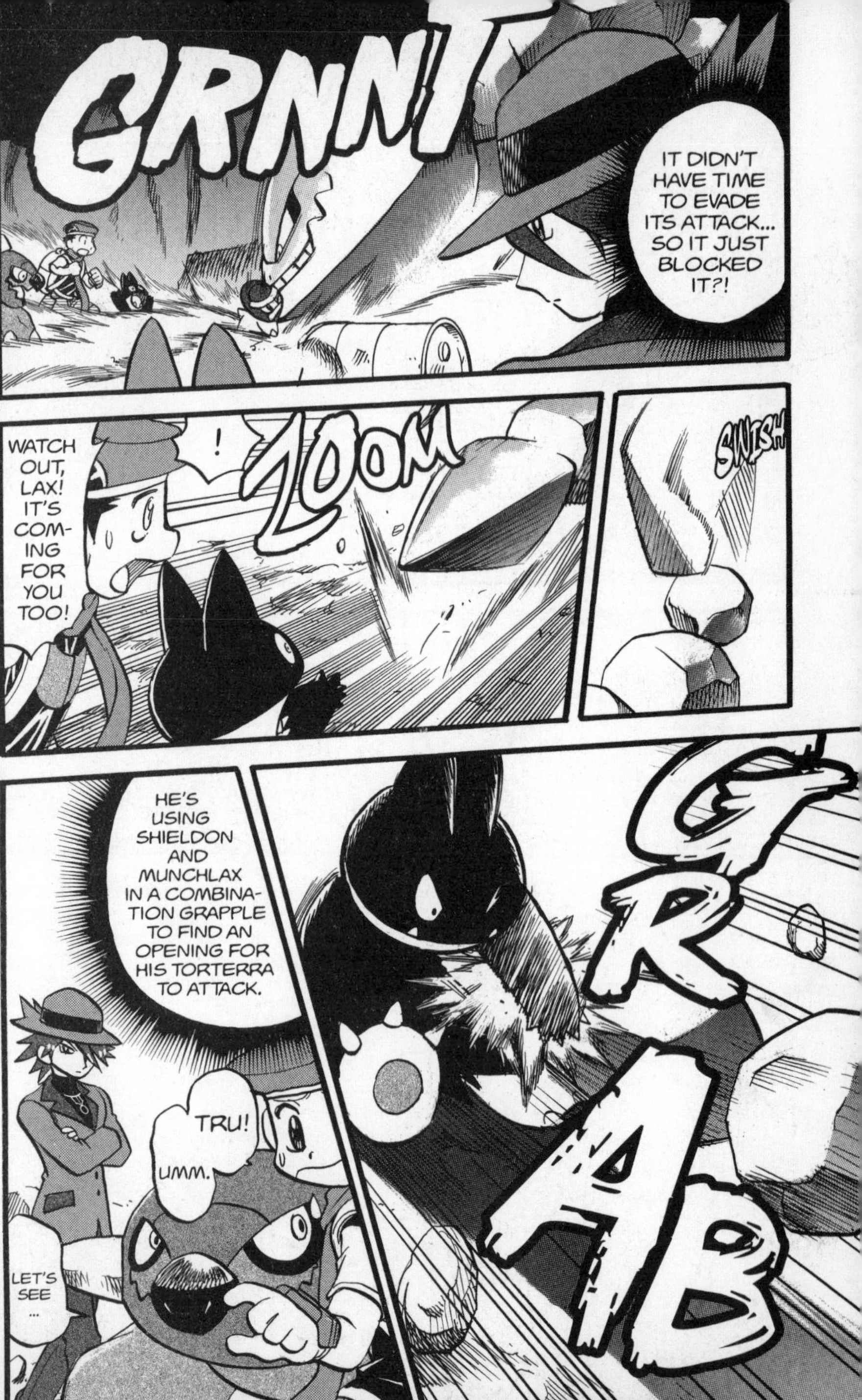
GRNNT
IT DIDN'T HAVE TIME TO EVADE ITS ATTACK... SO IT JUST BLOCKED IT?!
SWISH
ZOOM
!
WATCH OUT, LAX! IT'S COM-ING FOR YOU TOO!
GRAB
HE'S USING SHIELDON AND MUNCHLAX IN A COMBINA-TION GRAPPLE TO FIND AN OPENING FOR HIS TORTERRA TO ATTACK.
TRU!
UMM.
LET'S SEE ...

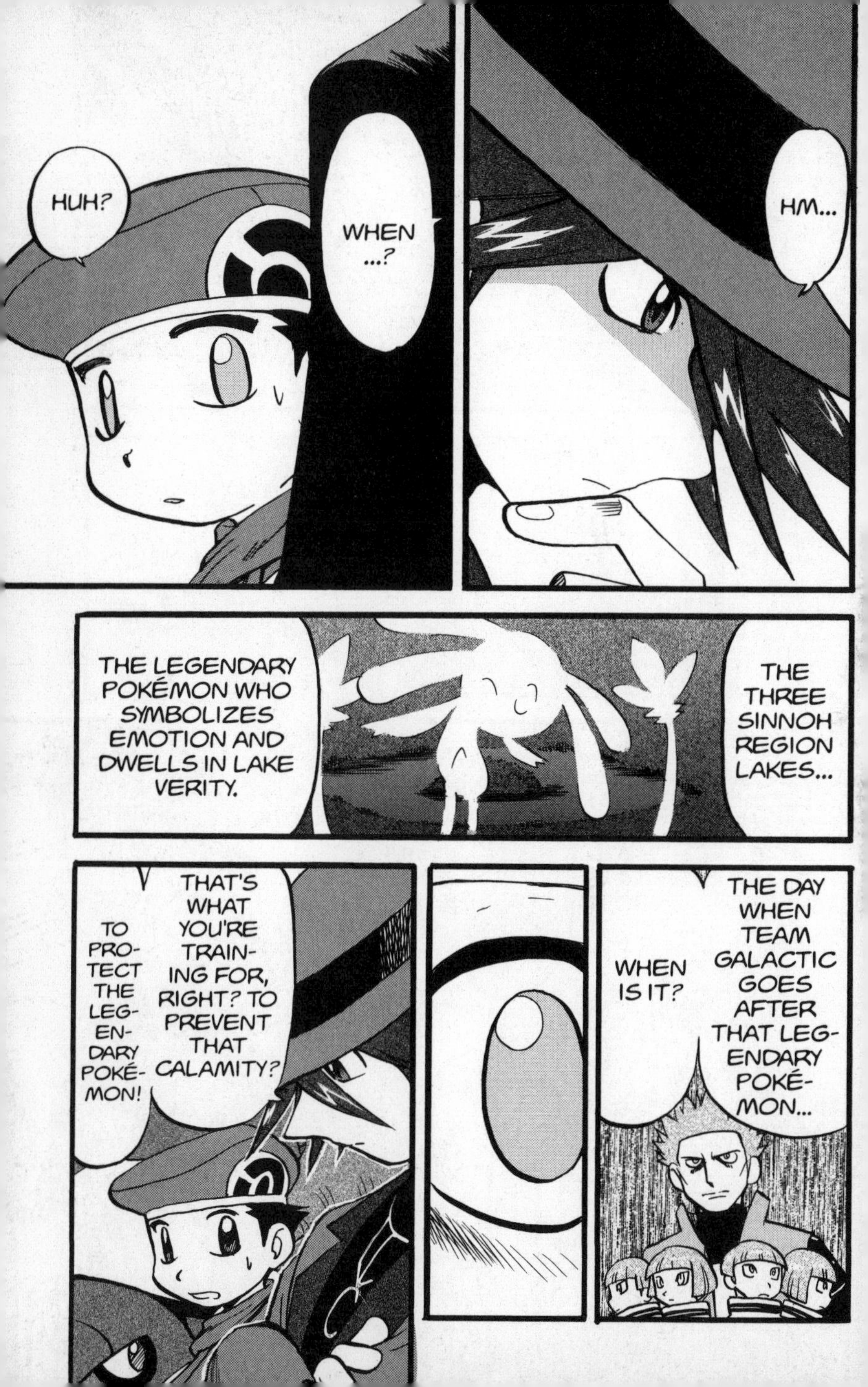

HM...
WHEN ...?
HUH?
THE THREE SINNOH REGION LAKES...
THE LEGENDARY POKÉMON WHO SYMBOLIZES EMOTION AND DWELLS IN LAKE VERITY.
THE DAY WHEN TEAM GALACTIC GOES AFTER THAT LEGENDARY POKÉMON...
WHEN IS IT?
THAT'S WHAT YOU'RE TRAINING FOR, RIGHT? TO PREVENT THAT CALAMITY?
TO PROTECT THE LEGENDARY POKÉMON!

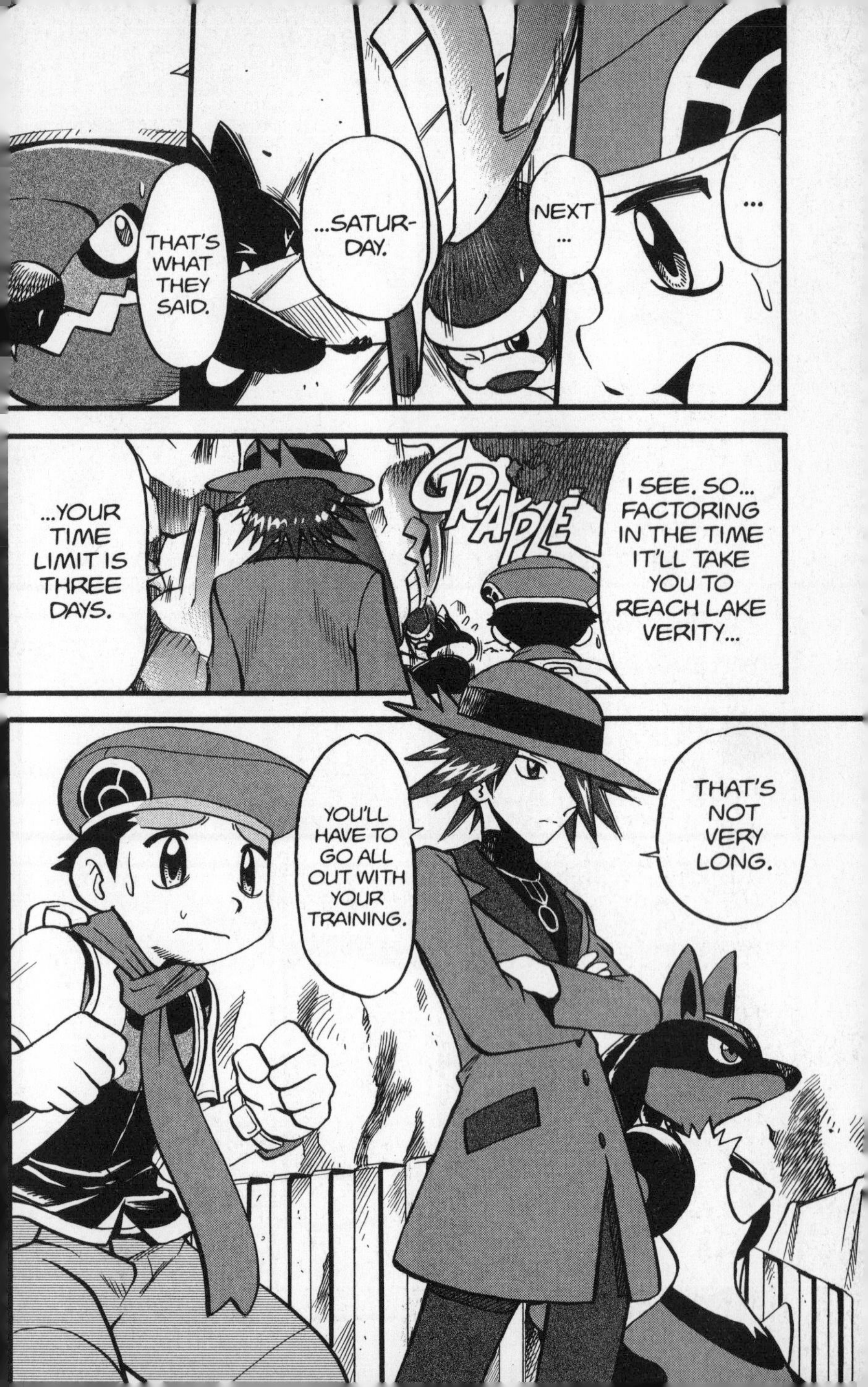
...
NEXT ...
...SATUR-DAY.
THAT'S WHAT THEY SAID.
I SEE. SO... FACTORING IN THE TIME IT'LL TAKE YOU TO REACH LAKE VERITY...
GRAPLE
...YOUR TIME LIMIT IS THREE DAYS.
THAT'S NOT VERY LONG.
YOU'LL HAVE TO GO ALL OUT WITH YOUR TRAINING.

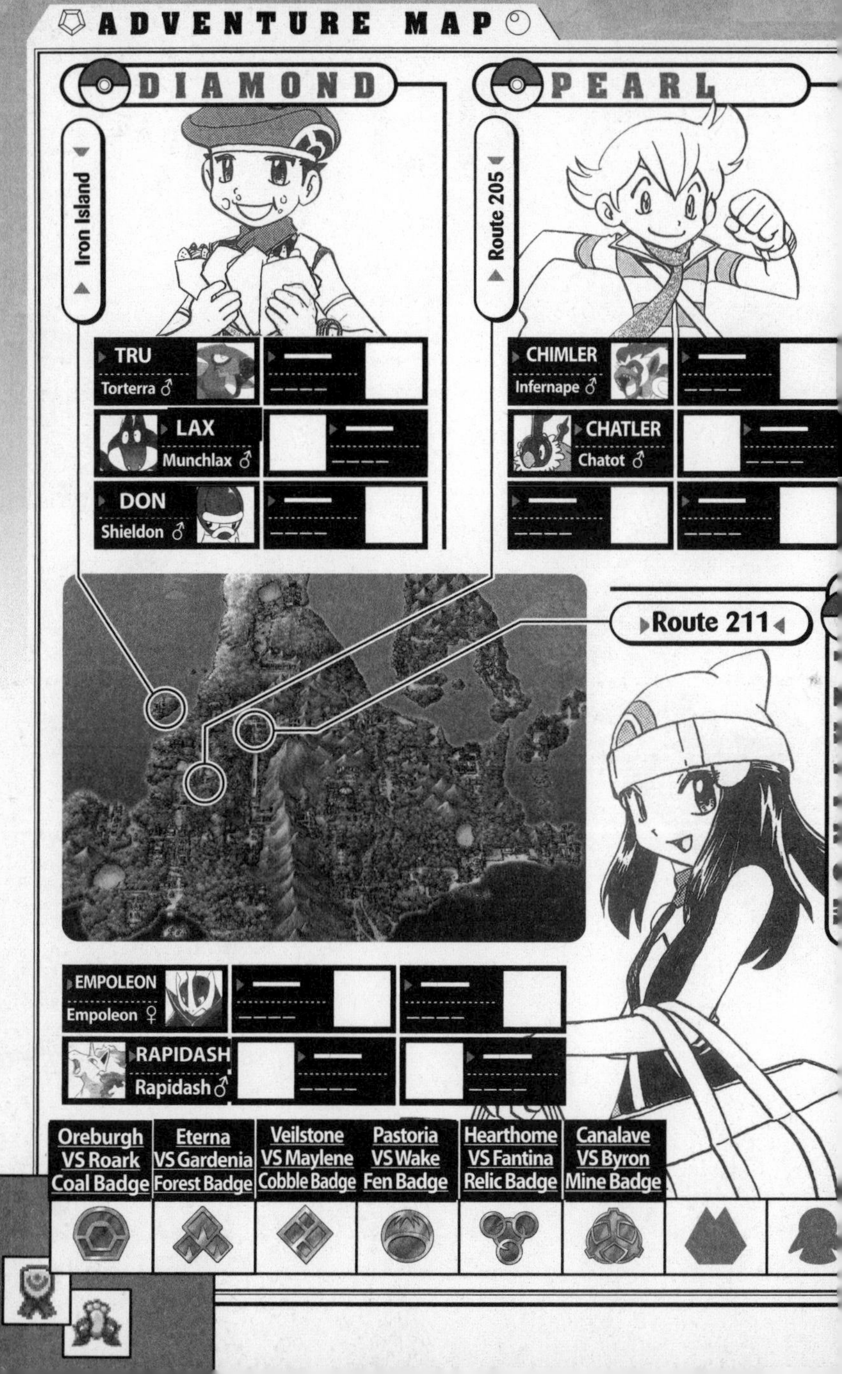
ADVENTURE MAP
DIAMOND
Iron Island
TRU
Torterra ♂
LAX
Munchlax ♂
DON
Shieldon ♂
PEARL
Route 205
CHIMLER
Infernape ♂
CHATLER
Chatot ♂
Route 211
EMPOLEON
Empoleon ♀
RAPIDASH
Rapidash ♂
Oreburgh
VS Roark
Coal Badge
Eterna
VS Gardenia
Forest Badge
Veilstone
VS Maylene
Cobble Badge
Pastoria
VS Wake
Fen Badge
Hearthome
VS Fantina
Relic Badge
Canalave
VS Byron
Mine Badge

43

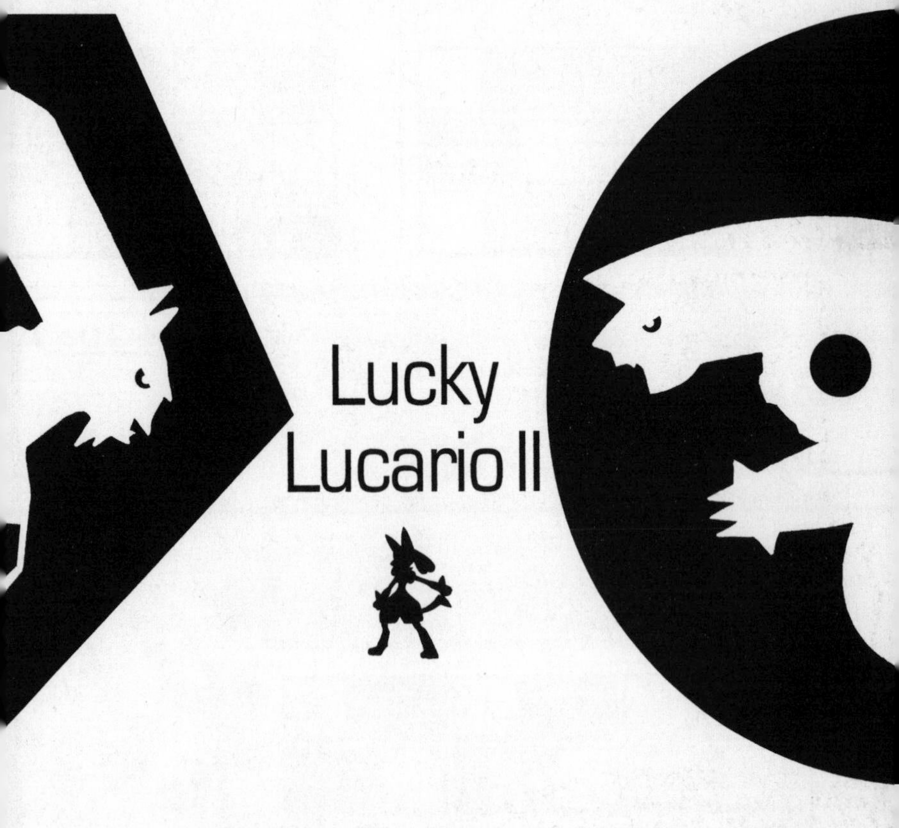

Lucky Lucario II

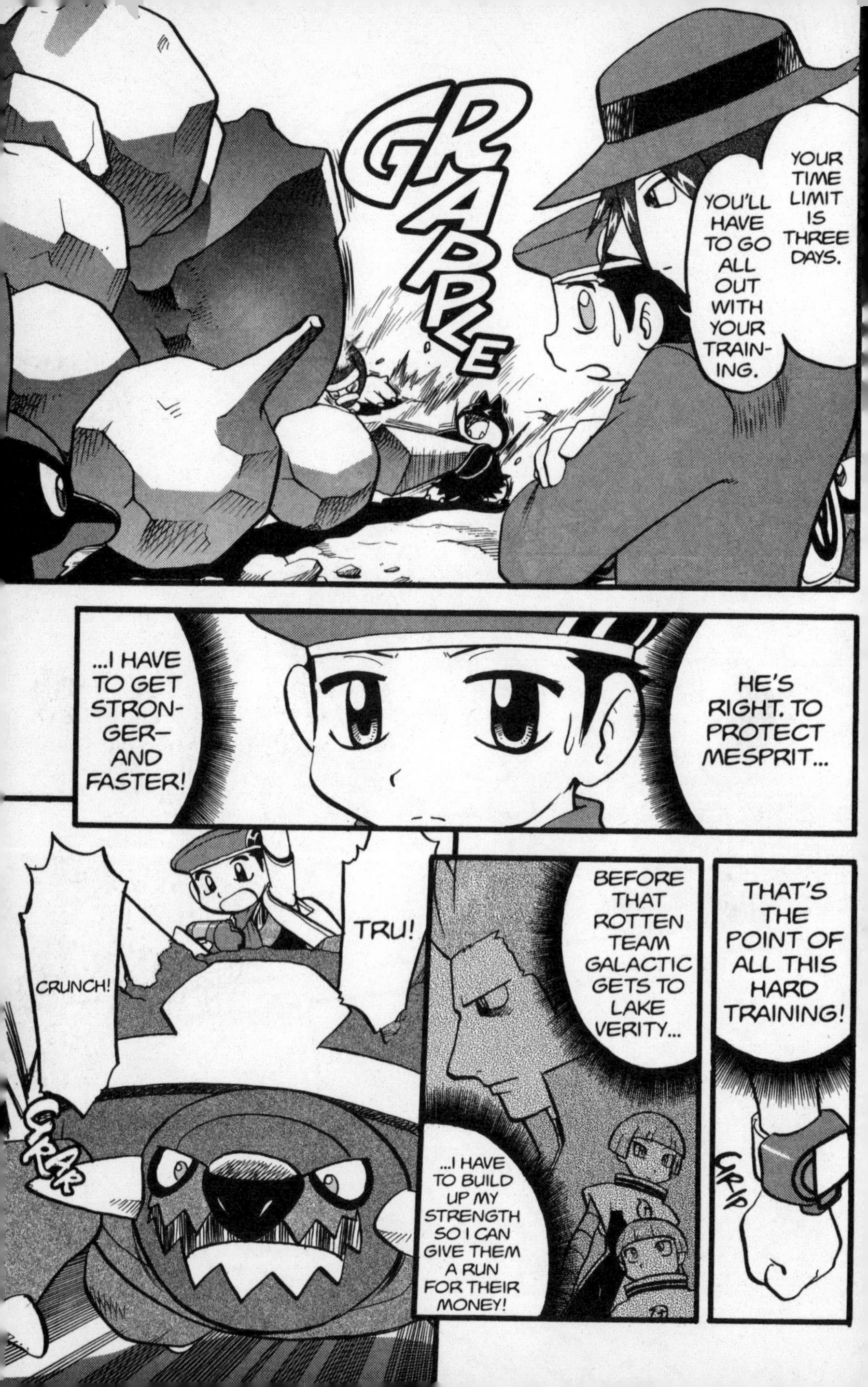
YOUR TIME LIMIT IS THREE DAYS.
YOU'LL HAVE TO GO ALL OUT WITH YOUR TRAIN-ING.
GRAPPLE
HE'S RIGHT. TO PROTECT MESPRIT...
...I HAVE TO GET STRON-GER—AND FASTER!
THAT'S THE POINT OF ALL THIS HARD TRAINING!
GRIP
BEFORE THAT ROTTEN TEAM GALACTIC GETS TO LAKE VERITY...
...I HAVE TO BUILD UP MY STRENGTH SO I CAN GIVE THEM A RUN FOR THEIR MONEY!
TRU!
CRUNCH!
GRAR

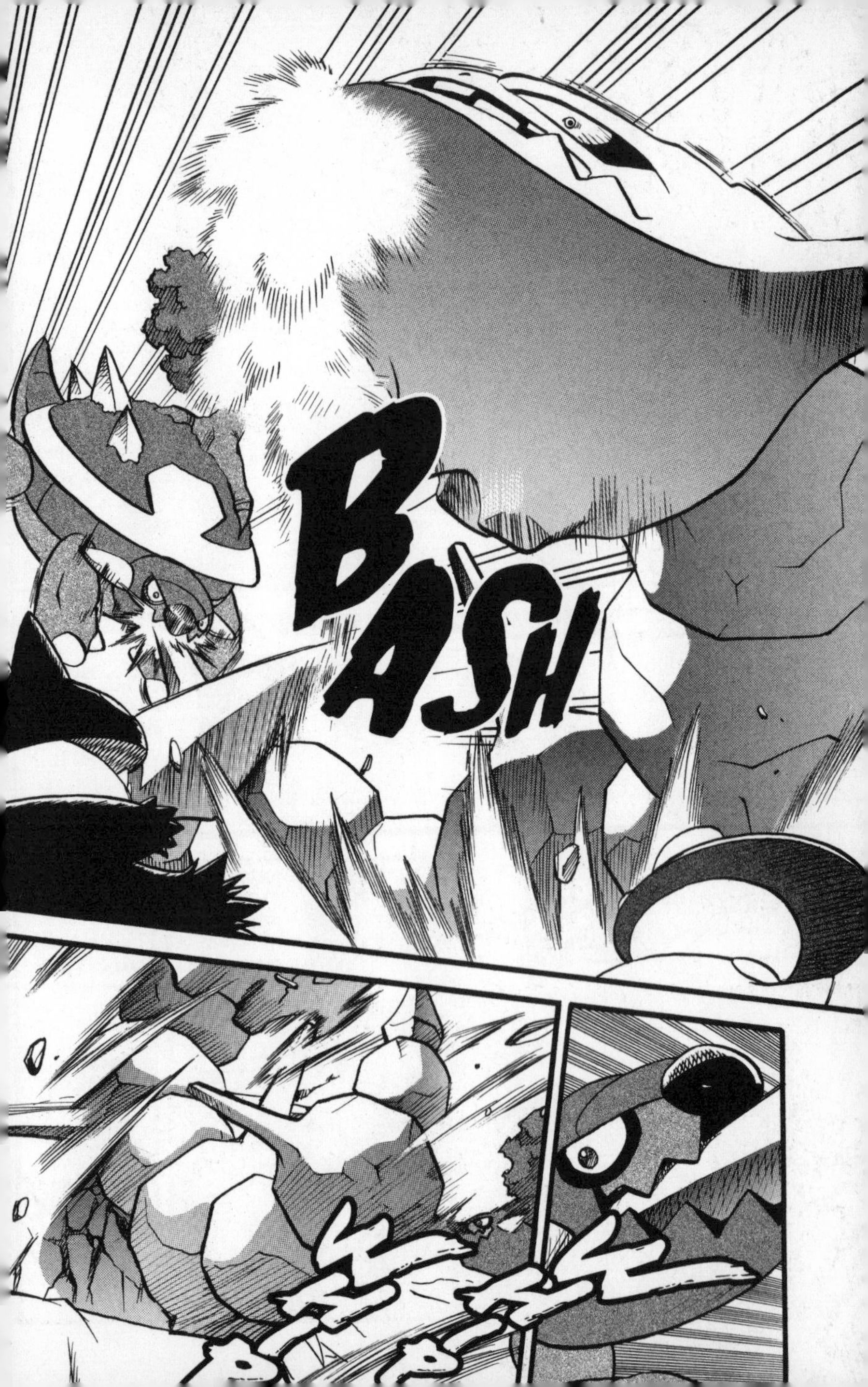
BASH

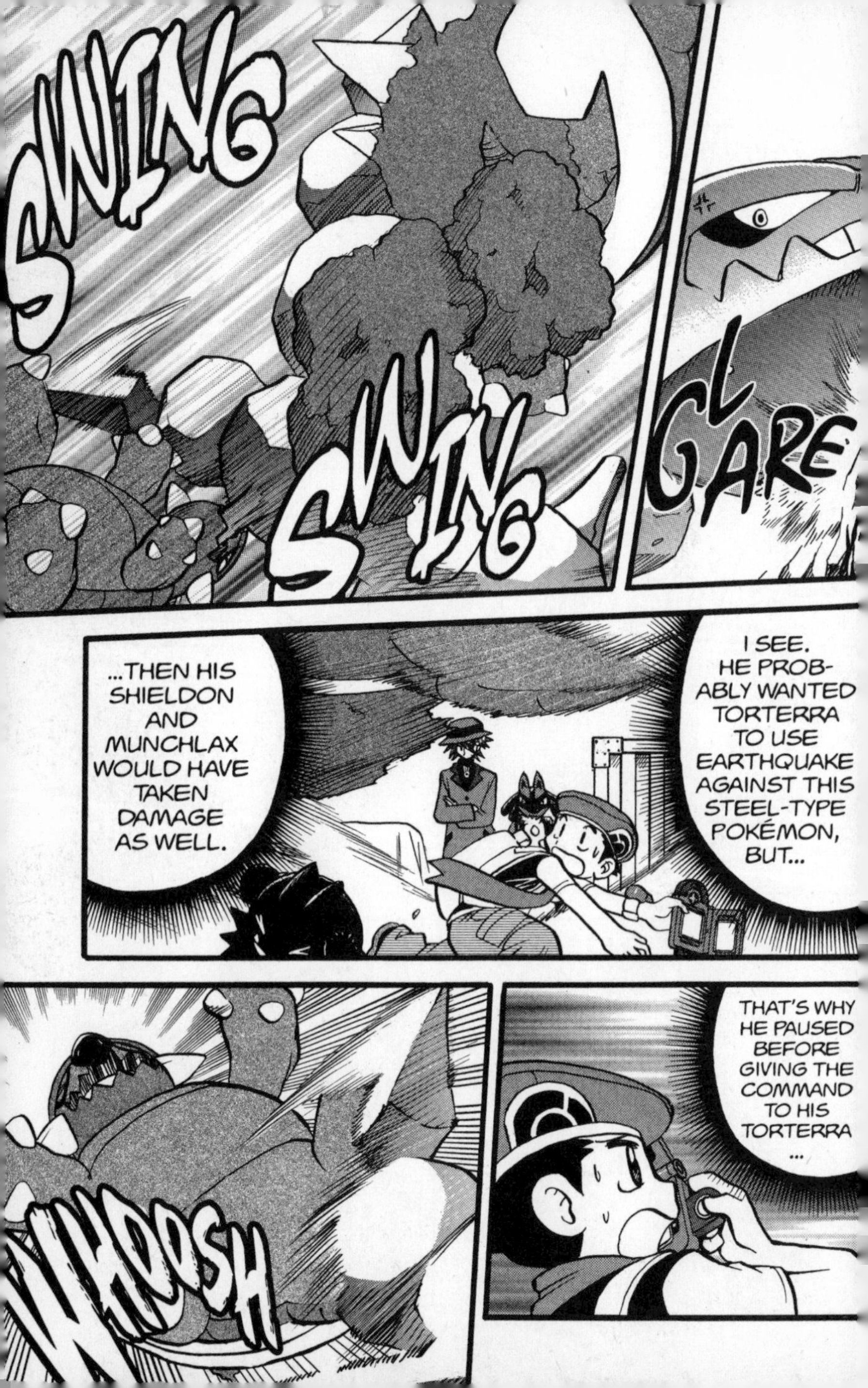
GLARE
SWING
SWING
I SEE. HE PROB-ABLY WANTED TORTERRA TO USE EARTHQUAKE AGAINST THIS STEEL-TYPE POKÉMON, BUT...
...THEN HIS SHIELDON AND MUNCHLAX WOULD HAVE TAKEN DAMAGE AS WELL.
THAT'S WHY HE PAUSED BEFORE GIVING THE COMMAND TO HIS TORTERRA ...
WHOOSH

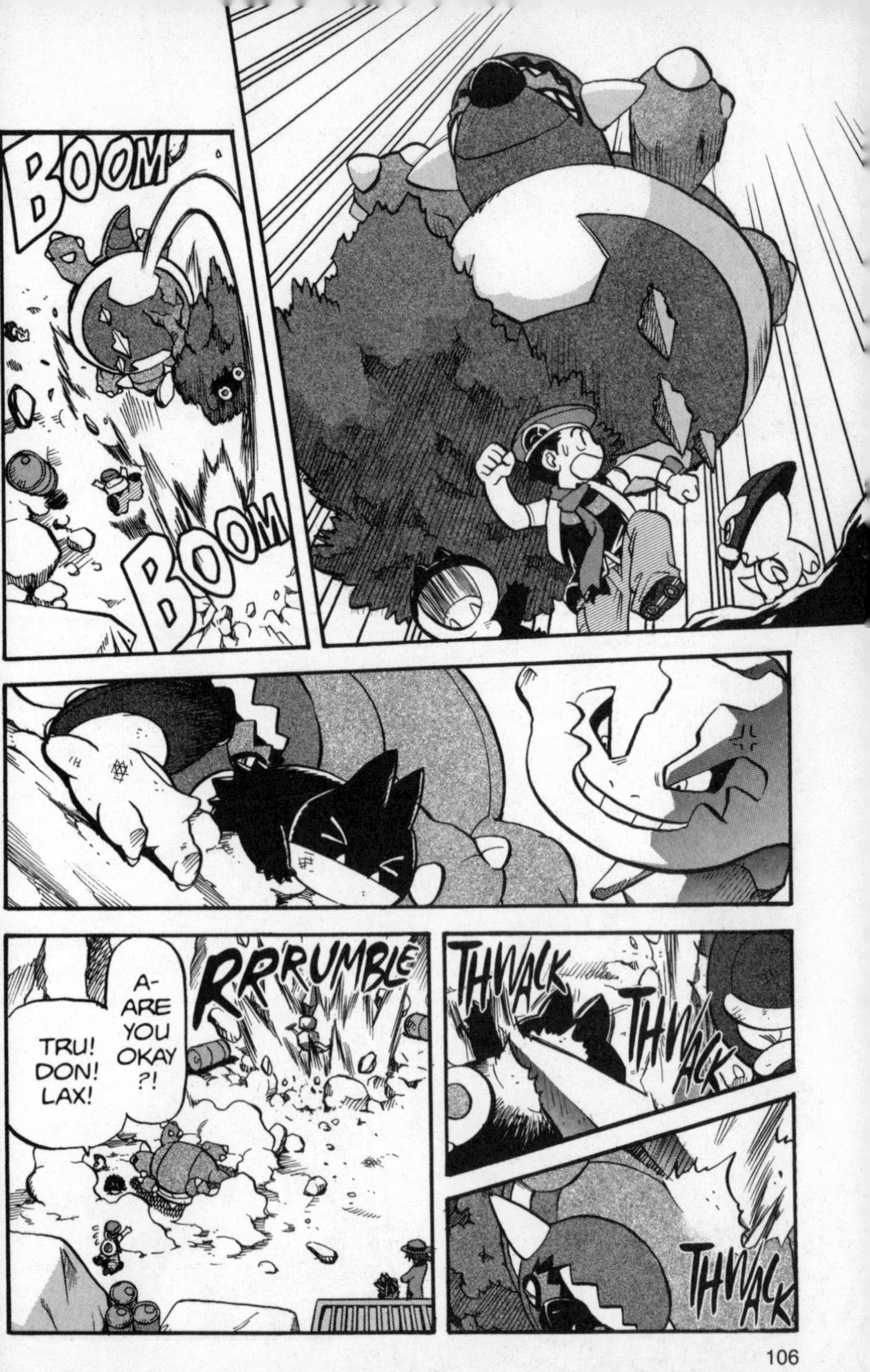
BOOM
BOOM
THWACK
THWACK
THWACK
RRRUMBLE
A-ARE YOU OKAY?!
TRU! DON! LAX!

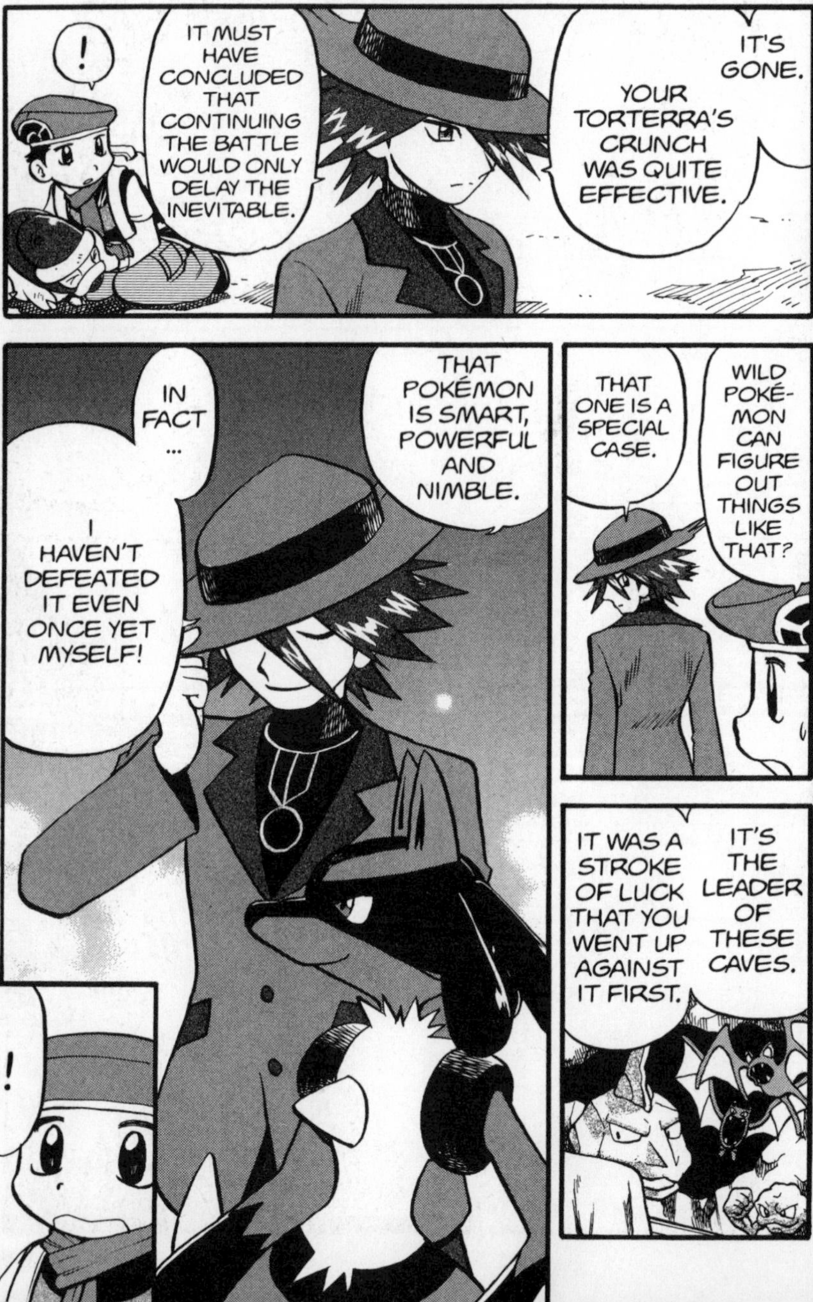
IT'S GONE.
YOUR TORTERRA'S CRUNCH WAS QUITE EFFECTIVE.
IT MUST HAVE CONCLUDED THAT CONTINUING THE BATTLE WOULD ONLY DELAY THE INEVITABLE.
!
WILD POKÉMON CAN FIGURE OUT THINGS LIKE THAT?
THAT ONE IS A SPECIAL CASE.
IT'S THE LEADER OF THESE CAVES.
IT WAS A STROKE OF LUCK THAT YOU WENT UP AGAINST IT FIRST.
THAT POKÉMON IS SMART, POWERFUL AND NIMBLE.
IN FACT ...
I HAVEN'T DEFEATED IT EVEN ONCE YET MYSELF!
!

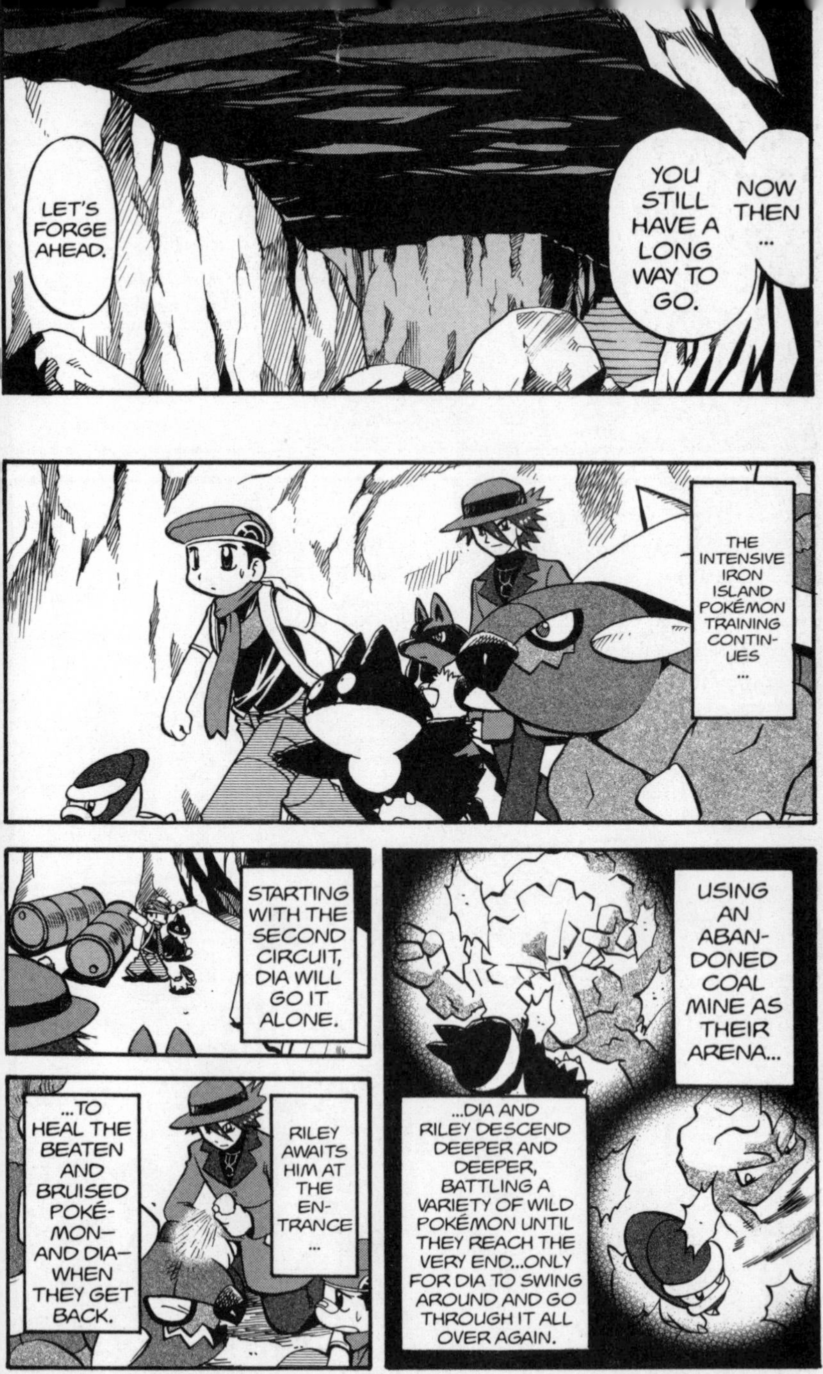
NOW THEN ...
YOU STILL HAVE A LONG WAY TO GO.
LET'S FORGE AHEAD.
THE INTENSIVE IRON ISLAND POKÉMON TRAINING CONTIN-UES ...
USING AN ABAN-DONED COAL MINE AS THEIR ARENA...
...DIA AND RILEY DESCEND DEEPER AND DEEPER, BATTLING A VARIETY OF WILD POKÉMON UNTIL THEY REACH THE VERY END...ONLY FOR DIA TO SWING AROUND AND GO THROUGH IT ALL OVER AGAIN.
STARTING WITH THE SECOND CIRCUIT, DIA WILL GO IT ALONE.
RILEY AWAITS HIM AT THE EN-TRANCE ...
...TO HEAL THE BEATEN AND BRUISED POKÉ-MON—AND DIA—WHEN THEY GET BACK.

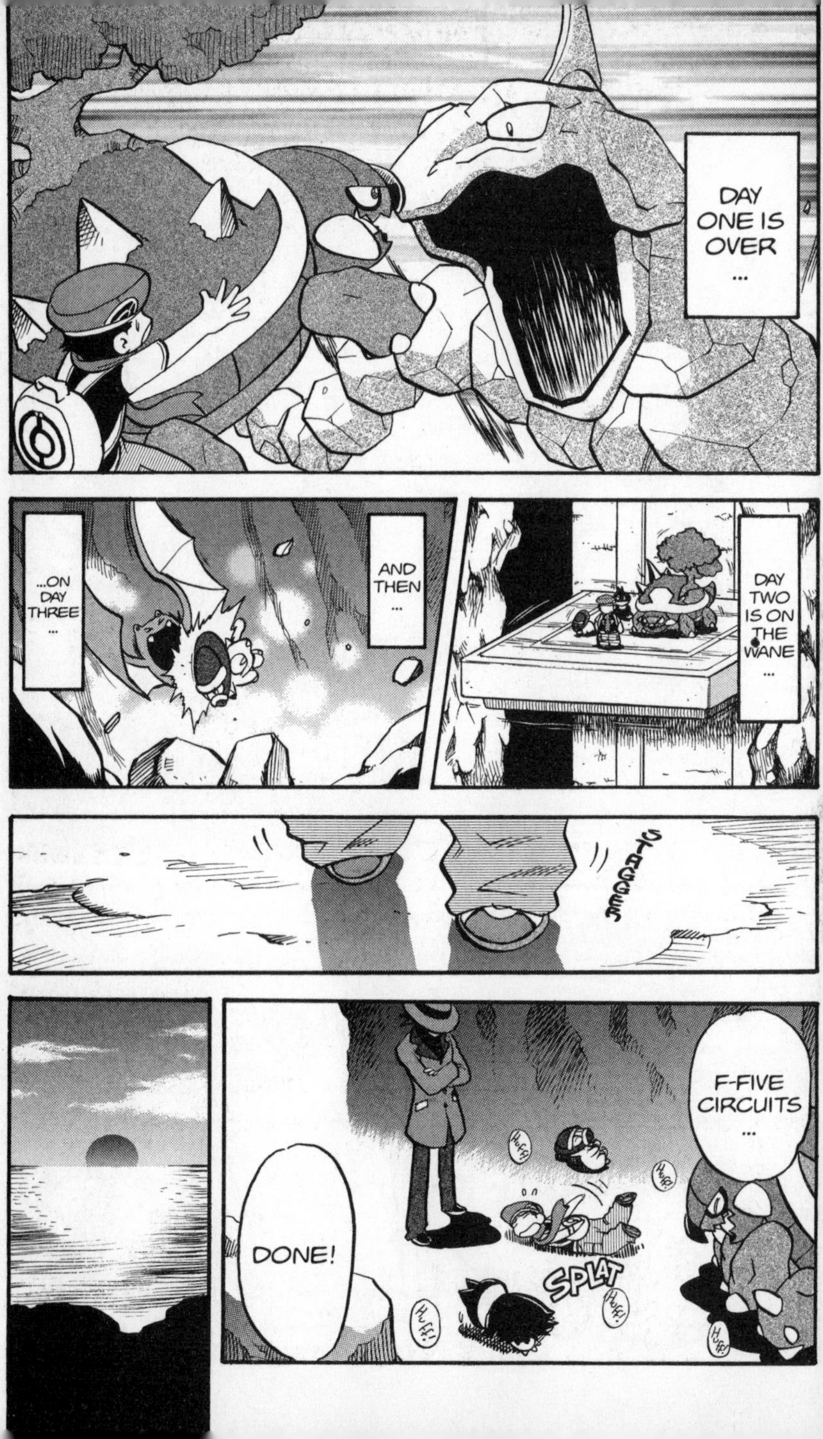

DAY ONE IS OVER ...
DAY TWO IS ON THE WANE ...
AND THEN ...
...ON DAY THREE ...
STAGGER
F-FIVE CIRCUITS ...
HUFF!
HUFF!
HUFF!
SPLAT
HUFF!
HUFF!
DONE!

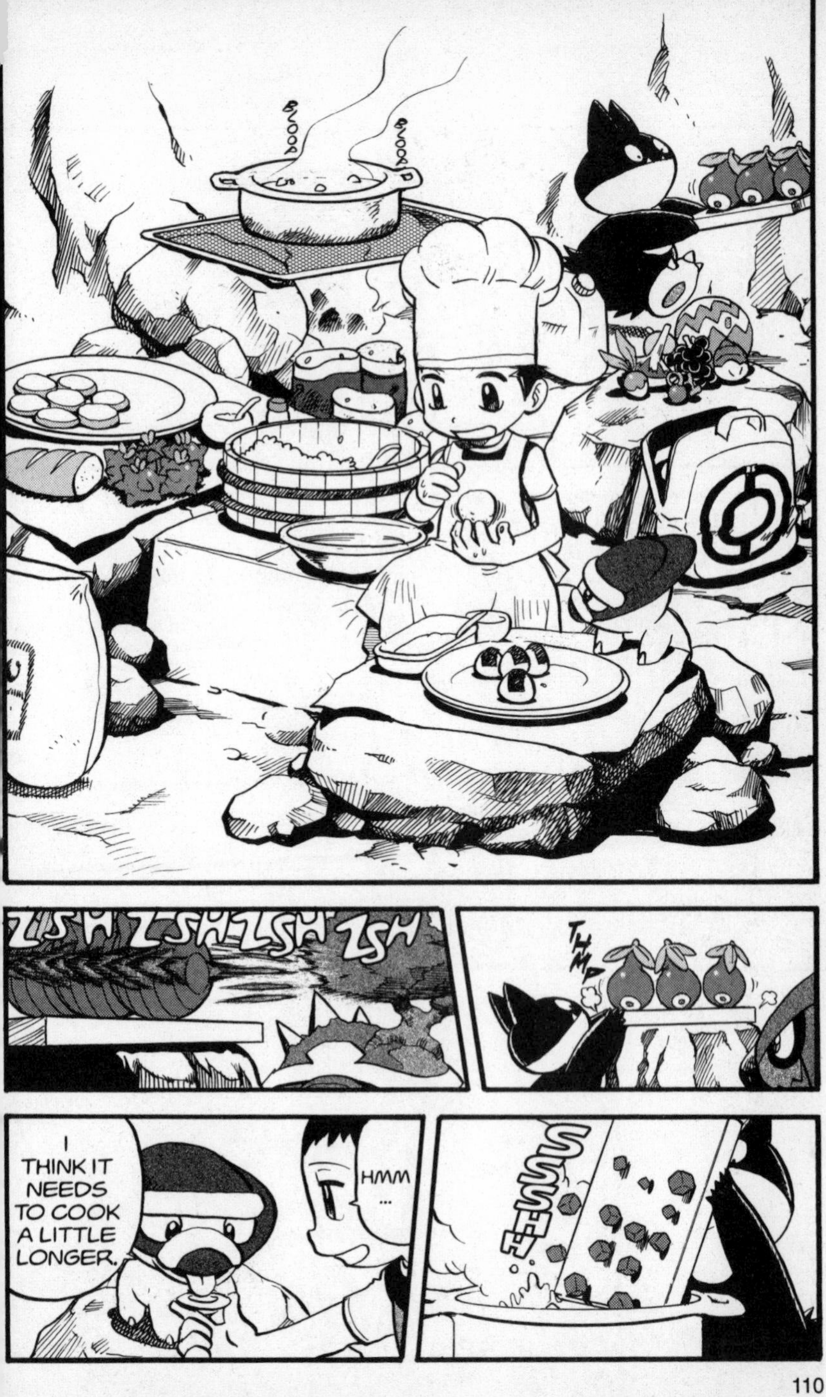
BLOOP
BLOOP
THMP
ZSH ZSH ZSH ZSH
SSSHH
HMM ...
I THINK IT NEEDS TO COOK A LITTLE LONGER.

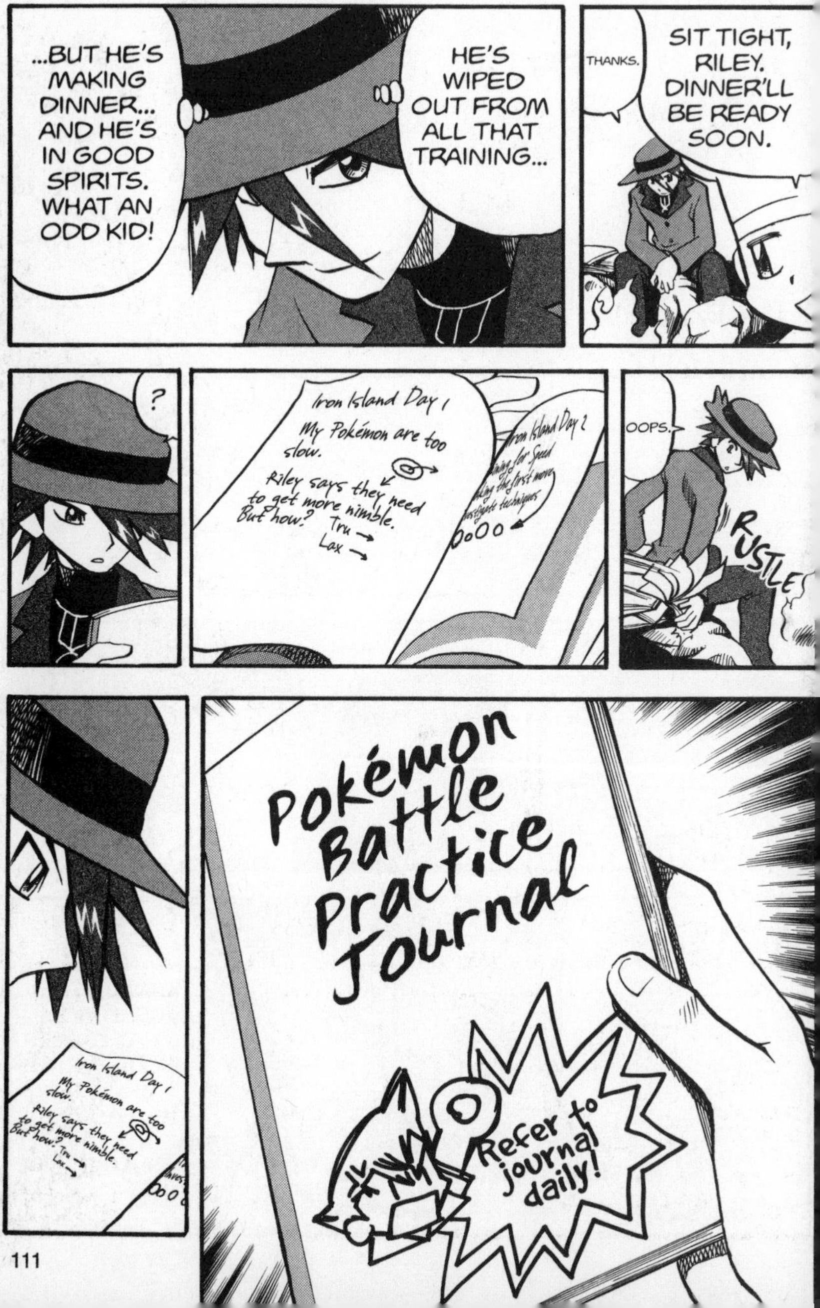
SIT TIGHT, RILEY. DINNER'LL BE READY SOON.
THANKS.
HE'S WIPED OUT FROM ALL THAT TRAINING...
...BUT HE'S MAKING DINNER... AND HE'S IN GOOD SPIRITS. WHAT AN ODD KID!
OOPS.
RUSTLE
Iron Island Day 1
My Pokémon are too slow.
Riley says they need to get more nimble. But how?
Tru →
Lax →
Iron Island Day 2
?
Pokémon Battle Practice Journal
Refer to journal daily!
Iron Island Day 1
My Pokémon are too slow.
Riley says they need to get more nimble. But how?
Tru →
Lax →

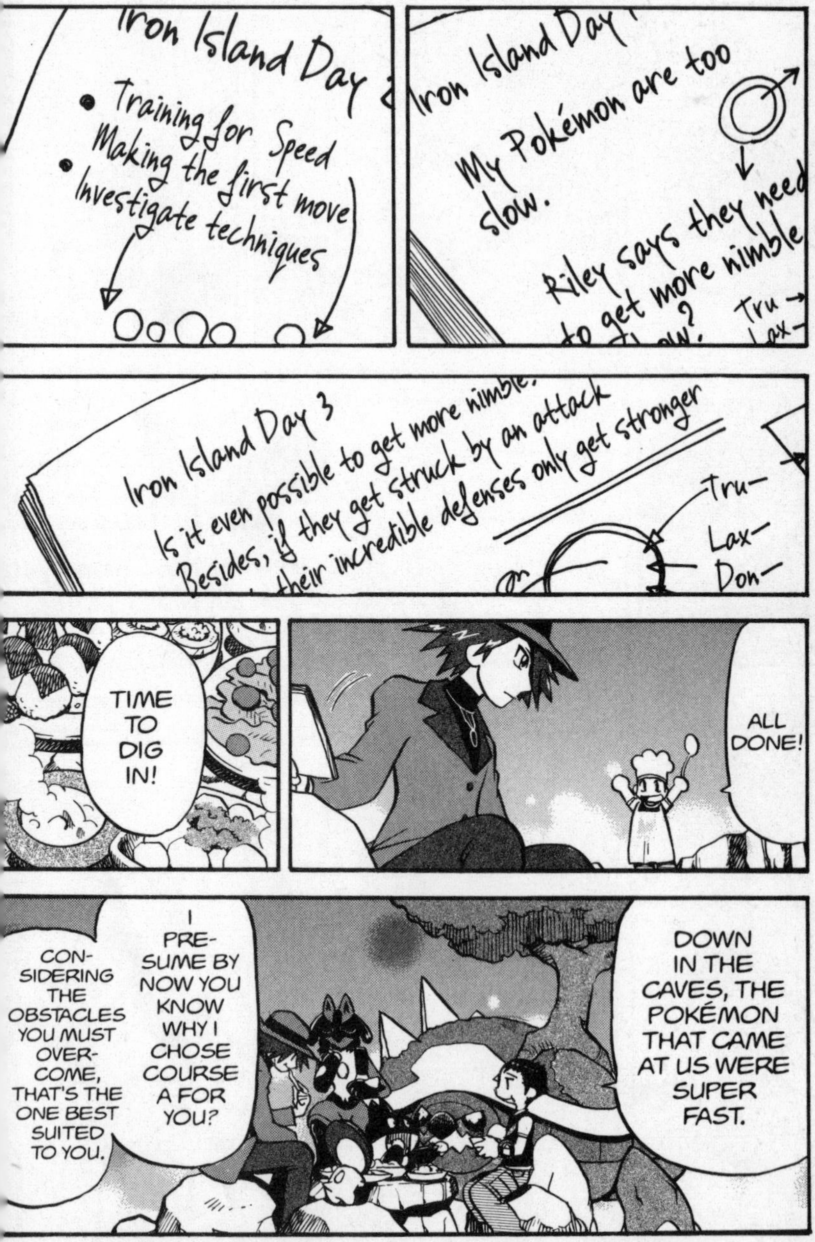
Iron Island Day
My Pokémon are too slow.
Riley says they need to get more nimble
Tru
Lax
Iron Island Day
Training for Speed
Making the first move
Investigate techniques
Iron Island Day 3
Is it even possible to get more nimble?
Besides, if they get struck by an attack their incredible defenses only get stronger
Tru
Lax
Don
ALL DONE!
TIME TO DIG IN!
DOWN IN THE CAVES, THE POKÉMON THAT CAME AT US WERE SUPER FAST.
I PRESUME BY NOW YOU KNOW WHY I CHOSE COURSE A FOR YOU?
CONSIDERING THE OBSTACLES YOU MUST OVERCOME, THAT'S THE ONE BEST SUITED TO YOU.

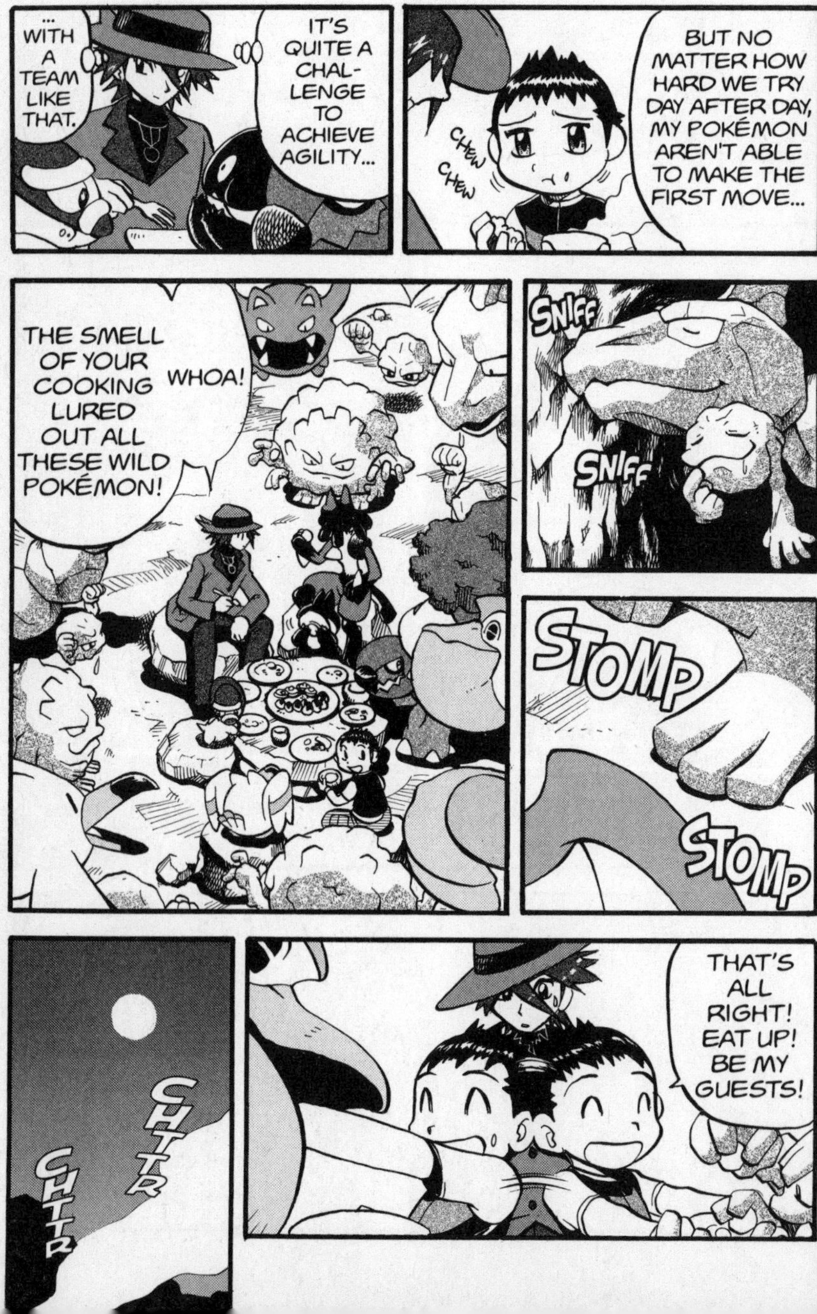
BUT NO MATTER HOW HARD WE TRY DAY AFTER DAY, MY POKÉMON AREN'T ABLE TO MAKE THE FIRST MOVE...
CHEW CHEW
IT'S QUITE A CHAL-LENGE TO ACHIEVE AGILITY...
...WITH A TEAM LIKE THAT.
SNIFF
SNIFF
STOMP
STOMP
WHOA!
THE SMELL OF YOUR COOKING LURED OUT ALL THESE WILD POKÉMON!
THAT'S ALL RIGHT! EAT UP! BE MY GUESTS!
CHTTR
CHTTR

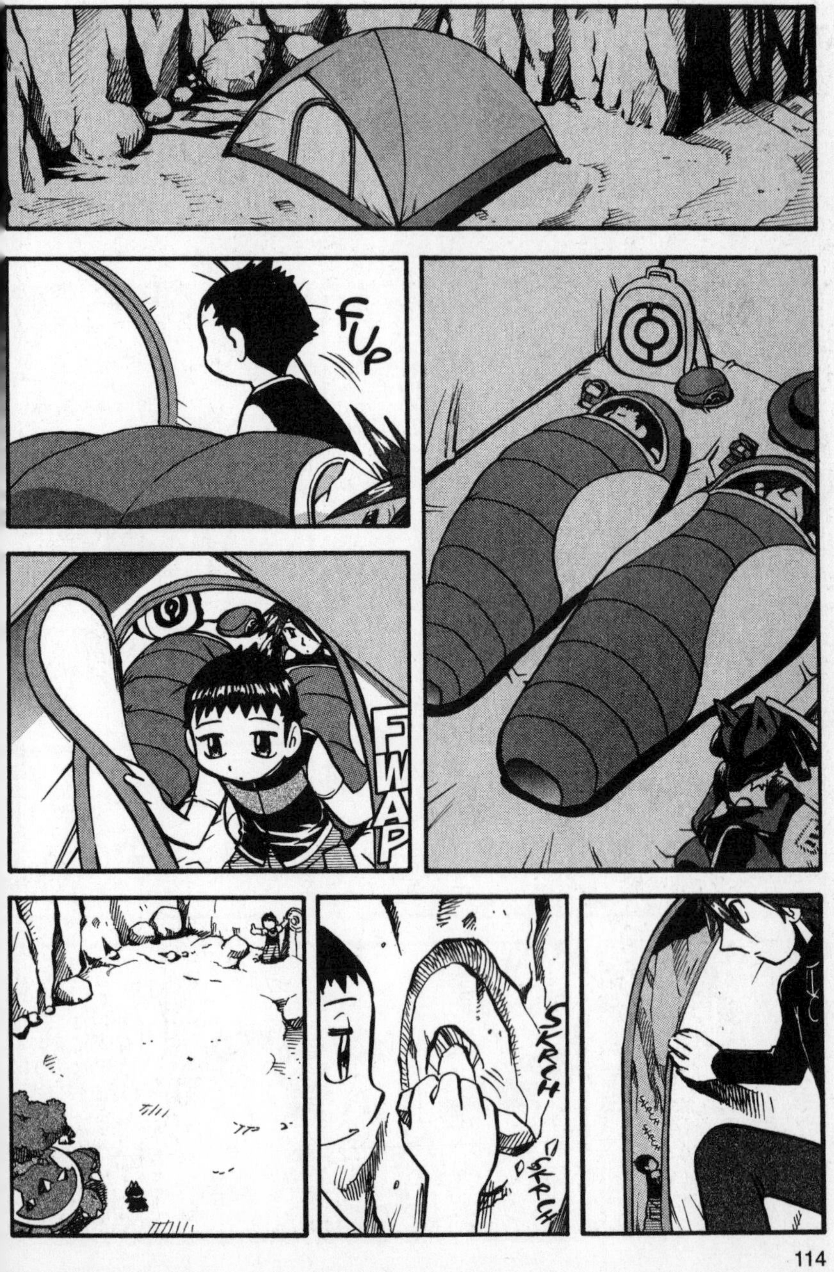
FUP
FWAP
SKRCH
SKRCH
SKRCH
SKRCH
SKRCH

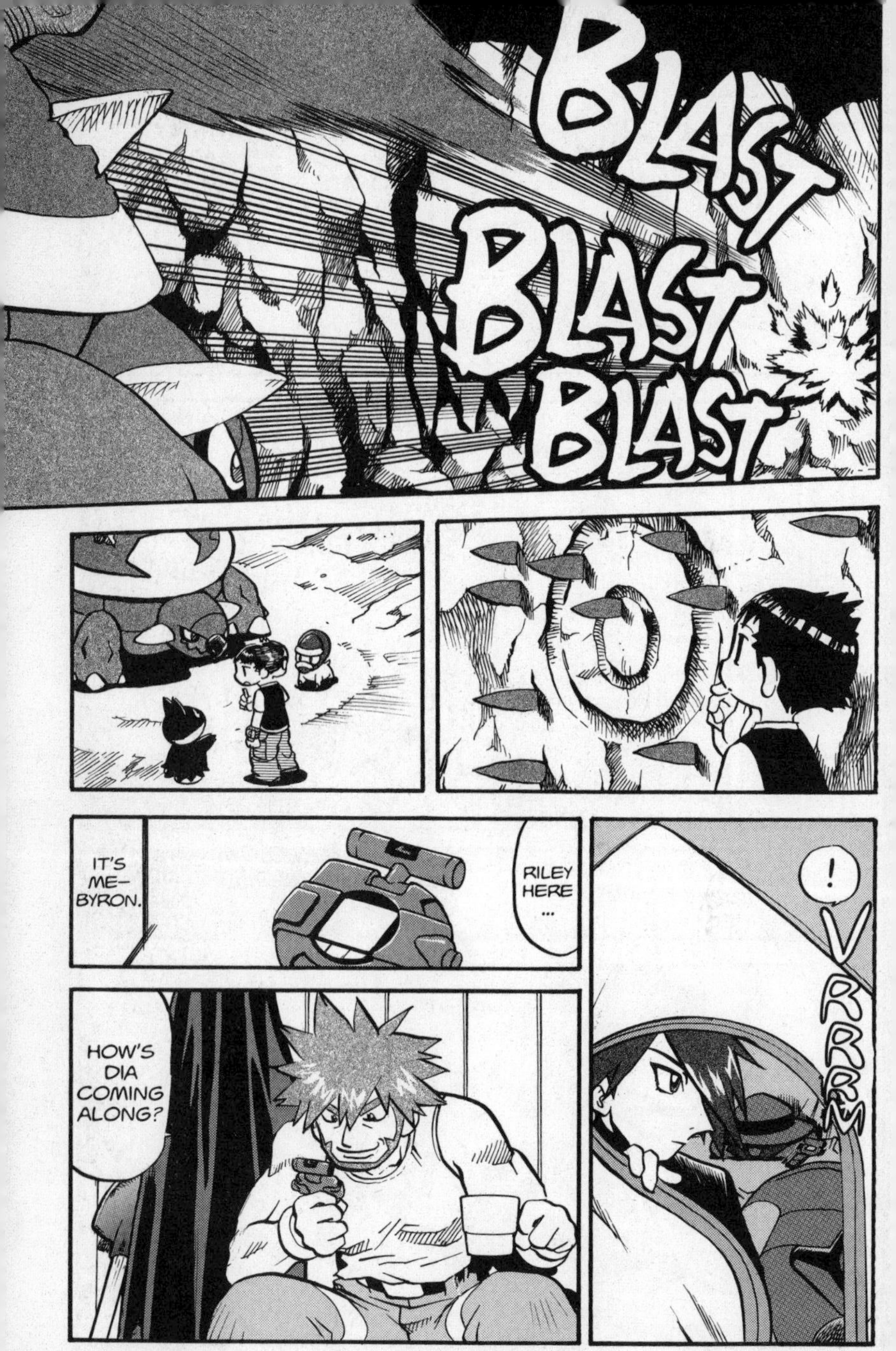
BLAST
BLAST
BLAST
!
VRRRRM
RILEY HERE ...
IT'S ME—BYRON.
HOW'S DIA COMING ALONG?

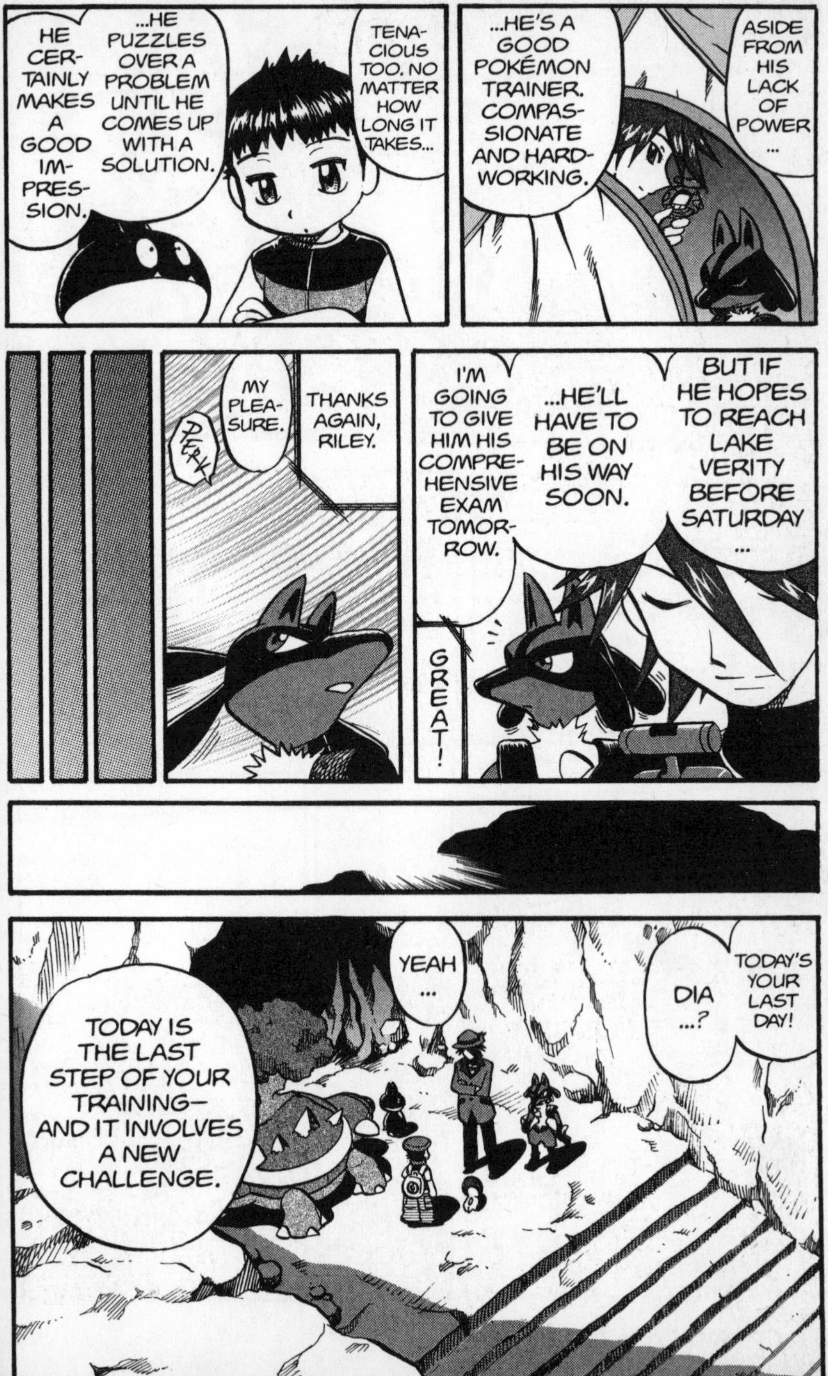
ASIDE FROM HIS LACK OF POWER...
...HE'S A GOOD POKÉMON TRAINER. COMPASSIONATE AND HARD-WORKING.
TENACIOUS TOO. NO MATTER HOW LONG IT TAKES...
...HE PUZZLES OVER A PROBLEM UNTIL HE COMES UP WITH A SOLUTION.
HE CERTAINLY MAKES A GOOD IMPRESSION.
BUT IF HE HOPES TO REACH LAKE VERITY BEFORE SATURDAY...
...HE'LL HAVE TO BE ON HIS WAY SOON.
I'M GOING TO GIVE HIM HIS COMPREHENSIVE EXAM TOMORROW.
GREAT!
THANKS AGAIN, RILEY.
MY PLEASURE.
PERK
TODAY'S YOUR LAST DAY!
DIA...?
YEAH...
TODAY IS THE LAST STEP OF YOUR TRAINING—AND IT INVOLVES A NEW CHALLENGE.

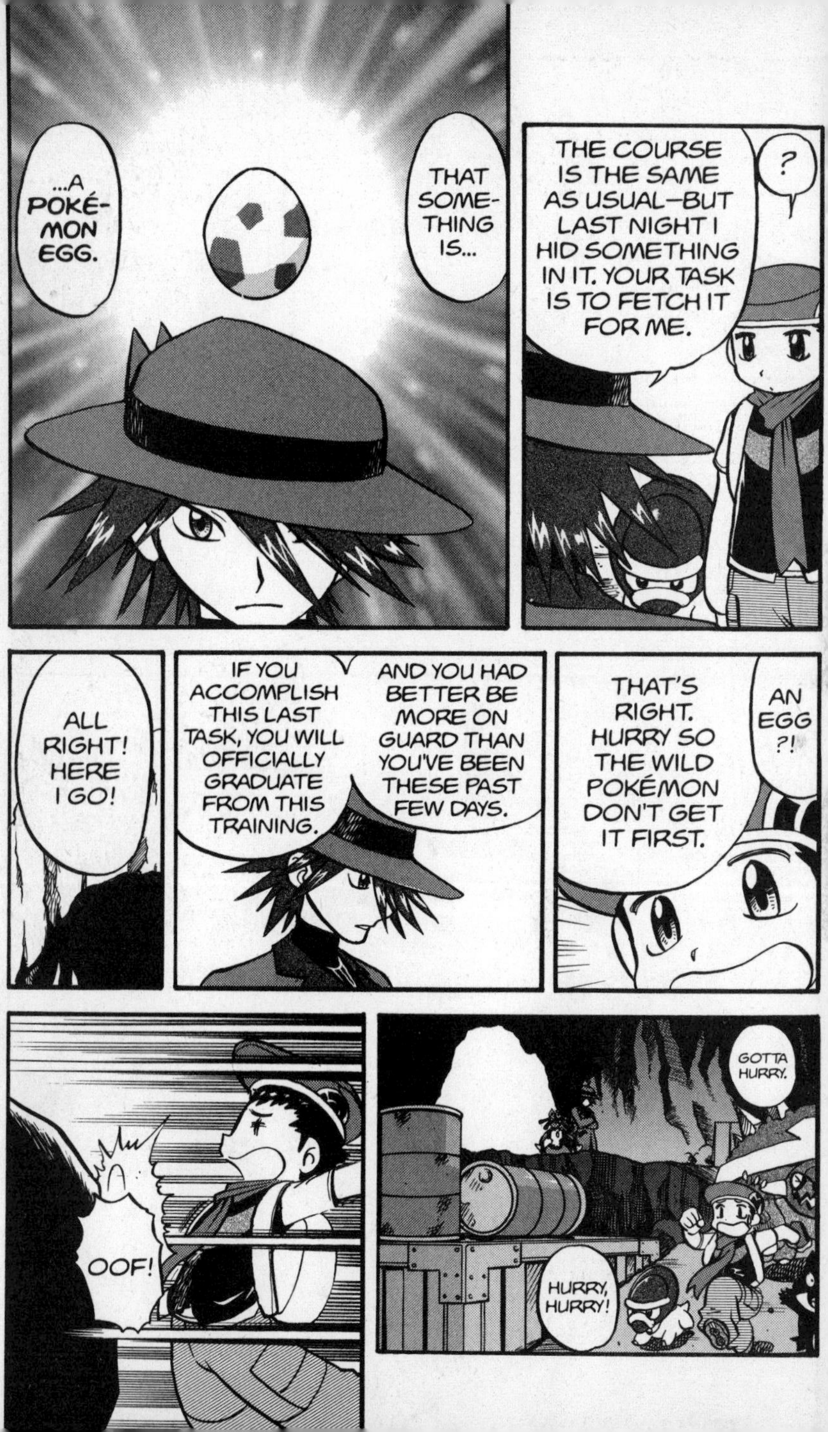
?
THE COURSE IS THE SAME AS USUAL—BUT LAST NIGHT I HID SOMETHING IN IT. YOUR TASK IS TO FETCH IT FOR ME.
THAT SOMETHING IS...
...A POKÉMON EGG.
AN EGG ?!
THAT'S RIGHT. HURRY SO THE WILD POKÉMON DON'T GET IT FIRST.
IF YOU ACCOMPLISH THIS LAST TASK, YOU WILL OFFICIALLY GRADUATE FROM THIS TRAINING.
AND YOU HAD BETTER BE MORE ON GUARD THAN YOU'VE BEEN THESE PAST FEW DAYS.
ALL RIGHT! HERE I GO!
GOTTA HURRY.
HURRY, HURRY!
OOF!

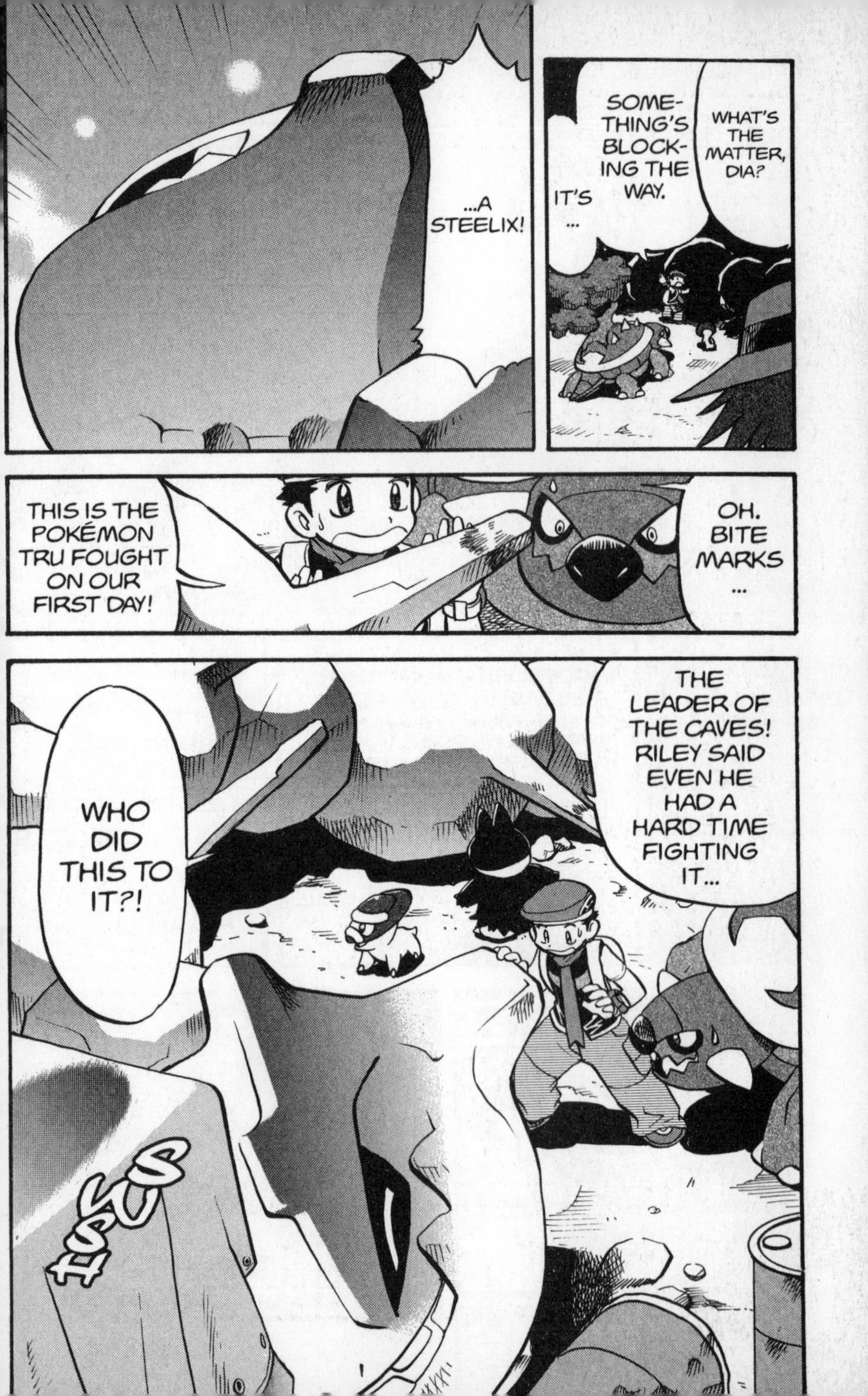
WHAT'S THE MATTER, DIA?
SOME-THING'S BLOCK-ING THE WAY.
IT'S ...
...A STEELIX!
OH. BITE MARKS ...
THIS IS THE POKÉMON TRU FOUGHT ON OUR FIRST DAY!
THE LEADER OF THE CAVES! RILEY SAID EVEN HE HAD A HARD TIME FIGHTING IT...
WHO DID THIS TO IT?!

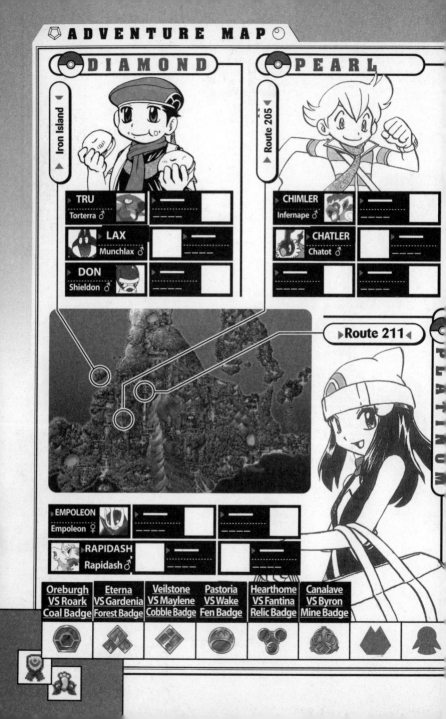

ADVENTURE MAP

DIAMOND

Iron Island

TRU
Torterra ♂

LAX
Munchlax ♂

DON
Shieldon ♂

EMPOLEON
Empoleon ♀

RAPIDASH
Rapidash ♂

PEARL

Route 205

CHIMLER
Infernape ♂

CHATLER
Chatot ♂

Route 211

PLATINUM

| Oreburgh
VS Roark
Coal Badge | Eterna
VS Gardenia
Forest Badge | Veilstone
VS Maylene
Cobble Badge | Pastoria
VS Wake
Fen Badge | Hearthome
VS Fantina
Relic Badge | Canalave
VS Byron
Mine Badge |

44

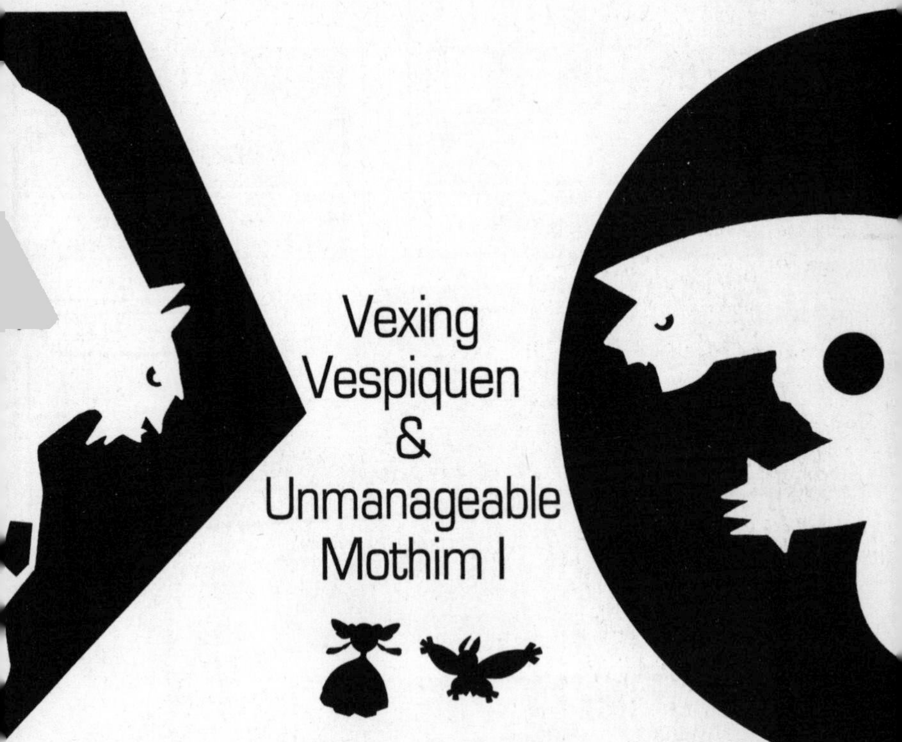

Vexing Vespiquen & Unmanageable Mothim I

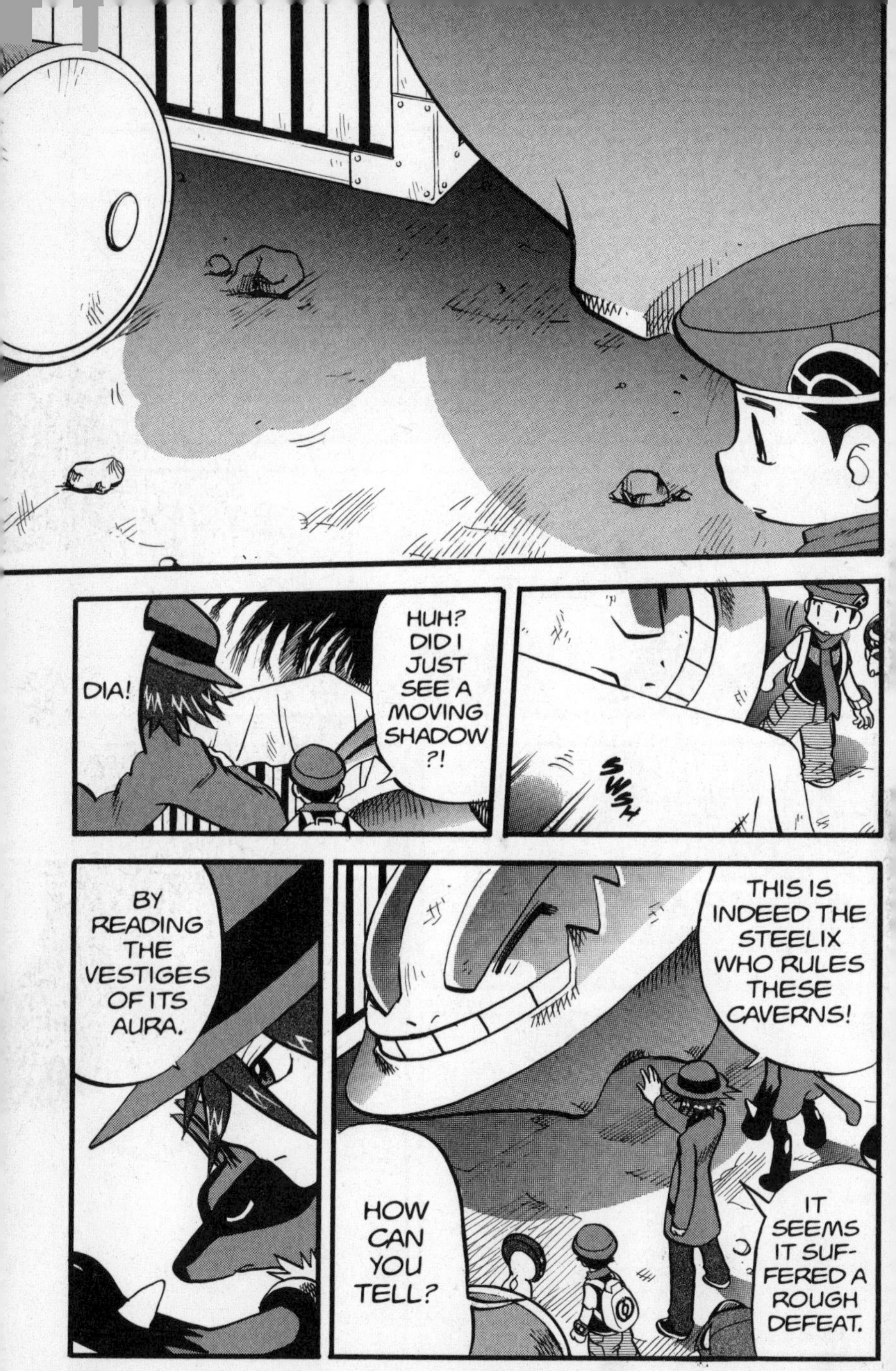
SWSH
HUH? DID I JUST SEE A MOVING SHADOW?!
DIA!
THIS IS INDEED THE STEELIX WHO RULES THESE CAVERNS!
IT SEEMS IT SUFFERED A ROUGH DEFEAT.
HOW CAN YOU TELL?
BY READING THE VESTIGES OF ITS AURA.

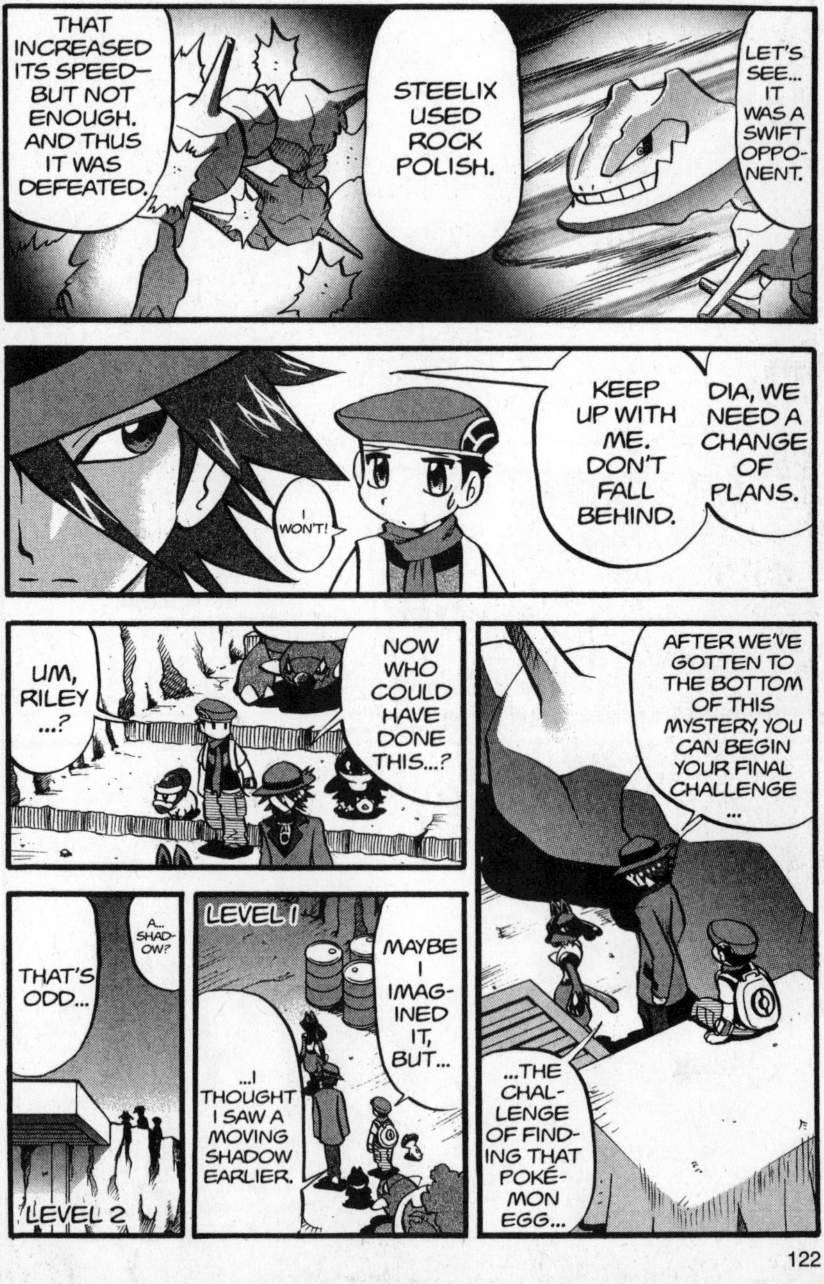
LET'S SEE... IT WAS A SWIFT OPPONENT.
STEELIX USED ROCK POLISH.
THAT INCREASED ITS SPEED—BUT NOT ENOUGH. AND THUS IT WAS DEFEATED.
DIA, WE NEED A CHANGE OF PLANS.
KEEP UP WITH ME. DON'T FALL BEHIND.
I WON'T!
AFTER WE'VE GOTTEN TO THE BOTTOM OF THIS MYSTERY, YOU CAN BEGIN YOUR FINAL CHALLENGE...
...THE CHALLENGE OF FINDING THAT POKÉMON EGG...
NOW WHO COULD HAVE DONE THIS...?
UM, RILEY...?
LEVEL 1
MAYBE I IMAGINED IT, BUT...
...I THOUGHT I SAW A MOVING SHADOW EARLIER.
A... SHADOW?
THAT'S ODD...
LEVEL 2

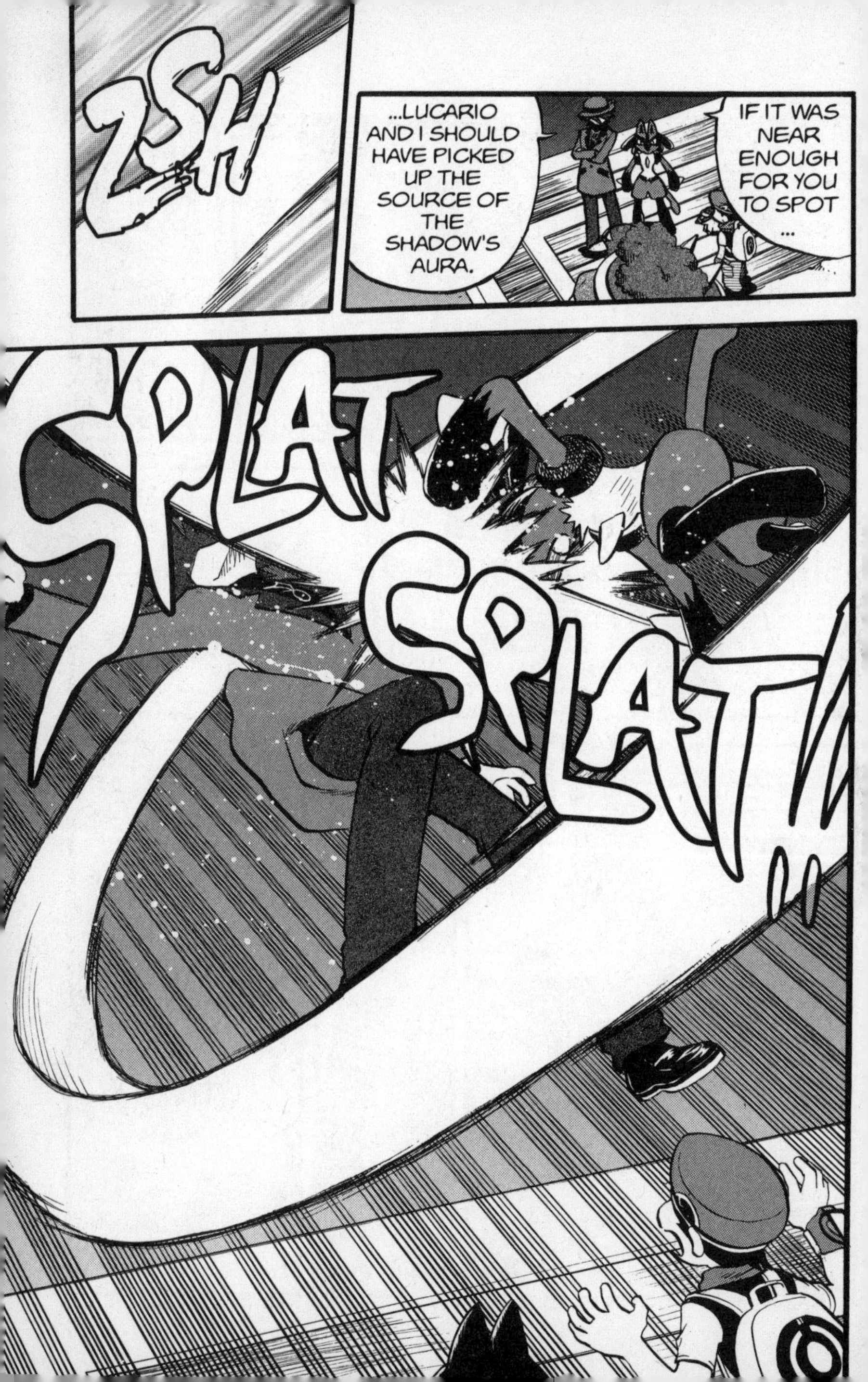
IF IT WAS NEAR ENOUGH FOR YOU TO SPOT ...
...LUCARIO AND I SHOULD HAVE PICKED UP THE SOURCE OF THE SHADOW'S AURA.
ZSH
SPLAT
SPLAT!!

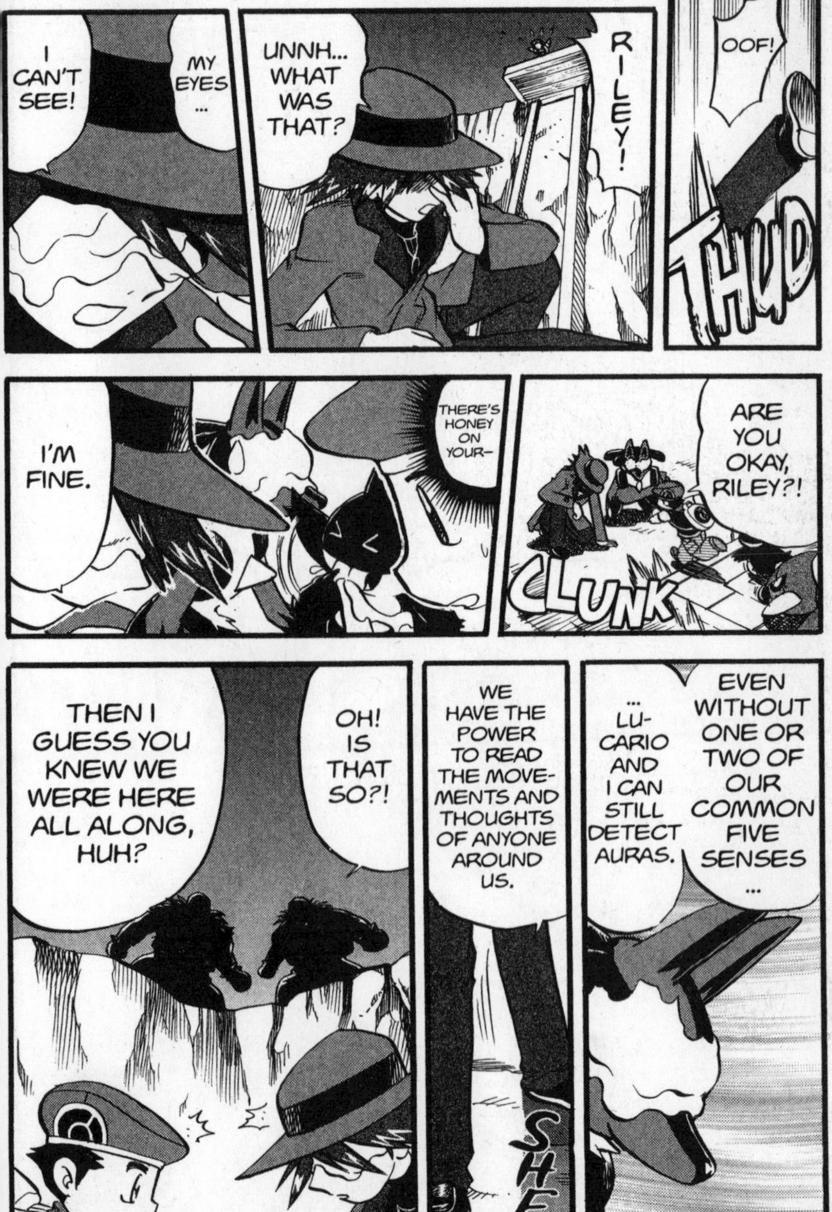
OOF!
THUD
RILEY!
UNNH... WHAT WAS THAT?
MY EYES ...
I CAN'T SEE!
ARE YOU OKAY, RILEY?!
CLUNK
THERE'S HONEY ON YOUR—
I'M FINE.
EVEN WITHOUT ONE OR TWO OF OUR COMMON FIVE SENSES ...
... LU-CARIO AND I CAN STILL DETECT AURAS.
WE HAVE THE POWER TO READ THE MOVE-MENTS AND THOUGHTS OF ANYONE AROUND US.
SHF
OH! IS THAT SO?!
THEN I GUESS YOU KNEW WE WERE HERE ALL ALONG, HUH?

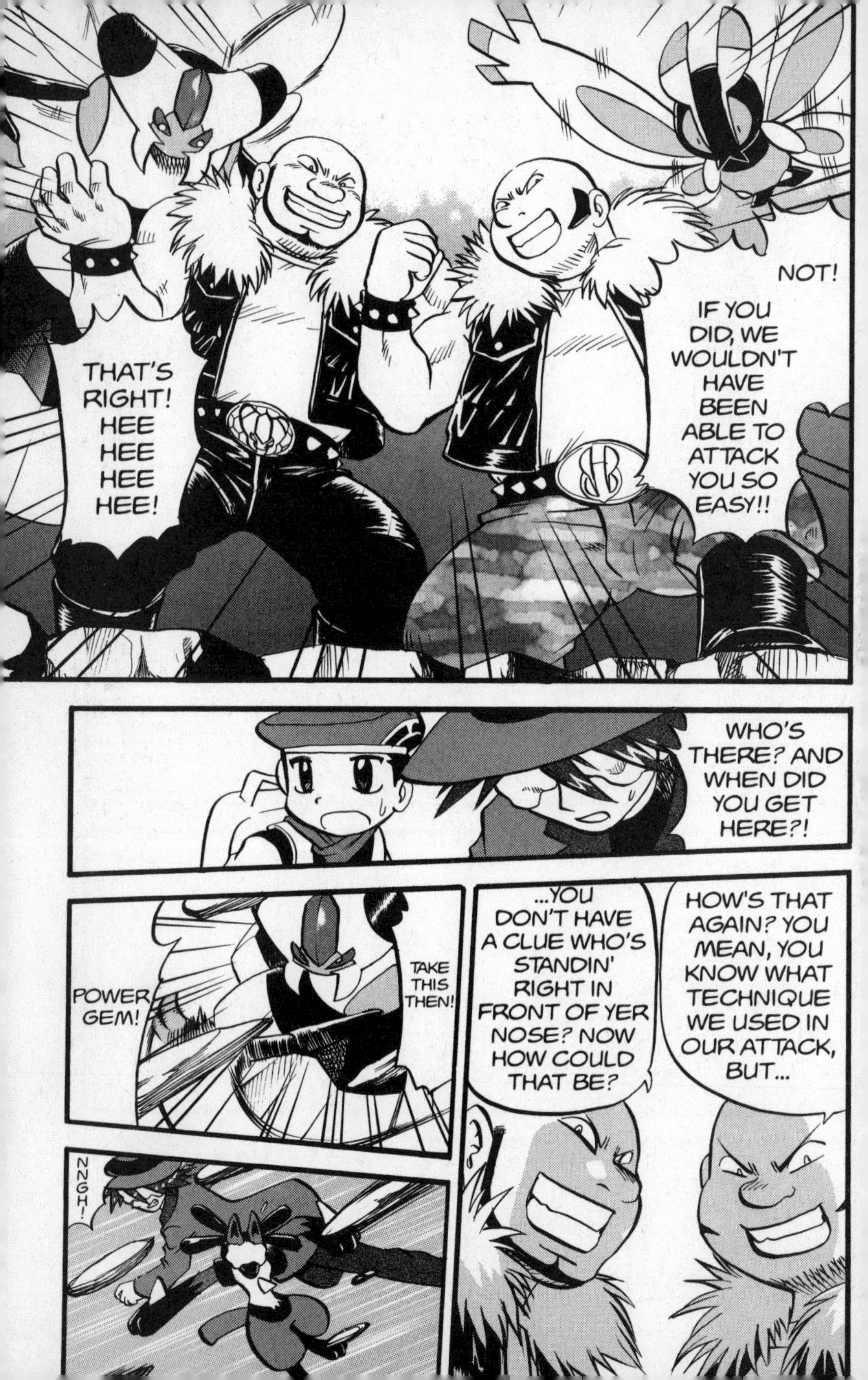
NOT!
IF YOU DID, WE WOULDN'T HAVE BEEN ABLE TO ATTACK YOU SO EASY!!
THAT'S RIGHT! HEE HEE HEE HEE!
WHO'S THERE? AND WHEN DID YOU GET HERE?!
HOW'S THAT AGAIN? YOU MEAN, YOU KNOW WHAT TECHNIQUE WE USED IN OUR ATTACK, BUT...
...YOU DON'T HAVE A CLUE WHO'S STANDIN' RIGHT IN FRONT OF YER NOSE? NOW HOW COULD THAT BE?
TAKE THIS THEN!
POWER GEM!
NNGH!

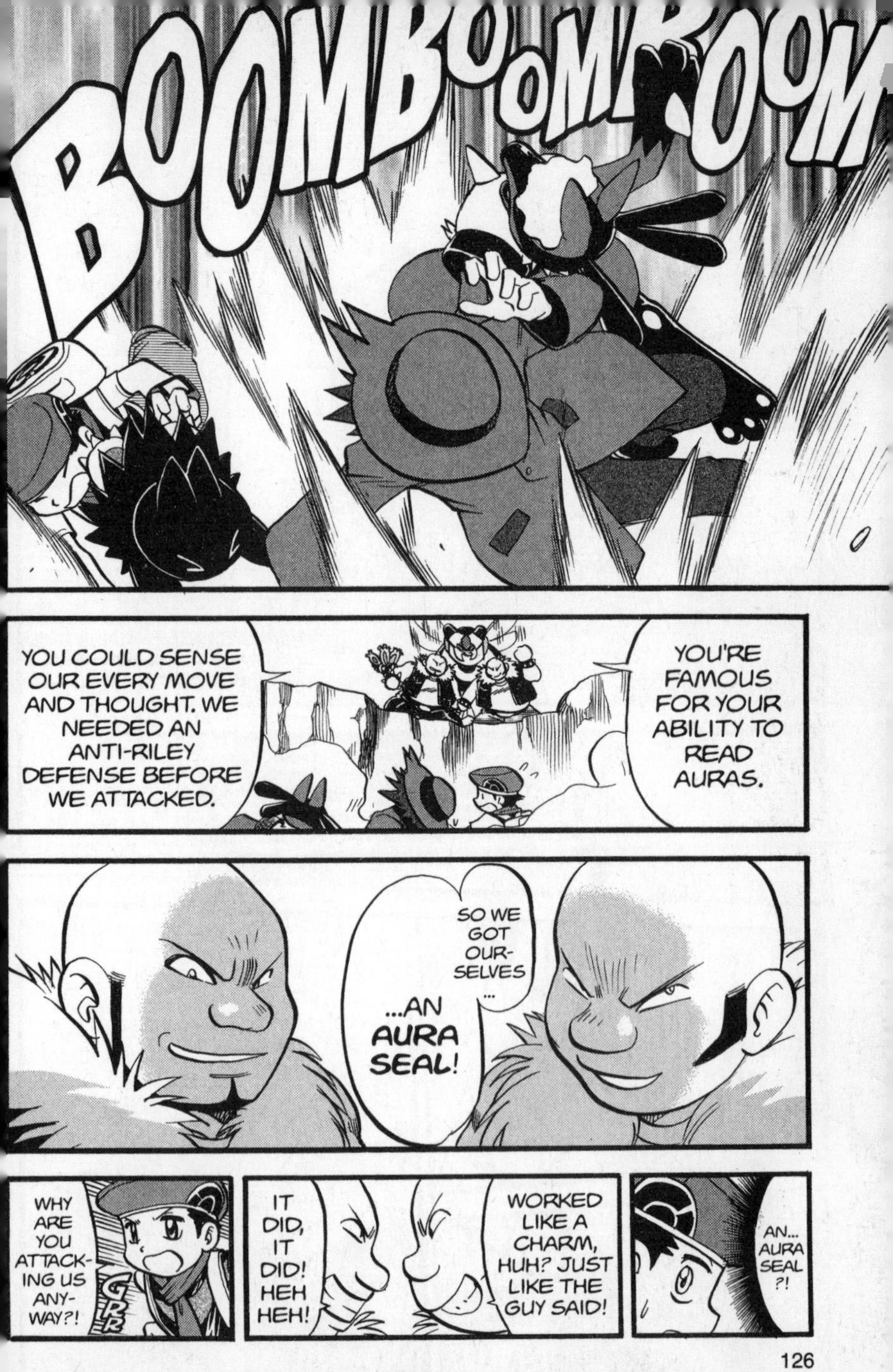
BOOMBOOMBOOM
YOU'RE FAMOUS FOR YOUR ABILITY TO READ AURAS.
YOU COULD SENSE OUR EVERY MOVE AND THOUGHT. WE NEEDED AN ANTI-RILEY DEFENSE BEFORE WE ATTACKED.
SO WE GOT OURSELVES ...
...AN AURA SEAL!
AN... AURA SEAL?!
WORKED LIKE A CHARM, HUH? JUST LIKE THE GUY SAID!
IT DID, IT DID! HEH HEH!
WHY ARE YOU ATTACKING US ANYWAY?!
GRR

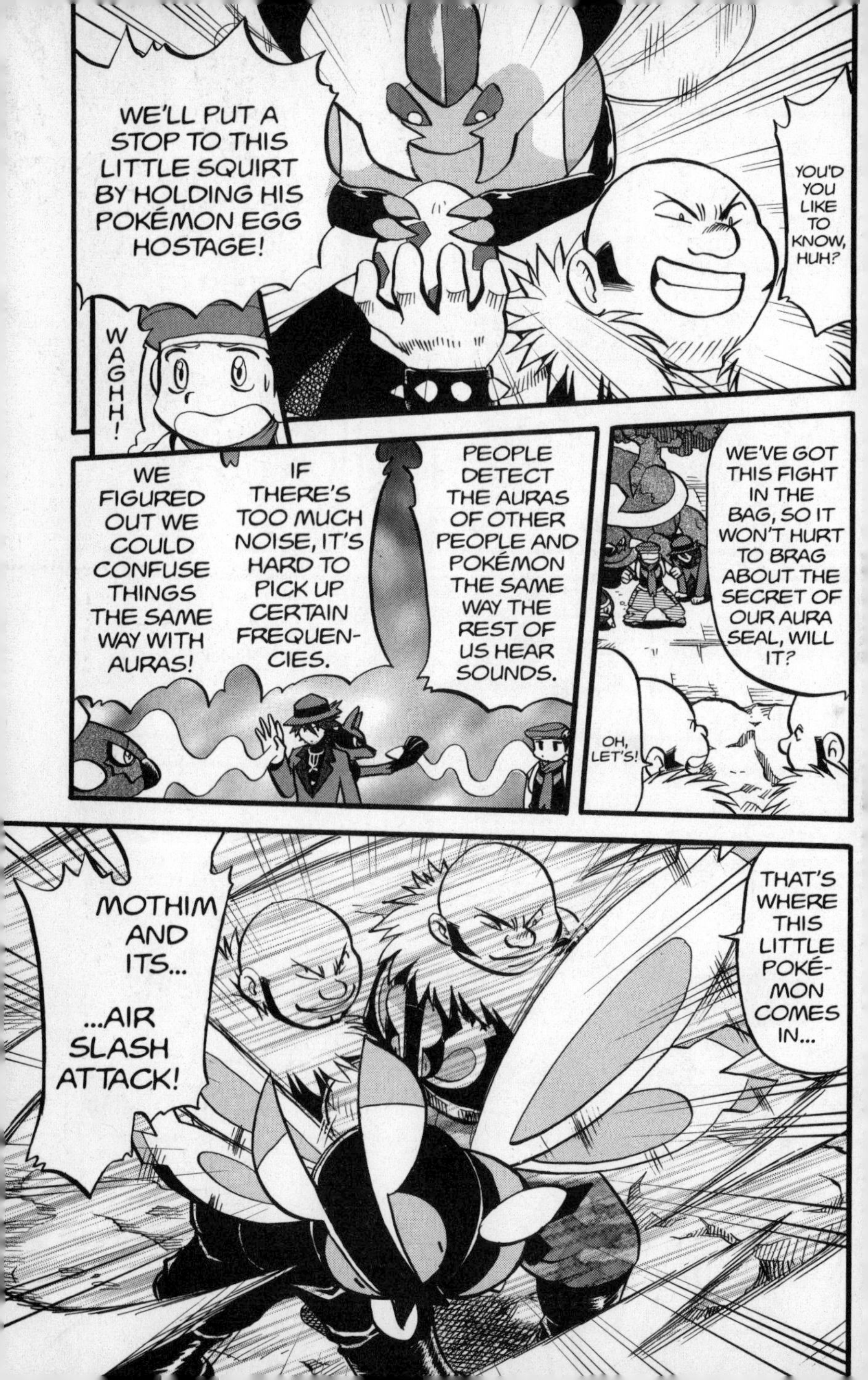
YOU'D YOU LIKE TO KNOW, HUH?
WE'LL PUT A STOP TO THIS LITTLE SQUIRT BY HOLDING HIS POKÉMON EGG HOSTAGE!
WAGHH!
WE'VE GOT THIS FIGHT IN THE BAG, SO IT WON'T HURT TO BRAG ABOUT THE SECRET OF OUR AURA SEAL, WILL IT?
OH, LET'S!
PEOPLE DETECT THE AURAS OF OTHER PEOPLE AND POKÉMON THE SAME WAY THE REST OF US HEAR SOUNDS.
IF THERE'S TOO MUCH NOISE, IT'S HARD TO PICK UP CERTAIN FREQUEN-CIES.
WE FIGURED OUT WE COULD CONFUSE THINGS THE SAME WAY WITH AURAS!
THAT'S WHERE THIS LITTLE POKÉ-MON COMES IN...
MOTHIM AND ITS...
...AIR SLASH ATTACK!

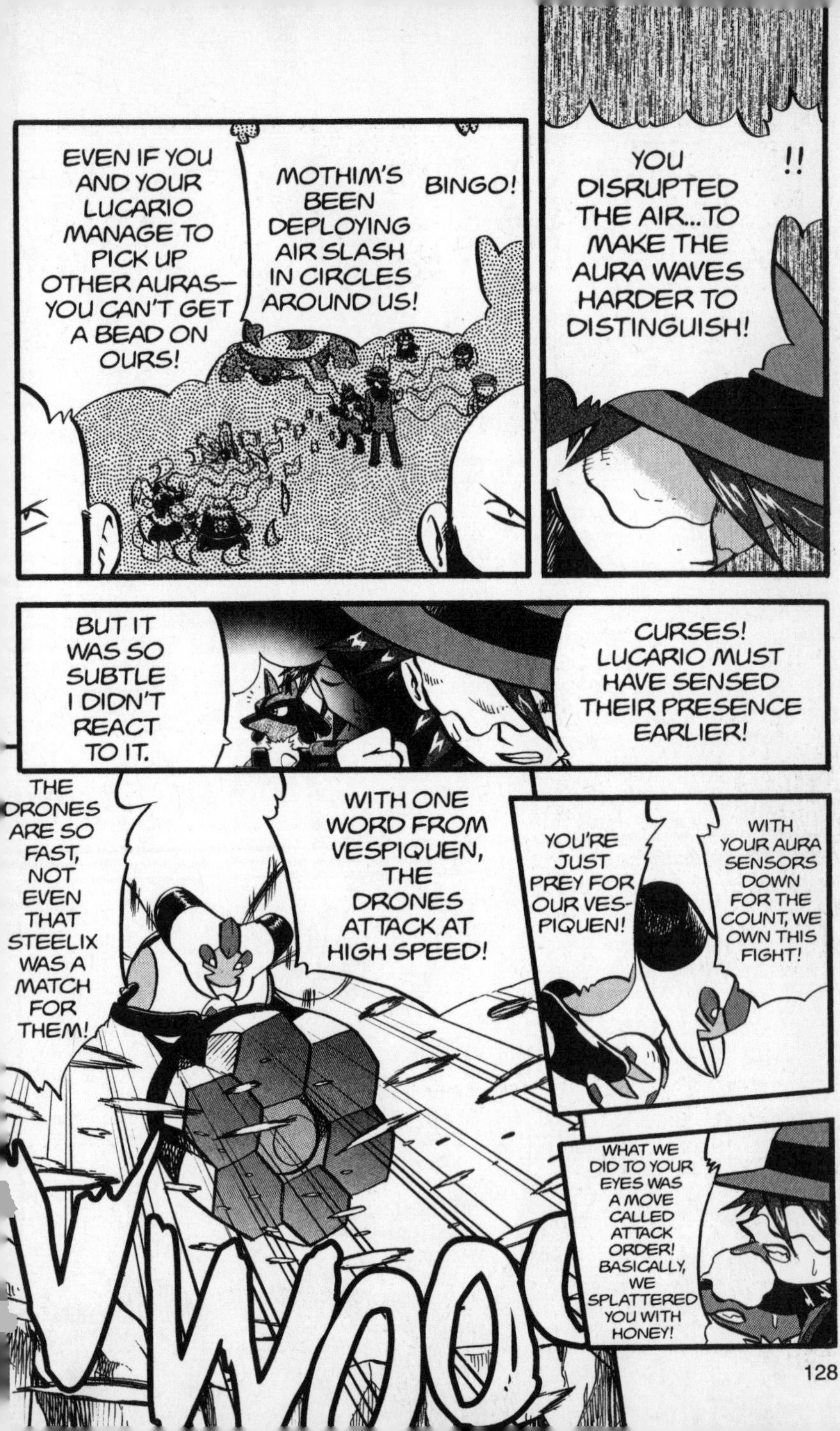
!!
YOU DISRUPTED THE AIR...TO MAKE THE AURA WAVES HARDER TO DISTINGUISH!
BINGO!
MOTHIM'S BEEN DEPLOYING AIR SLASH IN CIRCLES AROUND US!
EVEN IF YOU AND YOUR LUCARIO MANAGE TO PICK UP OTHER AURAS—YOU CAN'T GET A BEAD ON OURS!
CURSES! LUCARIO MUST HAVE SENSED THEIR PRESENCE EARLIER!
BUT IT WAS SO SUBTLE I DIDN'T REACT TO IT.
WITH YOUR AURA SENSORS DOWN FOR THE COUNT, WE OWN THIS FIGHT!
YOU'RE JUST PREY FOR OUR VES-PIQUEN!
WHAT WE DID TO YOUR EYES WAS A MOVE CALLED ATTACK ORDER! BASICALLY, WE SPLATTERED YOU WITH HONEY!
WITH ONE WORD FROM VESPIQUEN, THE DRONES ATTACK AT HIGH SPEED!
THE DRONES ARE SO FAST, NOT EVEN THAT STEELIX WAS A MATCH FOR THEM!
WHOO

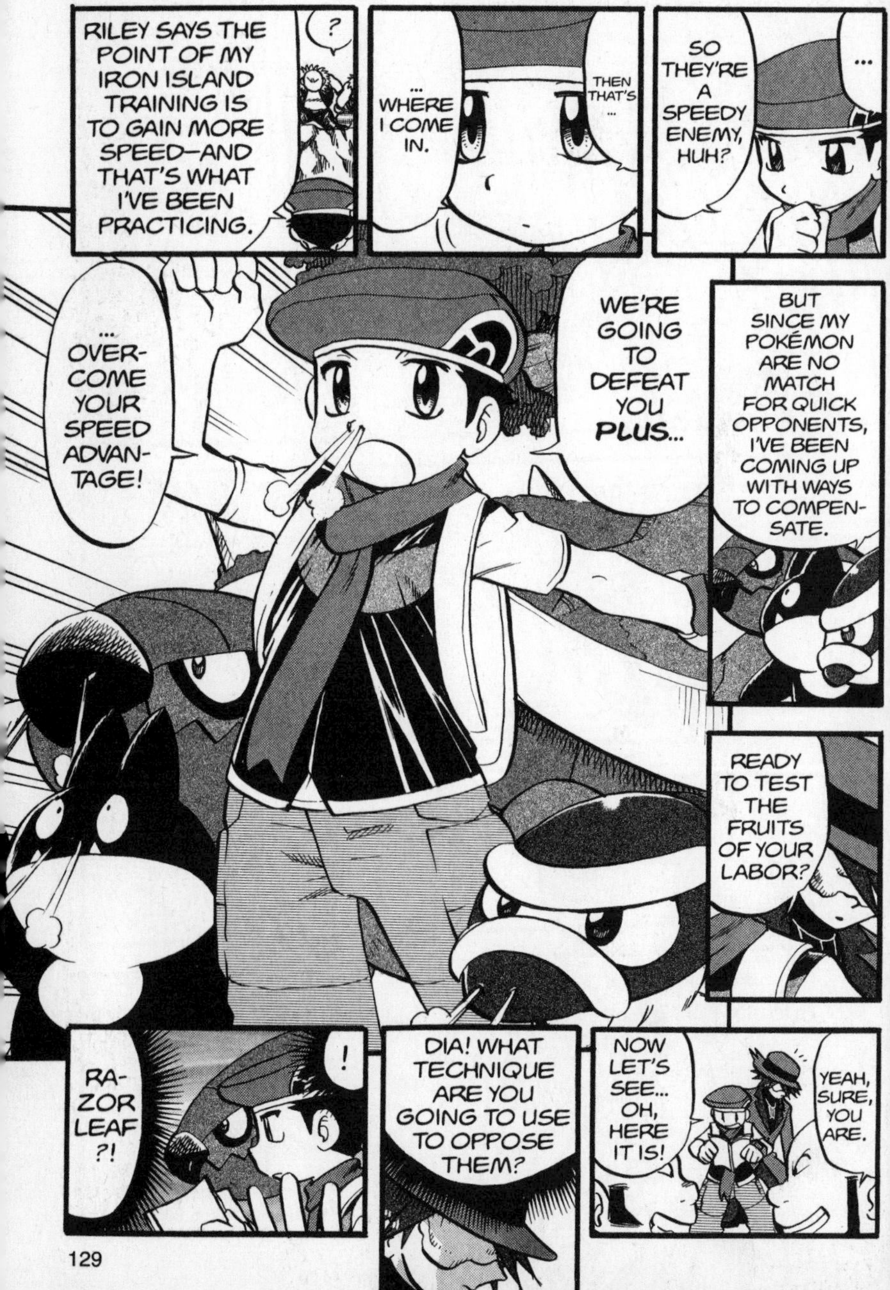
...
SO THEY'RE A SPEEDY ENEMY, HUH?
THEN THAT'S ...
... WHERE I COME IN.
?
RILEY SAYS THE POINT OF MY IRON ISLAND TRAINING IS TO GAIN MORE SPEED—AND THAT'S WHAT I'VE BEEN PRACTICING.
BUT SINCE MY POKÉMON ARE NO MATCH FOR QUICK OPPONENTS, I'VE BEEN COMING UP WITH WAYS TO COMPEN-SATE.
READY TO TEST THE FRUITS OF YOUR LABOR?
WE'RE GOING TO DEFEAT YOU **PLUS...**
... OVER-COME YOUR SPEED ADVAN-TAGE!
YEAH, SURE, YOU ARE.
NOW LET'S SEE... OH, HERE IT IS!
DIA! WHAT TECHNIQUE ARE YOU GOING TO USE TO OPPOSE THEM?
!
RA-ZOR LEAF ?!

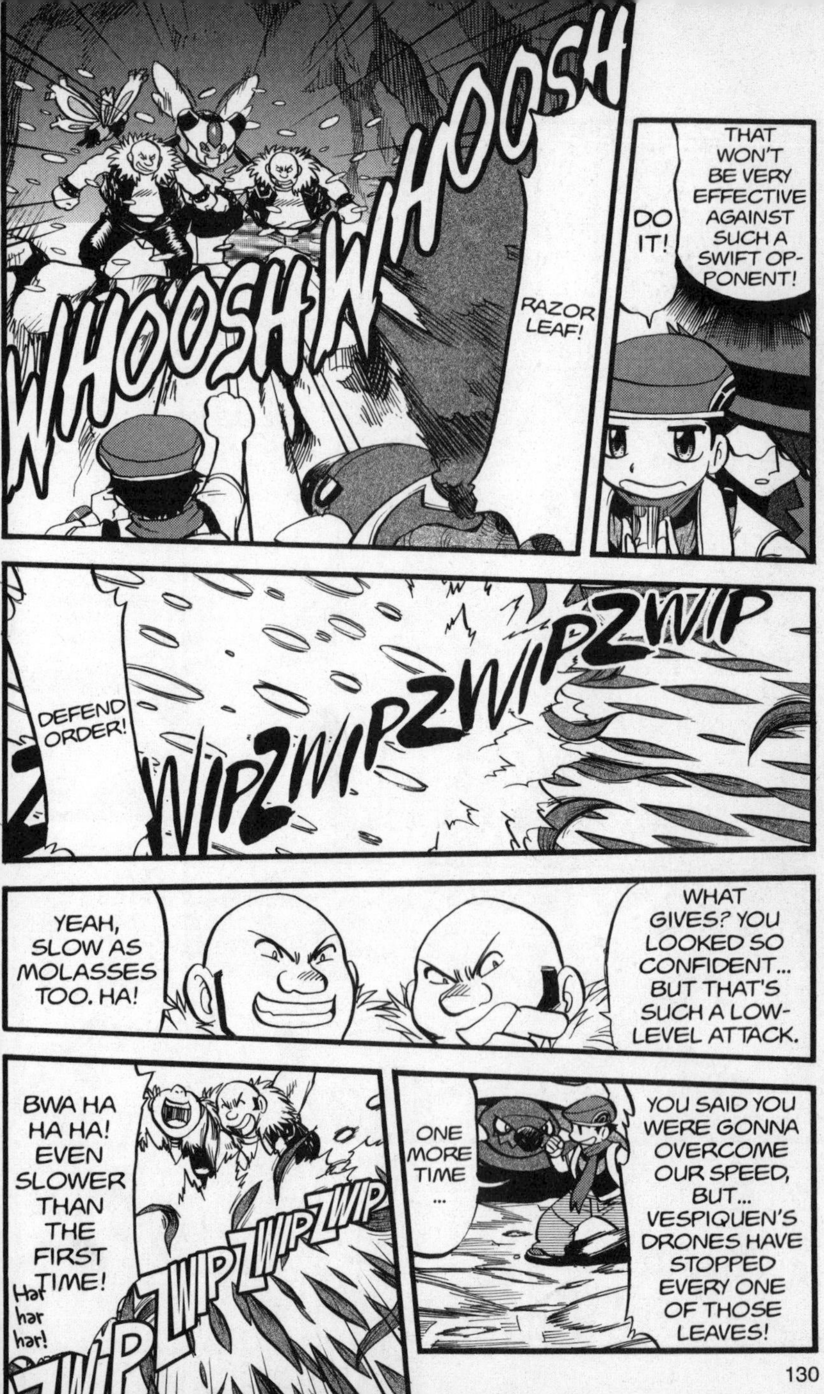
THAT WON'T BE VERY EFFECTIVE AGAINST SUCH A SWIFT OP-PONENT!
DO IT!
RAZOR LEAF!
WHOOSH
WHOOSH
ZWIP ZWIP ZWIP ZWIP
DEFEND ORDER!
WHAT GIVES? YOU LOOKED SO CONFIDENT... BUT THAT'S SUCH A LOW-LEVEL ATTACK.
YEAH, SLOW AS MOLASSES TOO. HA!
YOU SAID YOU WERE GONNA OVERCOME OUR SPEED, BUT... VESPIQUEN'S DRONES HAVE STOPPED EVERY ONE OF THOSE LEAVES!
ONE MORE TIME...
BWA HA HA HA! EVEN SLOWER THAN THE FIRST TIME!
ZWIP ZWIP ZWIP ZWIP
Har har har!

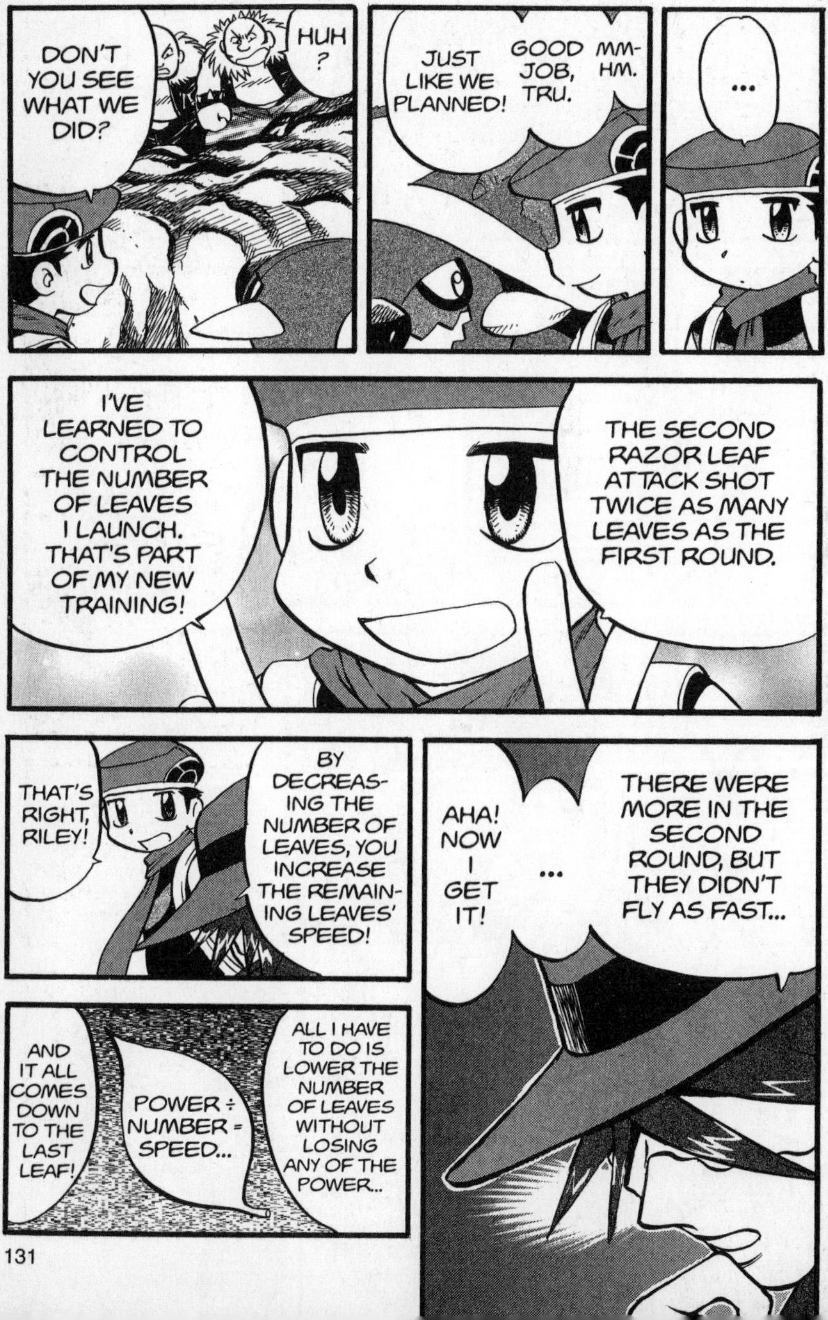
...
MM-HM.
GOOD JOB, TRU.
JUST LIKE WE PLANNED!
HUH?
DON'T YOU SEE WHAT WE DID?
THE SECOND RAZOR LEAF ATTACK SHOT TWICE AS MANY LEAVES AS THE FIRST ROUND.
I'VE LEARNED TO CONTROL THE NUMBER OF LEAVES I LAUNCH. THAT'S PART OF MY NEW TRAINING!
THERE WERE MORE IN THE SECOND ROUND, BUT THEY DIDN'T FLY AS FAST...
...
AHA! NOW I GET IT!
BY DECREAS-ING THE NUMBER OF LEAVES, YOU INCREASE THE REMAIN-ING LEAVES' SPEED!
THAT'S RIGHT, RILEY!
ALL I HAVE TO DO IS LOWER THE NUMBER OF LEAVES WITHOUT LOSING ANY OF THE POWER...
POWER ÷ NUMBER = SPEED...
AND IT ALL COMES DOWN TO THE LAST LEAF!

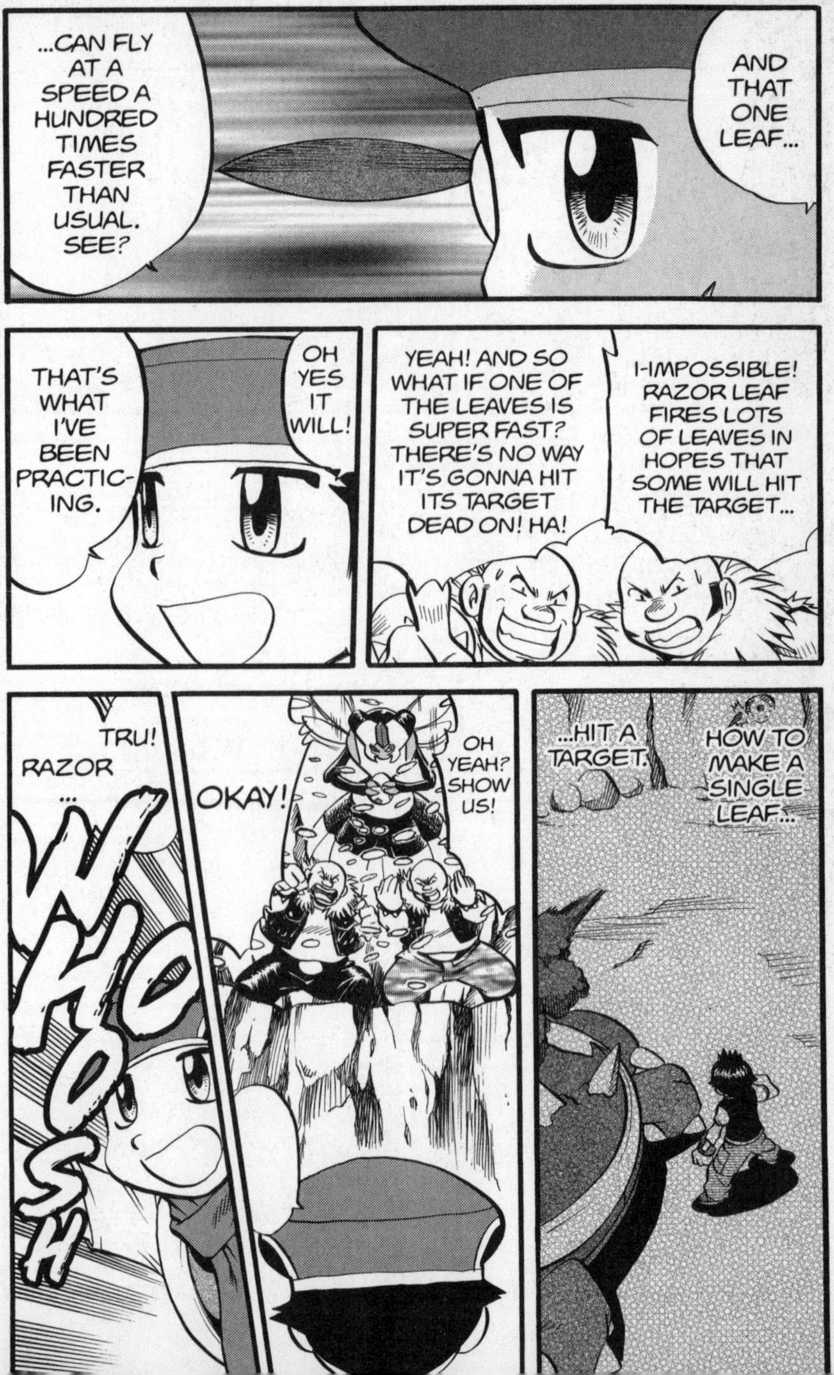
AND THAT ONE LEAF...
...CAN FLY AT A SPEED A HUNDRED TIMES FASTER THAN USUAL. SEE?
I-IMPOSSIBLE! RAZOR LEAF FIRES LOTS OF LEAVES IN HOPES THAT SOME WILL HIT THE TARGET...
YEAH! AND SO WHAT IF ONE OF THE LEAVES IS SUPER FAST? THERE'S NO WAY IT'S GONNA HIT ITS TARGET DEAD ON! HA!
OH YES IT WILL!
THAT'S WHAT I'VE BEEN PRACTICING.
HOW TO MAKE A SINGLE LEAF...
...HIT A TARGET.
OH YEAH? SHOW US!
OKAY!
TRU! RAZOR...
WHOOSH

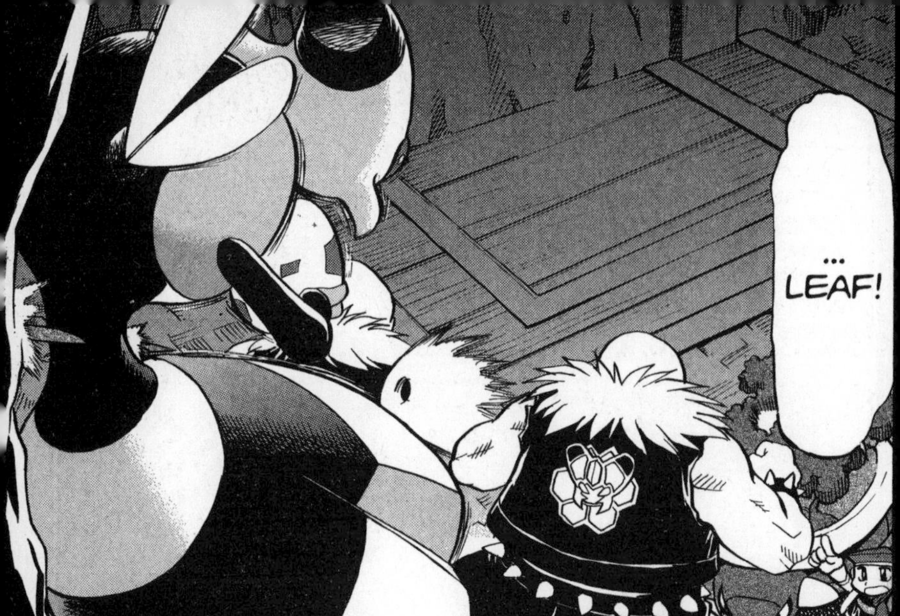
... LEAF!

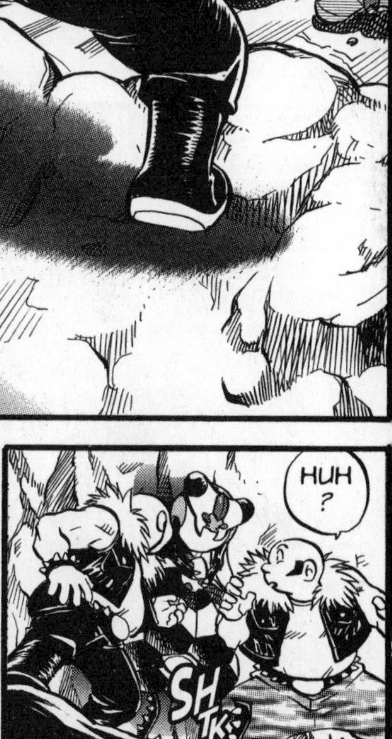
HUH ?
SHTK

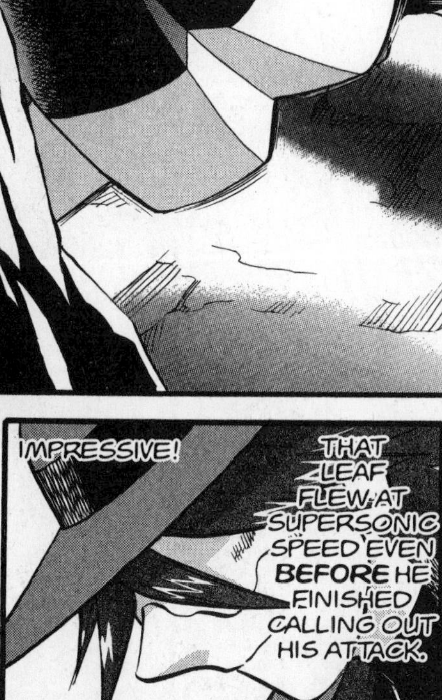
IMPRESSIVE!
THAT LEAF FLEW AT SUPERSONIC SPEED EVEN **BEFORE** HE FINISHED CALLING OUT HIS ATTACK.

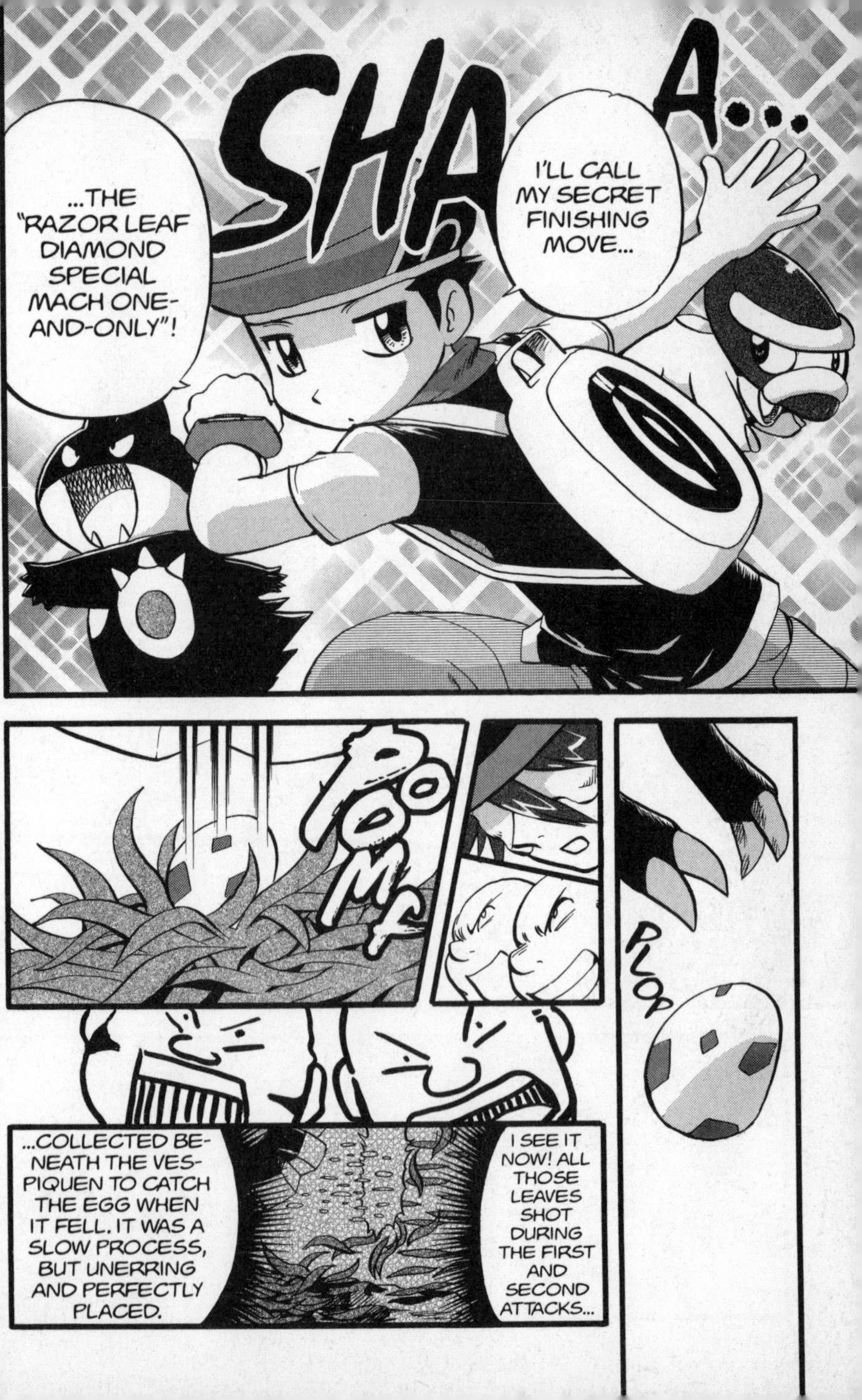
SHA A...
I'LL CALL MY SECRET FINISHING MOVE...
...THE "RAZOR LEAF DIAMOND SPECIAL MACH ONE-AND-ONLY"!
PLOP
POOMF
I SEE IT NOW! ALL THOSE LEAVES SHOT DURING THE FIRST AND SECOND ATTACKS...
...COLLECTED BENEATH THE VESPIQUEN TO CATCH THE EGG WHEN IT FELL. IT WAS A SLOW PROCESS, BUT UNERRING AND PERFECTLY PLACED.

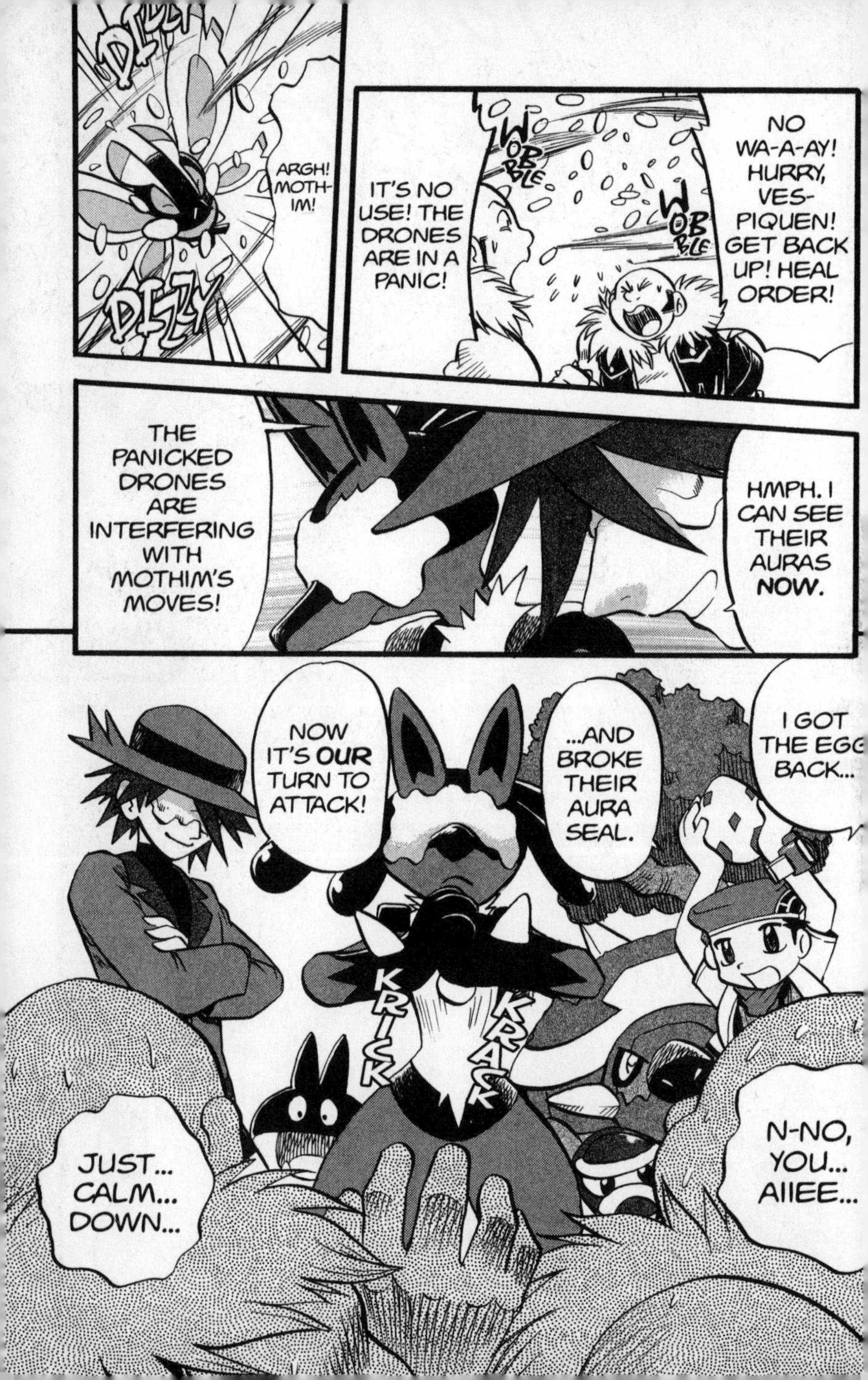
NO WA-A-AY! HURRY, VES-PIQUEN! GET BACK UP! HEAL ORDER!
WOBBLE
WOBBLE
IT'S NO USE! THE DRONES ARE IN A PANIC!
DIZZY
ARGH! MOTH-IM!
DIZZY
HMPH. I CAN SEE THEIR AURAS **NOW.**
THE PANICKED DRONES ARE INTERFERING WITH MOTHIM'S MOVES!
I GOT THE EGG BACK...
...AND BROKE THEIR AURA SEAL.
NOW IT'S **OUR** TURN TO ATTACK!
N-NO, YOU... AIIEE...
KRACK
KRICK
JUST... CALM... DOWN...

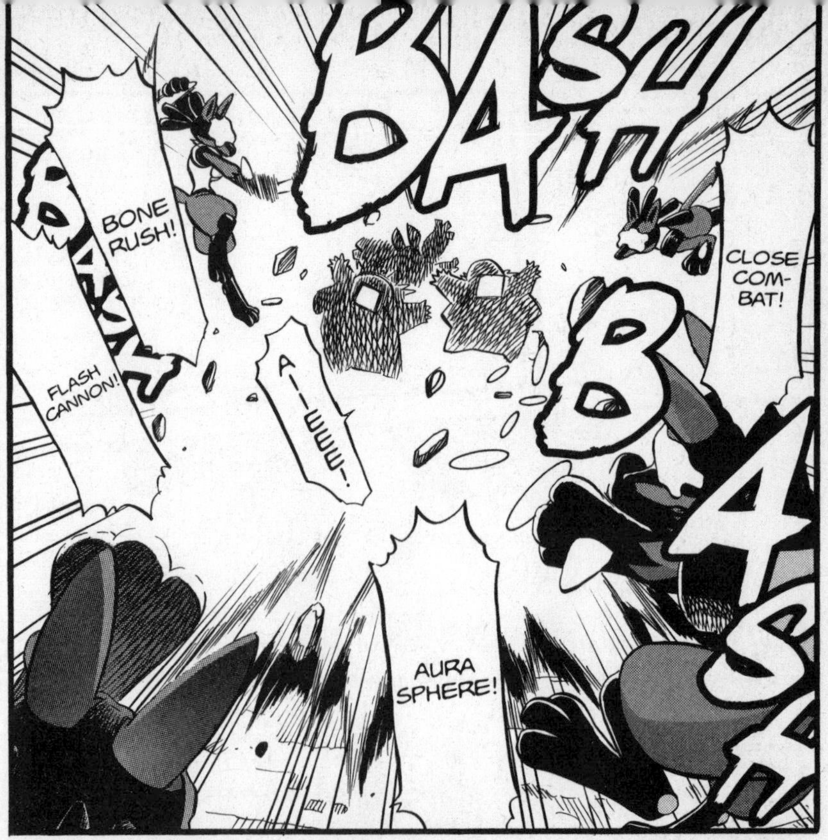
BASH
CLOSE COMBAT!
BASH
BONE RUSH!
A-IEEEE!
FLASH CANNON!
AURA SPHERE!

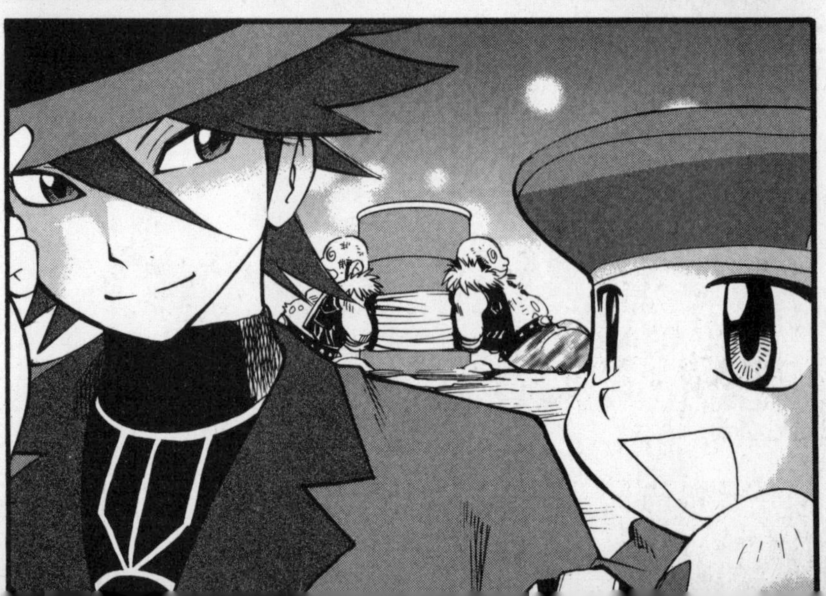

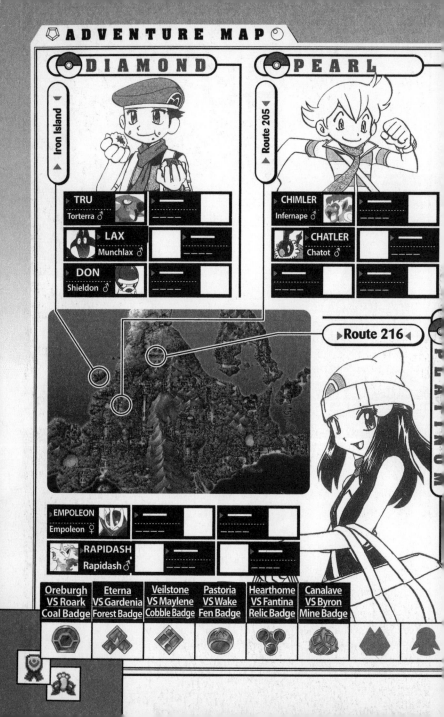

DIAMOND

▼ Iron Island ▲

PEARL

▲ Route 205 ▼

▶ **TRU**
Torterra ♂

▶ **LAX**
Munchlax ♂

▶ **DON**
Shieldon ♂

▶ **CHIMLER**
Infernape ♂

▶ **CHATLER**
Chatot ♂

▶ **Route 216** ◀

PLATINUM

▶ **EMPOLEON**
Empoleon ♀

▶ **RAPIDASH**
Rapidash ♂

Oreburgh	Eterna	Veilstone	Pastoria	Hearthome	Canalave
VS Roark	VS Gardenia	VS Maylene	VS Wake	VS Fantina	VS Byron
Coal Badge	Forest Badge	Cobble Badge	Fen Badge	Relic Badge	Mine Badge

45

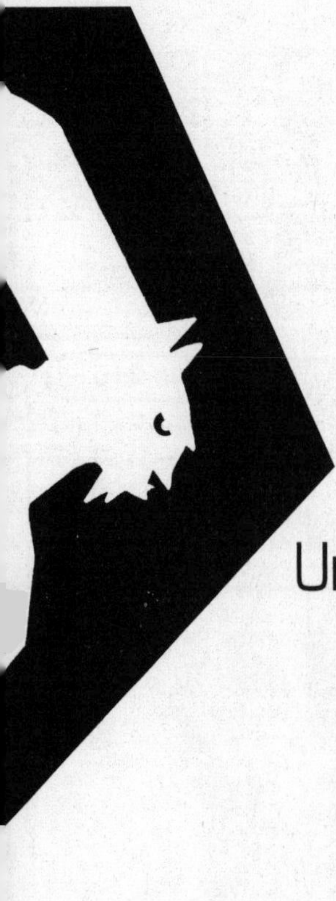

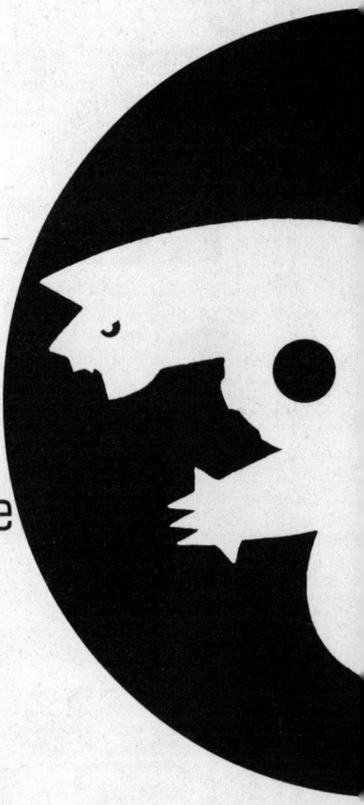

Vexing Vespiquen & Unmanageable Mothim II

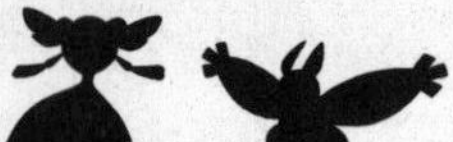

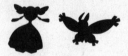

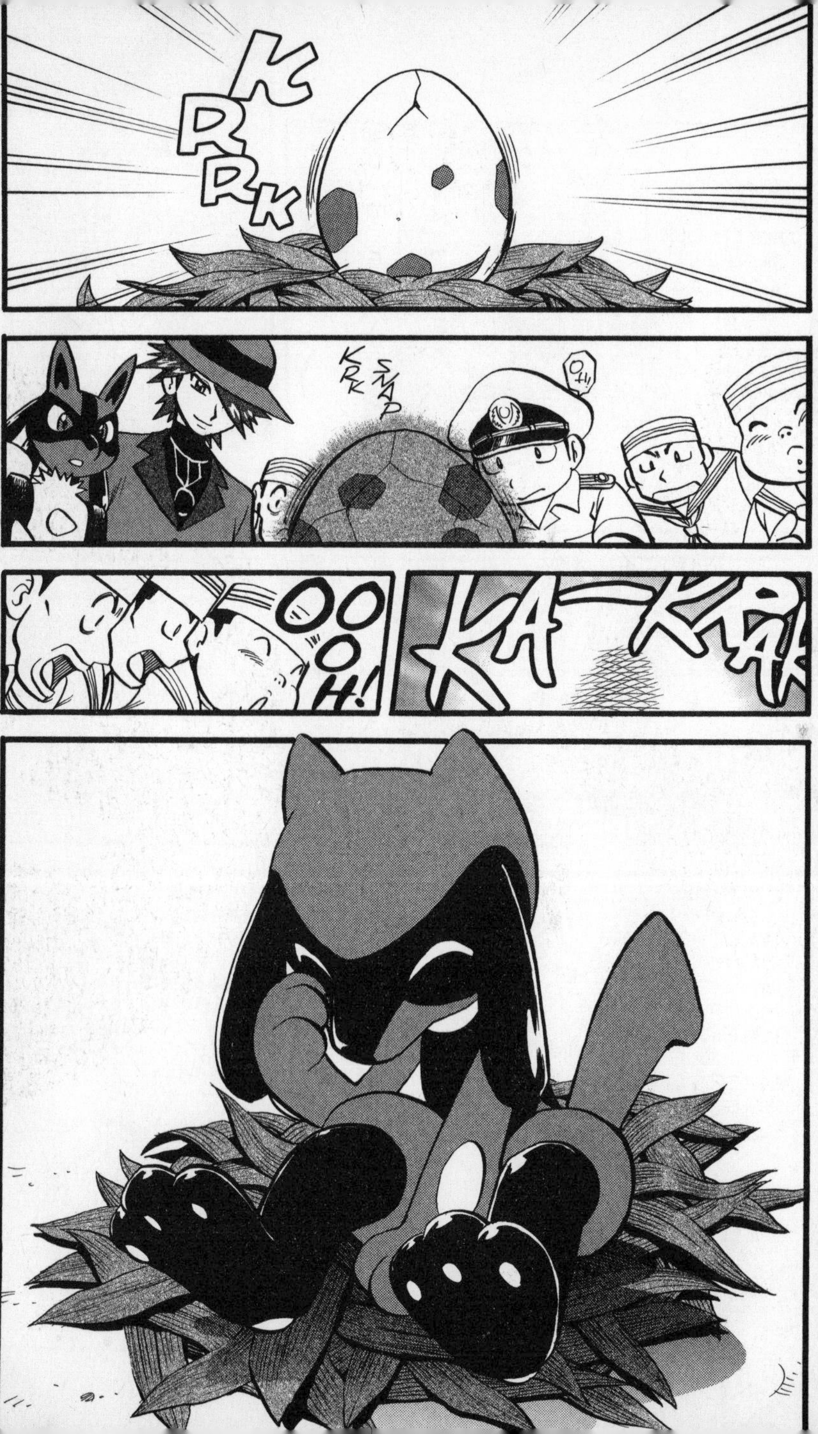
KRRK
SNAP
KRRK
Oh!!
KA-RAK
OOOH!

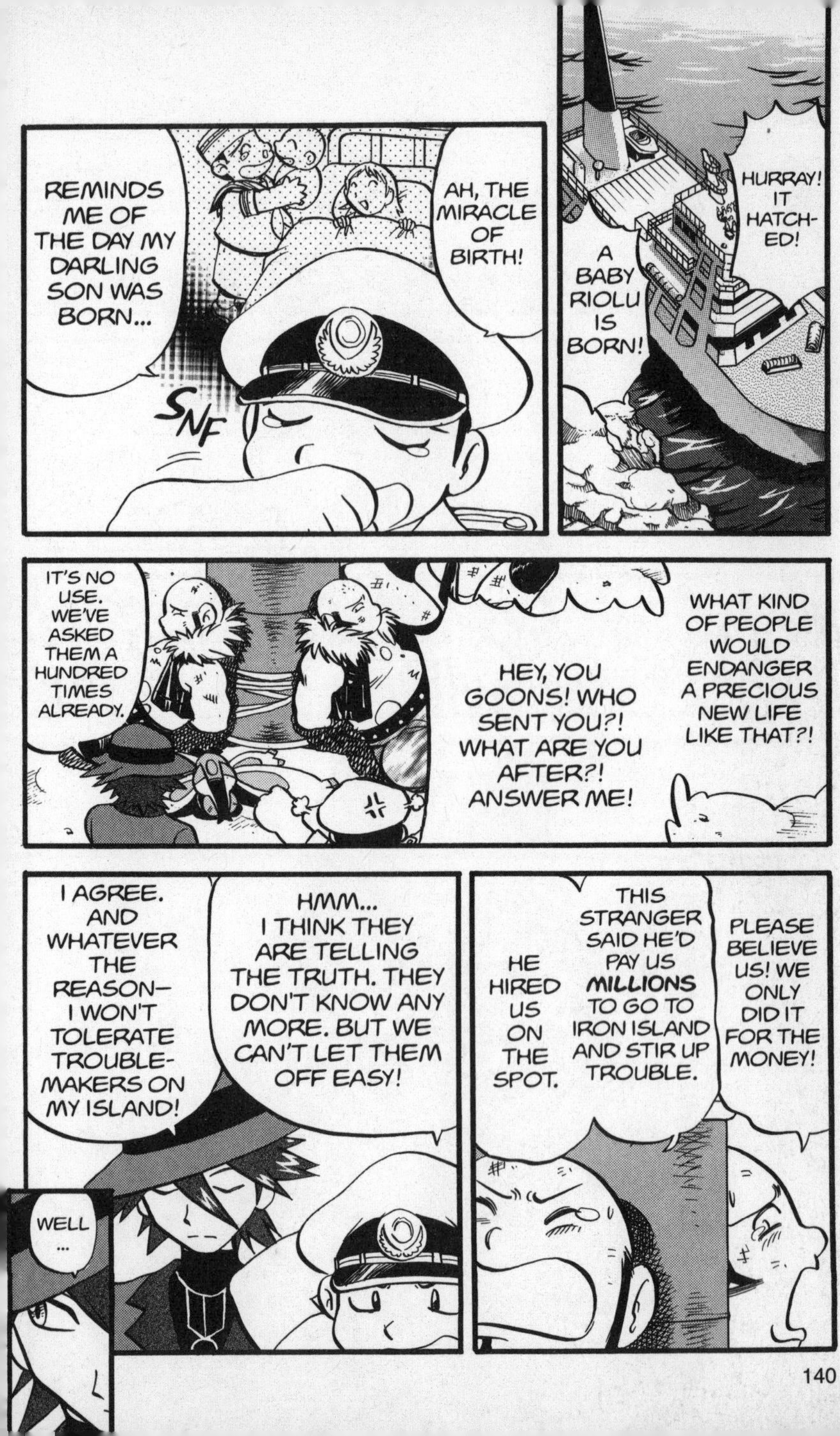
HURRAY! IT HATCHED!
A BABY RIOLU IS BORN!
AH, THE MIRACLE OF BIRTH!
REMINDS ME OF THE DAY MY DARLING SON WAS BORN...
SNF
WHAT KIND OF PEOPLE WOULD ENDANGER A PRECIOUS NEW LIFE LIKE THAT?!
HEY, YOU GOONS! WHO SENT YOU?! WHAT ARE YOU AFTER?! ANSWER ME!
IT'S NO USE. WE'VE ASKED THEM A HUNDRED TIMES ALREADY.
PLEASE BELIEVE US! WE ONLY DID IT FOR THE MONEY!
THIS STRANGER SAID HE'D PAY US **MILLIONS** TO GO TO IRON ISLAND AND STIR UP TROUBLE.
HE HIRED US ON THE SPOT.
HMM... I THINK THEY ARE TELLING THE TRUTH. THEY DON'T KNOW ANY MORE. BUT WE CAN'T LET THEM OFF EASY!
I AGREE. AND WHATEVER THE REASON— I WON'T TOLERATE TROUBLE-MAKERS ON MY ISLAND!
WELL ...

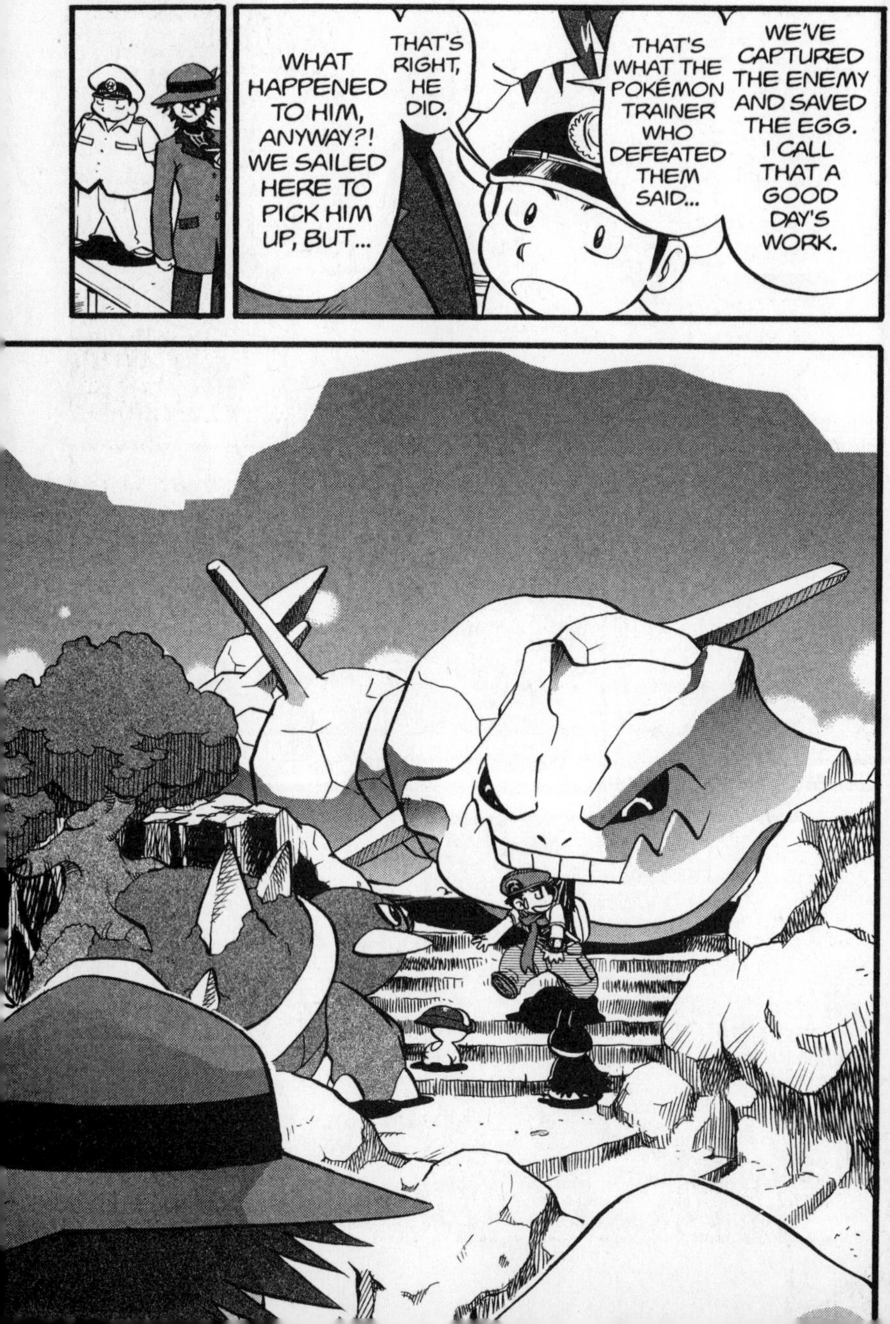
WE'VE CAPTURED THE ENEMY AND SAVED THE EGG. I CALL THAT A GOOD DAY'S WORK.
THAT'S WHAT THE POKÉMON TRAINER WHO DEFEATED THEM SAID...
THAT'S RIGHT, HE DID.
WHAT HAPPENED TO HIM, ANYWAY?! WE SAILED HERE TO PICK HIM UP, BUT...

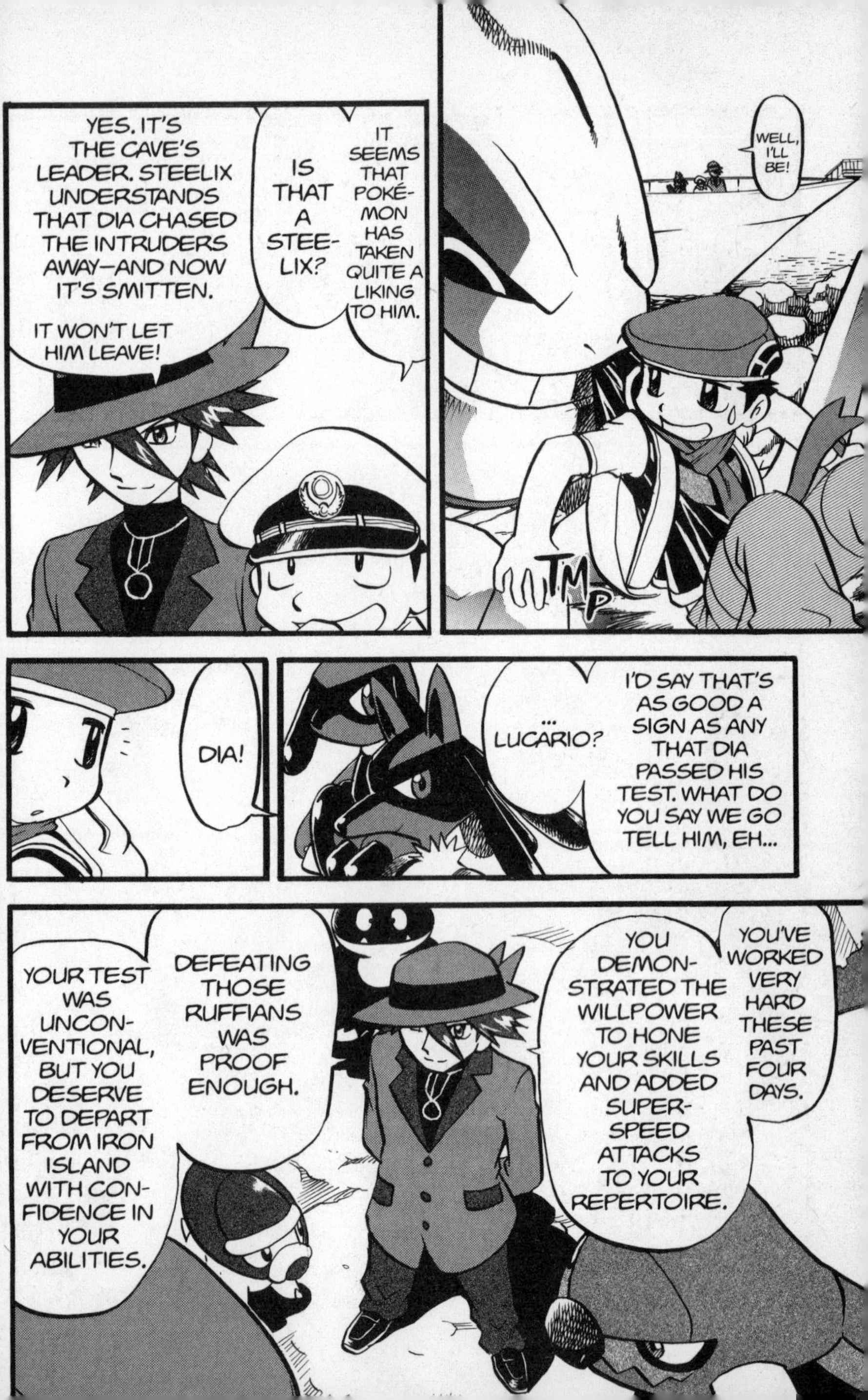
WELL, I'LL BE!
TMP
IT SEEMS THAT POKÉMON HAS TAKEN QUITE A LIKING TO HIM.
IS THAT A STEELIX?
YES. IT'S THE CAVE'S LEADER. STEELIX UNDERSTANDS THAT DIA CHASED THE INTRUDERS AWAY—AND NOW IT'S SMITTEN.
IT WON'T LET HIM LEAVE!
I'D SAY THAT'S AS GOOD A SIGN AS ANY THAT DIA PASSED HIS TEST. WHAT DO YOU SAY WE GO TELL HIM, EH...
... LUCARIO?
DIA!
YOU'VE WORKED VERY HARD THESE PAST FOUR DAYS.
YOU DEMONSTRATED THE WILLPOWER TO HONE YOUR SKILLS AND ADDED SUPER-SPEED ATTACKS TO YOUR REPERTOIRE.
DEFEATING THOSE RUFFIANS WAS PROOF ENOUGH.
YOUR TEST WAS UNCONVENTIONAL, BUT YOU DESERVE TO DEPART FROM IRON ISLAND WITH CONFIDENCE IN YOUR ABILITIES.

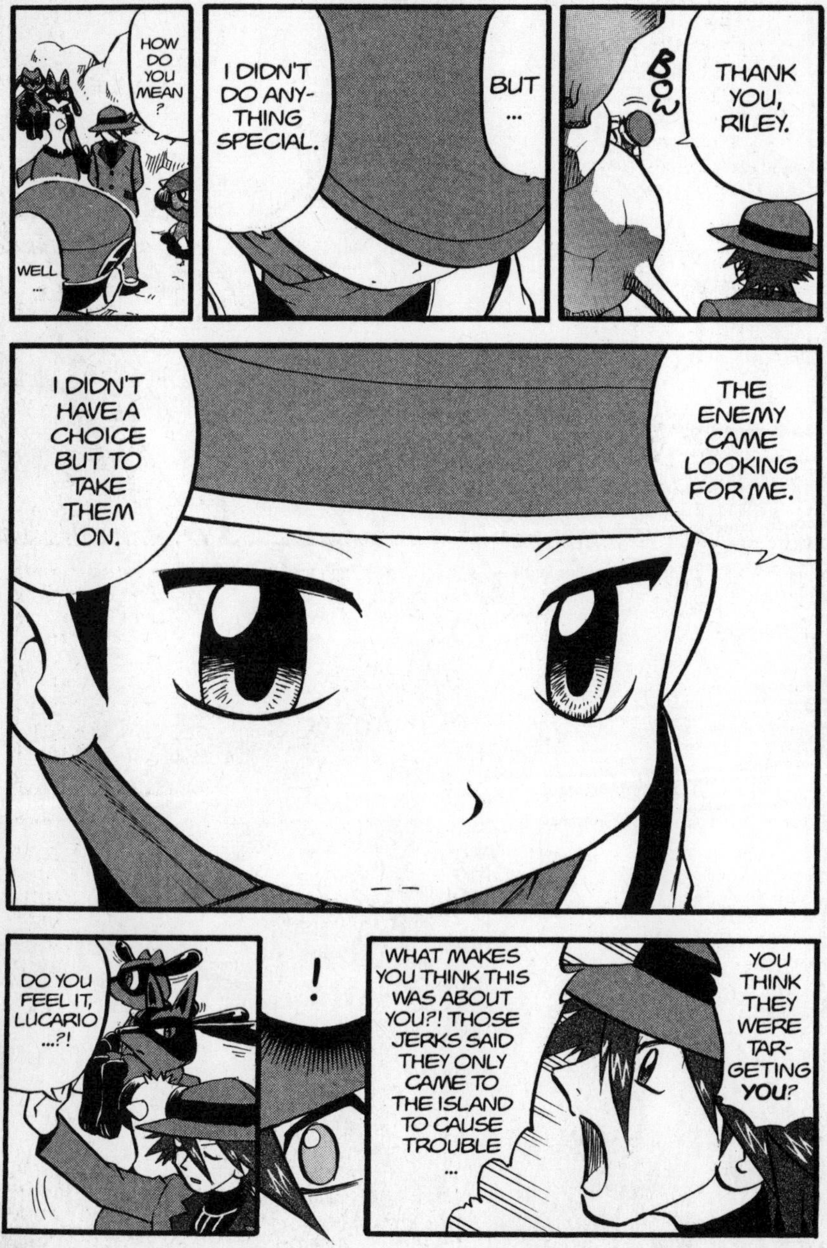
THANK YOU, RILEY.
BOW
BUT ...
I DIDN'T DO ANY-THING SPECIAL.
HOW DO YOU MEAN ?
WELL ...
THE ENEMY CAME LOOKING FOR ME.
I DIDN'T HAVE A CHOICE BUT TO TAKE THEM ON.
YOU THINK THEY WERE TAR-GETING YOU?
WHAT MAKES YOU THINK THIS WAS ABOUT YOU?! THOSE JERKS SAID THEY ONLY CAME TO THE ISLAND TO CAUSE TROUBLE ...
!
DO YOU FEEL IT, LUCARIO ...?!

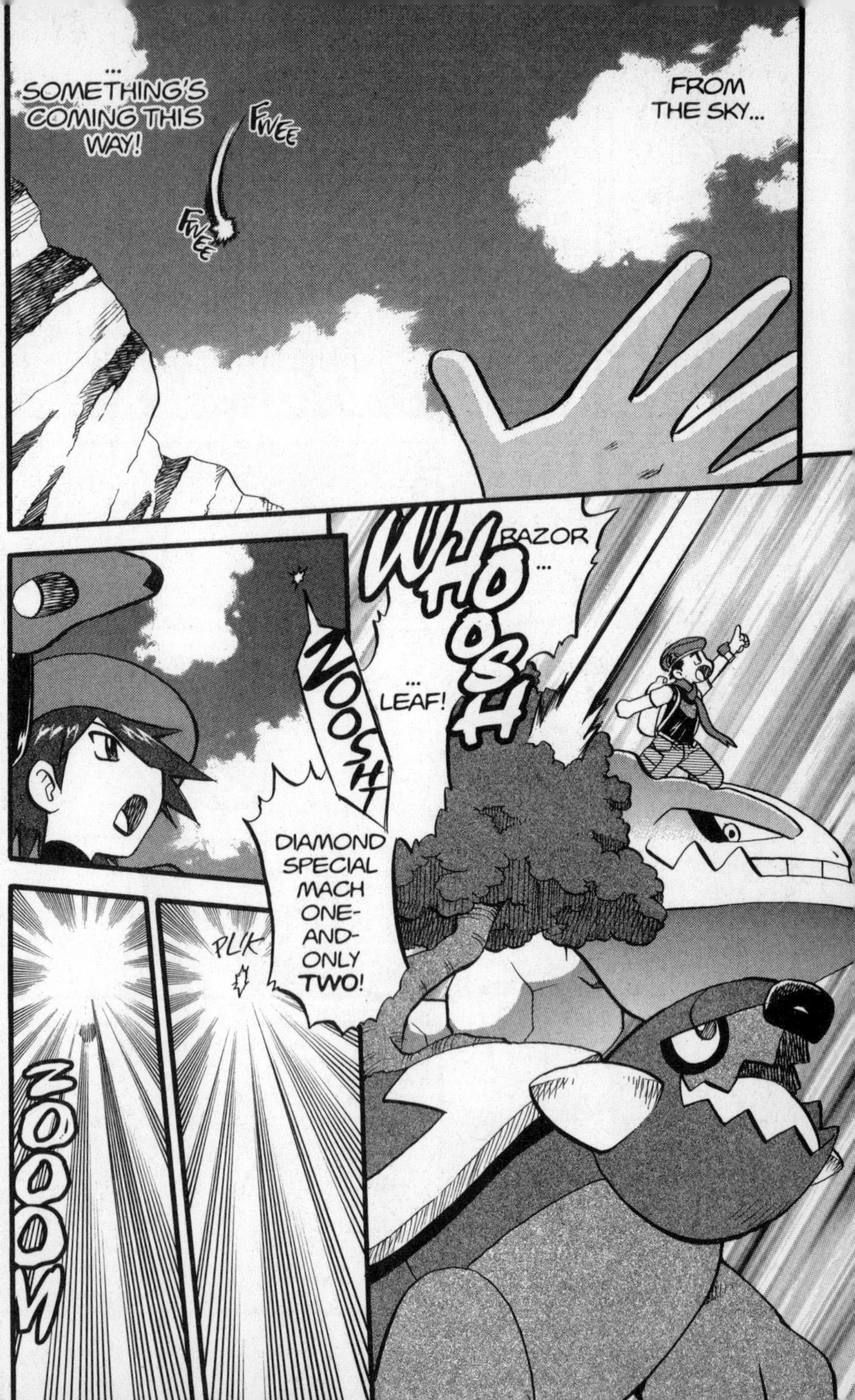
FROM THE SKY...
...SOMETHING'S COMING THIS WAY!
FWEE
FWEE
RAZOR...
WHOOSH
...LEAF!
WOOSH
DIAMOND SPECIAL MACH ONE-AND-ONLY TWO!
PLIK
ZOOOOM

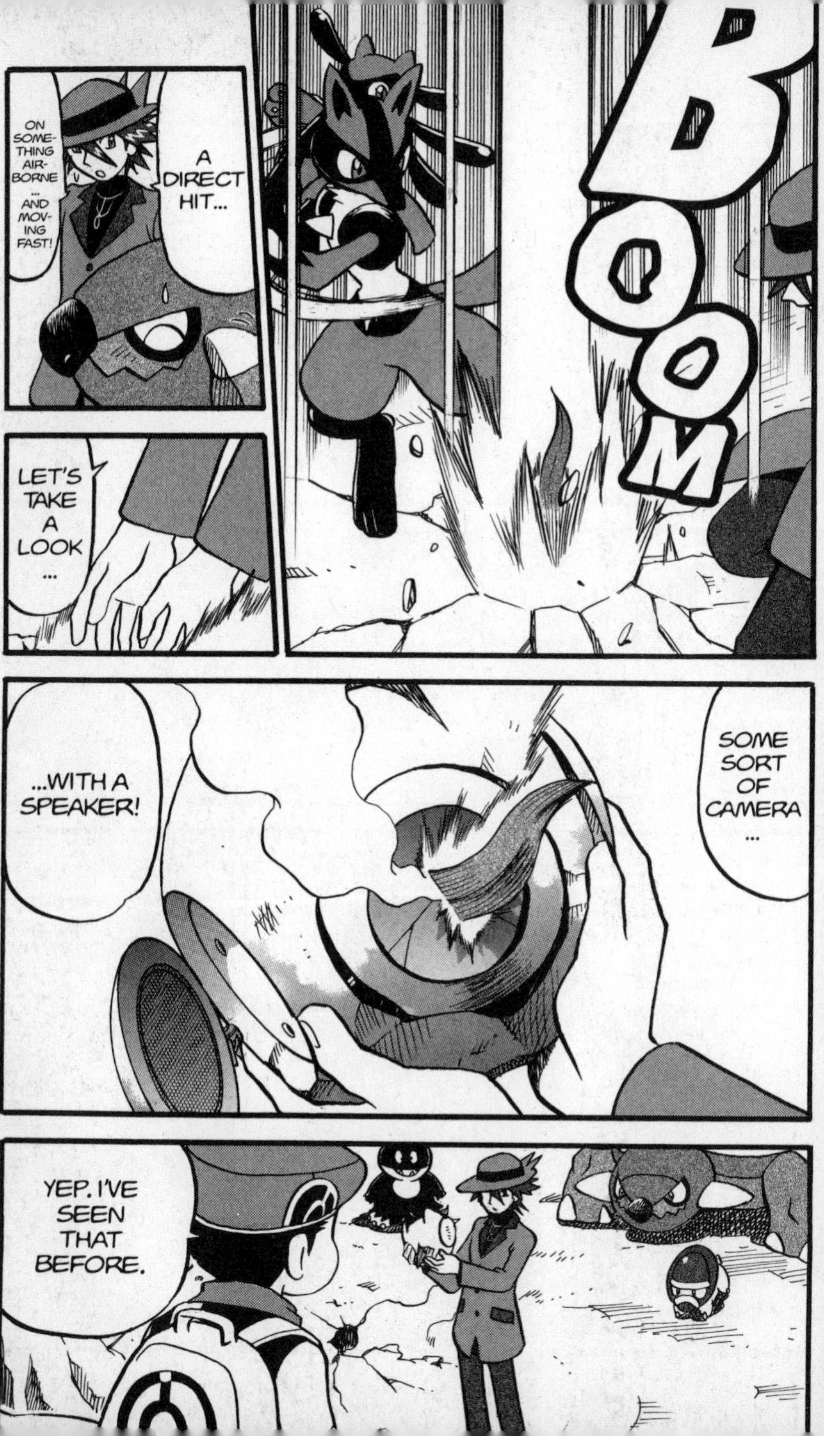
BOOM
A DIRECT HIT...
ON SOMETHING AIRBORNE ... AND MOVING FAST!
LET'S TAKE A LOOK ...
SOME SORT OF CAMERA ...
...WITH A SPEAKER!
YEP. I'VE SEEN THAT BEFORE.

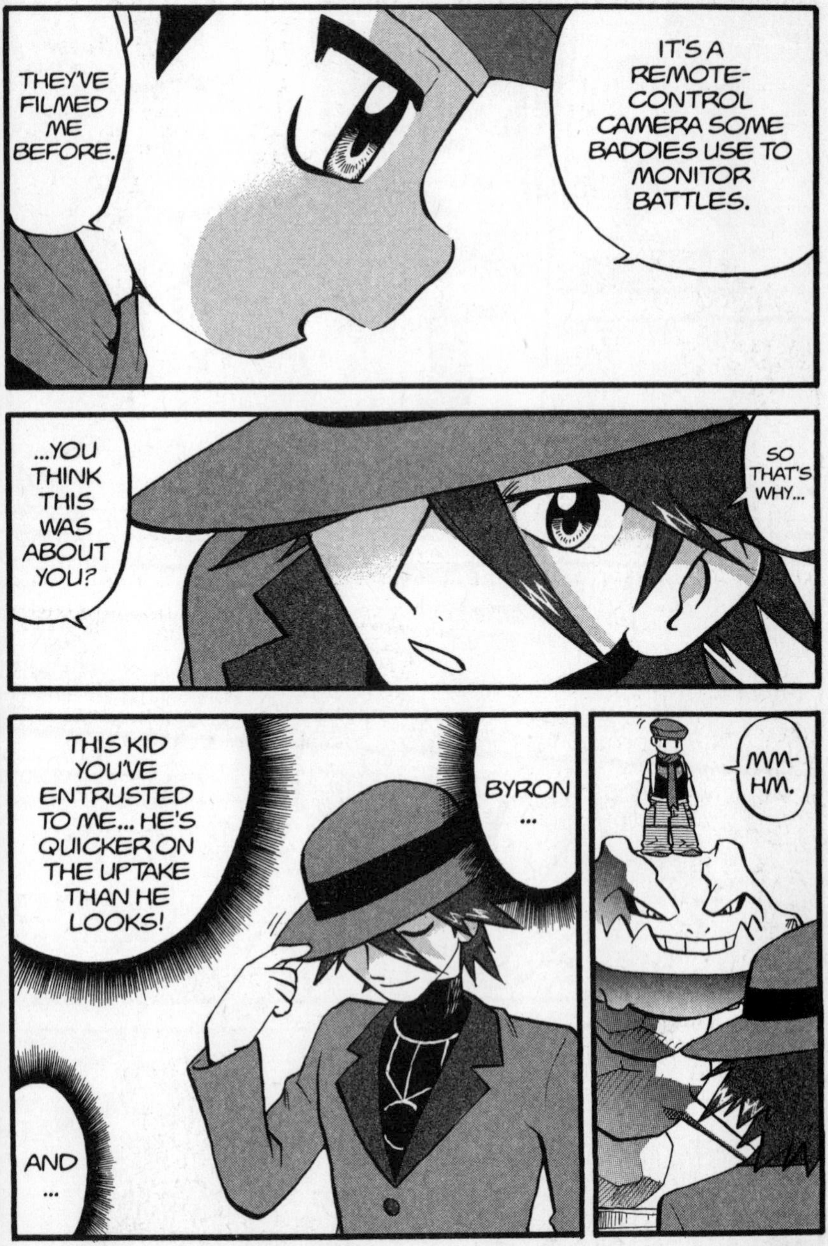
IT'S A REMOTE-CONTROL CAMERA SOME BADDIES USE TO MONITOR BATTLES.
THEY'VE FILMED ME BEFORE.
SO THAT'S WHY...
...YOU THINK THIS WAS ABOUT YOU?
MM-HM.
BYRON...
THIS KID YOU'VE ENTRUSTED TO ME... HE'S QUICKER ON THE UPTAKE THAN HE LOOKS!
AND...

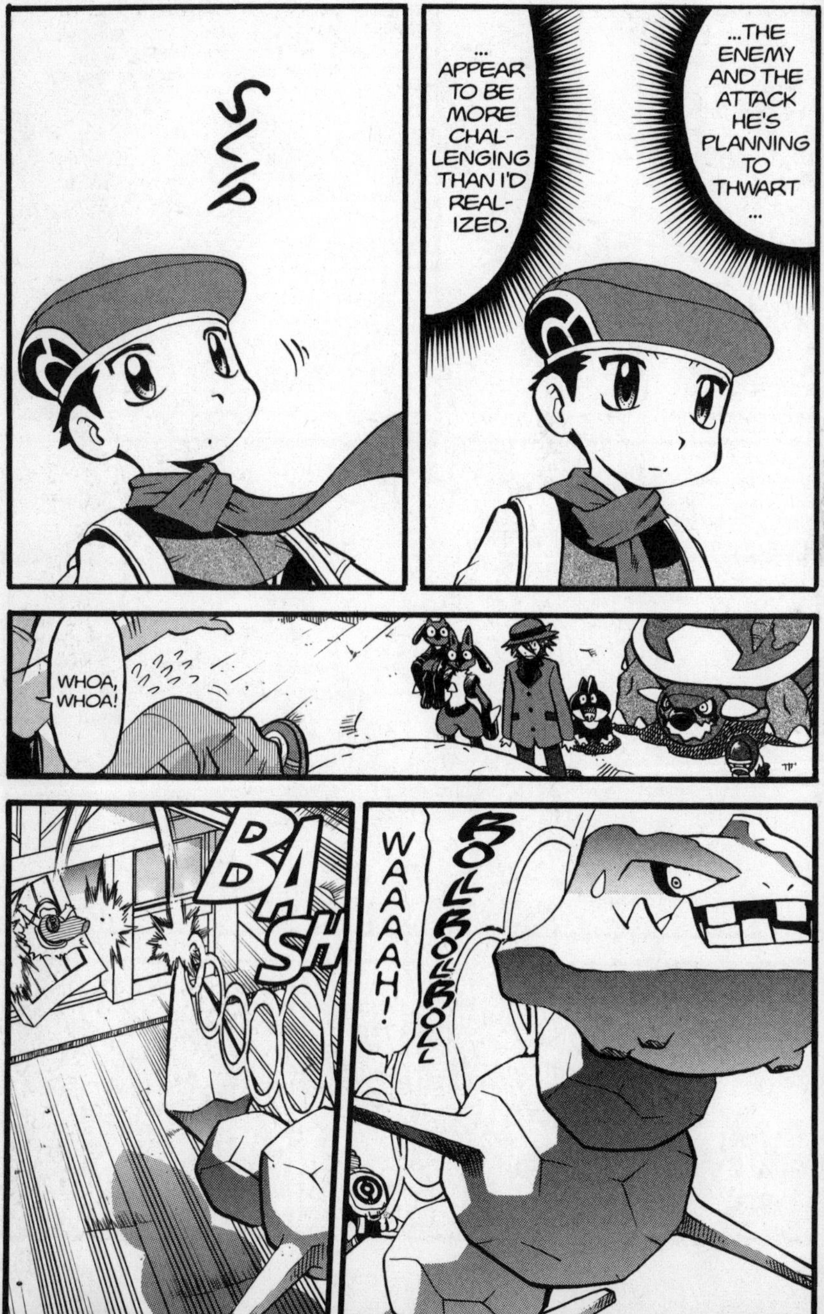
...THE ENEMY AND THE ATTACK HE'S PLANNING TO THWART ...
... APPEAR TO BE MORE CHAL-LENGING THAN I'D REAL-IZED.
SLIP
WHOA, WHOA!
ROLLROLLROLL
WAAAAAH!
BASH

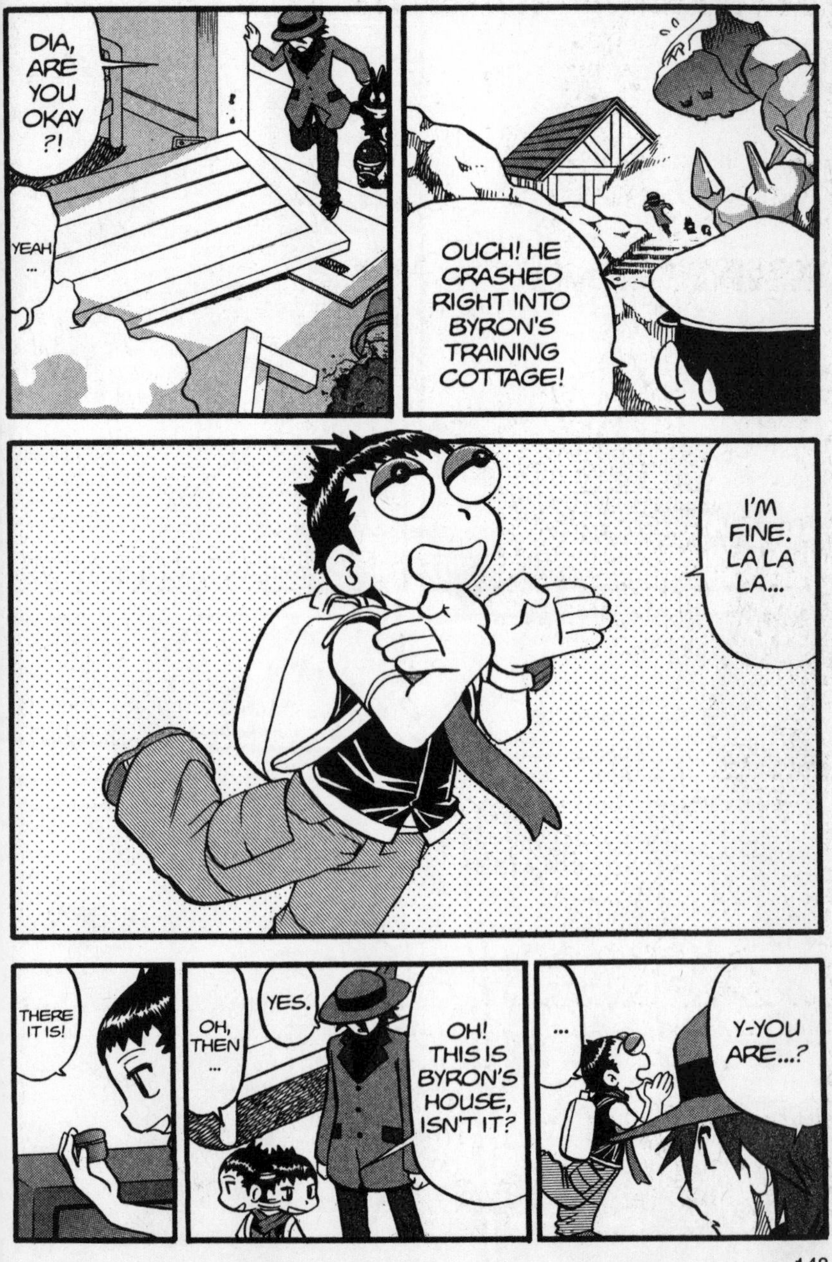
OUCH! HE CRASHED RIGHT INTO BYRON'S TRAINING COTTAGE!
DIA, ARE YOU OKAY ?!
YEAH ...
I'M FINE. LA LA LA...
Y-YOU ARE...?
...
OH! THIS IS BYRON'S HOUSE, ISN'T IT?
YES.
OH, THEN ...
THERE IT IS!

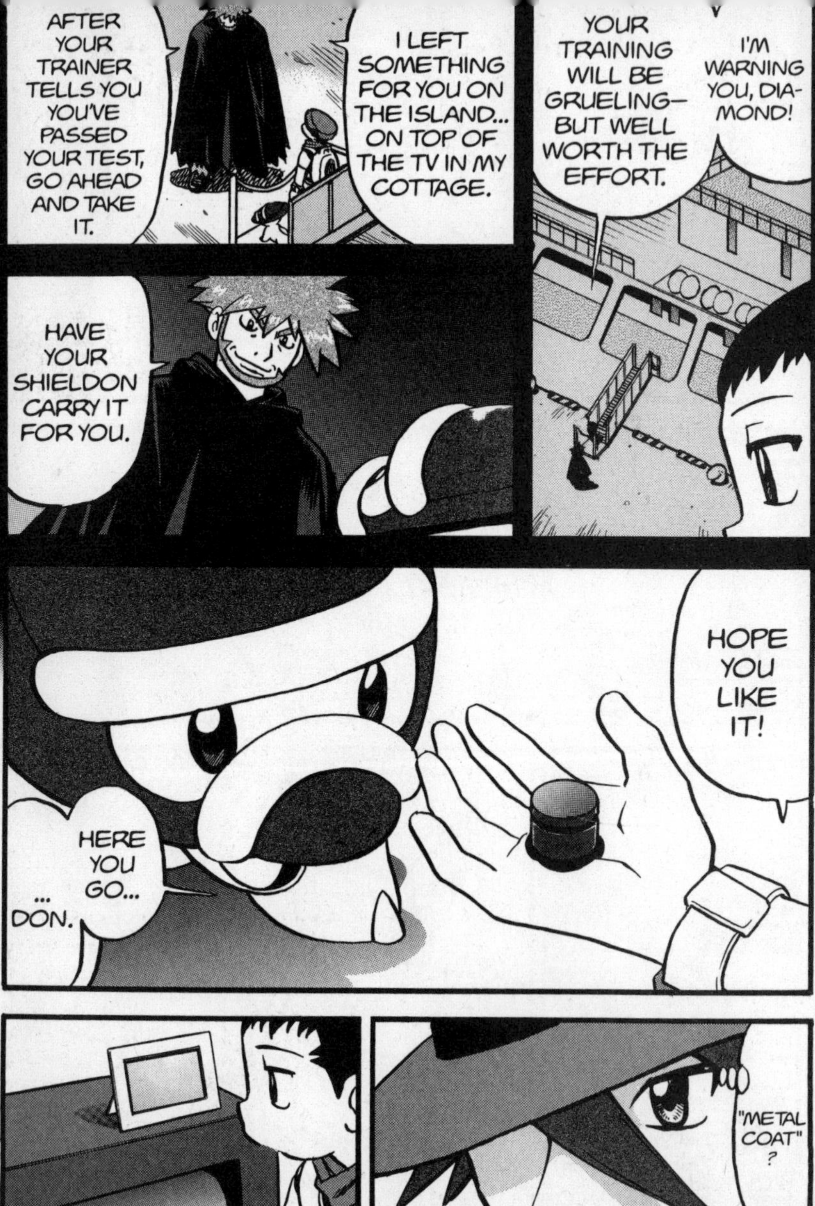
I'M WARNING YOU, DIAMOND!
YOUR TRAINING WILL BE GRUELING— BUT WELL WORTH THE EFFORT.
I LEFT SOMETHING FOR YOU ON THE ISLAND... ON TOP OF THE TV IN MY COTTAGE.
AFTER YOUR TRAINER TELLS YOU YOU'VE PASSED YOUR TEST, GO AHEAD AND TAKE IT.
HAVE YOUR SHIELDON CARRY IT FOR YOU.
HOPE YOU LIKE IT!
HERE YOU GO...
... DON.
"METAL COAT" ?

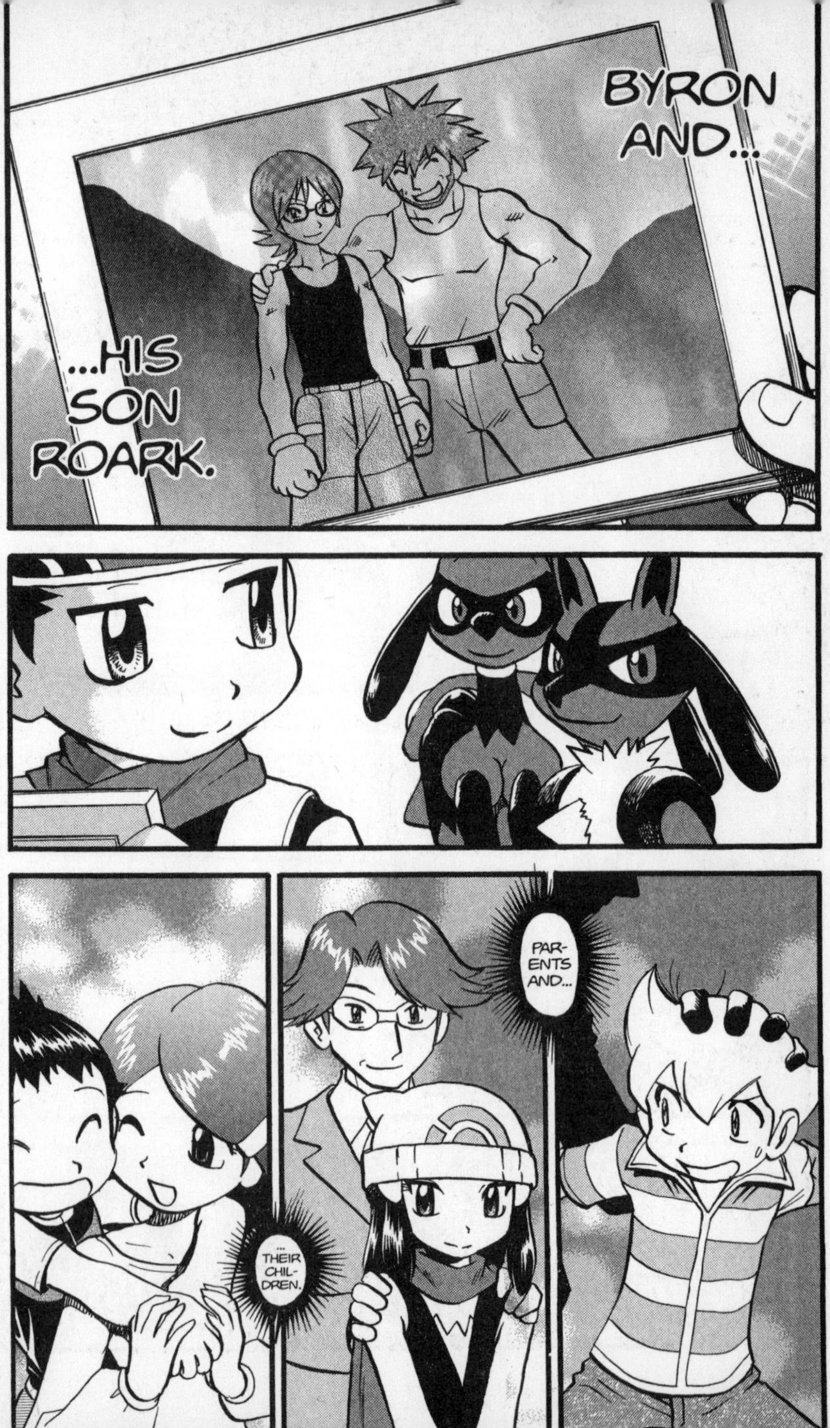
BYRON AND...
...HIS SON ROARK.
PAR-ENTS AND...
...THEIR CHIL-DREN.

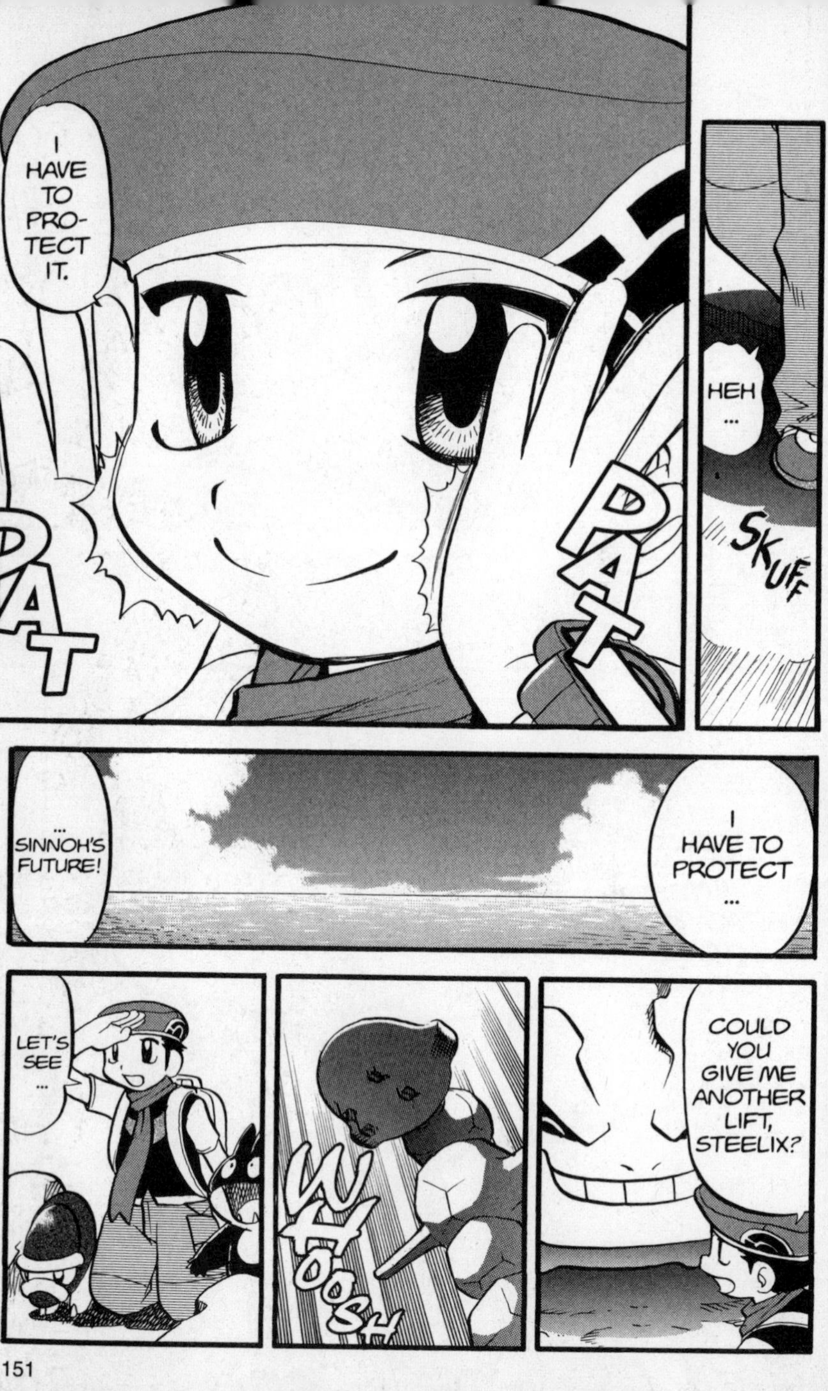
HEH ...
SKUFF
I HAVE TO PROTECT IT.
PAT
PAT
I HAVE TO PROTECT ...
... SINNOH'S FUTURE!
COULD YOU GIVE ME ANOTHER LIFT, STEELIX?
WHOOSH
LET'S SEE ...

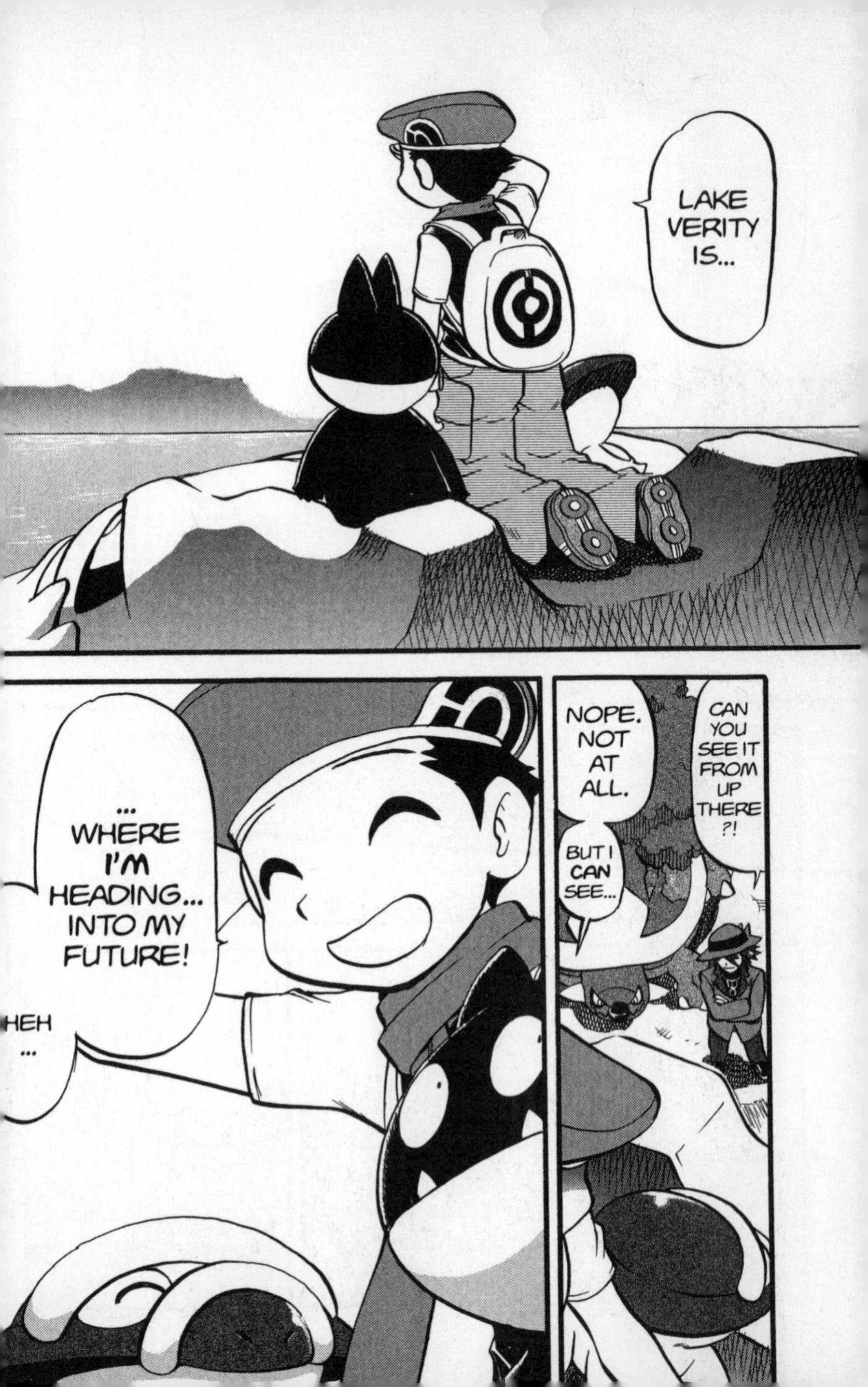
LAKE VERITY IS...
CAN YOU SEE IT FROM UP THERE?!
NOPE. NOT AT ALL.
BUT I CAN SEE...
... WHERE I'M HEADING... INTO MY FUTURE!
HEH ...

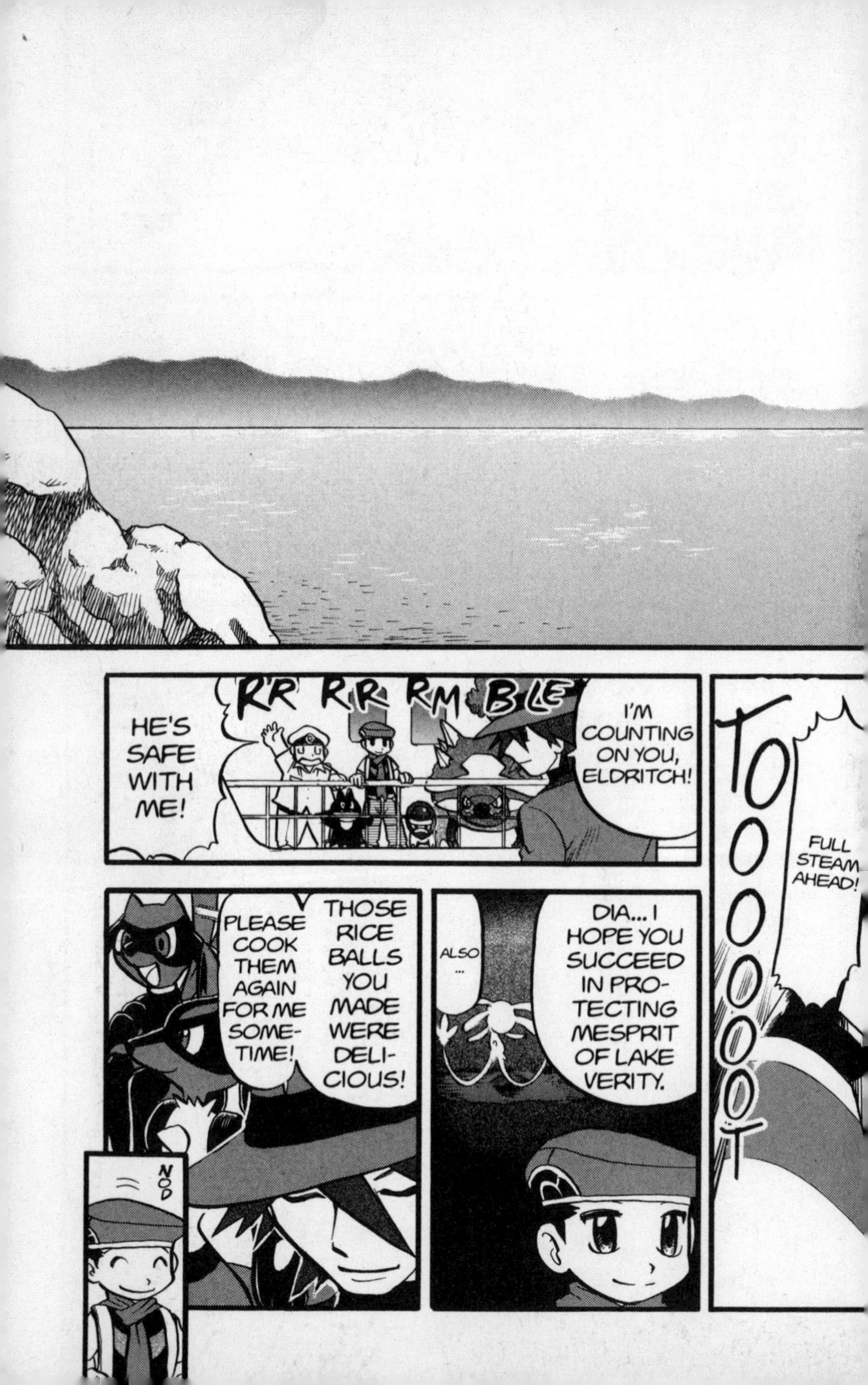
TOOOOOOT
FULL STEAM AHEAD!
I'M COUNTING ON YOU, ELDRITCH!
RRRRRMBLE
HE'S SAFE WITH ME!
DIA... I HOPE YOU SUCCEED IN PROTECTING MESPRIT OF LAKE VERITY.
ALSO...
THOSE RICE BALLS YOU MADE WERE DELICIOUS!
PLEASE COOK THEM AGAIN FOR ME SOMETIME!
NOD

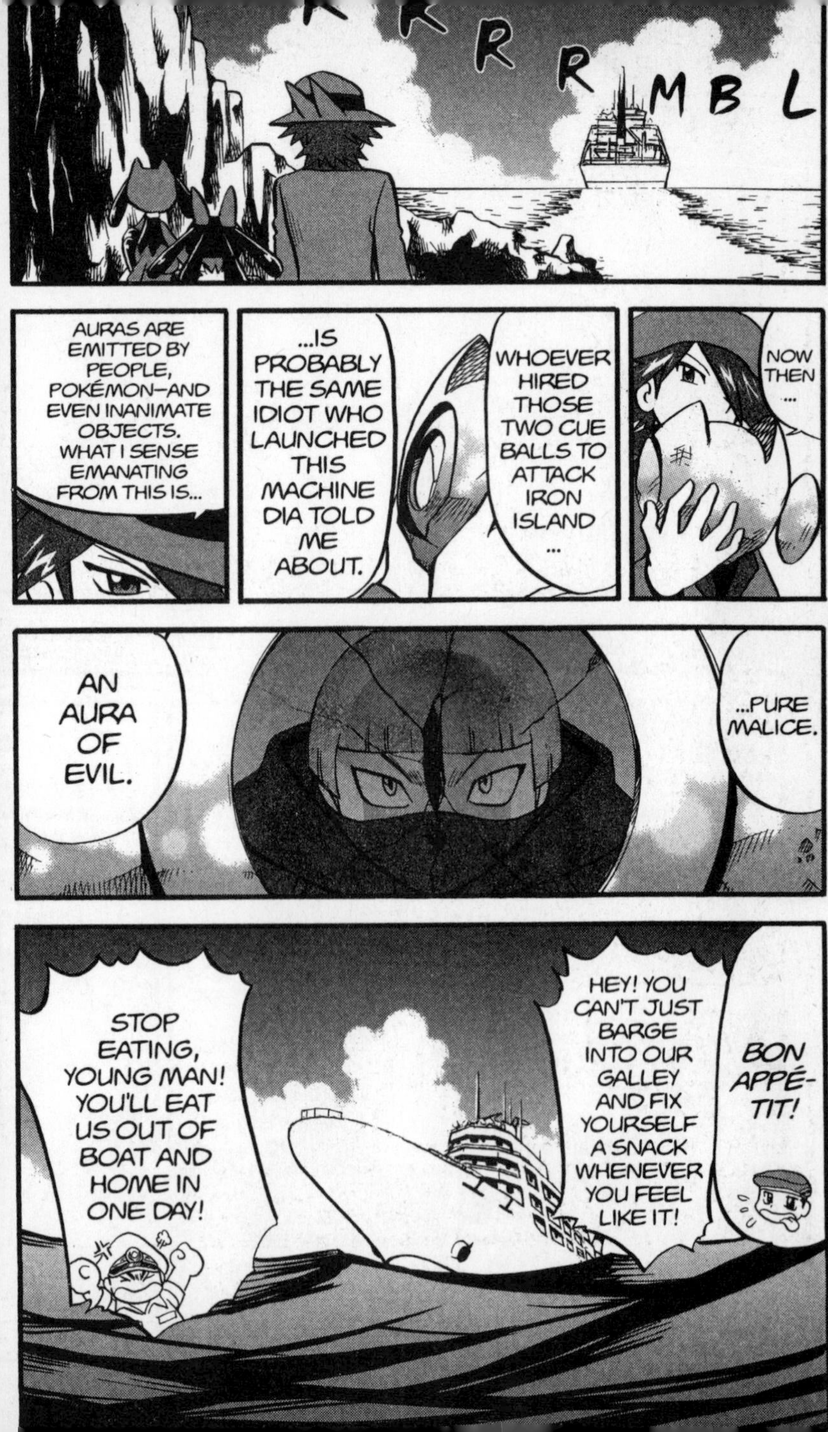

RRMBL
NOW THEN ...
WHOEVER HIRED THOSE TWO CUE BALLS TO ATTACK IRON ISLAND ...
...IS PROBABLY THE SAME IDIOT WHO LAUNCHED THIS MACHINE DIA TOLD ME ABOUT.
AURAS ARE EMITTED BY PEOPLE, POKÉMON—AND EVEN INANIMATE OBJECTS. WHAT I SENSE EMANATING FROM THIS IS...
...PURE MALICE.
AN AURA OF EVIL.
BON APPÉ-TIT!
HEY! YOU CAN'T JUST BARGE INTO OUR GALLEY AND FIX YOURSELF A SNACK WHENEVER YOU FEEL LIKE IT!
STOP EATING, YOUNG MAN! YOU'LL EAT US OUT OF BOAT AND HOME IN ONE DAY!

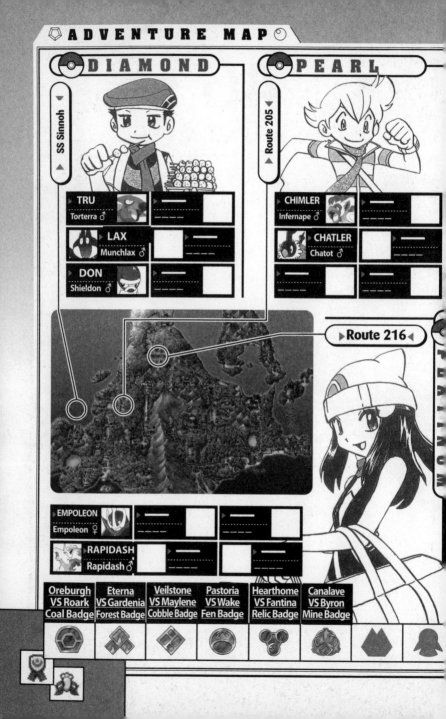

DIAMOND

SS Sinnoh

TRU
Torterra ♂

▶ **LAX**
Munchlax ♂

DON
Shieldon ♂

PEARL

Route 205

CHIMLER
Infernape ♂

CHATLER
Chatot ♂

▶Route 216◀

P L A T I N U M

▶ **EMPOLEON**
Empoleon ♀

RAPIDASH
Rapidash ♂

| Oreburgh VS Roark Coal Badge | Eterna VS Gardenia Forest Badge | Veilstone VS Maylene Cobble Badge | Pastoria VS Wake Fen Badge | Hearthome VS Fantina Relic Badge | Canalave VS Byron Mine Badge | | |

46

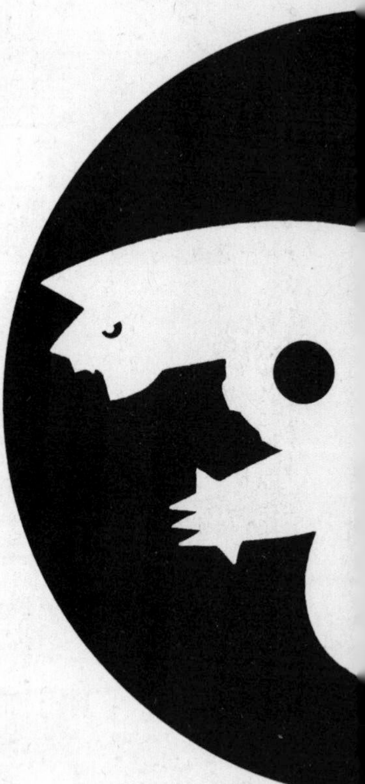

Winning Over Wingull

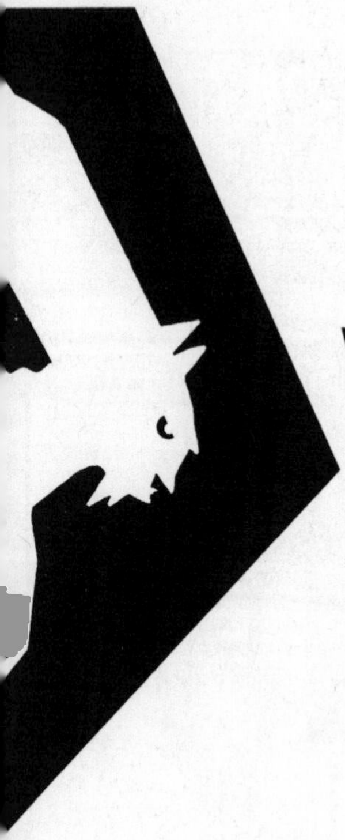

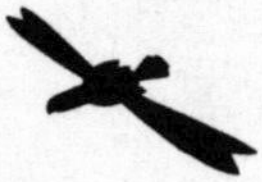

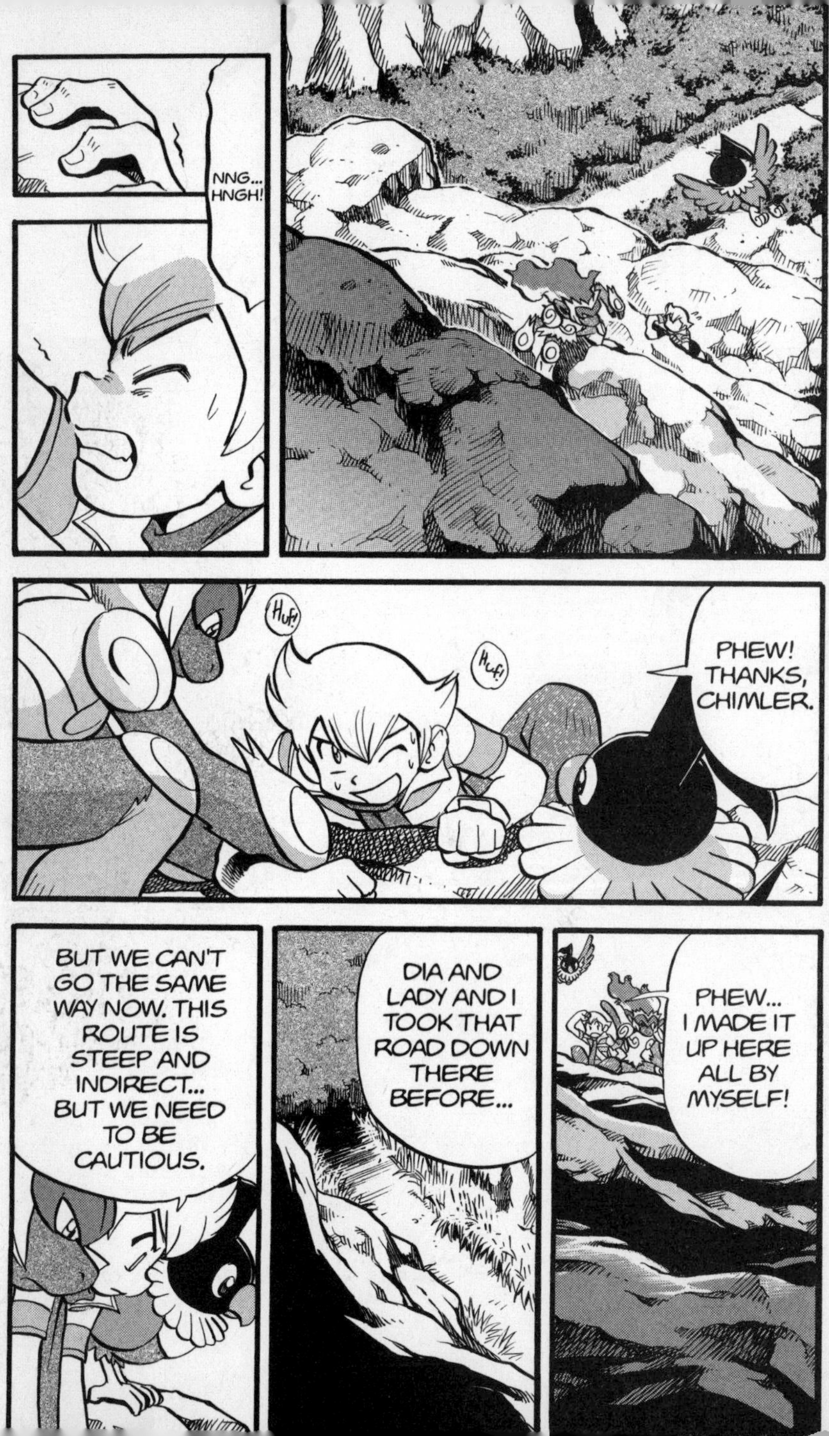
NNG... HNGH!
Huf!
Huf!
PHEW! THANKS, CHIMLER.
PHEW... I MADE IT UP HERE ALL BY MYSELF!
DIA AND LADY AND I TOOK THAT ROAD DOWN THERE BEFORE...
BUT WE CAN'T GO THE SAME WAY NOW. THIS ROUTE IS STEEP AND INDIRECT... BUT WE NEED TO BE CAUTIOUS.

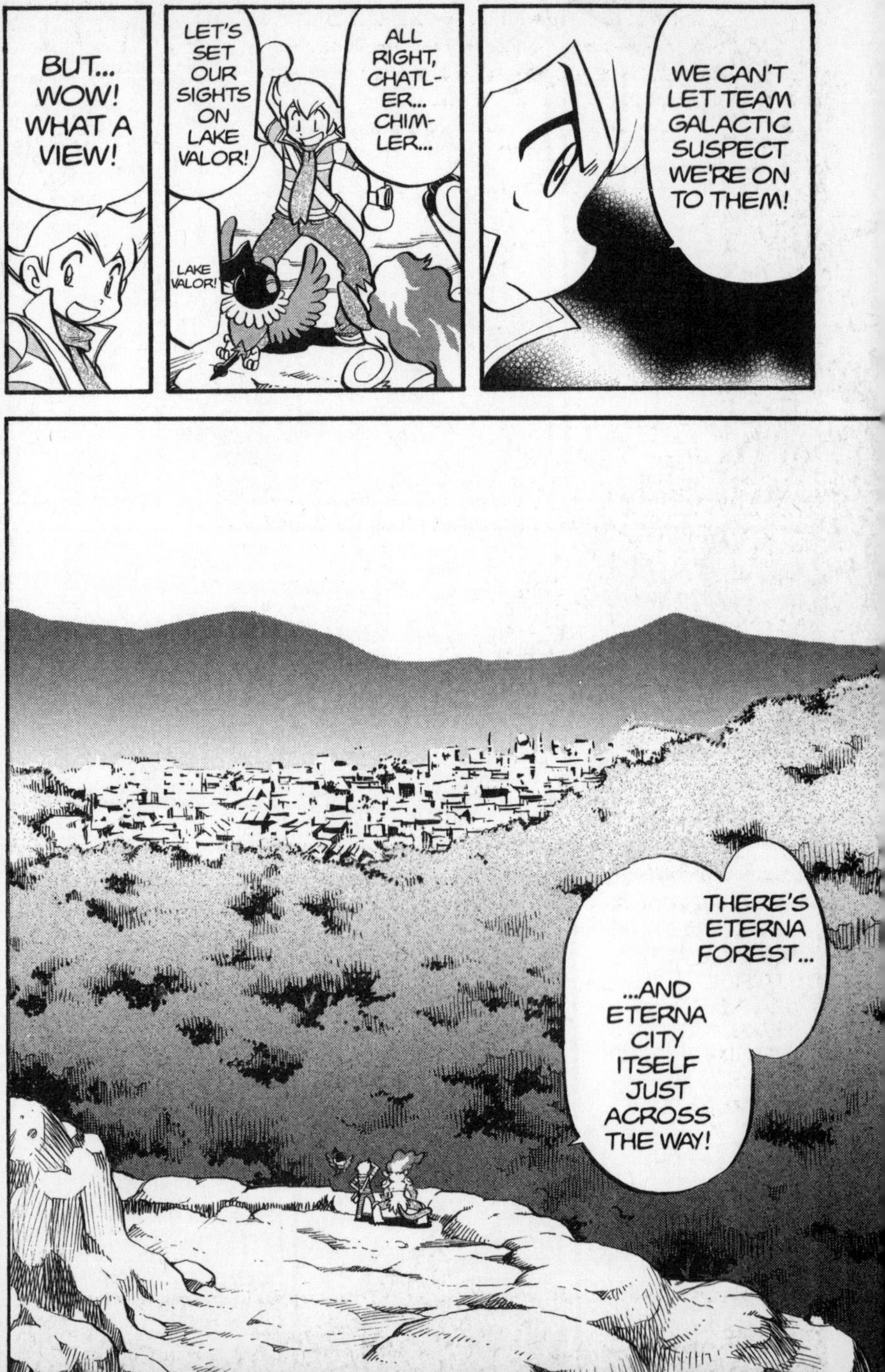
WE CAN'T LET TEAM GALACTIC SUSPECT WE'RE ON TO THEM!
ALL RIGHT, CHATL-ER... CHIM-LER...
LET'S SET OUR SIGHTS ON LAKE VALOR!
LAKE VALOR!
BUT... WOW! WHAT A VIEW!
THERE'S ETERNA FOREST...
...AND ETERNA CITY ITSELF JUST ACROSS THE WAY!

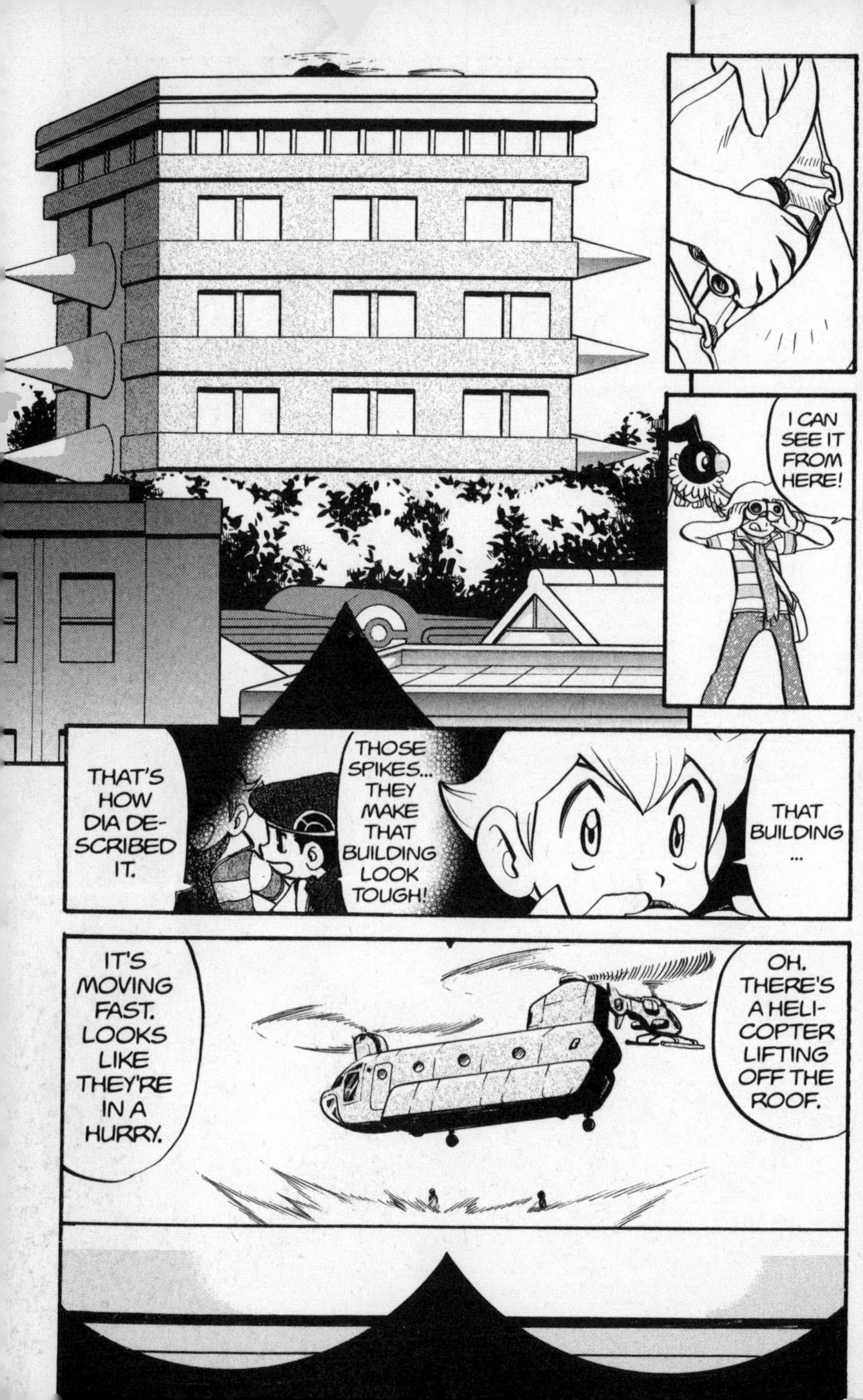
I CAN SEE IT FROM HERE!
THAT BUILDING ...
THOSE SPIKES... THEY MAKE THAT BUILDING LOOK TOUGH!
THAT'S HOW DIA DE-SCRIBED IT.
OH. THERE'S A HELI-COPTER LIFTING OFF THE ROOF.
IT'S MOVING FAST. LOOKS LIKE THEY'RE IN A HURRY.

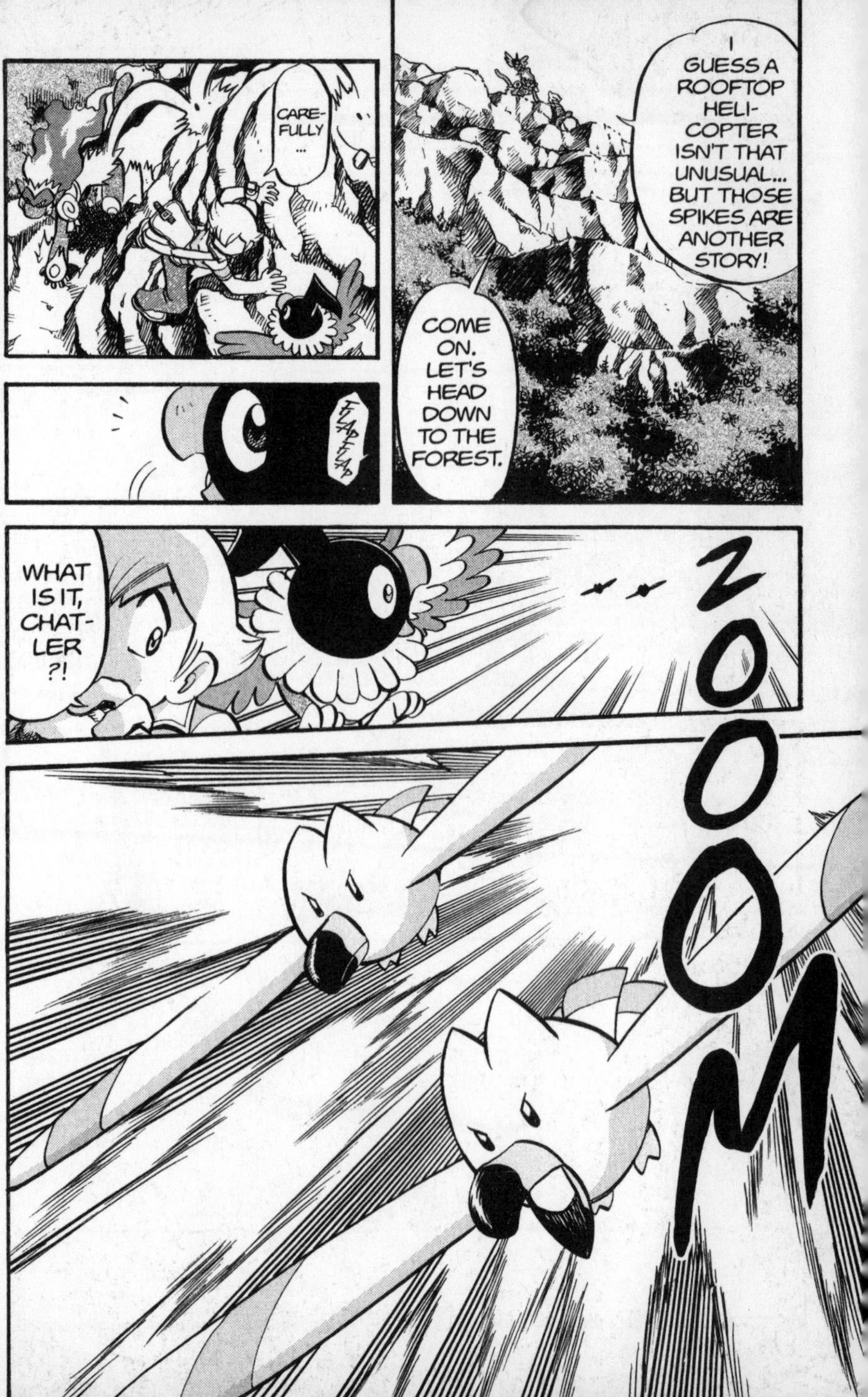
I GUESS A ROOFTOP HELI-COPTER ISN'T THAT UNUSUAL... BUT THOSE SPIKES ARE ANOTHER STORY!
COME ON. LET'S HEAD DOWN TO THE FOREST.
CARE-FULLY ...
FLAP FLAP
ZOOOOM
WHAT IS IT, CHAT-LER ?!

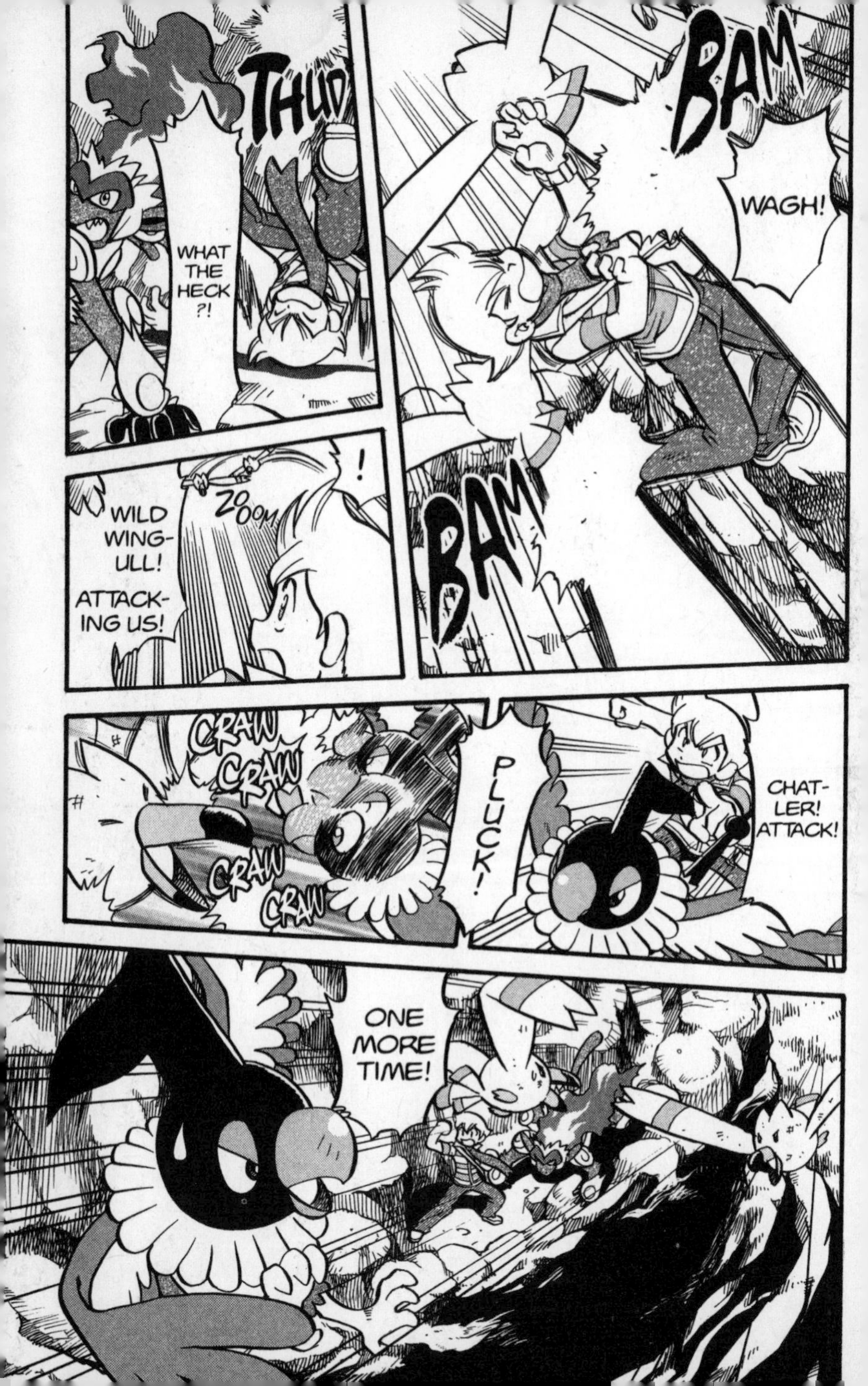
BAM
WAGH!
BAM
THUD
WHAT THE HECK ?!
!
ZOOOM
WILD WING-ULL!
ATTACK-ING US!
CHAT-LER! ATTACK!
PLUCK!
CRAW CRAW
CRAW CRAW
ONE MORE TIME!

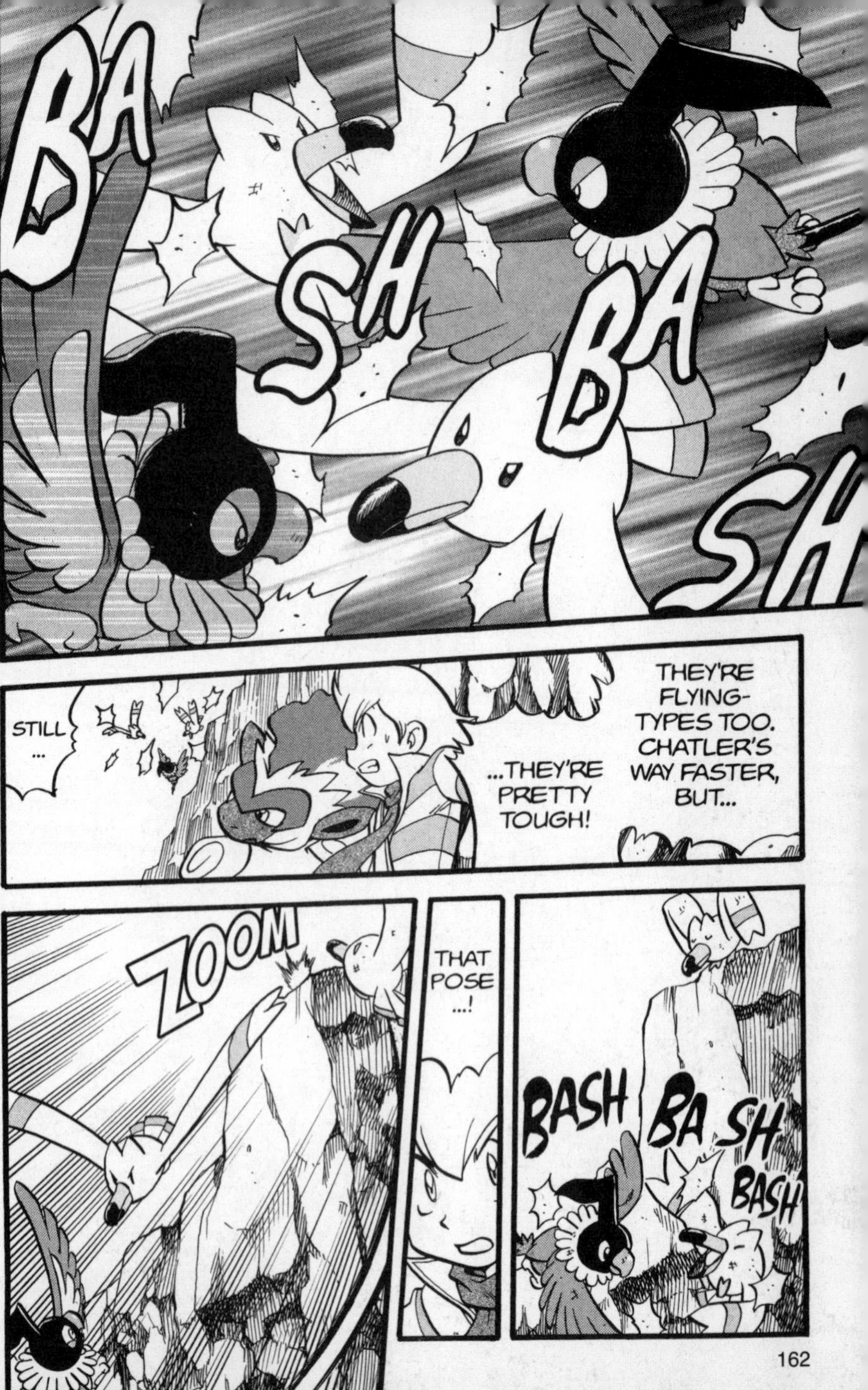
BASH
BASH
THEY'RE FLYING-TYPES TOO. CHATLER'S WAY FASTER, BUT...
...THEY'RE PRETTY TOUGH!
STILL ...
BASH
BASH
BASH
THAT POSE ...!
ZOOM

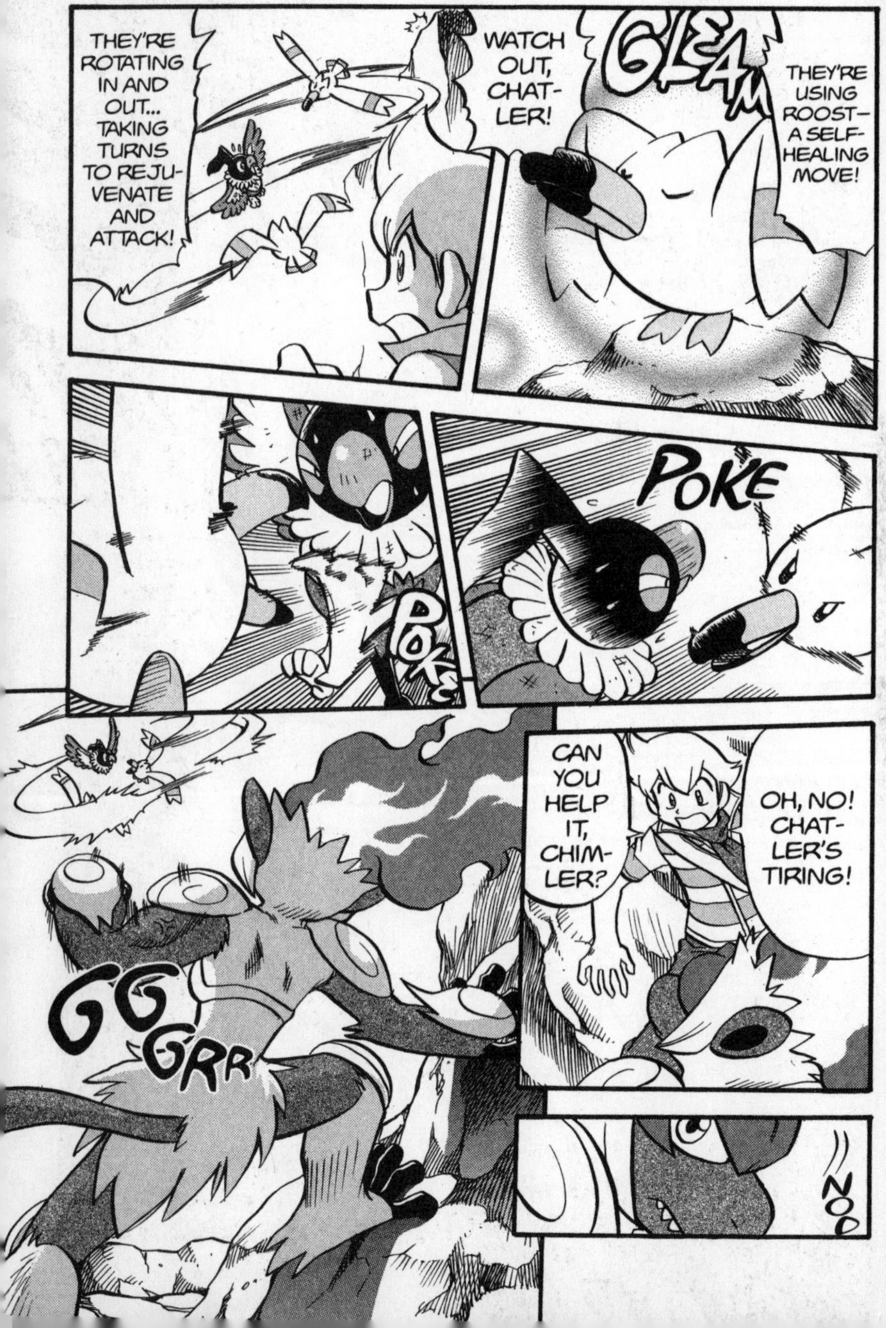
GLEAM
THEY'RE USING ROOST—A SELF-HEALING MOVE!
WATCH OUT, CHATLER!
THEY'RE ROTATING IN AND OUT... TAKING TURNS TO REJUVENATE AND ATTACK!
POKE
POKE
OH, NO! CHATLER'S TIRING!
CAN YOU HELP IT, CHIMLER?
NOD
GGGRR

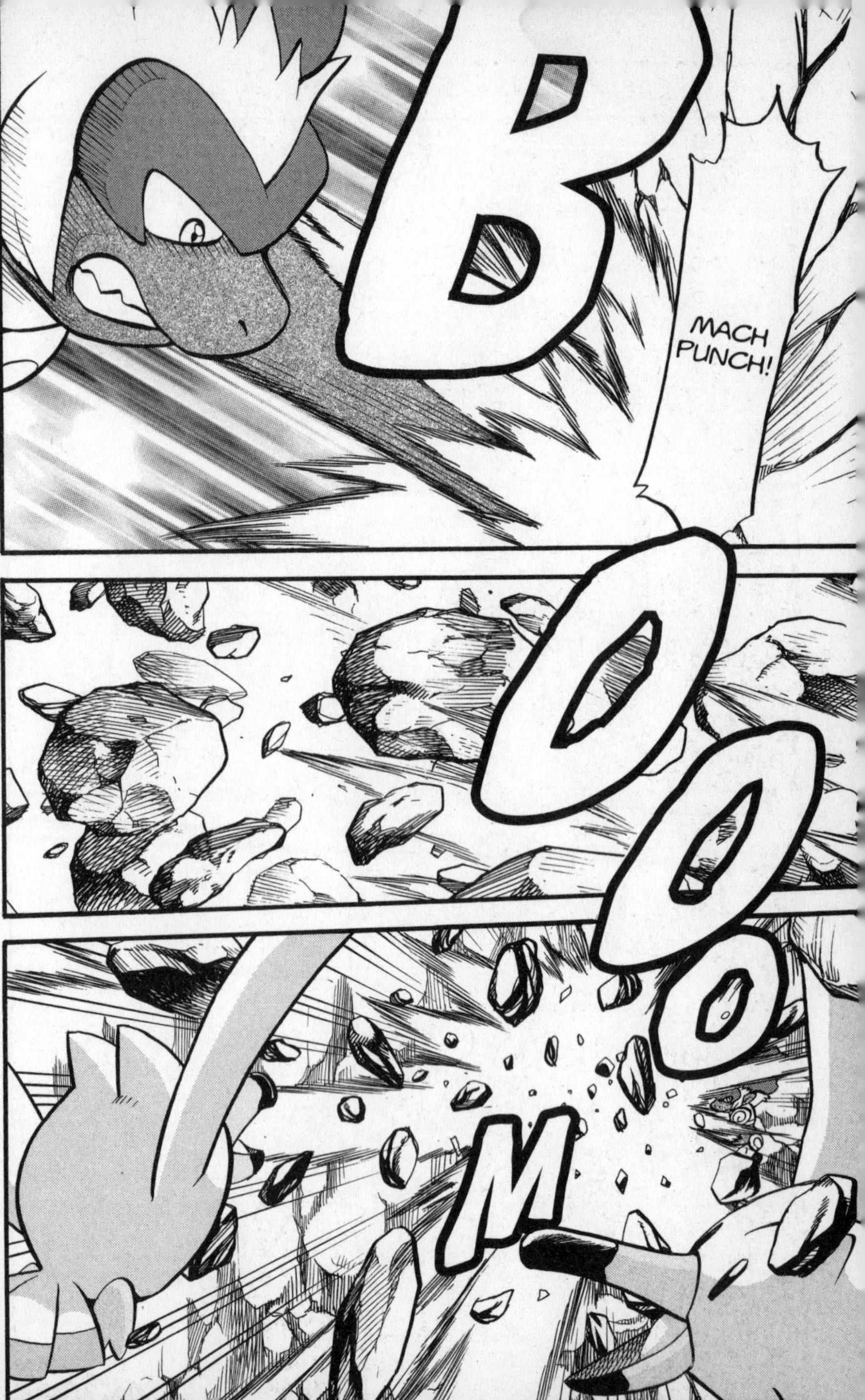
MACH PUNCH!
BOOOOM

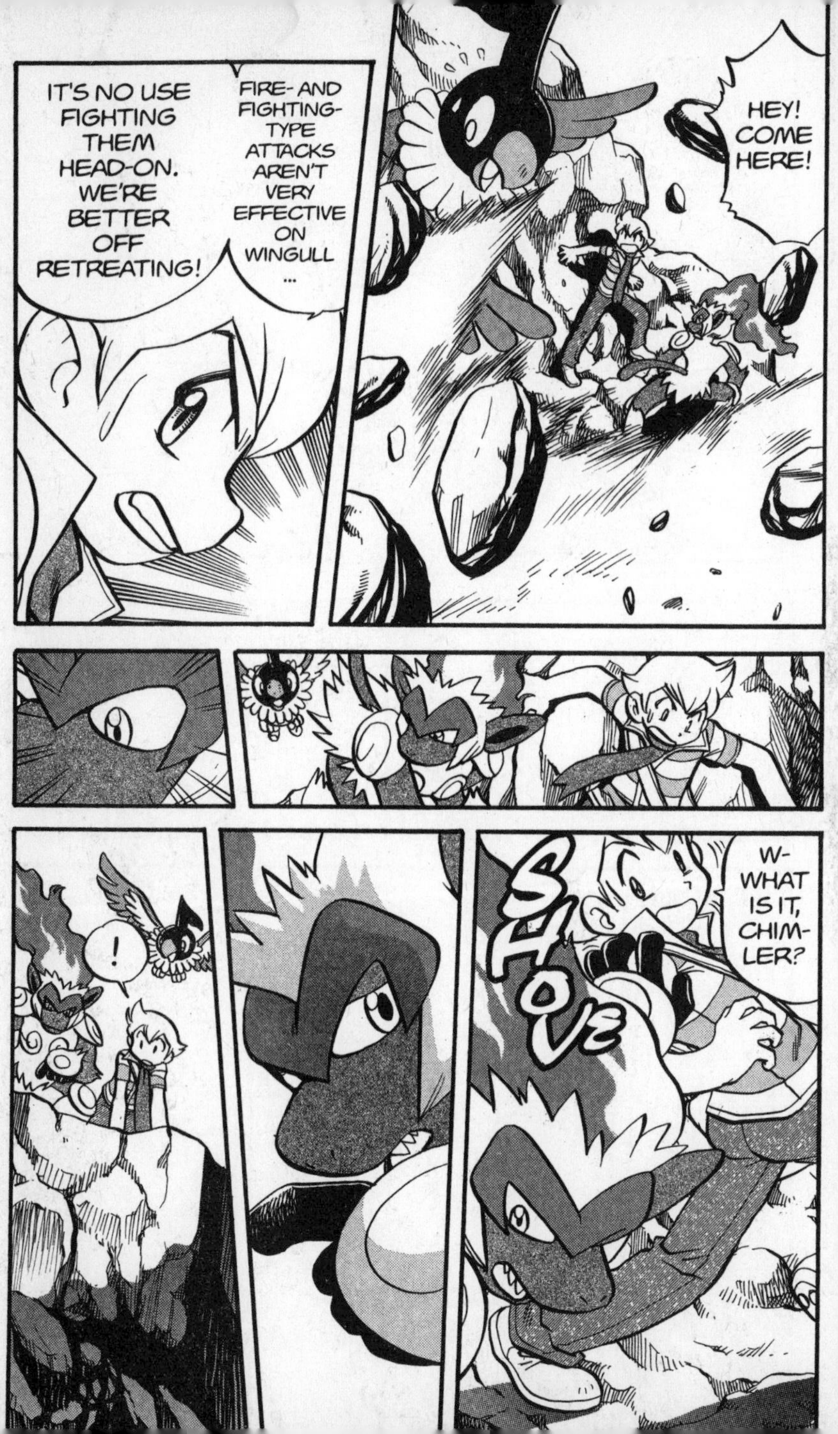
HEY! COME HERE!
FIRE- AND FIGHTING-TYPE ATTACKS AREN'T VERY EFFECTIVE ON WINGULL ...
IT'S NO USE FIGHTING THEM HEAD-ON. WE'RE BETTER OFF RETREATING!
W-WHAT IS IT, CHIMLER?
SHOVE
!

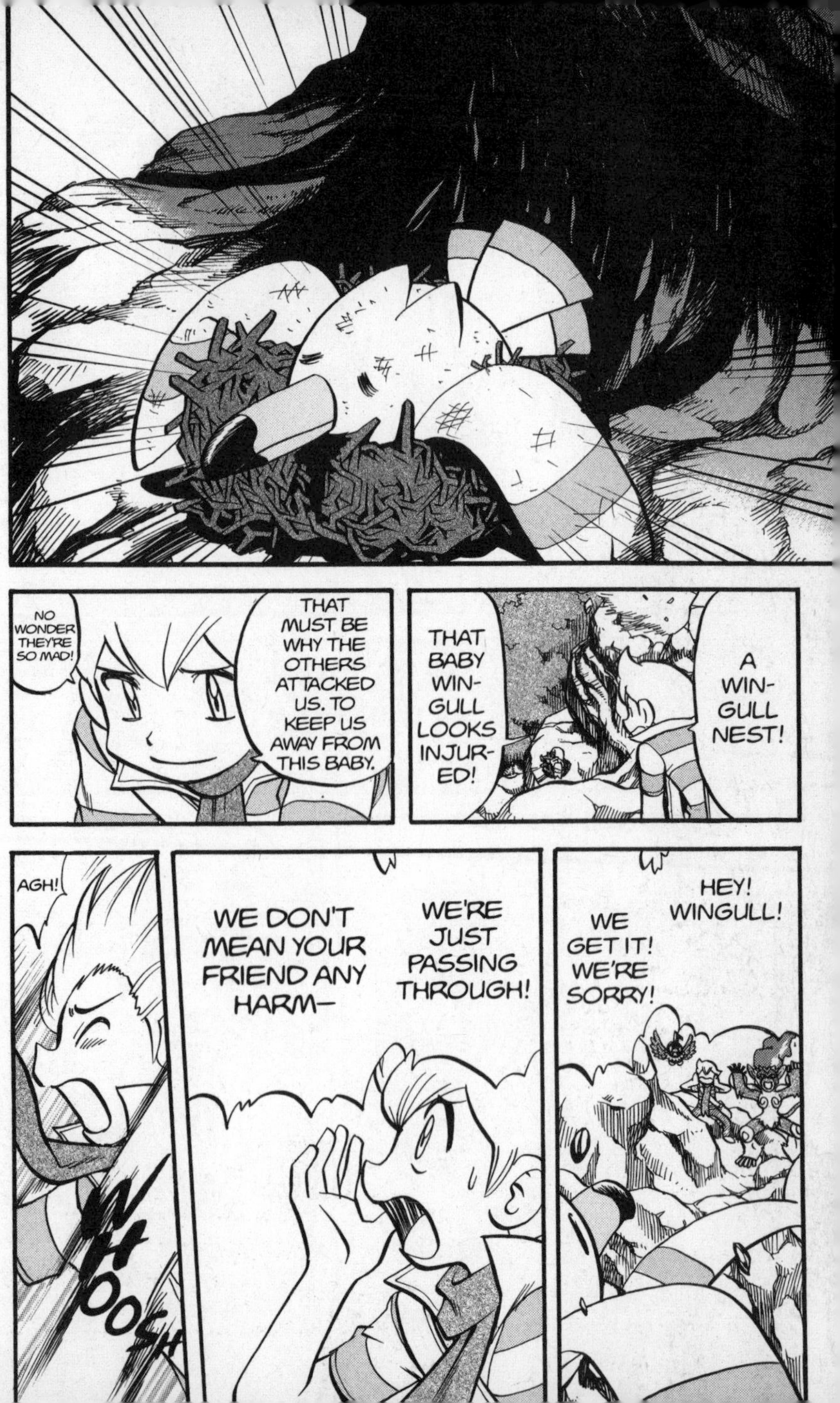
A WIN-GULL NEST!
THAT BABY WIN-GULL LOOKS INJUR-ED!
THAT MUST BE WHY THE OTHERS ATTACKED US. TO KEEP US AWAY FROM THIS BABY.
NO WONDER THEY'RE SO MAD!
HEY! WINGULL!
WE GET IT! WE'RE SORRY!
WE'RE JUST PASSING THROUGH!
WE DON'T MEAN YOUR FRIEND ANY HARM–
AGH!
WHOOSH

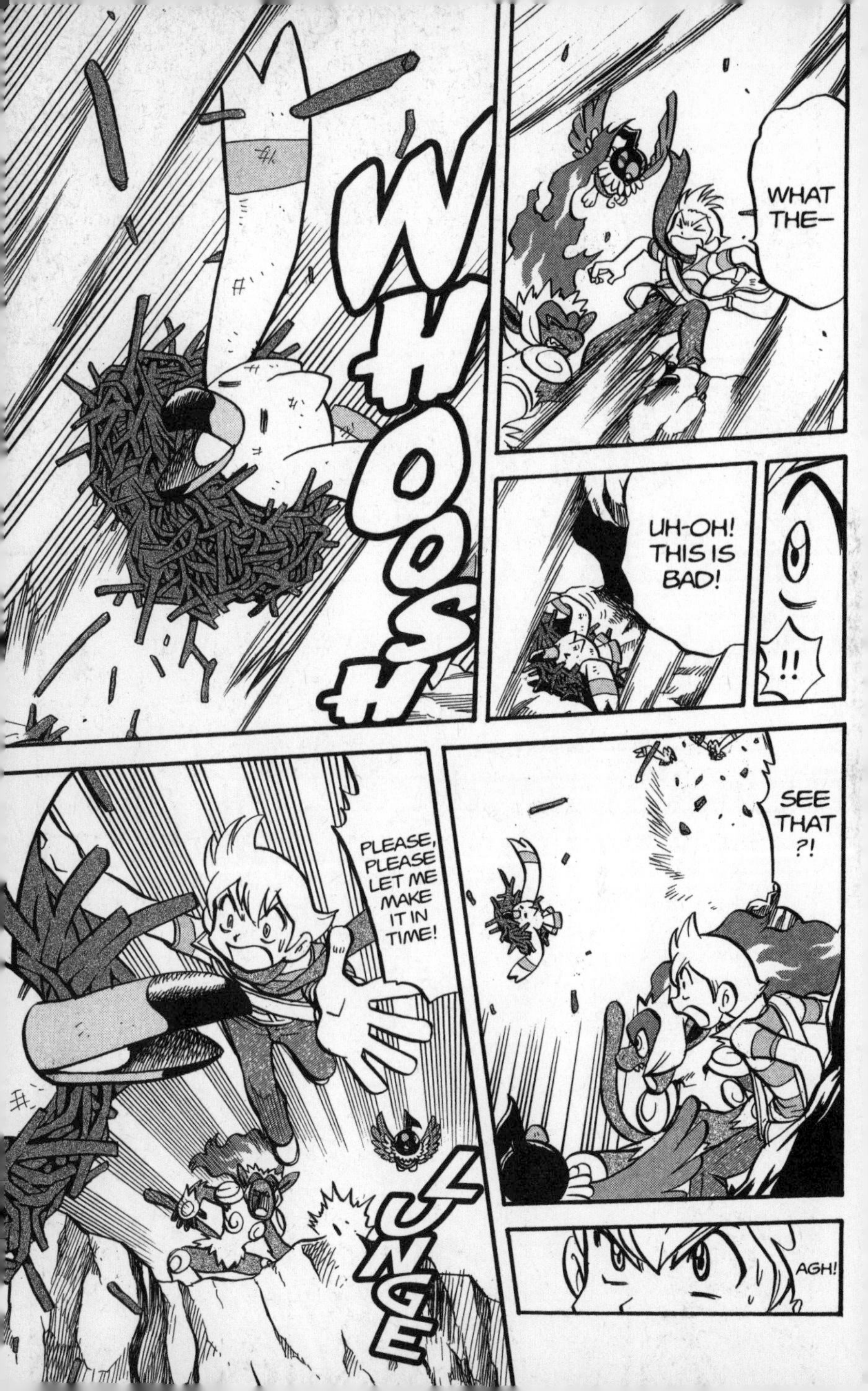
WHAT THE—
!!
UH-OH! THIS IS BAD!
WHOOSH
SEE THAT?!
AGH!
PLEASE, PLEASE LET ME MAKE IT IN TIME!
LUNGE

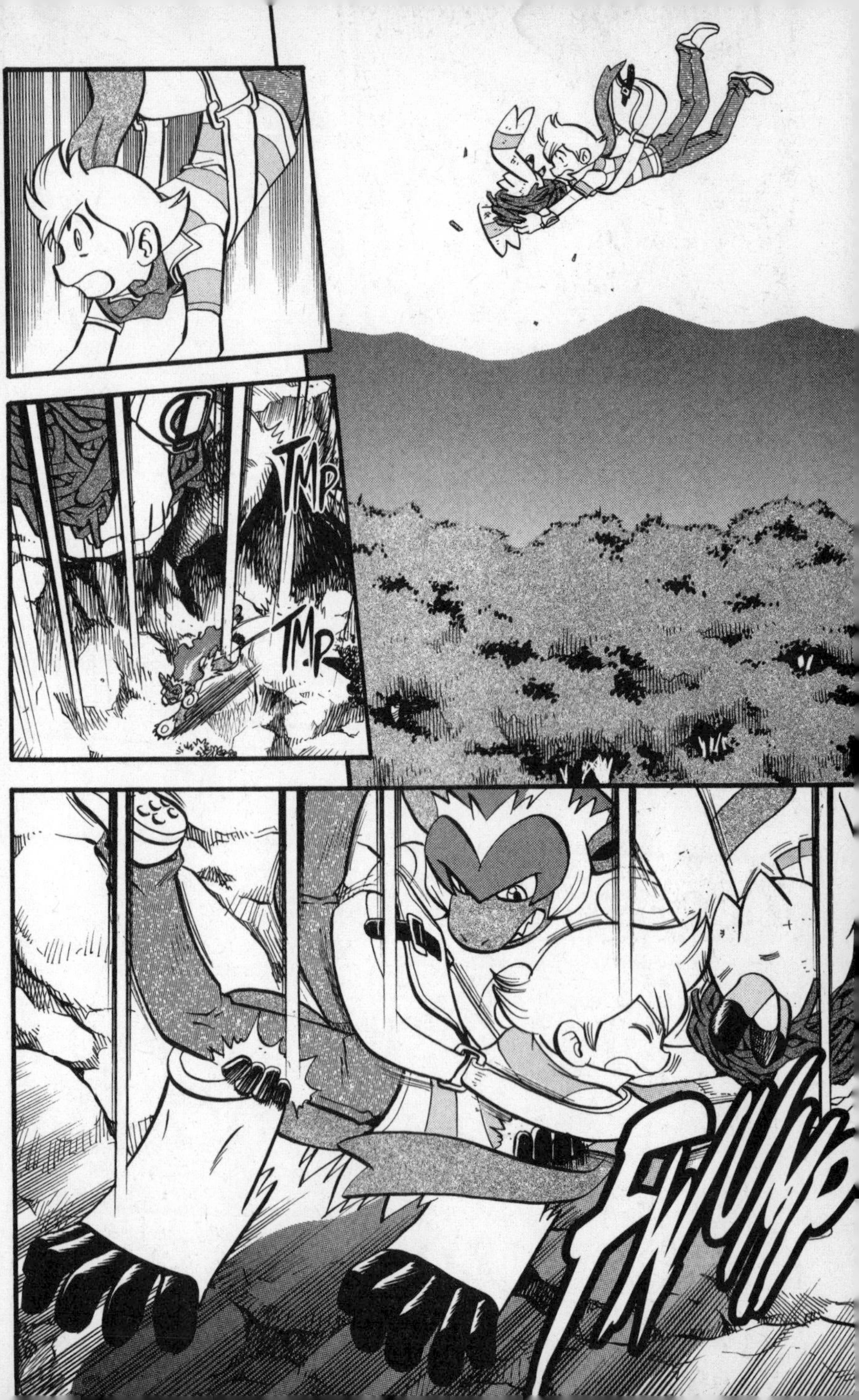
TMP
TMP
FWUMP

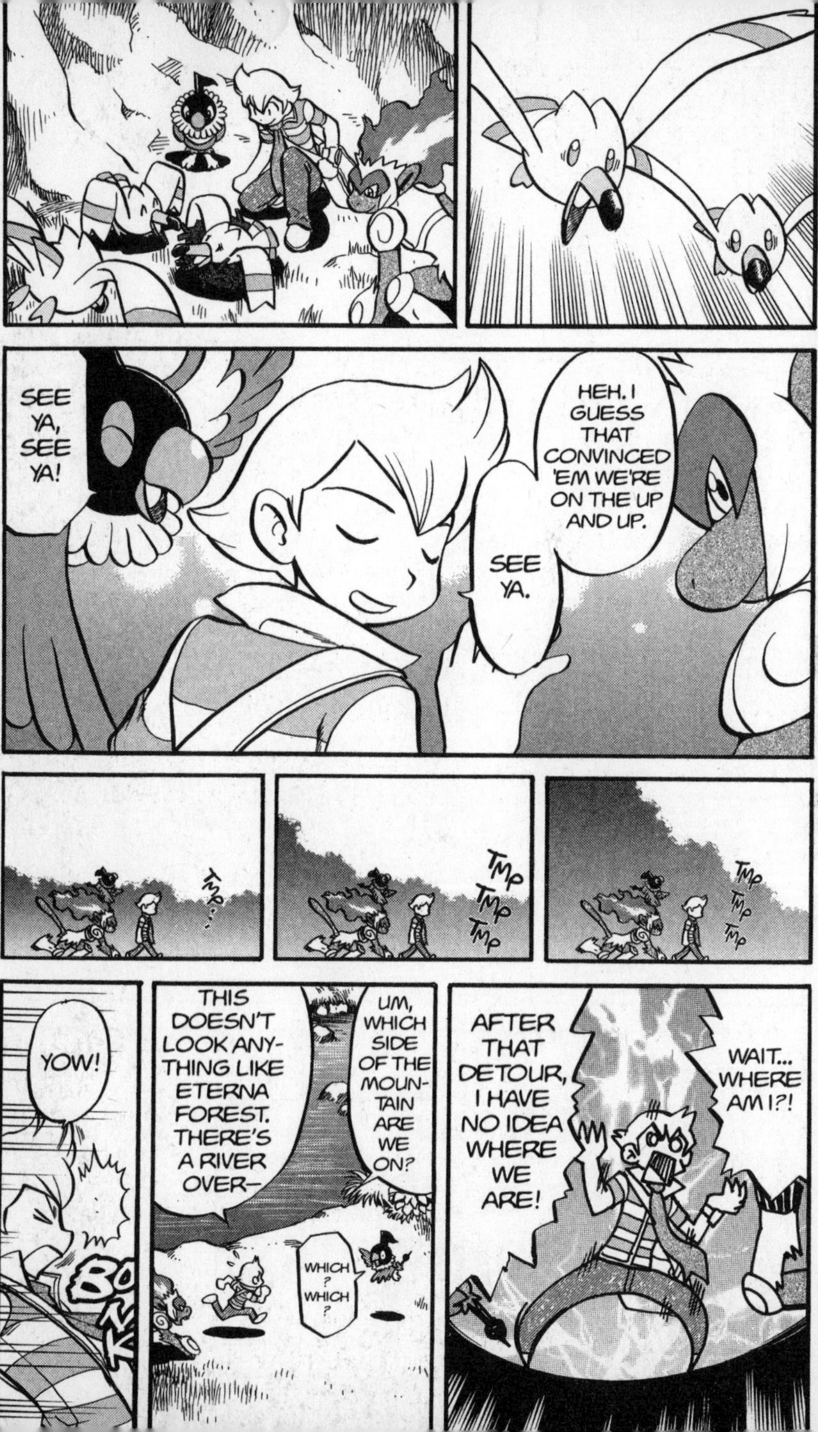
HEH. I GUESS THAT CONVINCED 'EM WE'RE ON THE UP AND UP.
SEE YA.
SEE YA, SEE YA!
TMP TMP TMP
TMP TMP TMP
TMP...
WAIT... WHERE AM I?!
AFTER THAT DETOUR, I HAVE NO IDEA WHERE WE ARE!
UM, WHICH SIDE OF THE MOUNTAIN ARE WE ON?
THIS DOESN'T LOOK ANYTHING LIKE ETERNA FOREST. THERE'S A RIVER OVER–
WHICH? WHICH?
YOW!

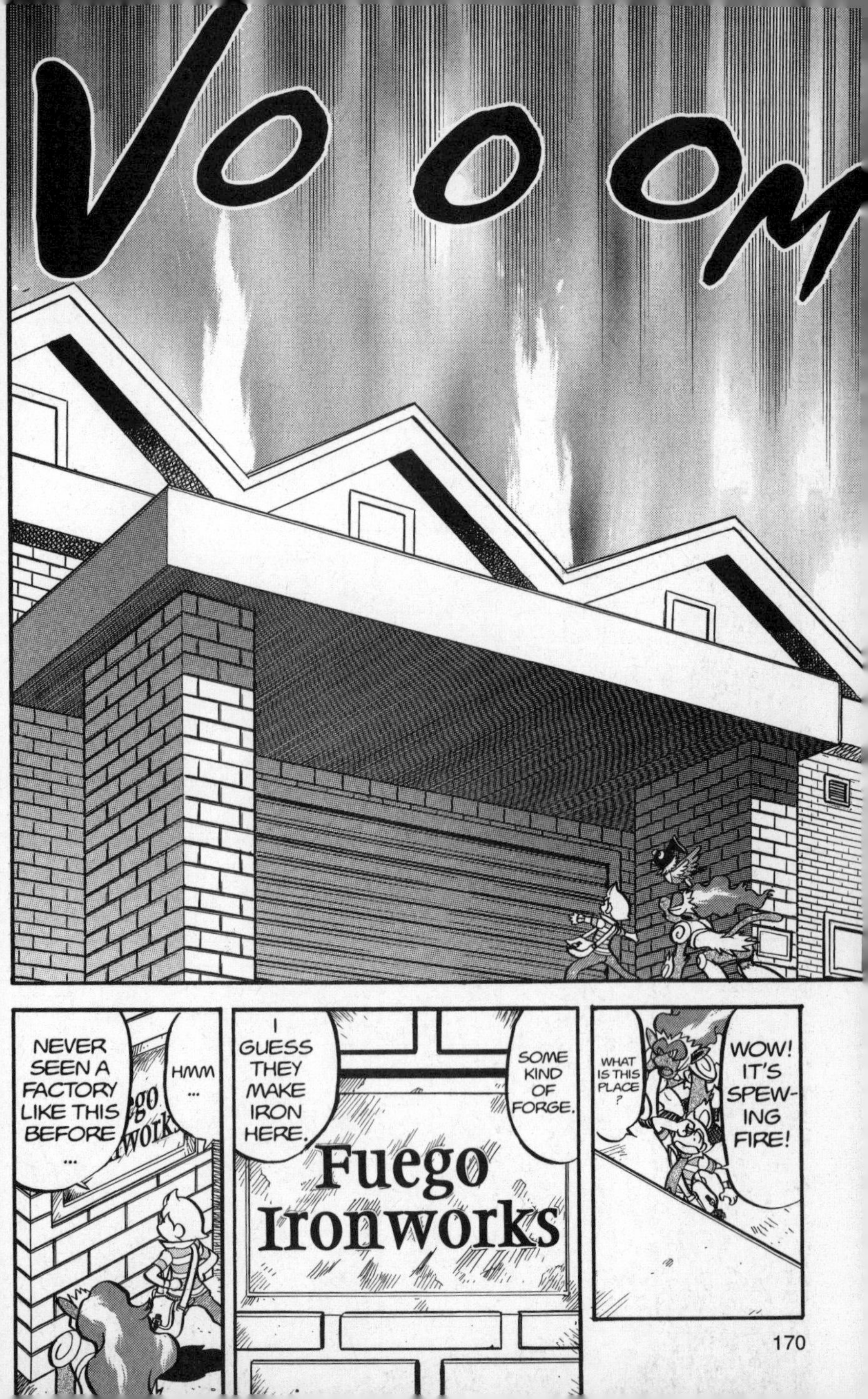
VOOM
WOW! IT'S SPEW-ING FIRE!
WHAT IS THIS PLACE?
SOME KIND OF FORGE.
I GUESS THEY MAKE IRON HERE.
Fuego Ironworks
HMM...
NEVER SEEN A FACTORY LIKE THIS BEFORE...

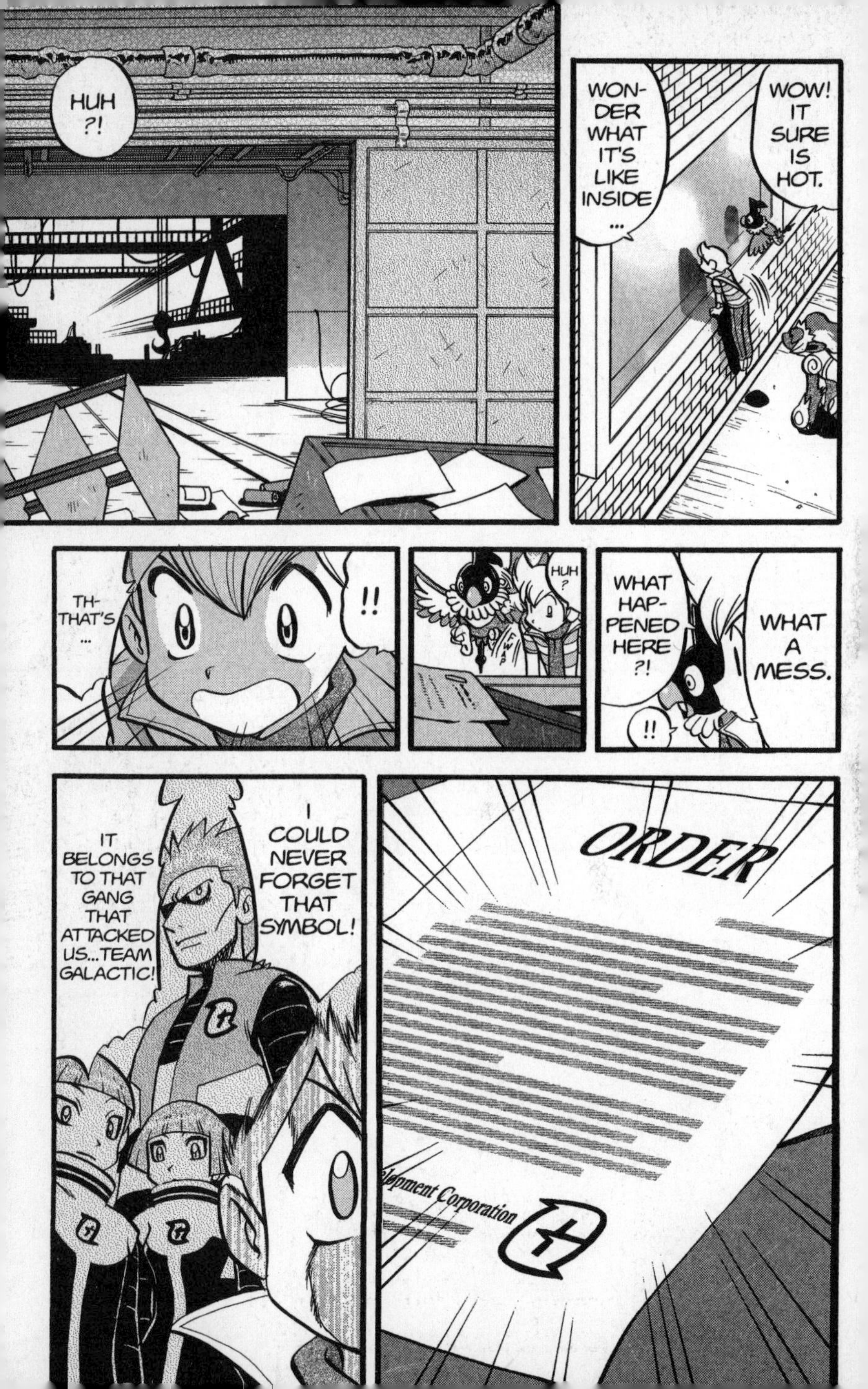
WOW! IT SURE IS HOT.
WON-DER WHAT IT'S LIKE INSIDE...
HUH?!
WHAT A MESS.
WHAT HAP-PENED HERE?!
!!
HUH?
!!
TH-THAT'S...
ORDER
elopment Corporation
I COULD NEVER FORGET THAT SYMBOL!
IT BELONGS TO THAT GANG THAT ATTACKED US...TEAM GALACTIC!

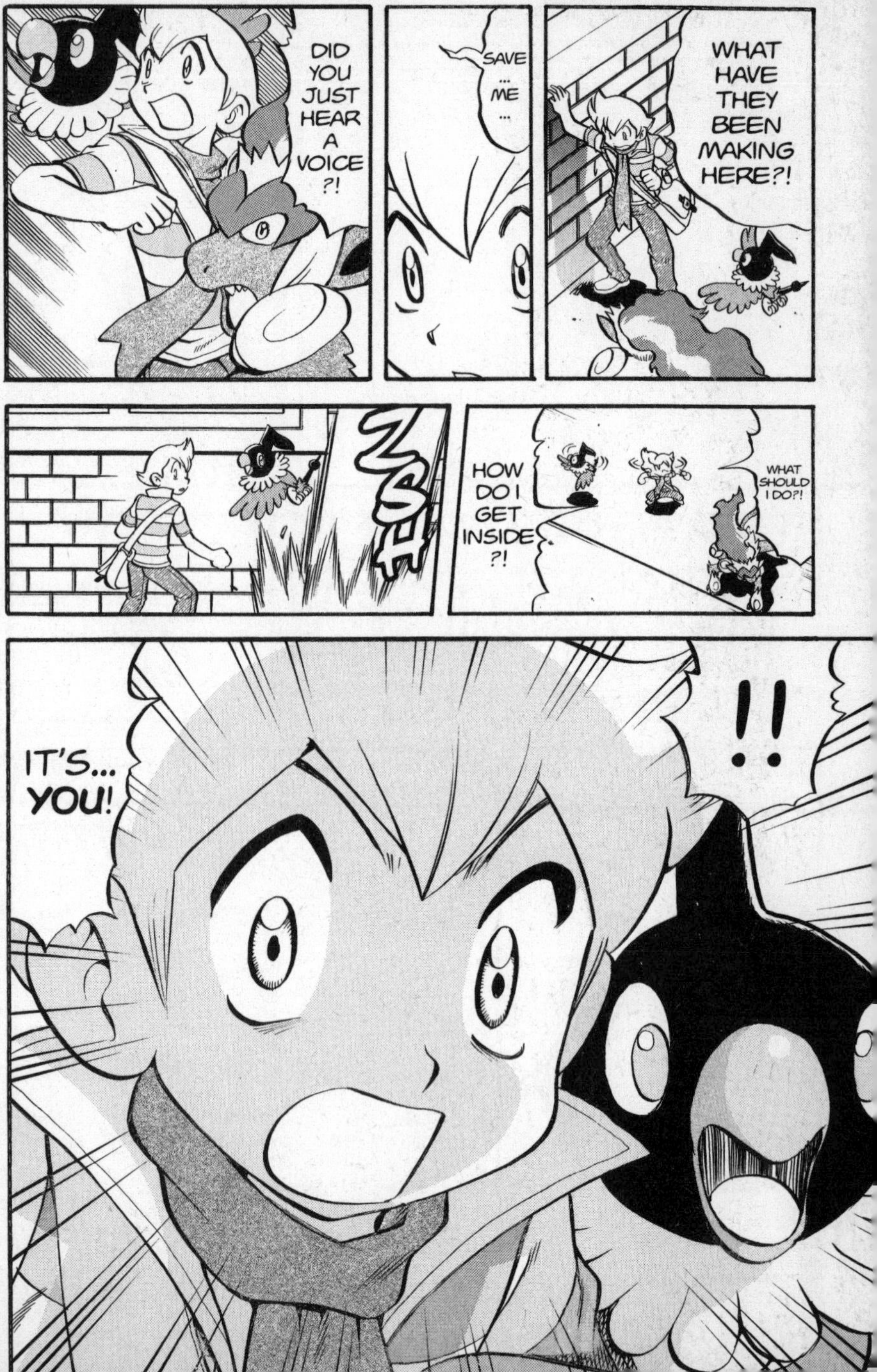
WHAT HAVE THEY BEEN MAKING HERE?!
SAVE ... ME ...
DID YOU JUST HEAR A VOICE ?!
WHAT SHOULD I DO?!
HOW DO I GET INSIDE ?!
WSH
!!
IT'S... YOU!

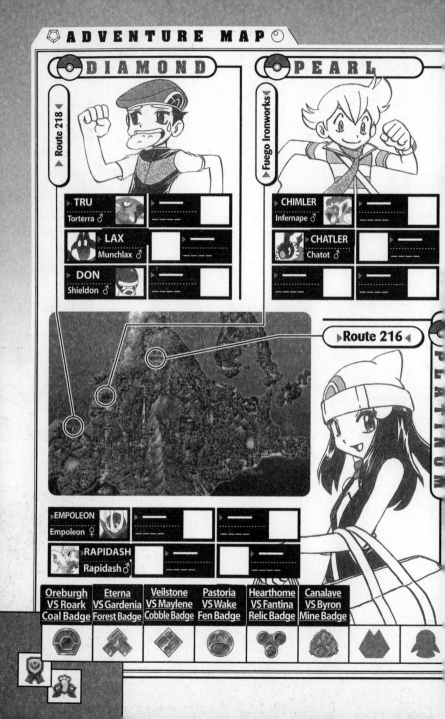

ADVENTURE MAP

DIAMOND

Route 218

Fuego Ironworks

PEARL

TRU
Torterra ♂

LAX
Munchlax ♂

DON
Shieldon ♂

CHIMLER
Infernape ♂

CHATLER
Chatot ♂

Route 216

PLATINUM

EMPOLEON
Empoleon ♀

RAPIDASH
Rapidash ♂

Oreburgh VS Roark Coal Badge	Eterna VS Gardenia Forest Badge	Veilstone VS Maylene Cobble Badge	Pastoria VS Wake Fen Badge	Hearthome VS Fantina Relic Badge	Canalave VS Byron Mine Badge

47

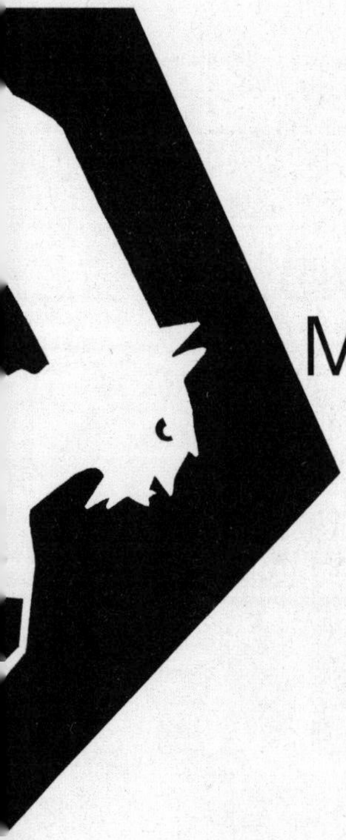

Maddening Magby

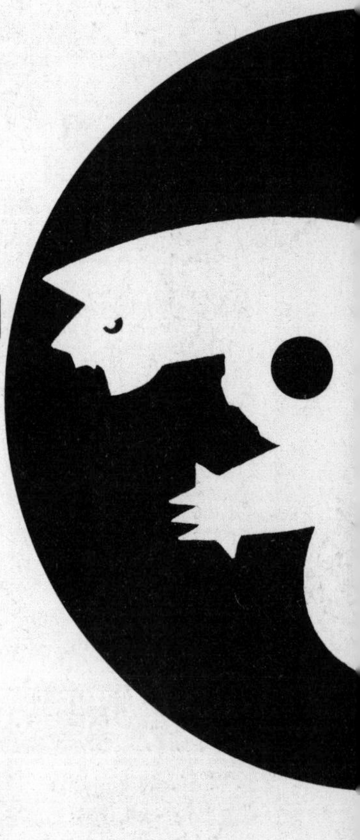

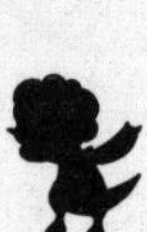

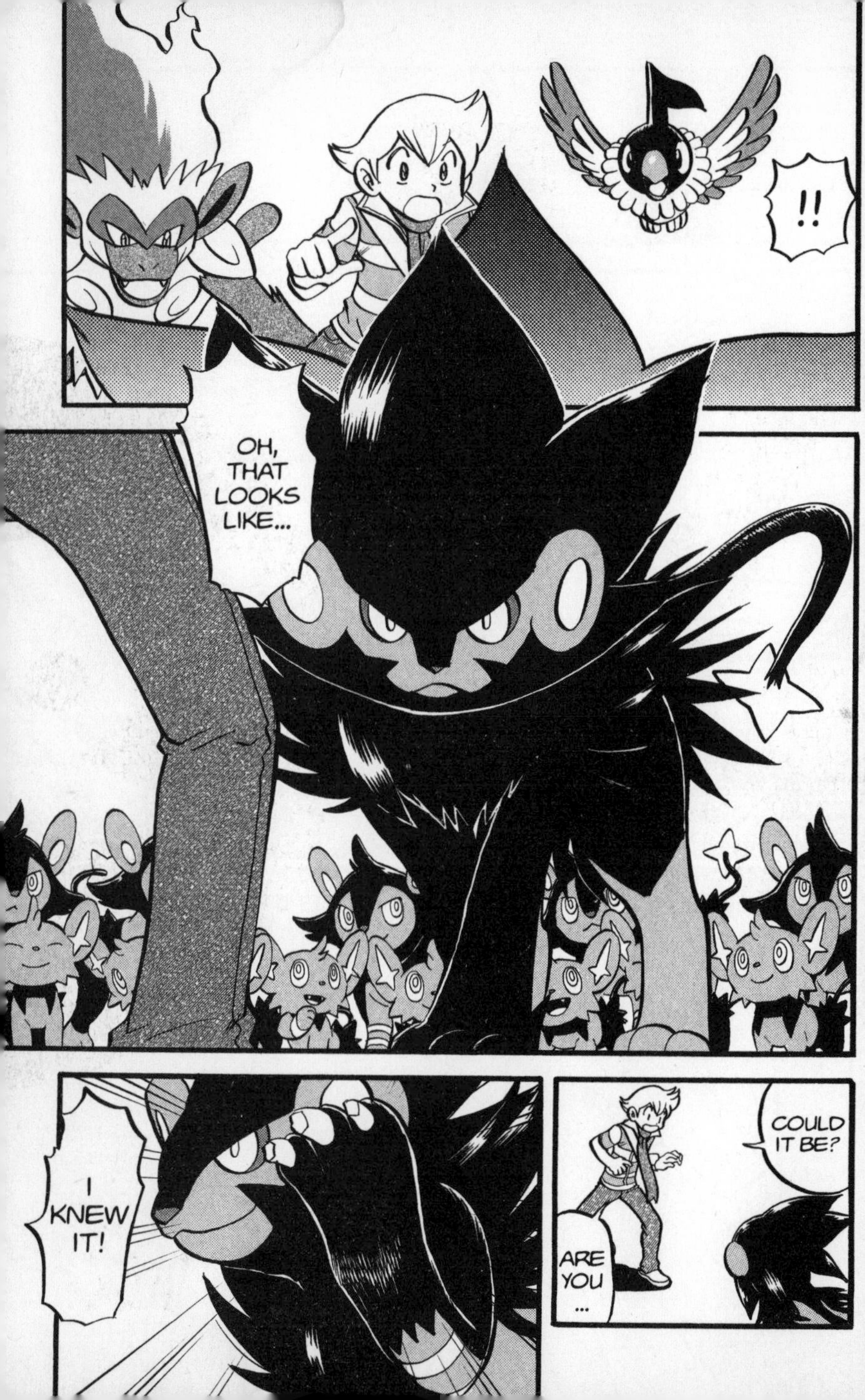
!!
OH, THAT LOOKS LIKE...
COULD IT BE?
ARE YOU ...
I KNEW IT!

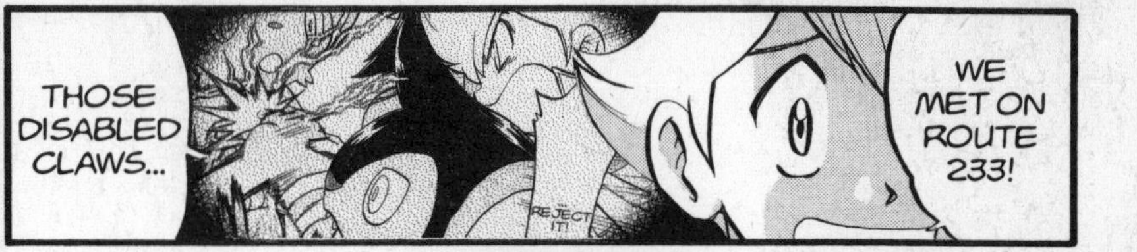
WE MET ON ROUTE 233!
THOSE DISABLED CLAWS...
REJECT IT!

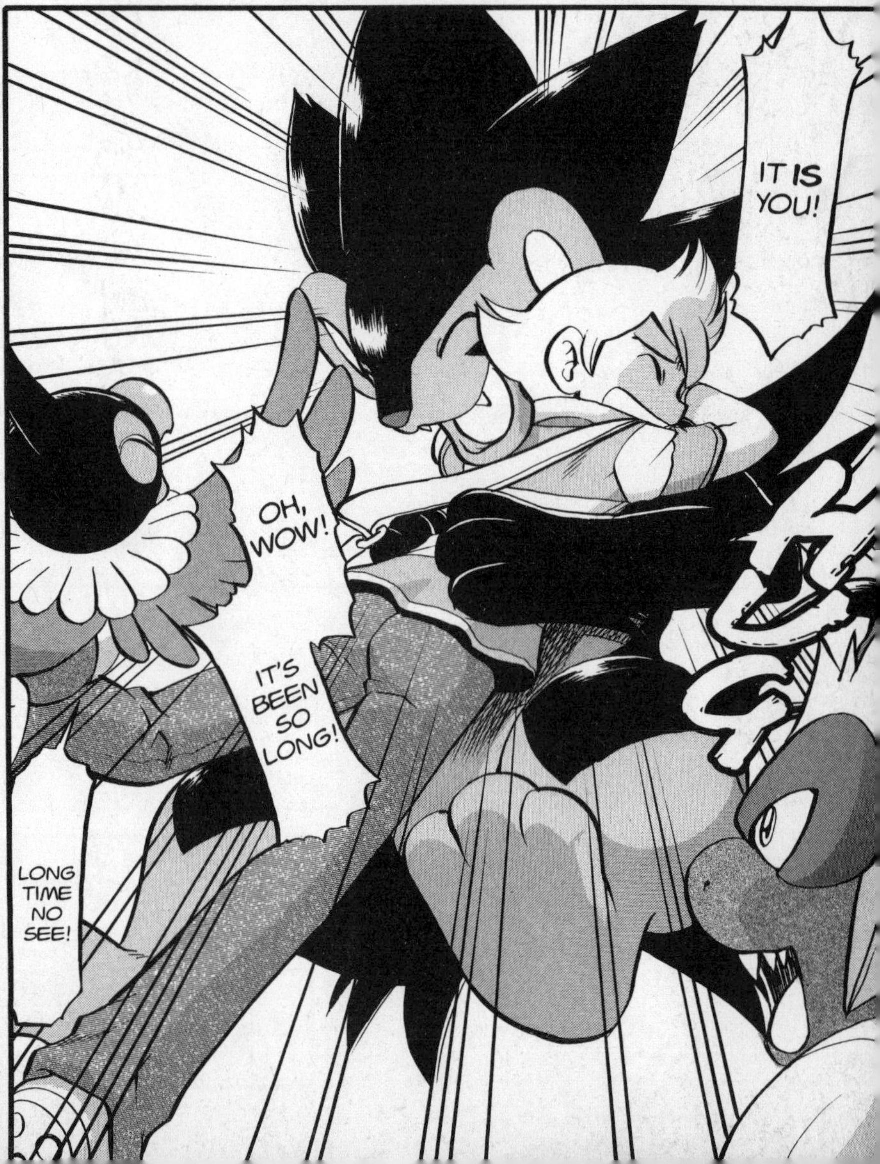
IT IS YOU!
OH, WOW!
IT'S BEEN SO LONG!
LONG TIME NO SEE!

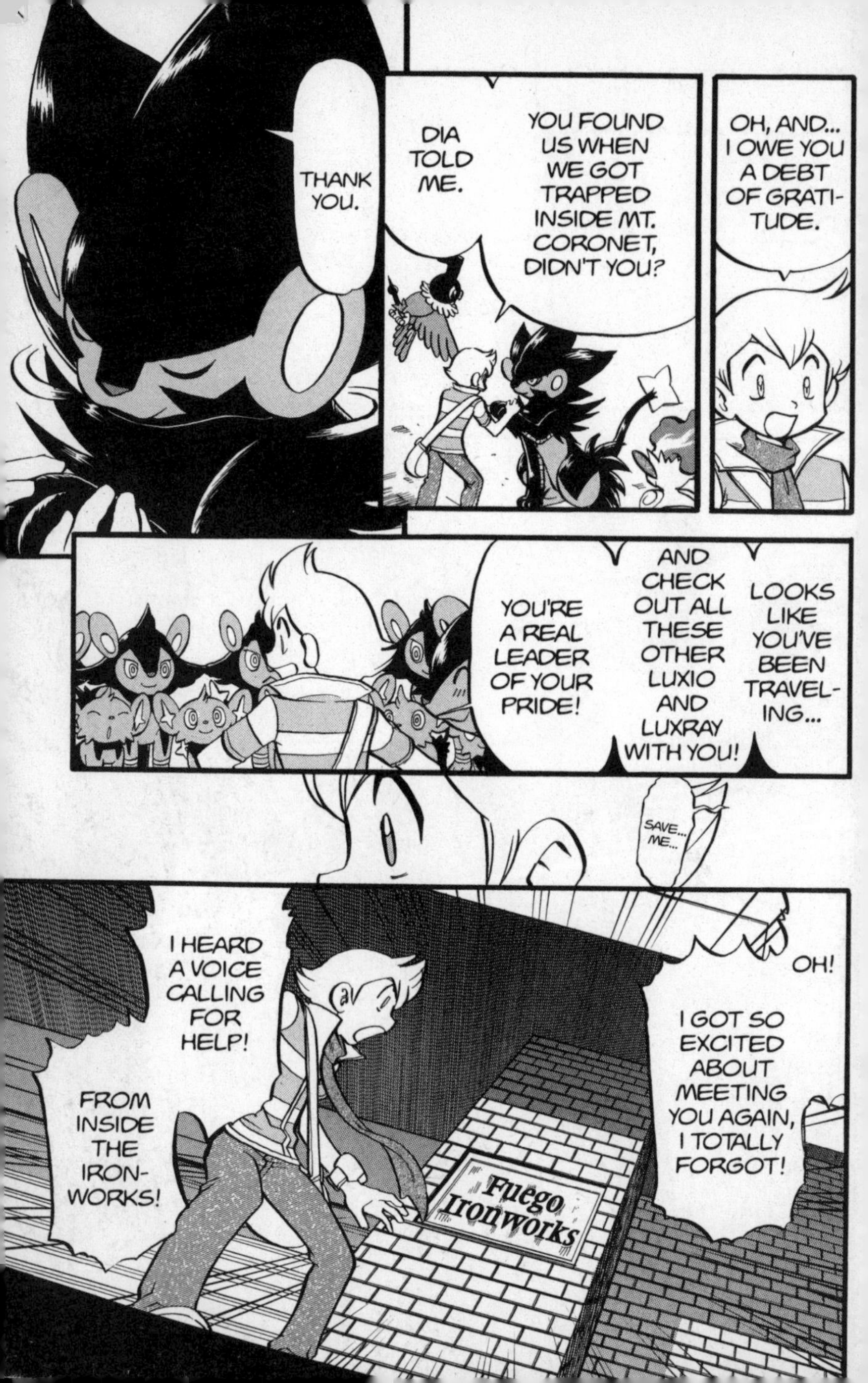
OH, AND... I OWE YOU A DEBT OF GRATI-TUDE.
YOU FOUND US WHEN WE GOT TRAPPED INSIDE MT. CORONET, DIDN'T YOU?
DIA TOLD ME.
THANK YOU.
LOOKS LIKE YOU'VE BEEN TRAVEL-ING...
AND CHECK OUT ALL THESE OTHER LUXIO AND LUXRAY WITH YOU!
YOU'RE A REAL LEADER OF YOUR PRIDE!
SAVE... ME...
OH!
I GOT SO EXCITED ABOUT MEETING YOU AGAIN, I TOTALLY FORGOT!
I HEARD A VOICE CALLING FOR HELP!
FROM INSIDE THE IRON-WORKS!
Fuego Ironworks

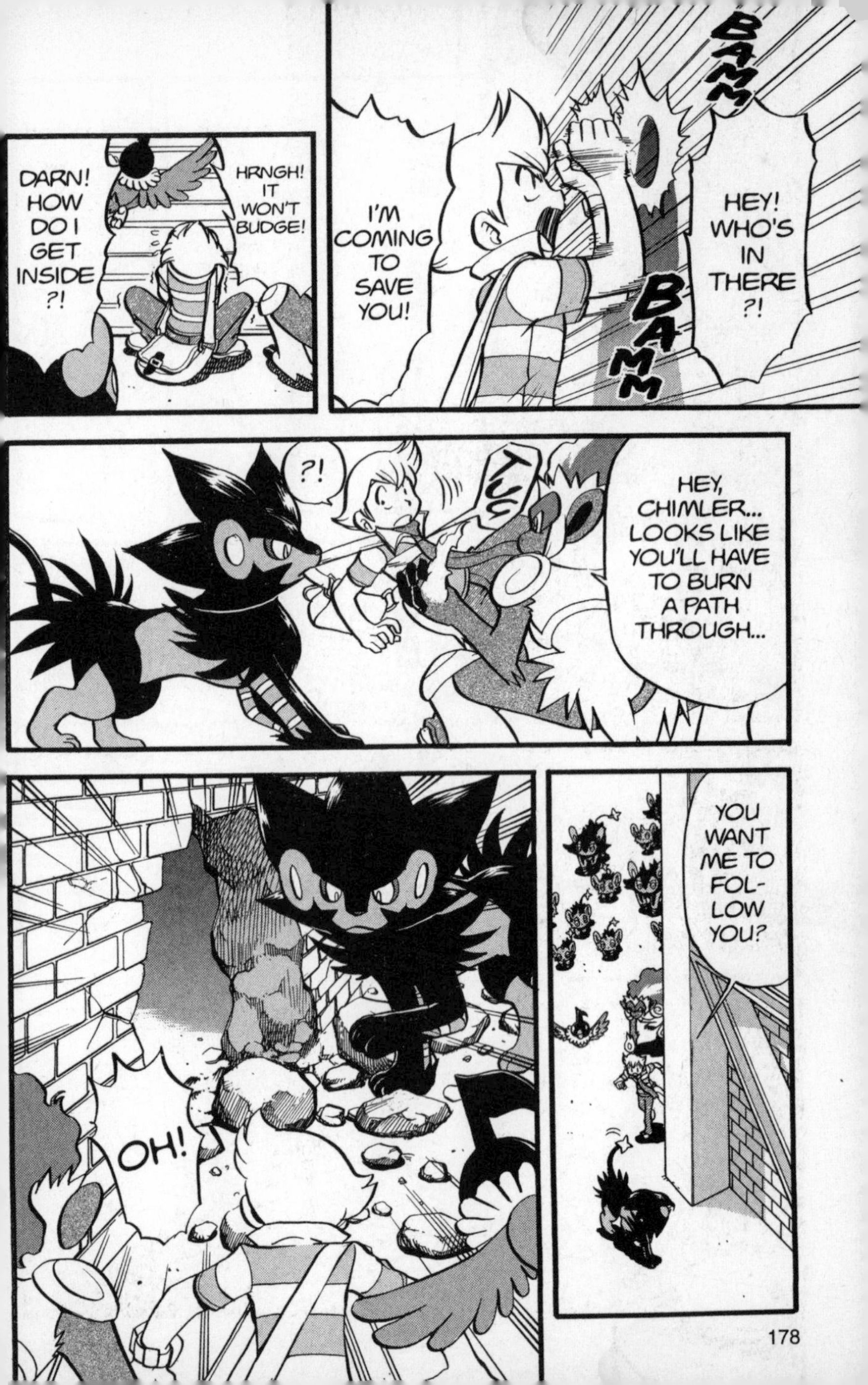
BAMM
HEY! WHO'S IN THERE ?!
BAMM
I'M COMING TO SAVE YOU!
HRNGH! IT WON'T BUDGE!
DARN! HOW DO I GET INSIDE ?!
HEY, CHIMLER... LOOKS LIKE YOU'LL HAVE TO BURN A PATH THROUGH...
TUG
?!
YOU WANT ME TO FOL-LOW YOU?
OH!

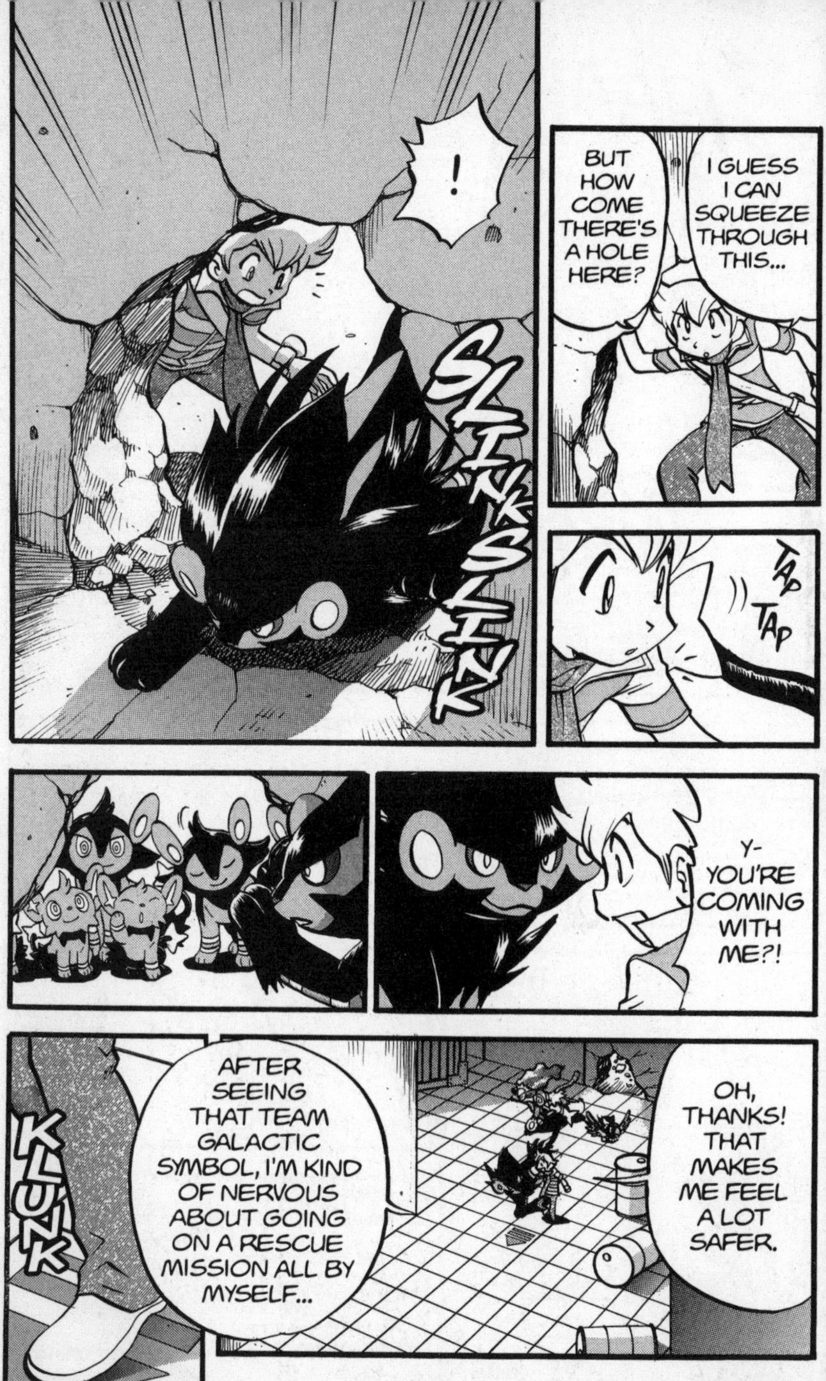
I GUESS I CAN SQUEEZE THROUGH THIS...
BUT HOW COME THERE'S A HOLE HERE?
TAP TAP
!
SLINK SLINK
Y-YOU'RE COMING WITH ME?!
OH, THANKS! THAT MAKES ME FEEL A LOT SAFER.
AFTER SEEING THAT TEAM GALACTIC SYMBOL, I'M KIND OF NERVOUS ABOUT GOING ON A RESCUE MISSION ALL BY MYSELF...
KLUNK

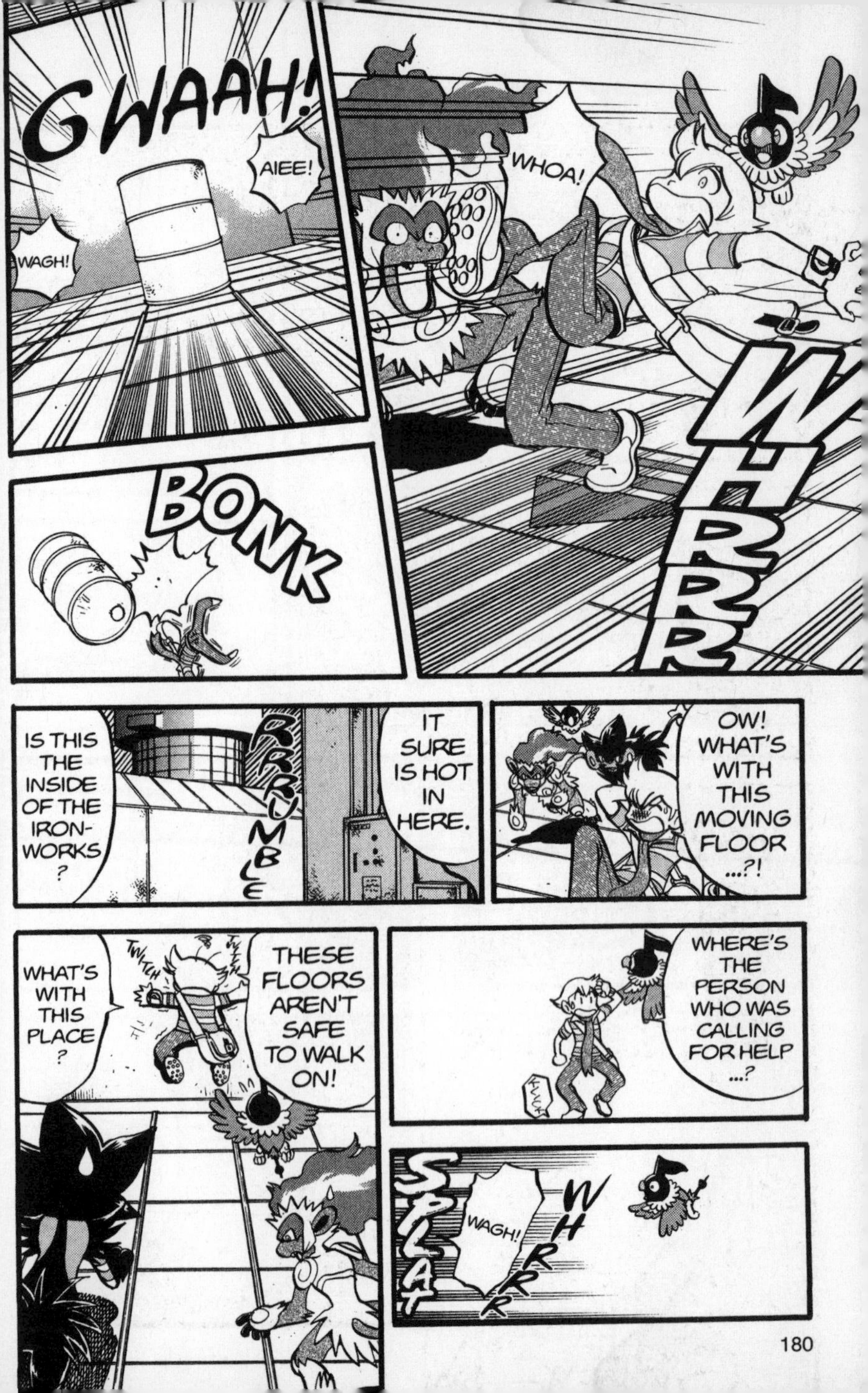
WHOA!
WHRRR
GWAAH!
AIEE!
WAGH!
BONK
OW! WHAT'S WITH THIS MOVING FLOOR ...?!
IT SURE IS HOT IN HERE.
RRRUMBLE
IS THIS THE INSIDE OF THE IRON-WORKS ?
WHERE'S THE PERSON WHO WAS CALLING FOR HELP ...?
WHRRRR
WAGH!
SPLAT
THESE FLOORS AREN'T SAFE TO WALK ON!
TWITCH
WHAT'S WITH THIS PLACE ?

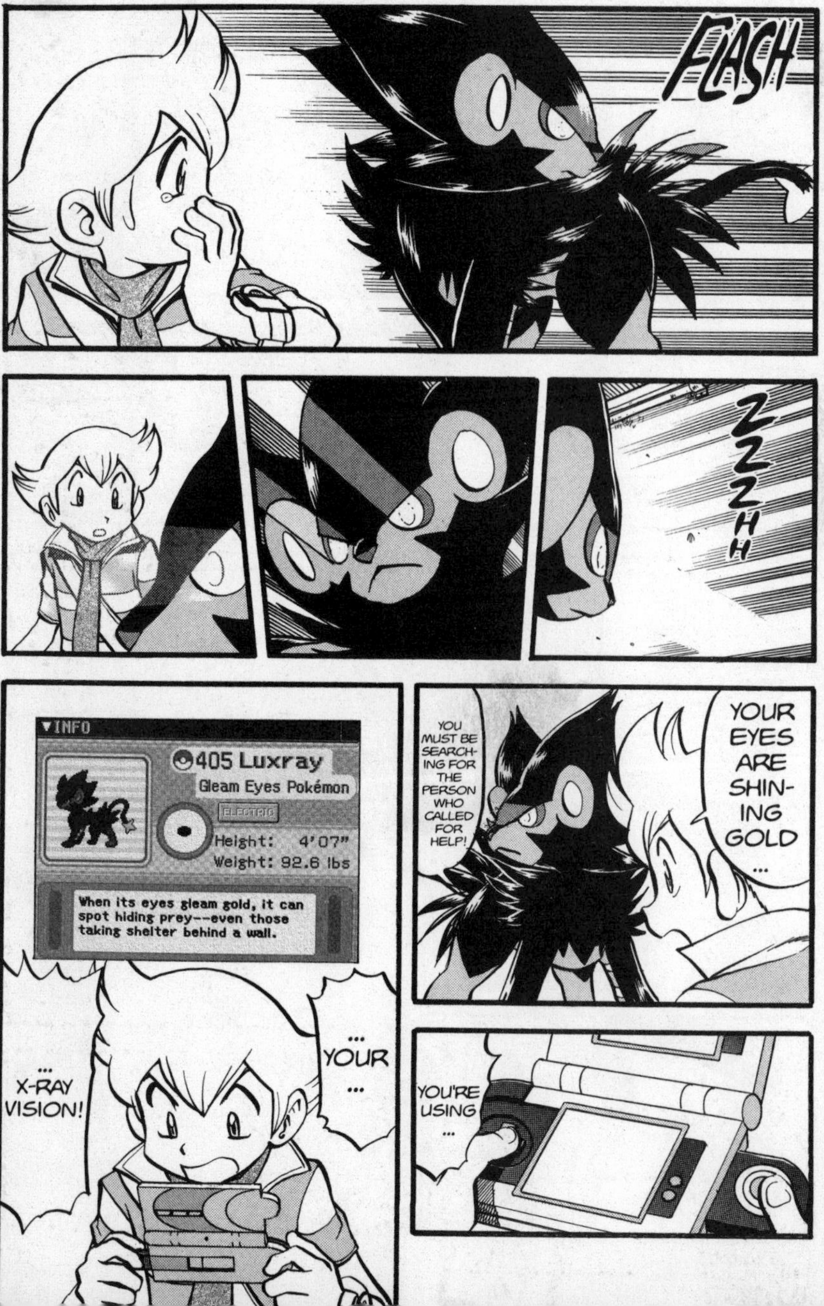

FLASH
ZZZZHHH
YOUR EYES ARE SHINING GOLD...
YOU MUST BE SEARCHING FOR THE PERSON WHO CALLED FOR HELP!
YOU'RE USING...
▼INFO
405 Luxray
Gleam Eyes Pokémon
ELECTRIC
Height: 4'07"
Weight: 92.6 lbs
When its eyes gleam gold, it can spot hiding prey--even those taking shelter behind a wall.
...YOUR...
...X-RAY VISION!

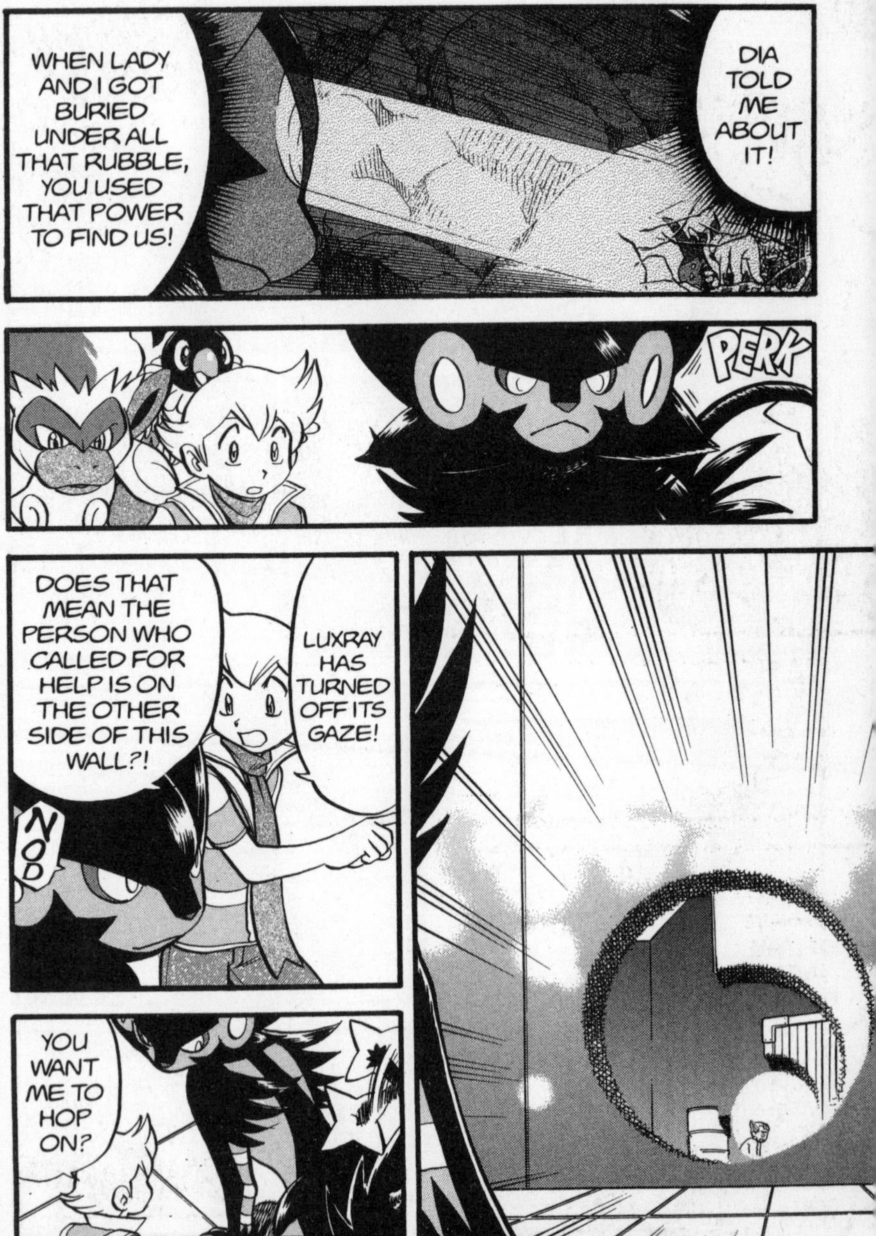
DIA TOLD ME ABOUT IT!
WHEN LADY AND I GOT BURIED UNDER ALL THAT RUBBLE, YOU USED THAT POWER TO FIND US!
PERK
LUXRAY HAS TURNED OFF ITS GAZE!
DOES THAT MEAN THE PERSON WHO CALLED FOR HELP IS ON THE OTHER SIDE OF THIS WALL?!
NOD
YOU WANT ME TO HOP ON?

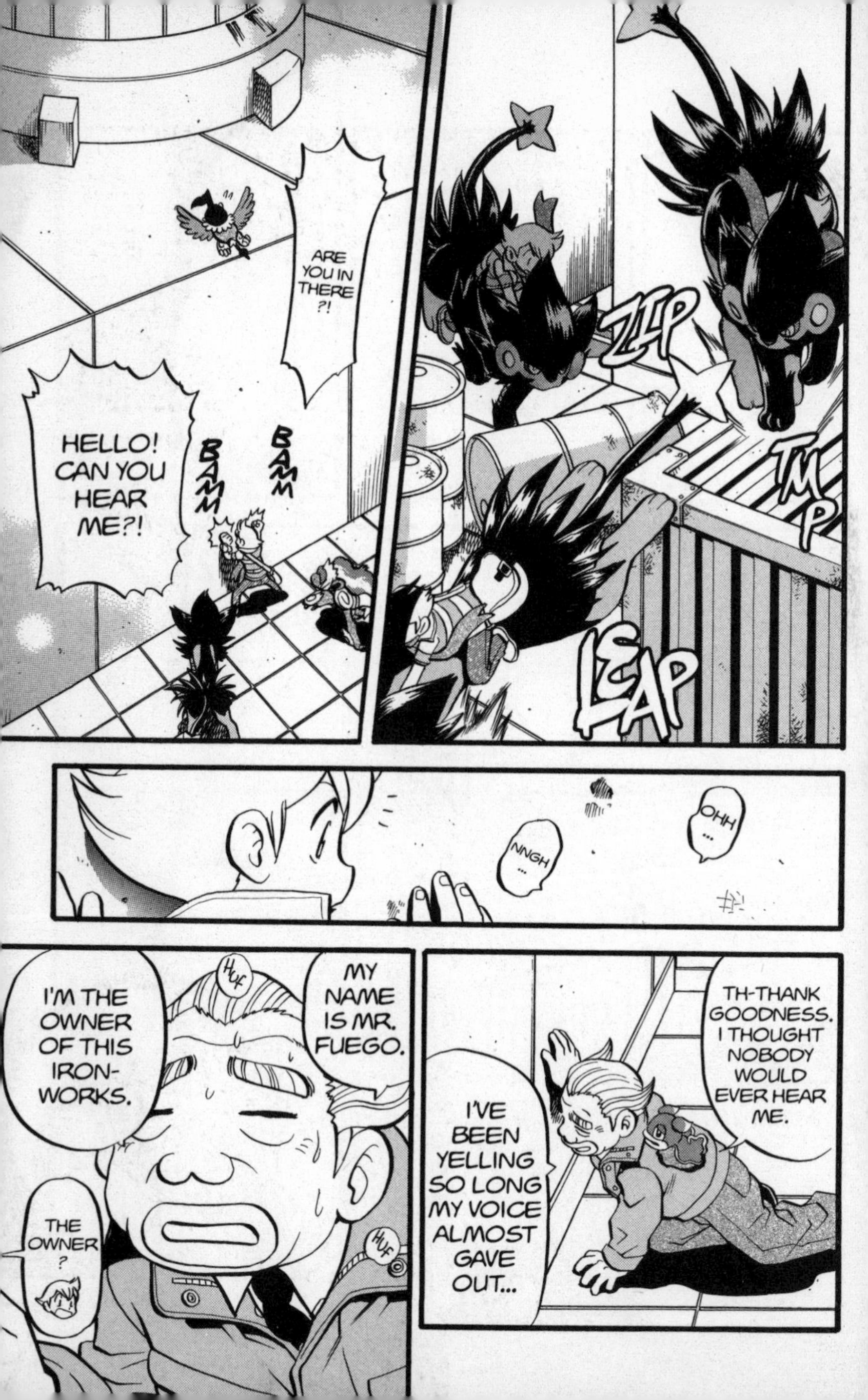
ZIP
TMP
LEAP
ARE YOU IN THERE?!
BAMM
BAMM
HELLO! CAN YOU HEAR ME?!
OHH...
NNGH...
TH-THANK GOODNESS. I THOUGHT NOBODY WOULD EVER HEAR ME.
I'VE BEEN YELLING SO LONG MY VOICE ALMOST GAVE OUT...
HUF
MY NAME IS MR. FUEGO.
I'M THE OWNER OF THIS IRON-WORKS.
HUF
THE OWNER?

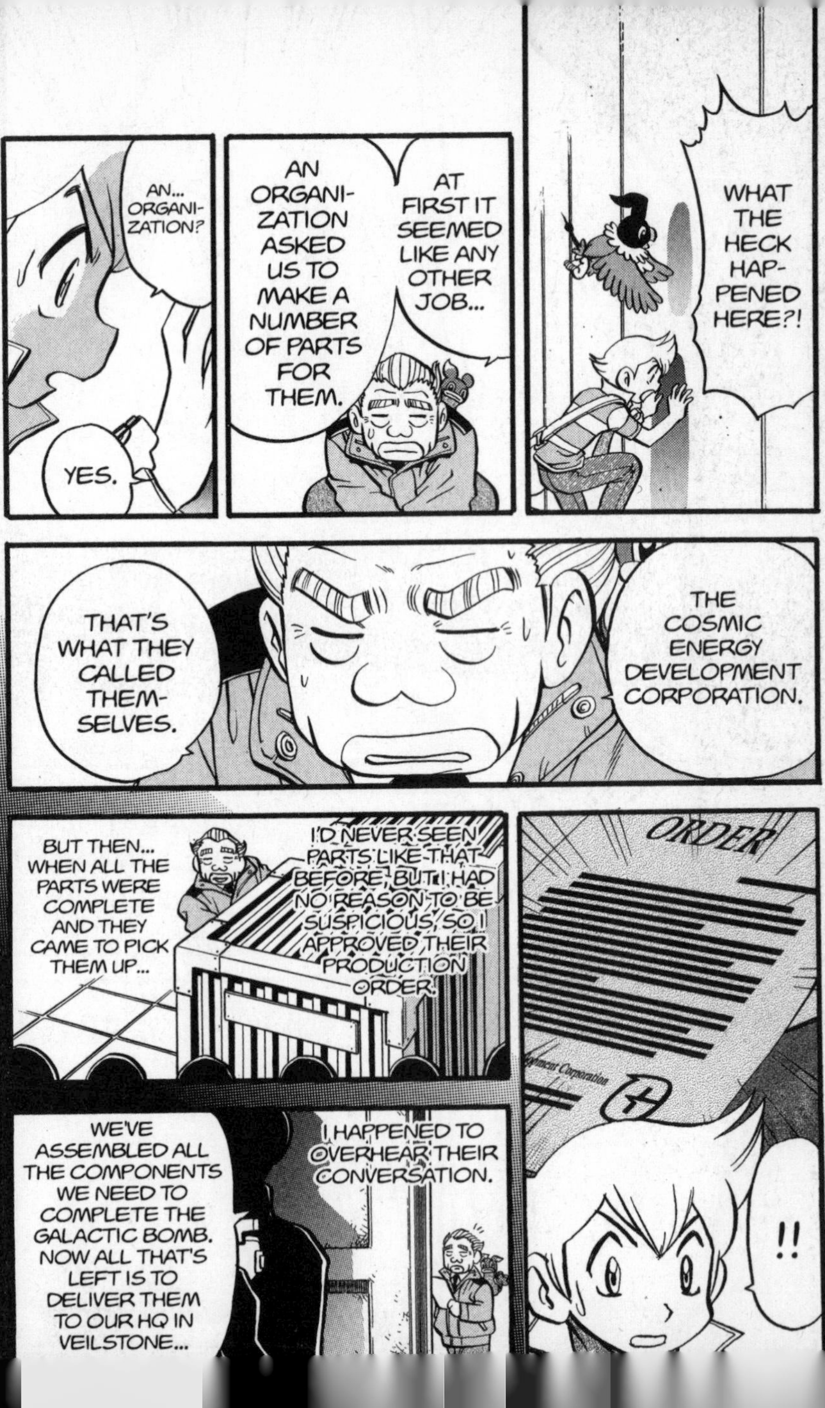
WHAT THE HECK HAPPENED HERE?!
AT FIRST IT SEEMED LIKE ANY OTHER JOB...
AN ORGANIZATION ASKED US TO MAKE A NUMBER OF PARTS FOR THEM.
AN... ORGANIZATION?
YES.
THE COSMIC ENERGY DEVELOPMENT CORPORATION.
THAT'S WHAT THEY CALLED THEMSELVES.
ORDER
!!
I'D NEVER SEEN PARTS LIKE THAT BEFORE, BUT I HAD NO REASON TO BE SUSPICIOUS, SO I APPROVED THEIR PRODUCTION ORDER.
BUT THEN... WHEN ALL THE PARTS WERE COMPLETE AND THEY CAME TO PICK THEM UP...
I HAPPENED TO OVERHEAR THEIR CONVERSATION.
WE'VE ASSEMBLED ALL THE COMPONENTS WE NEED TO COMPLETE THE GALACTIC BOMB. NOW ALL THAT'S LEFT IS TO DELIVER THEM TO OUR HQ IN VEILSTONE...

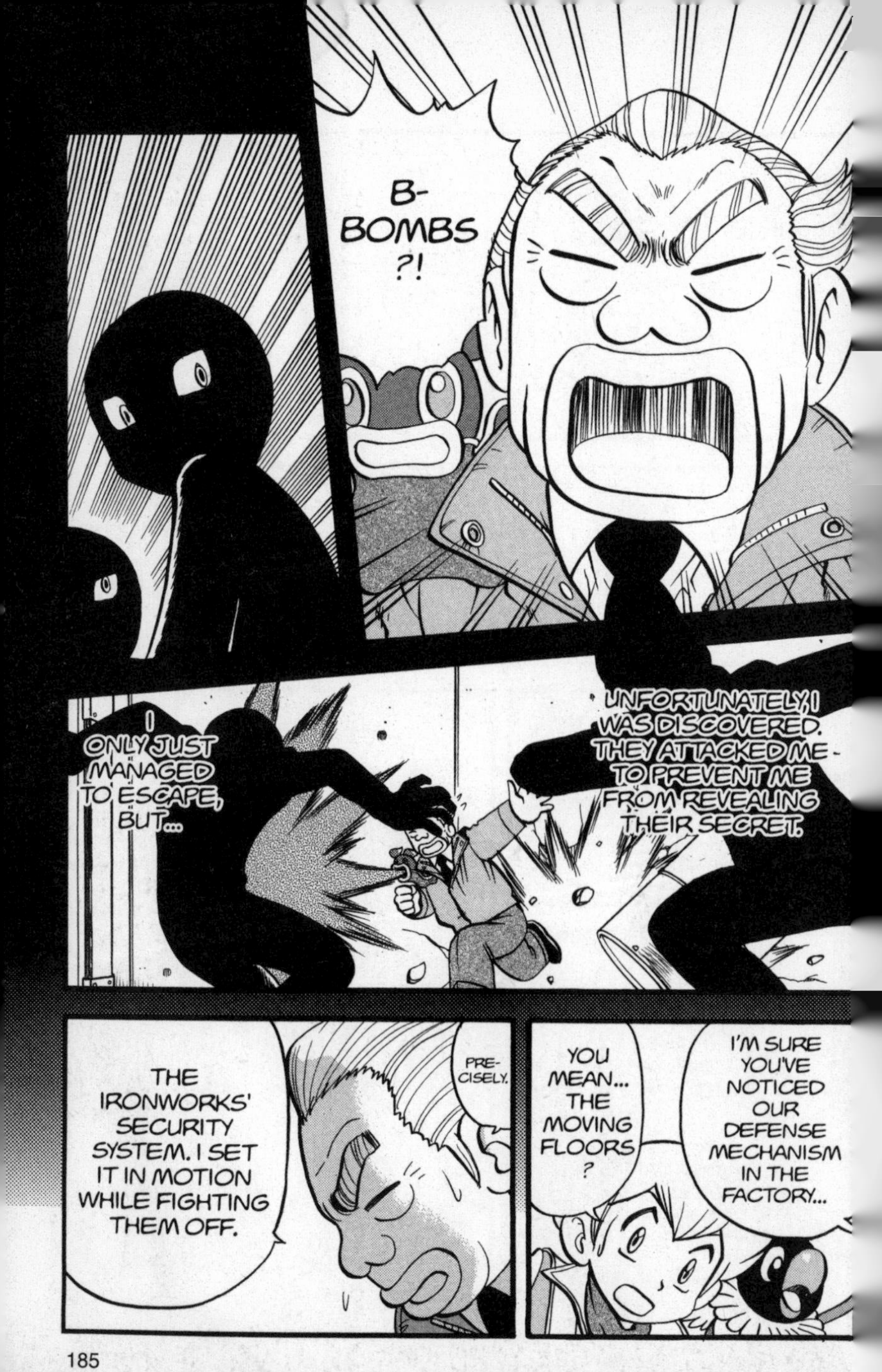
B-BOMBS ?!
UNFORTUNATELY, I WAS DISCOVERED. THEY ATTACKED ME TO PREVENT ME FROM REVEALING THEIR SECRET.
I ONLY JUST MANAGED TO ESCAPE, BUT...
I'M SURE YOU'VE NOTICED OUR DEFENSE MECHANISM IN THE FACTORY...
YOU MEAN... THE MOVING FLOORS?
PRECISELY.
THE IRONWORKS' SECURITY SYSTEM. I SET IT IN MOTION WHILE FIGHTING THEM OFF.

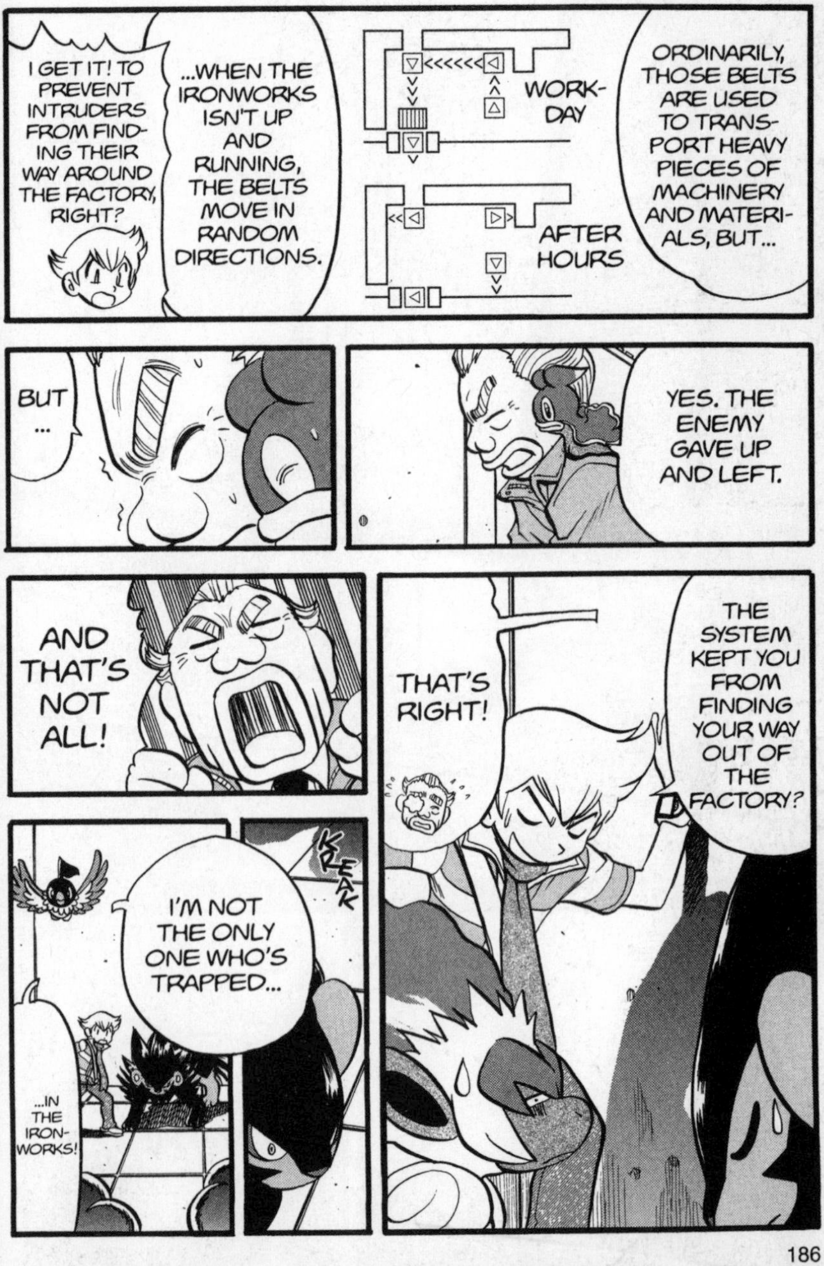
ORDINARILY, THOSE BELTS ARE USED TO TRANSPORT HEAVY PIECES OF MACHINERY AND MATERIALS, BUT...
WORK-DAY
AFTER HOURS
...WHEN THE IRONWORKS ISN'T UP AND RUNNING, THE BELTS MOVE IN RANDOM DIRECTIONS.
I GET IT! TO PREVENT INTRUDERS FROM FINDING THEIR WAY AROUND THE FACTORY, RIGHT?
YES. THE ENEMY GAVE UP AND LEFT.
BUT ...
THE SYSTEM KEPT YOU FROM FINDING YOUR WAY OUT OF THE FACTORY?
THAT'S RIGHT!
AND THAT'S NOT ALL!
KREAK
I'M NOT THE ONLY ONE WHO'S TRAPPED...
...IN THE IRONWORKS!

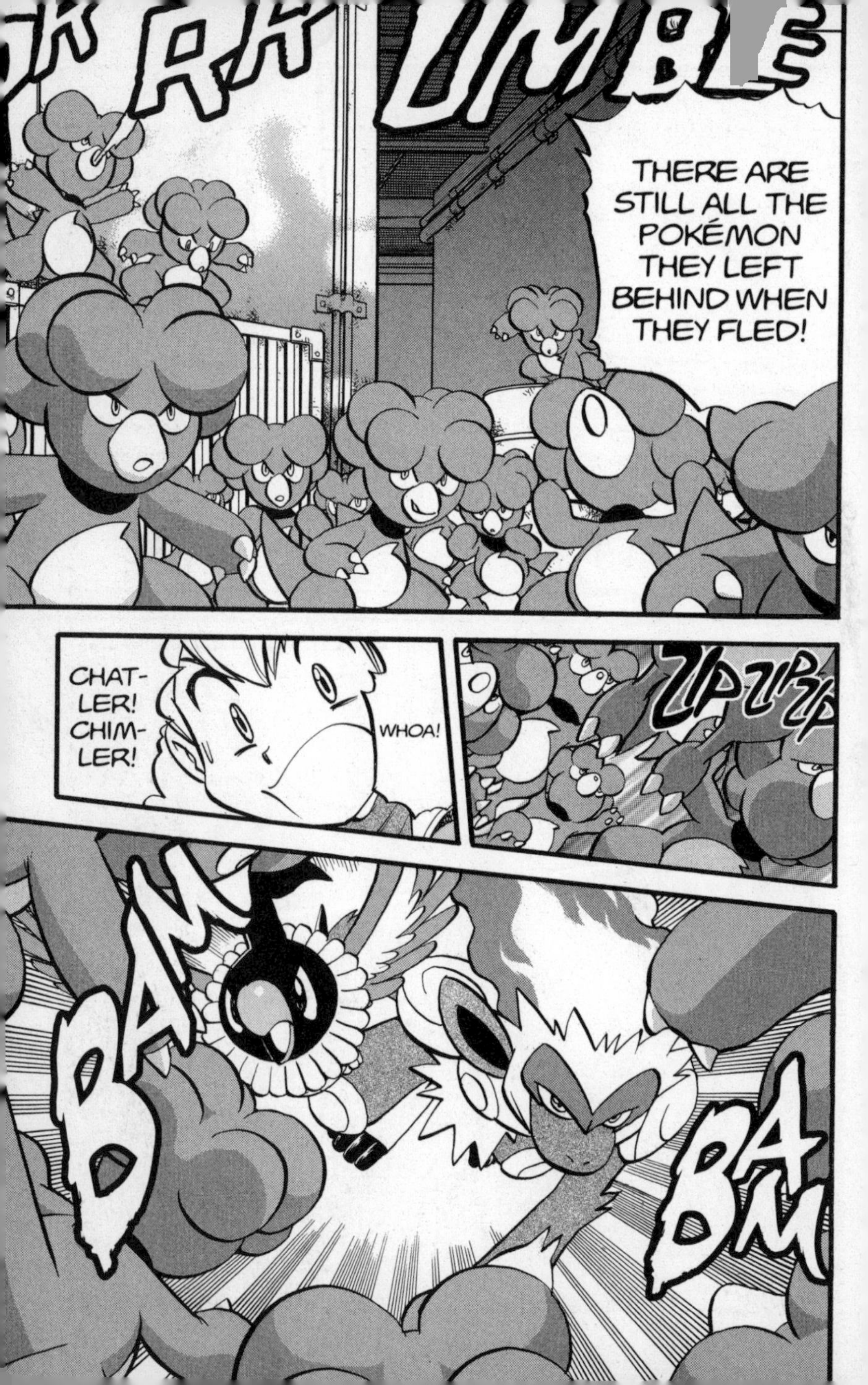
THERE ARE STILL ALL THE POKÉMON THEY LEFT BEHIND WHEN THEY FLED!
WHOA!
CHAT-LER! CHIM-LER!
BAM

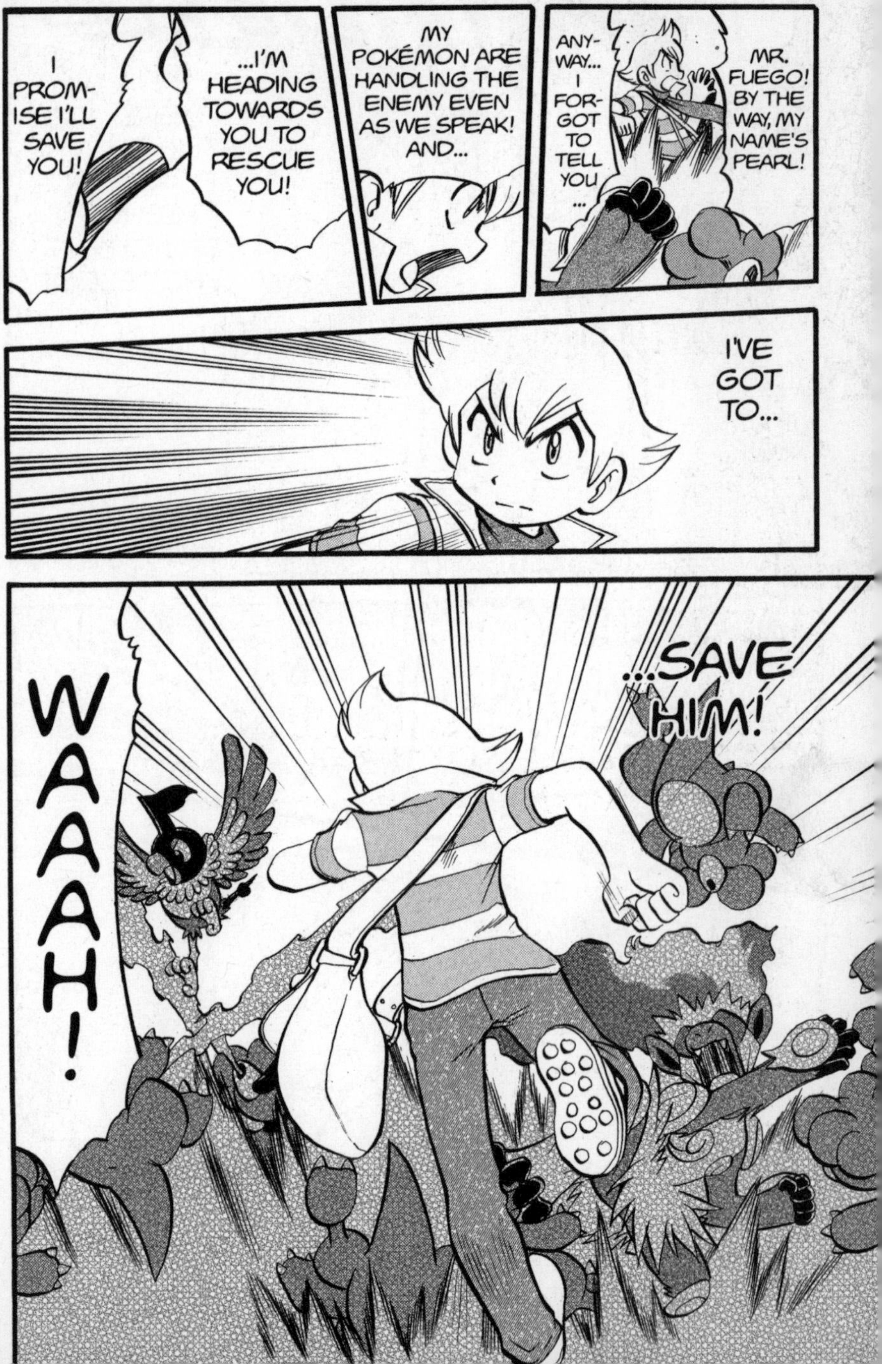
MR. FUEGO! BY THE WAY, MY NAME'S PEARL!
ANY-WAY... I FOR-GOT TO TELL YOU...
MY POKÉMON ARE HANDLING THE ENEMY EVEN AS WE SPEAK! AND...
...I'M HEADING TOWARDS YOU TO RESCUE YOU!
I PROM-ISE I'LL SAVE YOU!
I'VE GOT TO...
...SAVE HIM!
WAAAH!

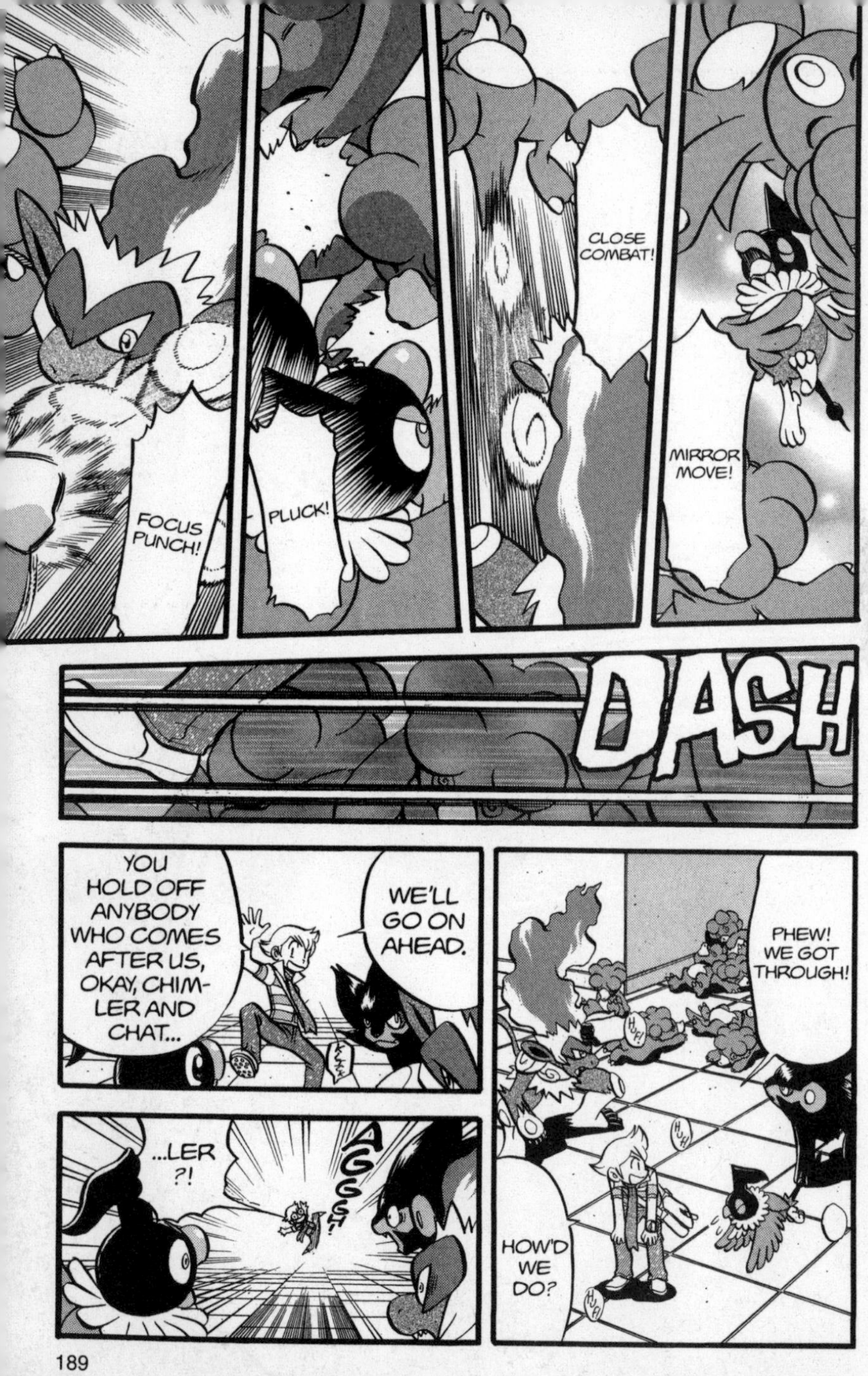
MIRROR MOVE!
CLOSE COMBAT!
PLUCK!
FOCUS PUNCH!
DASH
PHEW! WE GOT THROUGH!
HUH!
HUH!
HOW'D WE DO?
HUH!
WE'LL GO ON AHEAD.
YOU HOLD OFF ANYBODY WHO COMES AFTER US, OKAY, CHIM-LER AND CHAT...
AGGGH!
...LER ?!

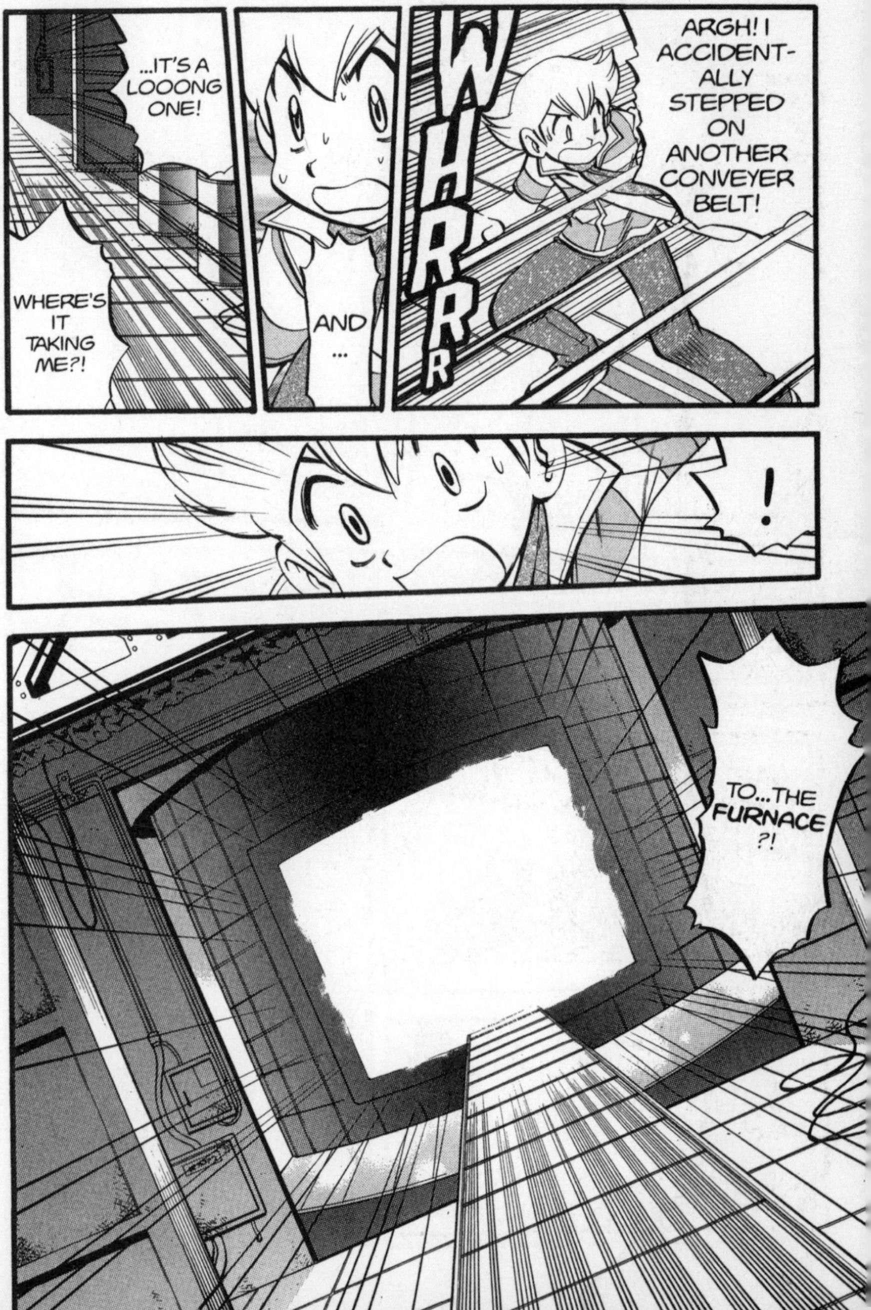

ARGH! I ACCIDENT-ALLY STEPPED ON ANOTHER CONVEYER BELT!
WHRRR
AND ...
...IT'S A LOOONG ONE!
WHERE'S IT TAKING ME?!
!
TO...THE FURNACE ?!

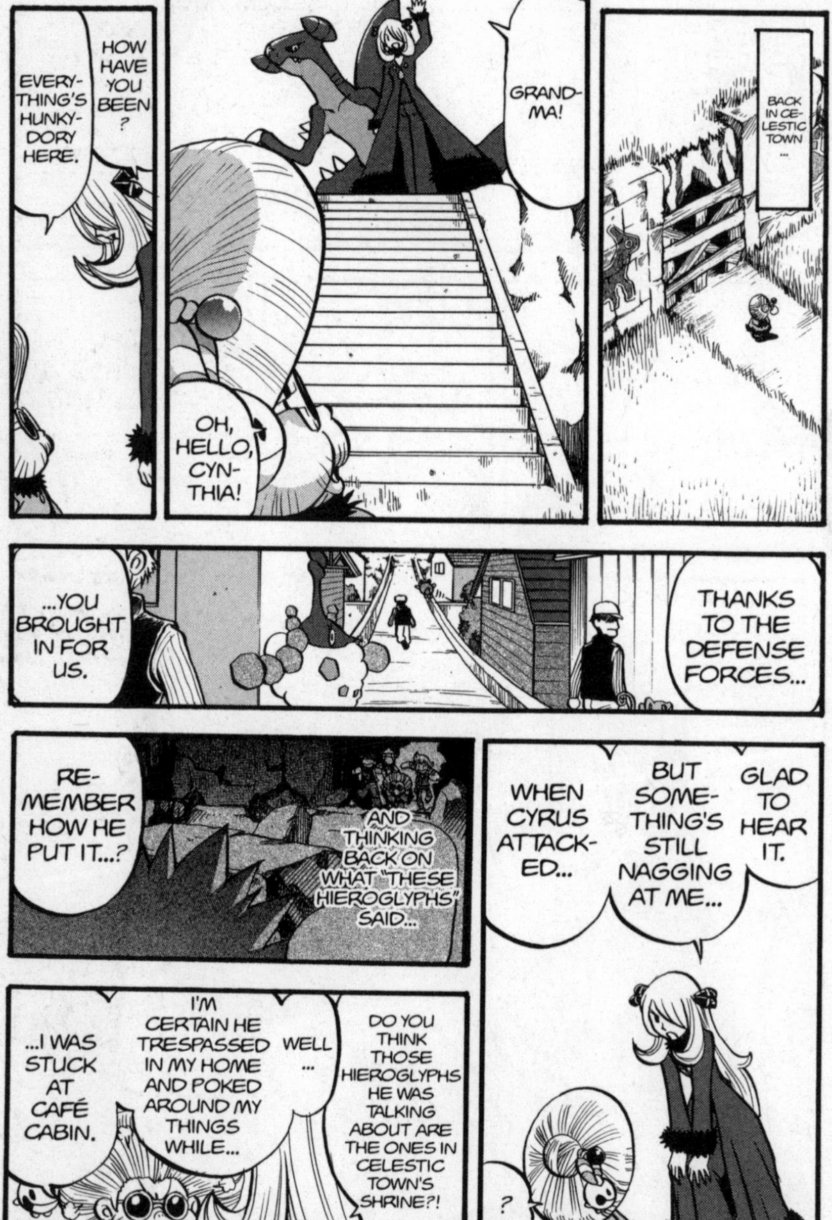
BACK IN CELESTIC TOWN...
GRANDMA!
OH, HELLO, CYNTHIA!
HOW HAVE YOU BEEN?
EVERYTHING'S HUNKY-DORY HERE.
THANKS TO THE DEFENSE FORCES...
...YOU BROUGHT IN FOR US.
GLAD TO HEAR IT.
BUT SOMETHING'S STILL NAGGING AT ME...
WHEN CYRUS ATTACKED...
?
AND THINKING BACK ON WHAT "THESE HIEROGLYPHS" SAID...
REMEMBER HOW HE PUT IT...?
DO YOU THINK THOSE HIEROGLYPHS HE WAS TALKING ABOUT ARE THE ONES IN CELESTIC TOWN'S SHRINE?!
WELL...
I'M CERTAIN HE TRESPASSED IN MY HOME AND POKED AROUND MY THINGS WHILE...
...I WAS STUCK AT CAFÉ CABIN.

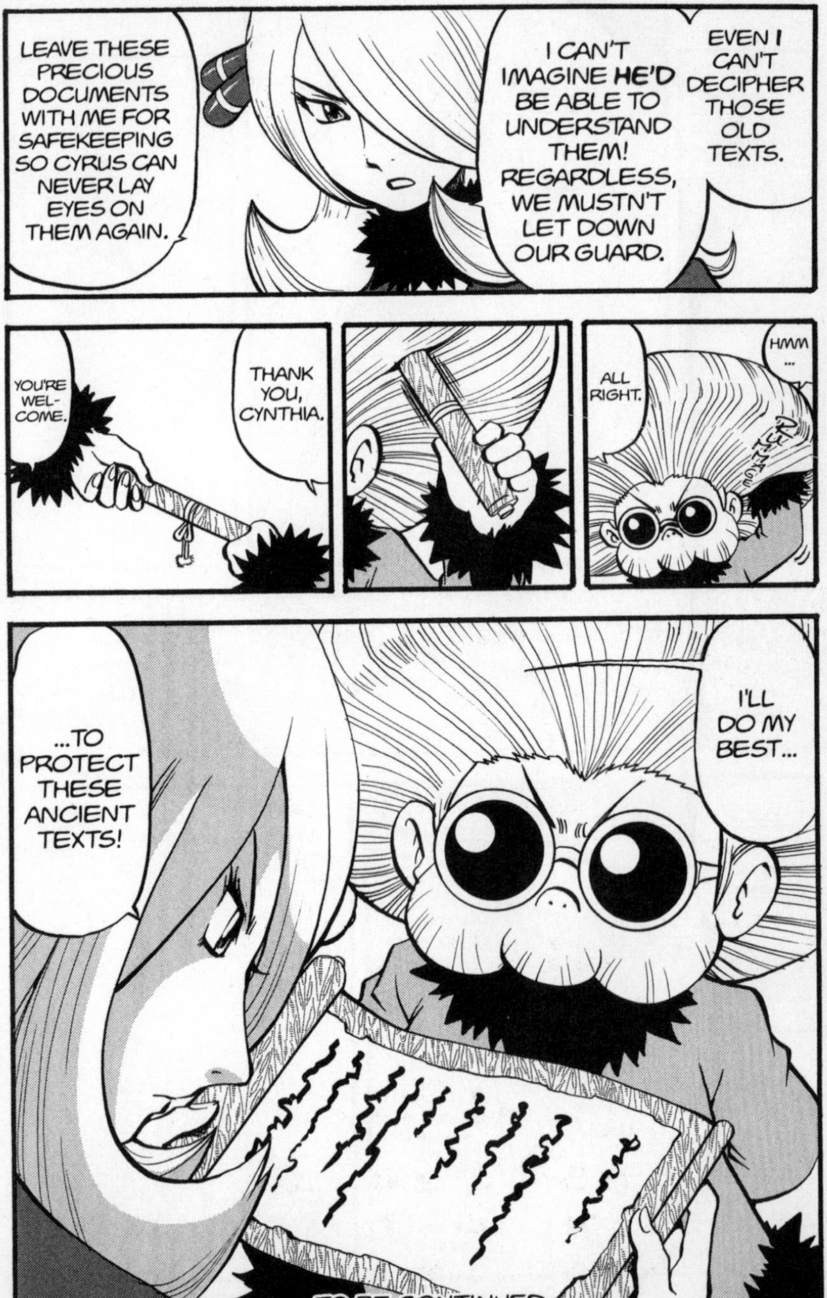
EVEN I CAN'T DECIPHER THOSE OLD TEXTS.
I CAN'T IMAGINE **HE'D** BE ABLE TO UNDERSTAND THEM! REGARDLESS, WE MUSTN'T LET DOWN OUR GUARD.
LEAVE THESE PRECIOUS DOCUMENTS WITH ME FOR SAFEKEEPING SO CYRUS CAN NEVER LAY EYES ON THEM AGAIN.
HMM...
ALL RIGHT.
THANK YOU, CYNTHIA.
YOU'RE WEL-COME.
I'LL DO MY BEST...
...TO PROTECT THESE ANCIENT TEXTS!
TO BE CONTINUED...

END OF VOLUME BONUS

The Scoop on the Mysterious Organization Team Galactic!!

LURKING IN THE SHADOWS, TEAM GALACTIC IS THE EPITOME OF EVIL. THEIR PLANS ARE MOVING FORWARD AT BREAKNECK SPEED! CAN YOU FOLLOW THEM?!

Connect the dots to reveal their ultimate goal!

TEAM GALACTIC'S PLAN IS MOVING SLOWLY BUT SURELY TOWARD ITS IMPLEMENTATION! AND IT SEEMS TEAM GALACTIC IS BEHIND ALL THE STRANGE INCIDENTS BEFALLING THE SINNOH REGION LATELY. APPARENTLY UNRELATED EVENTS IN DIFFERENT TOWNS ARE ALL CONNECTED TO THEIR MASTER PLAN! LET'S REVISIT THE INCIDENTS DIA AND HIS FRIENDS ENCOUNTERED ON THEIR JOURNEY AND FIGURE OUT WHAT TEAM GALACTIC IS UP TO ONCE AND FOR ALL!

Incident 1

Valley Windworks

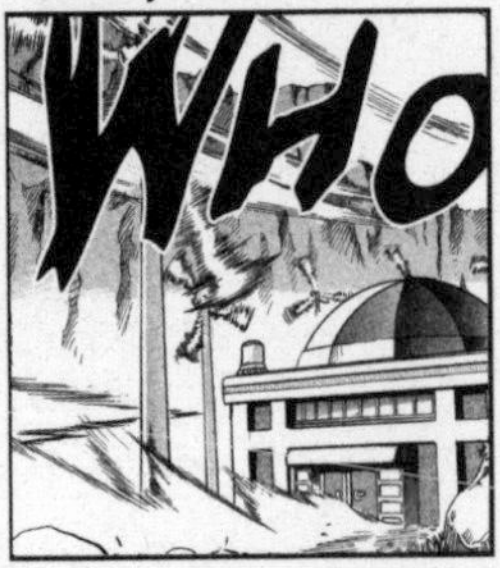

WHO

A tremendous amount of electricity is stolen!

NEAR FLOAROMA TOWN, SOMEBODY ATTACKS THE WIND-POWERED POWER PLANT! A SHOCKING THEFT OF ENERGY ENSUES!

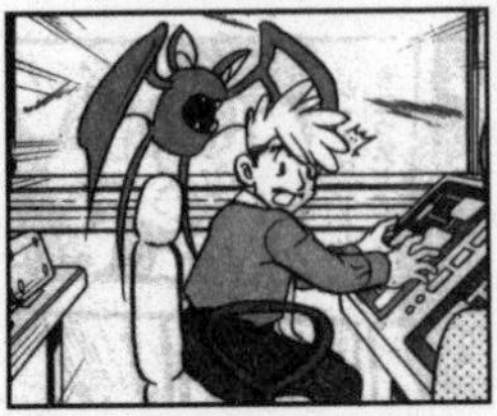

▲THE CHIEF OF THE POWER PLANT IS FRIGHTENED NEARLY TO DEATH! WHAT ARE THE CRIMINALS GOING TO USE ALL THAT ELECTRICITY FOR...?

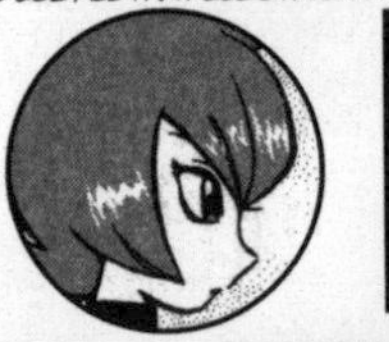

MARS

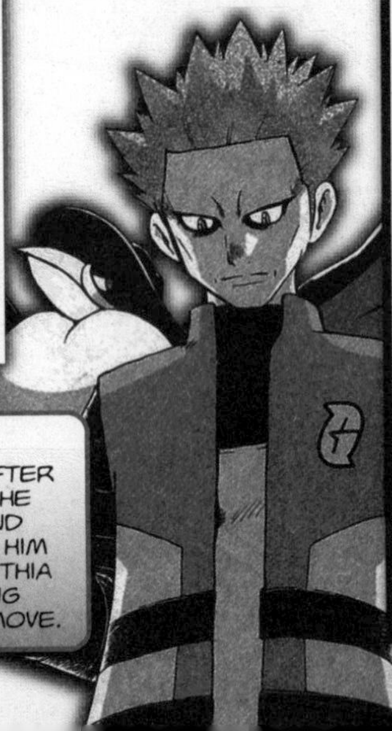

CYNTHIA IS DEPLOYED TO RESCUE RAD RICKSHAW. AFTER SOME DETECTIVE WORK, SHE ARRIVES ON THE SCENE AND SUCCESSFULLY RELEASES HIM WITHOUT BEING SEEN. CYNTHIA APPEARS TO BE FOLLOWING TEAM GALACTIC'S EVERY MOVE.

Incident 2

Eterna City

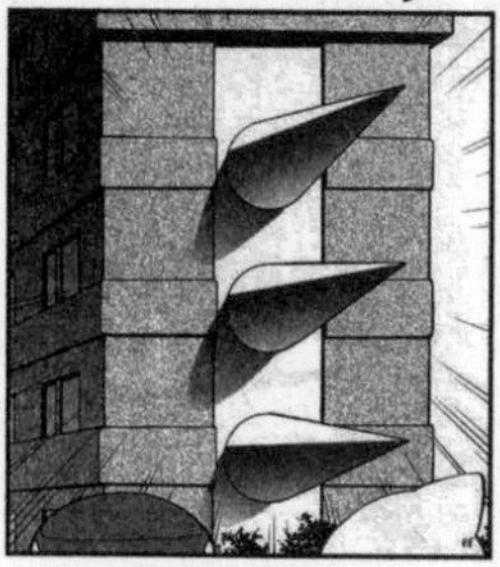

Cycle Shop Shopkeeper Kidnapped!

RAD RICKSHAW'S CYCLE SHOP HAS BEEN IN THE FAMILY FOR GENERATIONS. NOW RAD RICKSHAW IS ABDUCTED AND IMPRISONED IN AN EERIE SPIKED FORTRESS. APPARENTLY THE ENEMY WAS TRYING TO EXTRACT INFORMATION FROM HIM...

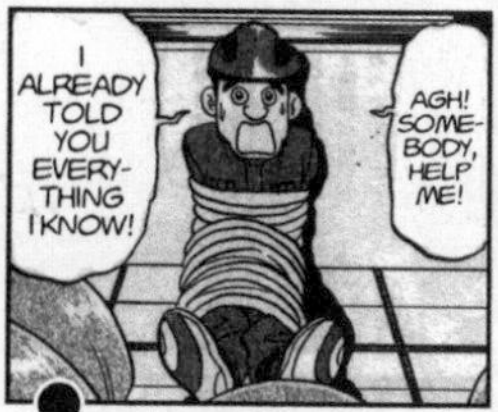
AGH! SOME-BODY, HELP ME!
I ALREADY TOLD YOU EVERY-THING I KNOW!

▲ HE INSISTS HE'S TOLD THEM EVERYTHING HE KNOWS—YET THEY REFUSE TO RELEASE HIM!

Galactic Grunts

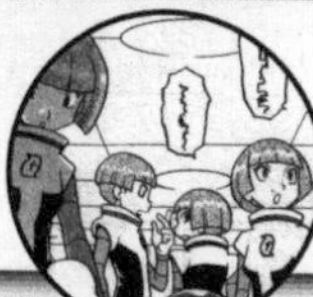

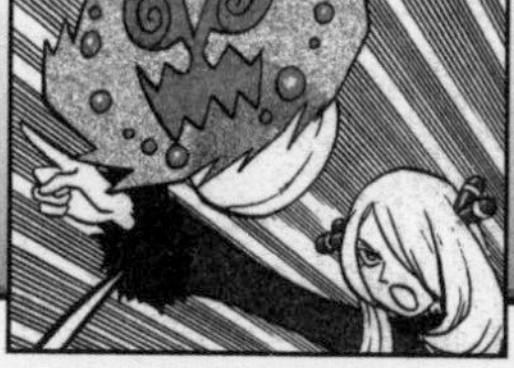

Incident 3

Mt. Coronet

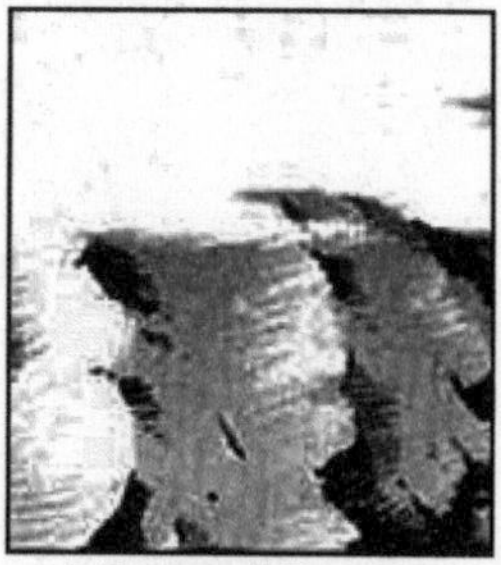

A Burst of Energy From the Ground!

MT. CORONET PIERCES THE VERY HEART OF SINNOH. A GREAT ENERGY BURSTS FORTH FROM WITHIN! THE ENSUING LANDSLIDE SWALLOWS UP PEOPLE AND POKÉMON ALIKE.

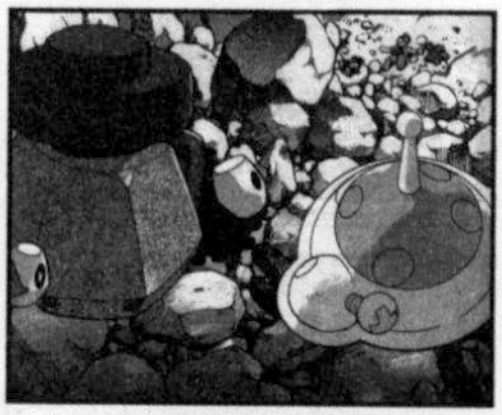

▲ FOR SOME REASON, IN THE AFTERMATH OF THIS EXPLOSION, POKÉMON EVOLVE! CYRUS EXCLAIMS THAT HE HAS COME TO EXPERIENCE THE BIRTH OF A WORLD!

Cyrus

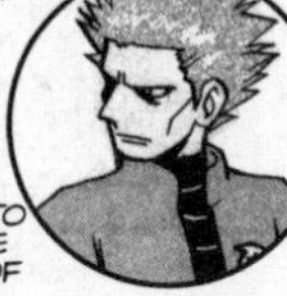

Incident 4

Lost Tower

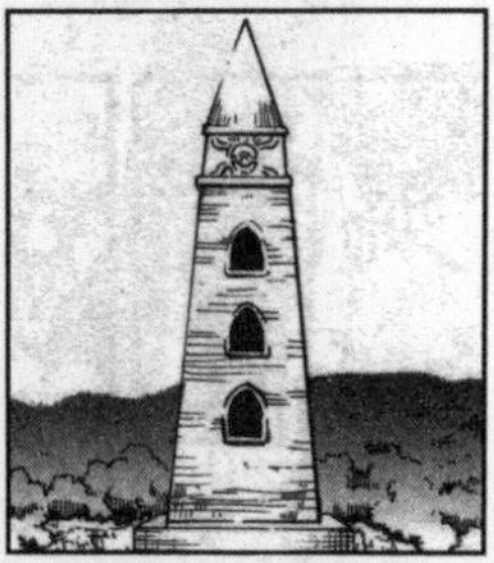

Desperate for Funding, Team Galactic Sets Its Sights on Lady!

TEAM GALACTIC NEEDS MONEY. AND TO GET IT, THEY TARGET THE WEALTHY BERLITZ FAMILY. THE DUO OF PROFESSIONAL BODY-GUARDS ORIGINALLY HIRED TO GUARD LADY ARE ATTACKED.

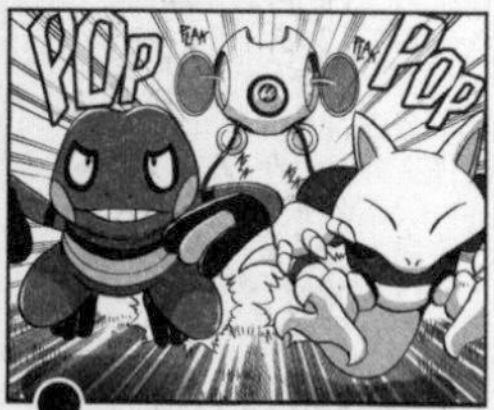
POP
POP

▲ A BATTLE BREAKS OUT IN THE LOST TOWER POKÉMON CEMETERY!

Saturn

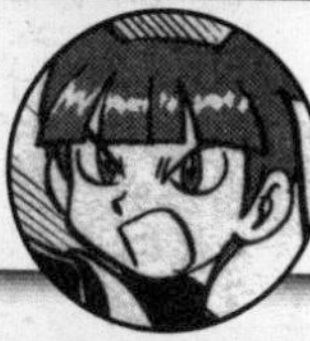

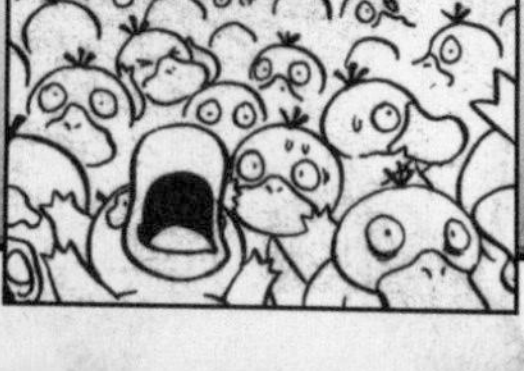

THE BATTLE IS FIERCE, BUT THE TWO BODYGUARDS ARE VICTORIOUS. SO THE ENEMY BLOCKADES ROUTE 210 WITH A FLOCK OF PSYDUCK, CUNNINGLY DIRECTING THE BODY-GUARDS TO VEILSTONE CITY.

Incident 5

Veilstone City

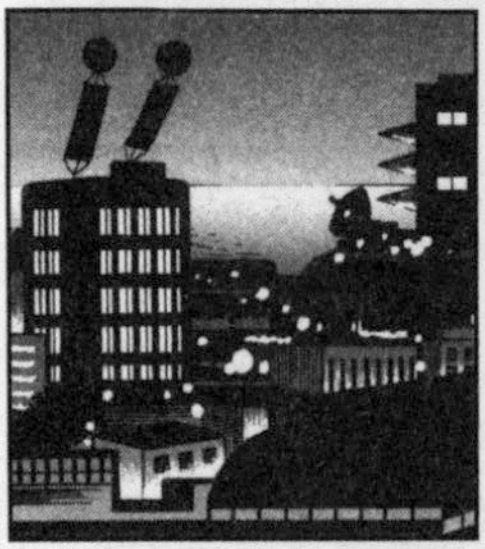

In the Dead of Night, the Town Is in Turmoil!

FALLING FOR TEAM GALACTIC'S TRICKS, OUR HEROES FIND THEMSELVES IN VEILSTONE BATTLING TOGETHER AT NIGHT. PEARL AND DIA ARE DETERMINED TO PROTECT LADY!

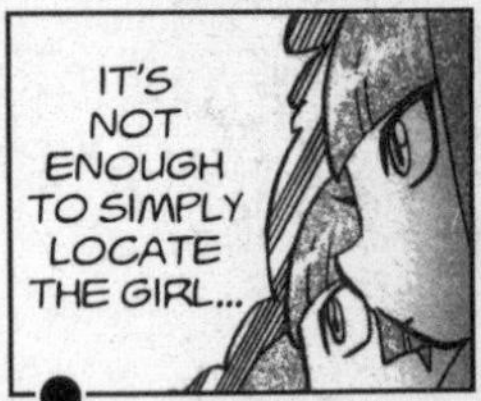
IT'S NOT ENOUGH TO SIMPLY LOCATE THE GIRL...

▲ THE ENEMY GROWS EVER MORE NEFARIOUS!

Saturn

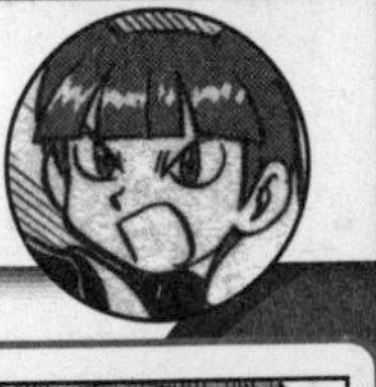

Incident 6

Lake Valor

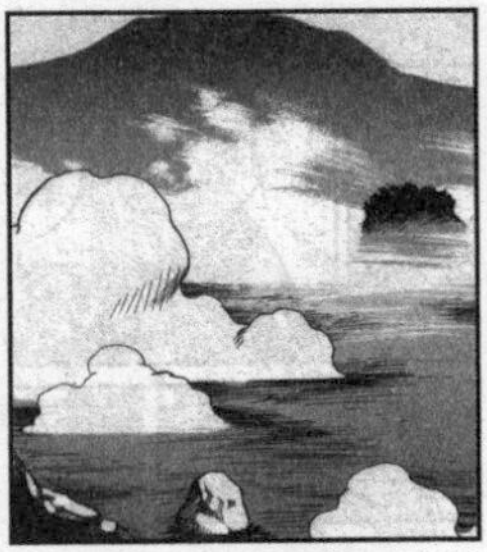

Why Are They Evacuating the Lake?!

"DO NOT ENTER" SIGNS ARE POSTED AROUND LAKE VALOR. OUR FRIENDS MANAGE TO GIVE THE GUARDS THE SLIP, BUT...

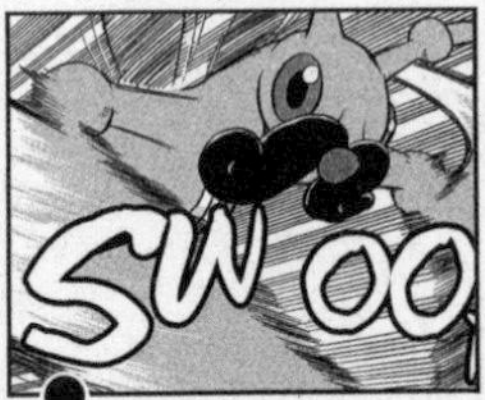
SWOO

▲ AN ENEMY POKÉMON WHO USES SONIC ATTACKS! BUT HOW TO STOP IT?

Scientists

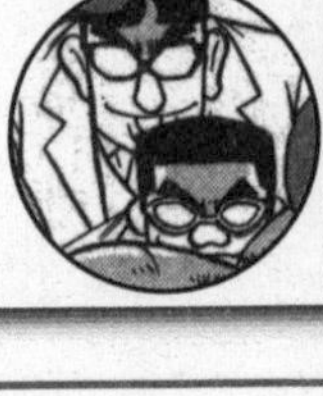

Incident 7

Celestic Town

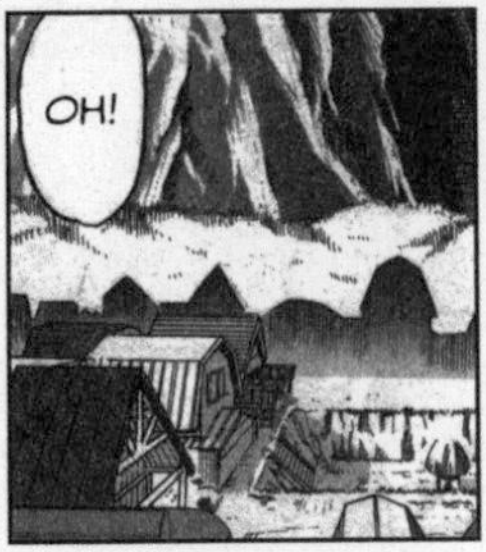
OH!

The Secret of the Ancient Ruin's Murals!

CELESTIC TOWN IS HOME TO ARCHEOLOGICAL TREASURES. WHAT WILL CYRUS DO WITH THE PHOTOS HE'S TAKEN OF THE ANCIENT MURALS THAT NO ONE IS MEANT TO LAY EYES ON?!

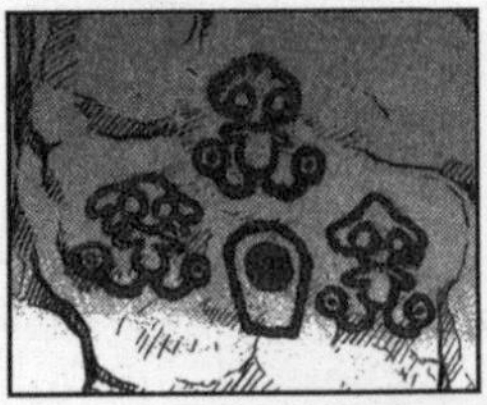

Cyrus

CYRUS ▲▶ IS CONNECTED TO THE INCIDENT BACK AT THE LAKE! WHAT DO THE MURALS SIGNIFY TO HIM?

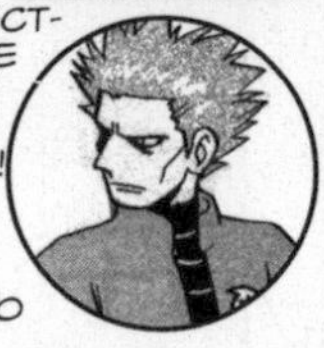

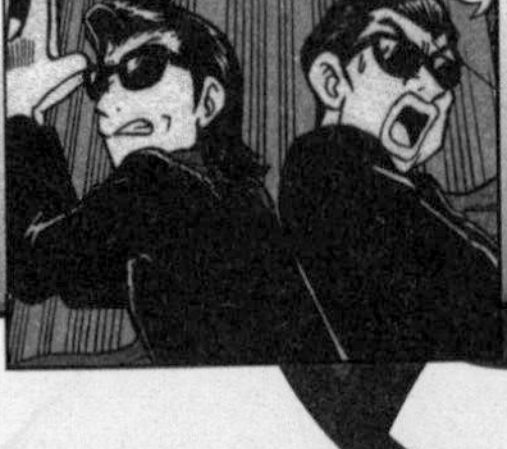

IN THE MIDST OF BATTLE, THE TWO BODYGUARDS ARE SWALLOWED UP BY A MYSTERIOUS LIGHT. IT'S A HAIR-RAISING SIGHT! WILL WE EVER SEE THEM AGAIN?

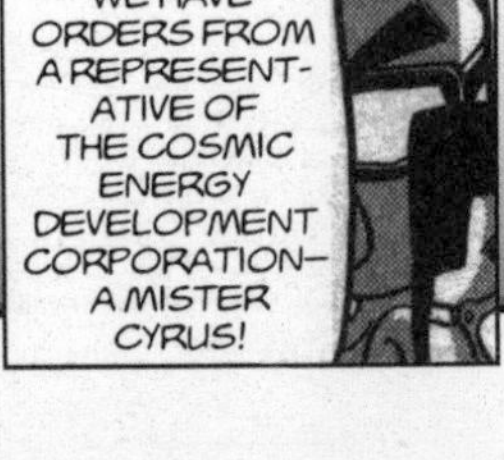
WE HAVE ORDERS FROM A REPRESENTATIVE OF THE COSMIC ENERGY DEVELOPMENT CORPORATION— A MISTER CYRUS!

Incident 8

Canalave City

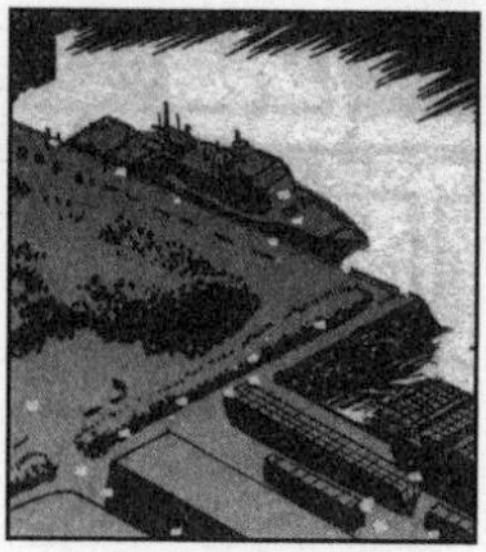

Extorted Money!

TEAM GALACTIC EXTORTS A RANSOM FROM SIR BERLITZ BY CLAIMING THEY HAVE KIDNAPPED HIS DAUGHTER (LADY). WHAT THEY PLAN TO SPEND THE MONEY ON FINALLY COMES TO LIGHT.

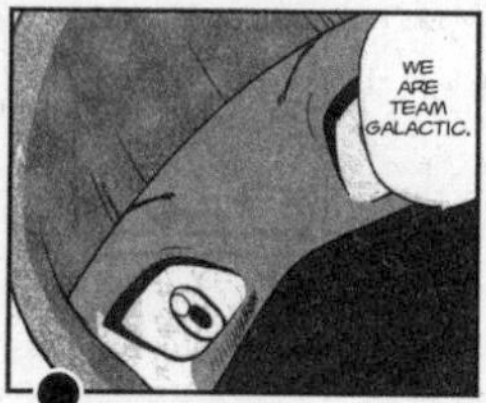
WE ARE TEAM GALACTIC.

▲▼THE NAME OF THE ORGANIZATION AND ITS SHOCKING INTENTIONS ARE NOW CLEAR!

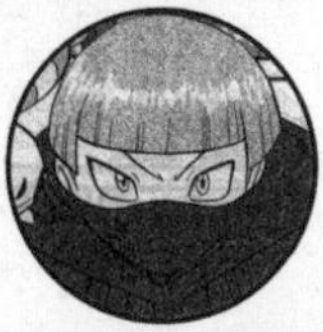

Incident 9

Iron Island

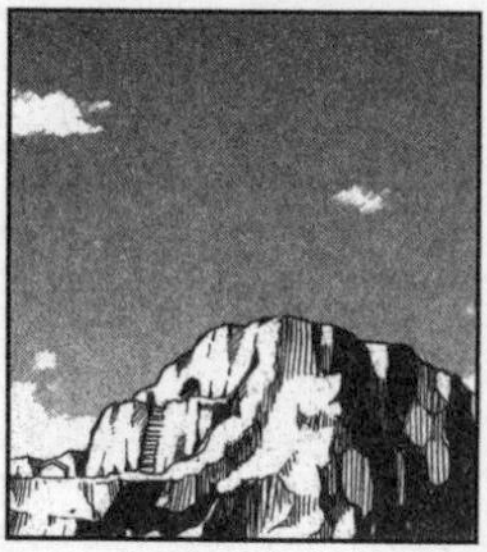

Chasing Down Evil!

THUGS PURSUE DIA, WHO IS UNDERGOING SPECIAL TRAINING, AND FILM THEIR BATTLE.

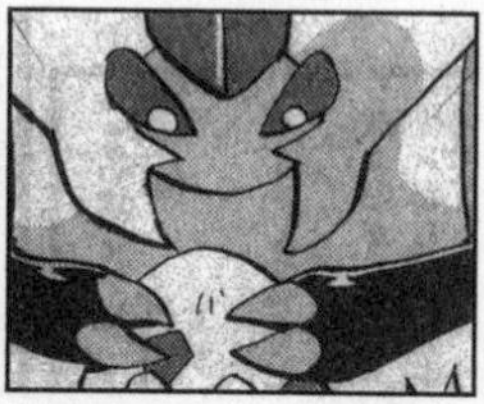

▲THE COWARDLY ENEMY HOLDS A POOR INNOCENT POKÉMON EGG HOSTAGE. WHO HIRED THESE THUGS TO BEHAVE SO BADLY?!

Cue Balls

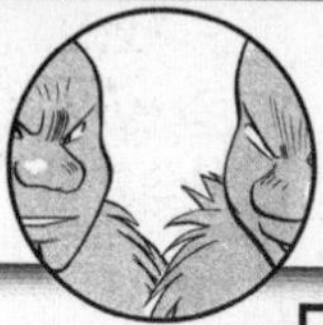

Their goal is... Cosmic!

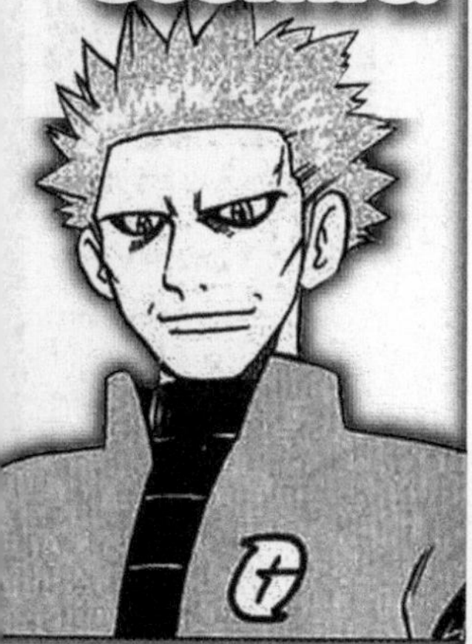

REFERENCES TO "SPACE" HAVE COME UP IN ONE INCIDENT TO THE NEXT. IT MUST BE SOMEHOW RELATED TO TEAM GALACTIC'S ULTIMATE GOAL. TIME FOR A CLOSER LOOK AT THIS ORGANIZATION AND ITS LEADERS.

THIS GRUNT DROPS THE NAME "COSMIC ENERGY DEVELOPMENT CORPORTION." THIS IS THE FIRST DIA AND FRIENDS HEAR OF CYRUS. JUST WHO IS HE?!

THE GYM LEADERS OF SINNOH ARE MONITORING TEAM GALACTIC'S SUSPICIOUS ACTIVITIES. ONE FATHER/SON TEAM IN PARTICULAR IS TAKING AN ACTIVE ROLE. THEY SHARE INFORMATION TO HELP THEM DEVELOP THEIR DEFENSE TOGETHER.

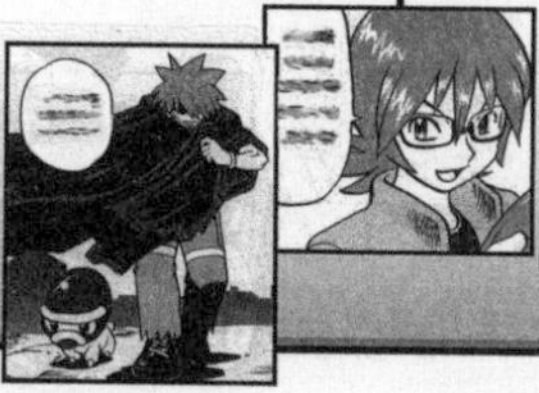

Team Galactic's boss is intense!
CYRUS

● Cyrus

CYRUS GIVES THE ORDERS AT TEAM GALACTIC. HE IS THE CHARISMATIC CORE OF THE ORGANIZATION, WIELDING ABSOLUTE AUTHORITY OVER ALL HIS MINIONS. HE MAINTAINS A COOL AND COLLECTED DEMEANOR AT ALL TIMES. SNAGS AND DISRUPTIONS IN HIS PLANS DON'T FAZE HIM.

The Man

His Prowess as a Trainer

CYRUS'S POKÉMON OBEY HIS ORDERS TO THE LETTER! NO ONE CAN MATCH THE AURA OF POWER HE EXUDES. HE IS ABSOLUTELY A FORCE TO BE RECKONED WITH.

▼ HE COULD LAY A TOWN FLAT IF HE WISHED.

HWOOOAAA!

THEY WANT TO HARNESS COSMIC ENERGY FOR EVERYONE.

THEY EVEN HAVE COMMERCIALS!

▲ He's the president of that company!

EXCEPT FOR THE INCIDENT AT LAKE VALOR, IT'S CLEAR THAT TEAM GALACTIC IS ESTABLISHING ITSELF AS A COMMERCIAL VENTURE. THEY EVEN ADVERTISE ON TV SO EVERYONE WILL BE FAMILIAR WITH THEIR BRAND.

A Plan to Create a New Universe!

CYRUS IS ADAMANT ABOUT HIS CONVICTIONS. ONCE HE PUTS HIS MIND TO SOMETHING, NOT EVEN THE STARS ARE THE LIMIT—SO TO SPEAK...

IT IS AS GRAND AS THE COSMOS.

▲ HIS VISION IS CLEAR!

Cyrus's Pokémon

THE TWO POKÉMON HE EVOLVED AT MT. CORONET WERE UNFORGETTABLE. BUT HE HAS OTHER POWERFUL TEAM-MATES, CREATING A BALANCE THAT LEAVES NO RESOURCE UNTAPPED.

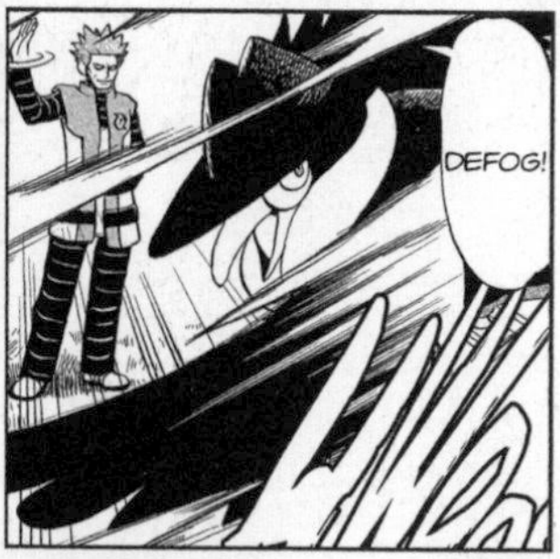
DEFOG!

▶ CAN EVEN MANIPULATE FOG!

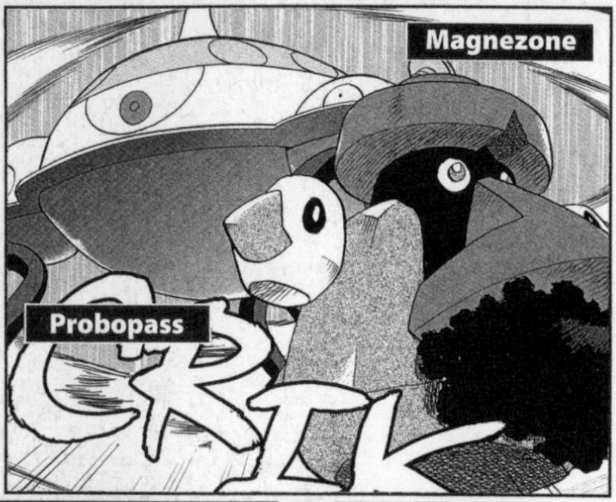
Magnezone
Probopass
CRIK

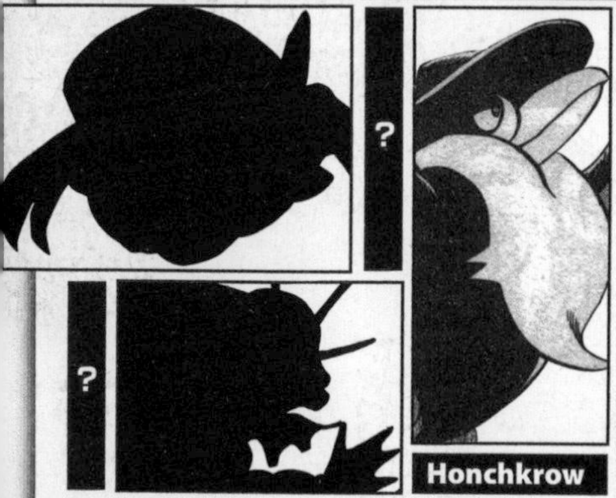
?
Honchkrow
?

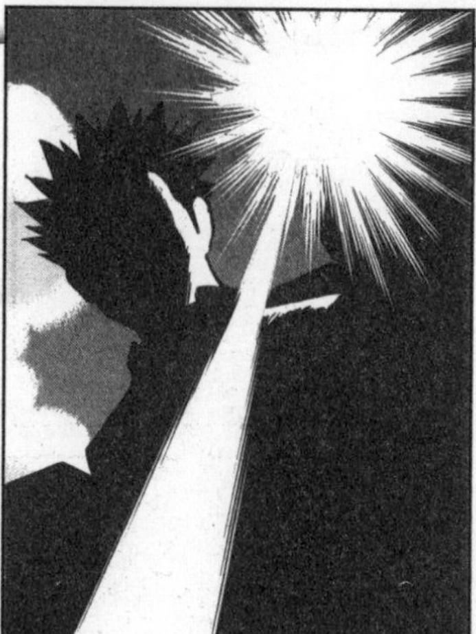

▲ CYRUS'S UPBRINGING IS SHROUDED IN MYSTERY.

Spent his Youth Tinkering with Machines

OVERHEARD WHISPERING THAT HIS HOMETOWN WAS BATHED IN SUNLIGHT. DID HIS LOVE AFFAIR WITH TECHNOLOGY BEGIN DURING HIS EARLY YEARS?

Equipment

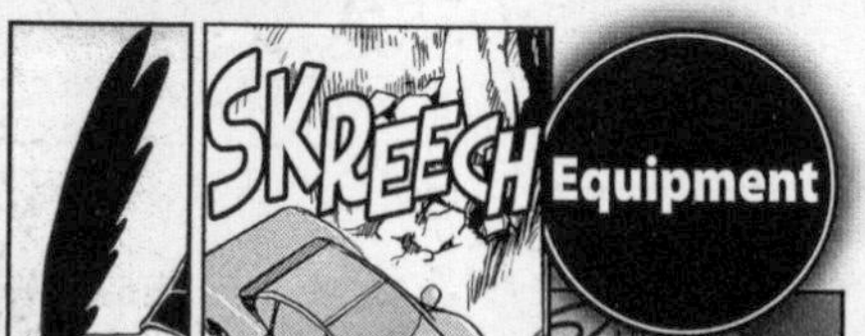
SKREECH

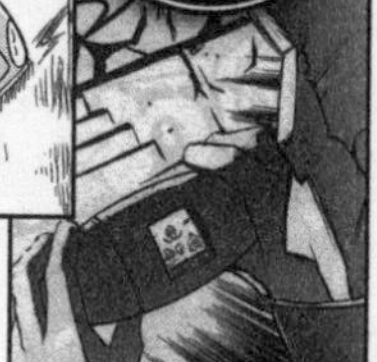

OWNS A HOVER CAR AND LOTS OF OTHER GADGETS—INCLUDING A DIGITAL CAMERA—AND CLASSIC TOOLS SUCH AS A PEN MADE FROM HIS HONCHKROW'S FEATHER.

She's a slippery one! And merciless!

Mars

THIS TEAM GALACTIC COMMANDER WALKS TO THE BEAT OF HER OWN DRUM. AT FIRST GLANCE, SHE COMES OFF AS CAREFREE. BEHIND THAT FAÇADE, SHE IS A METICULOUS PLANNER. SHE WAS IN CHARGE OF THE ELECTRICITY ROBBERY. THE PLUNDERED ELECTRICITY ALL WENT INTO THE CREATION OF THE GALACTIC BOMB!

YOU BETTER NOT CROSS THAT LINE! THIS IS MY STRATEGY ROOM!
OH, RIGHT ...
What a pain.

▲ HER TESTINESS RUBS SATURN THE WRONG WAY.

An explosives expert in charge of in-base operations.

Saturn

"REMOTE CONTROL" IS HIS FORTE, SO HE RARELY LEAVES HQ. SATURN IS THE ONE BEHIND THE FLYING CAMERA-SPEAKER APPARATUS WE'VE SEEN FLOATING AROUND. HE ALSO CAME UP WITH THE NEFARIOUS PLAN FOR PROCURING FUNDS.

BEFORE YOU PICK A FIGHT WITH ME, FULFILL YOUR DUTIES. ANY PROGRESS ON PROCURING A POWER SUPPLY?
THINGS ARE GOING AS PLANNED ON MY SIDE. THE GALACTIC BOMB IS NEARLY COMPLETE!

▲ THEY'VE PROCURED THE FUNDS AND COMPLETED THE GALACTIC BOMB. SOON THEY WILL CONQUER THE WORLD!

Jupiter is third in command.

Jupiter

WE HAVE YET TO MEET THIS THIRD TEAM LEADER. WHO IS SAID TO BE STRONGER THAN MARS OR SATURN AND TO BE A FORMIDABLE OPPONENT IN BATTLE. THIS LEADER'S APPEARANCE IS ANTICIPATED WITH GREAT FOREBODING.

▲ THIS LEADER'S EXPERTISE IN BATTLE TACTICS IS ALREADY CLEAR!

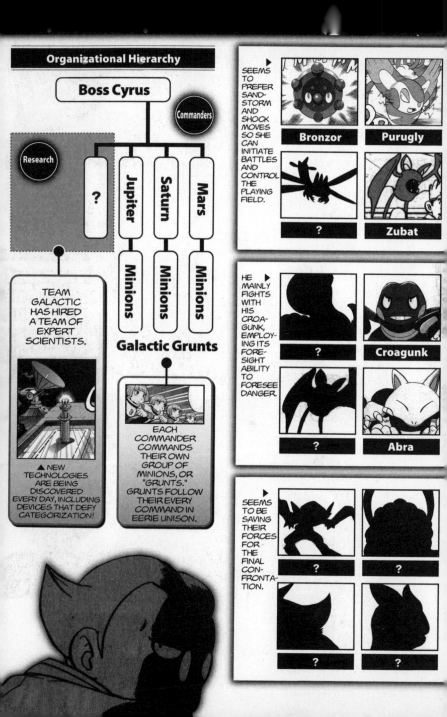

Organizational Hierarchy

Boss Cyrus

Commanders

- ?
- Jupiter — Minions
- Saturn — Minions
- Mars — Minions

Research

Galactic Grunts

TEAM GALACTIC HAS HIRED A TEAM OF EXPERT SCIENTISTS.

▲ NEW TECHNOLOGIES ARE BEING DISCOVERED EVERY DAY, INCLUDING DEVICES THAT DEFY CATEGORIZATION!

EACH COMMANDER COMMANDS THEIR OWN GROUP OF MINIONS, OR "GRUNTS." GRUNTS FOLLOW THEIR EVERY COMMAND IN EERIE UNISON.

▶ SEEMS TO PREFER SANDSTORM AND SHOCK MOVES SO SHE CAN INITIATE BATTLES AND CONTROL THE PLAYING FIELD.

Bronzor
Purugly
?
Zubat

▶ HE MAINLY FIGHTS WITH HIS CROAGUNK, EMPLOYING ITS FORESIGHT ABILITY TO FORESEE DANGER.

?
Croagunk
?
Abra

▶ SEEMS TO BE SAVING THEIR FORCES FOR THE FINAL CONFRONTATION.

?
?
?
?

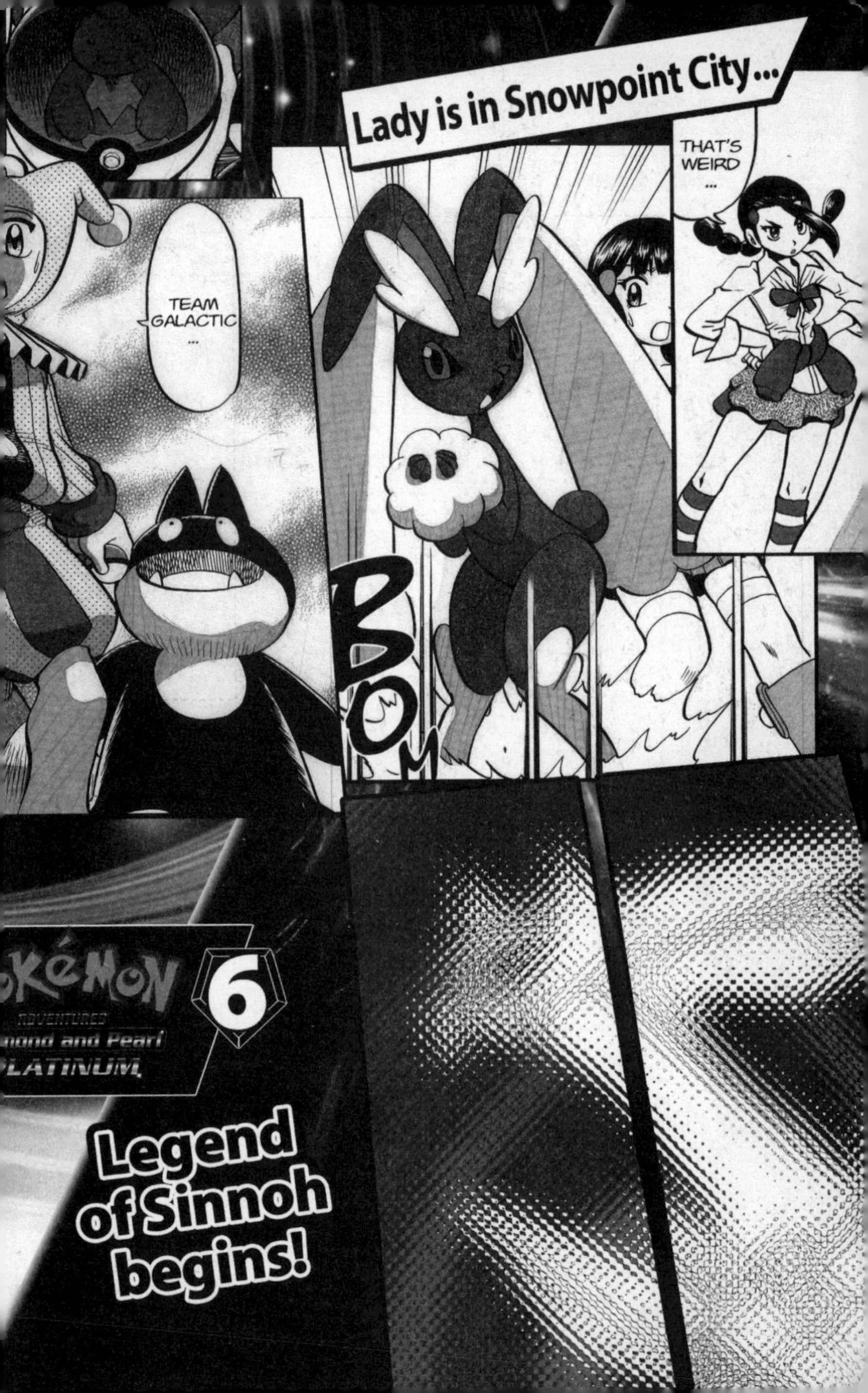
Lady is in Snowpoint City...
THAT'S WEIRD ...
BOOM
TEAM GALACTIC ...
OKÉMON
ADVENTURES
mond and Pearl
LATINUM
6
Legend of Sinnoh begins!

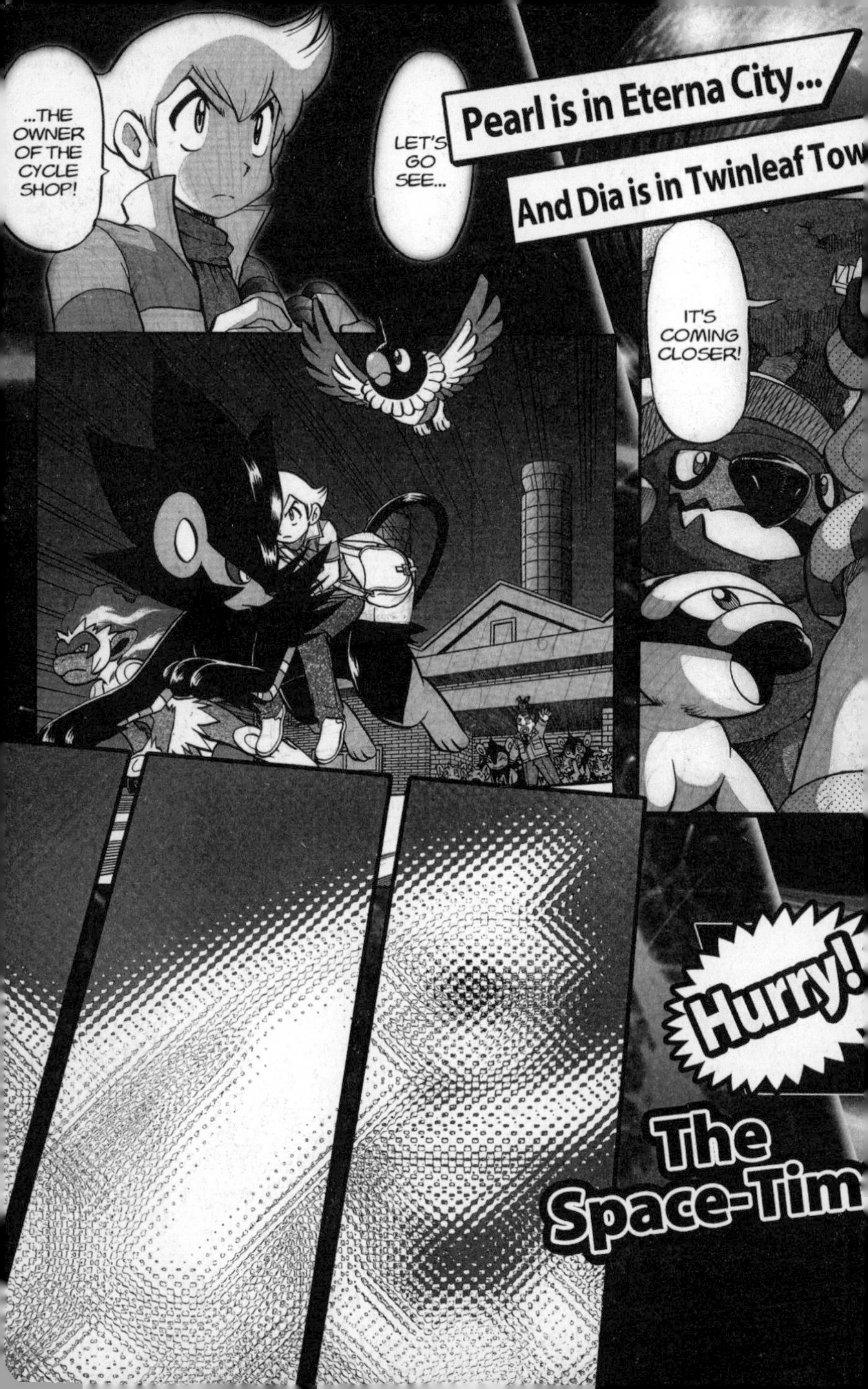

Pearl is in Eterna City...
And Dia is in Twinleaf Tow
IT'S COMING CLOSER!
LET'S GO SEE...
...THE OWNER OF THE CYCLE SHOP!
Hurry!
The Space-Tim

Message from
Hidenori Kusaka

These episodes are memorable for me, and I'm delighted to be able to share them with overseas readers. Our brave trio faces a crisis during their journey, and their complex emotions are evident in their faces. You'll see plenty of Pokémon characters too!! Enjoy!

Message from
Satoshi Yamamoto

The *Pokémon Adventures* series includes a lot of stories about the relationships between characters—particularly between father and child. Every parent and child has an intense relationship. What will Lady and her father, Sir Berlitz, grapple with when they finally meet again in this volume?

More Adventures Coming Soon...

Platinum gets a new Pokémon, and an old Pokémon friend gets a Trainer! Then, our trio divide and conquer. While Platinum skis the slopes and pursues her Glacier Badge, Pearl investigates Team Galactic, and Diamond stumbles upon a luxurious mansion staffed by a stuffy butler. Where could Diamond be...?!

Meanwhile, what is Team Galactic member Mars doing with that mysterious flying camera...?

Plus, meet Snover, Froslass, Lickilicky, Yanmega and many more Sinnoh Pokémon friends!

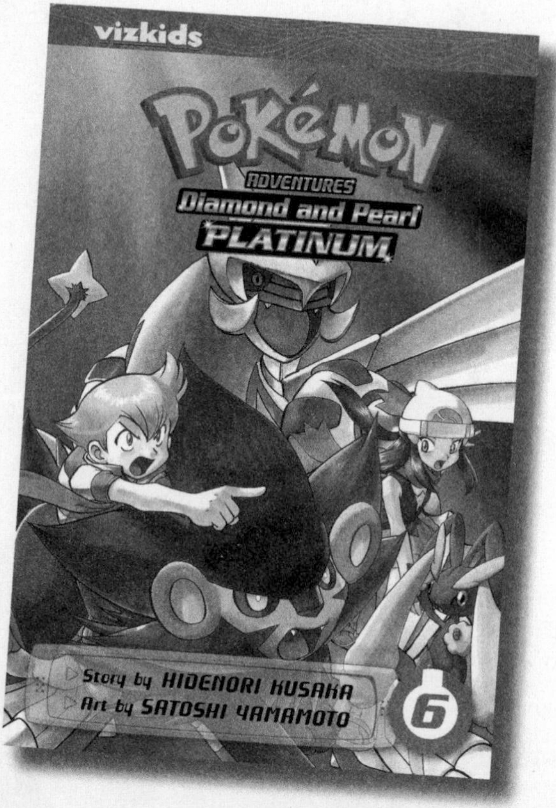
vizkids
POKÉMON
ADVENTURES
Diamond and Pearl
PLATINUM
Story by HIDENORI KUSAKA
Art by SATOSHI YAMAMOTO
6

AVAILABLE NOW!

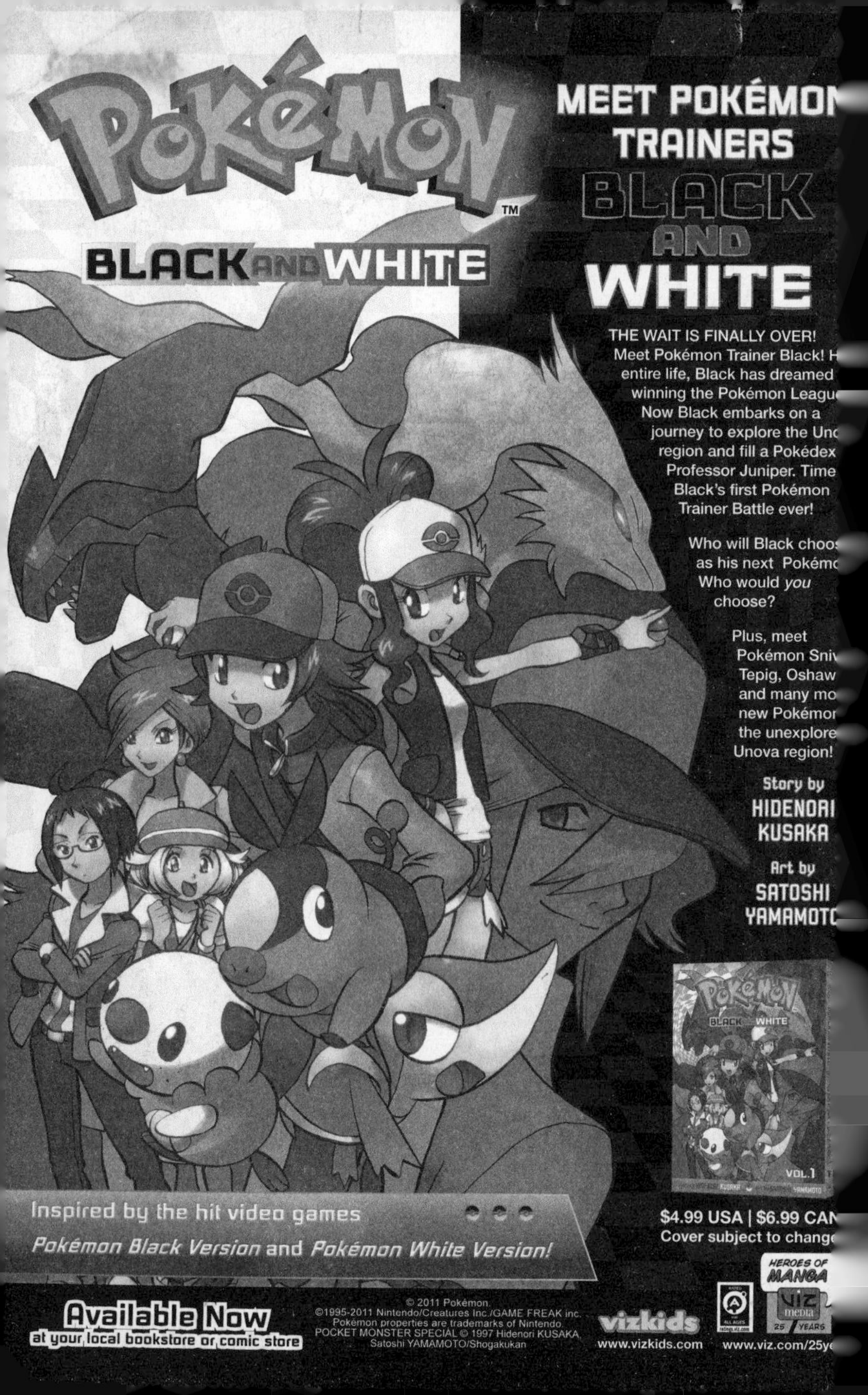

POKÉMON™
BLACK AND WHITE
MEET POKÉMON TRAINERS
BLACK AND WHITE
THE WAIT IS FINALLY OVER!
Meet Pokémon Trainer Black! H
entire life, Black has dreamed
winning the Pokémon Leagu
Now Black embarks on a
journey to explore the Un
region and fill a Pokédex
Professor Juniper. Time
Black's first Pokémon
Trainer Battle ever!
Who will Black choos
as his next Pokémo
Who would *you*
choose?
Plus, meet
Pokémon Sni
Tepig, Oshaw
and many mo
new Pokémon
the unexplore
Unova region!
Story by
HIDENORI
KUSAKA
Art by
SATOSHI
YAMAMOTO
VOL. 1
$4.99 USA | $6.99 CAN
Cover subject to chang
Inspired by the hit video games
Pokémon Black Version and *Pokémon White Version!*
Available Now
at your local bookstore or comic store
© 2011 Pokémon.
©1995-2011 Nintendo/Creatures Inc./GAME FREAK inc.
Pokémon properties are trademarks of Nintendo.
POCKET MONSTER SPECIAL © 1997 Hidenori KUSAKA,
Satoshi YAMAMOTO/Shogakukan
HEROES OF MANGA
vizkids
www.vizkids.com
VIZ media 25 YEARS
www.viz.com/25y

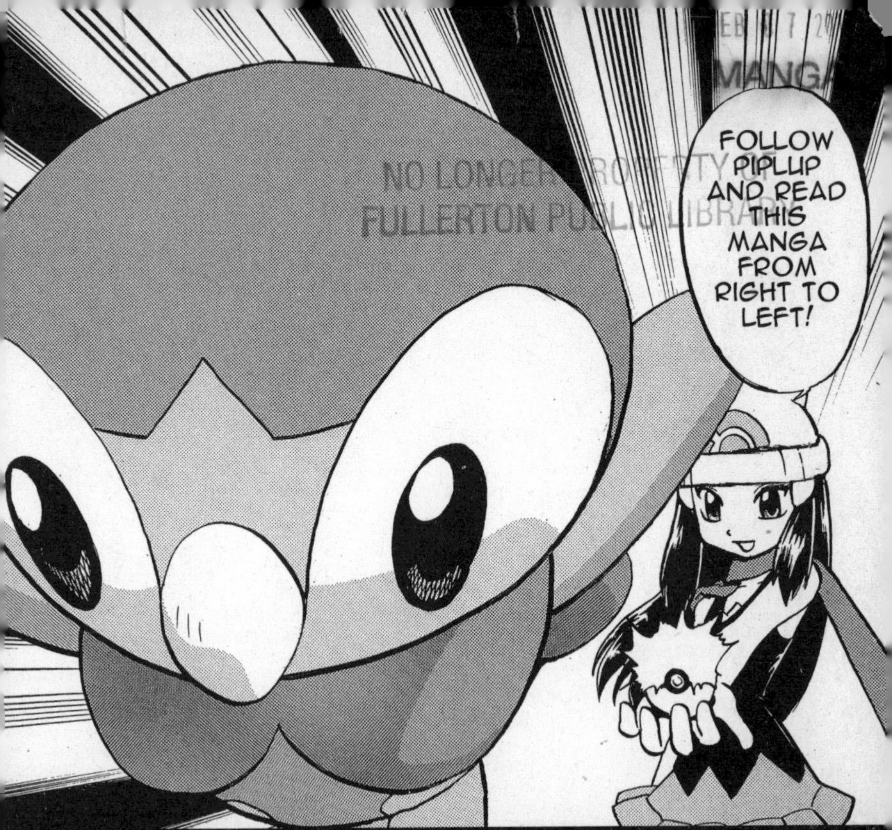
FOLLOW PIPLUP AND READ THIS MANGA FROM RIGHT TO LEFT!

THIS IS THE END OF THIS GRAPHIC NOVEL!

To properly enjoy this VIZ Media graphic novel, please turn it around and begin reading from right to left.

This book has been printed in the original Japanese format in order to preserve the orientation of the original artwork. Have fun with it!

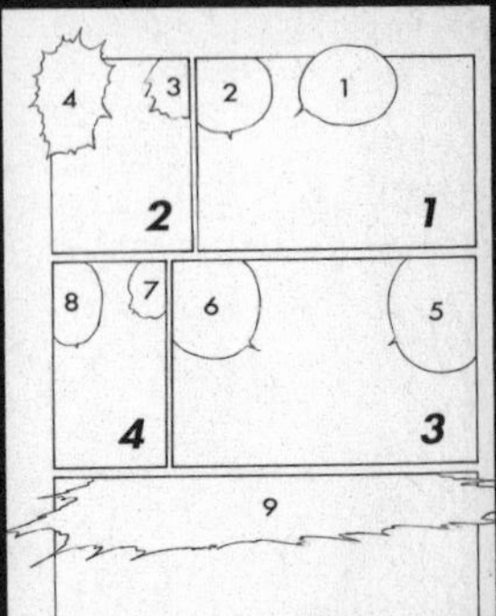

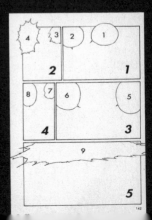